THE WARRIOR QUEEN CHRONICLES
BOOK ONE

Kellianna wrote the song *Warrior Queen* for her 2004 debut album, Lady Moon. The song is about a Queen who dies in battle, with the story beginning at her death. In early 2014, she decided to move forward with the creation of a book trilogy inspired by the song. *The Warrior Queen Chronicles* is a series of three books telling the story of the Queen's life, with the series ending where the song begins. Kellianna met Kaalii Cargill in Australia in October 2013 and again in the United Kingdom in the summer of 2014. When she picked up Kaalii's latest book, *Daughters of Time*, Kellianna knew that she had found the perfect person to help her bring her vision of the Warrior Queen's story to life . . .

TAPESTRY

OF

DARK AND LIGHT

Book One of

The Warrior Queen Chronicles

Kellianna Girouard

Kaalii Cargill

For all the girls who are called to be Warrior Queens

Sappho Books
71 Barkly Street,
St Kilda, Victoria, Australia 3182

www.sapphobooks.com

This paperback edition 2016
1

ISBN: 0997106905
ISBN-13: 978-0997106909

Cover design and art work by Kaalii Cargill and Leslie Baker

Cartography by Derek Debenham

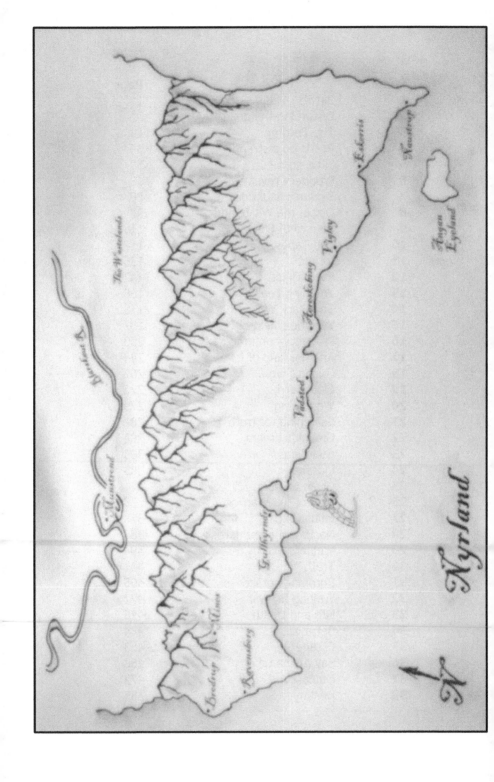

Nyrland

I will not flee, though death-fated you know I am. I was not conceived as a coward. I will have all of your loving advice as long as I live. - The Saga of the Völsungs

Night gave way to a new day. The sun glided over the land, bringing light and life to the harbor of Gullhyrndr. Seabirds called from the shore, and ravens took wing from the wildwood. An old woman stood at the parapet of Torten's tower, highest point of Gullhyrndr stronghold. She wrapped her arms around her chest and narrowed her eyes, seeking beyond the sea mists to a far island where women gathered to give thanks for the child born that night. Child of prophecy, child of dreams, child of hope . . .

"Faeoia!"

The old woman turned to answer the call, to tend the newborn babe as she had tended the mother twenty-five cycles ago and the mother's mother before that. Daughters born to serve, born to suffer, born to save the Land from darkness.

The blood rich smell of birth led Faeoia back to the Queen's rooms, where the child of prophecy snuffled at her mother's breast like any newborn creature.

"She was calling for you." Bera pulled Faeoia closer to the bed where the Queen lay, pale and beautiful.

"Something's wrong." The blood smell filled the room.

Faeoia smoothed the damp hair from Ronja's brow and said what must be said. "The price is paid. The child is the one." She gently closed Ronja's eyes, eased the nipple from the baby's mouth, and lifted the girl child into her arms.

"Blessings on this day
This day of your birth
Child of Golden Light
Child to heal the earth

Blessings on this hour
This hour of your birth
Born of love's pure light
Child of strength and might

Blessings on this moment
This moment of your birth
Child of golden light
Child to heal the earth."

Faeoia might have cried then - Ronja deserved her tears - but what use were tears, even tears of amber and gold? The Norns would have their way with or without an old woman's tears, and now there was a child to raise and a beloved one to lay on her pyre atop the cliffs of Gullhyrndr.

Two ravens sit on Óðin's shoulders, and into his ears they tell all the news they see or hear. Their names are Huginn and Muninn. - The Prose Edda.

Llianna needed a God.

She tucked her long plaits inside her leather vest and climbed out through the tower window. There were stories of maidens who used their hair as ladders, but Llianna used only the strength of her arms and legs to scale Torten's tower. She had been climbing the tower wall since she was old enough to drag a chest to the window and pull herself up onto the wide sill. From there she could see all the way to the sea, the far edge of her father's lands and the beginning of Aegir's watery world. Her father was King of Gullhyrndr, and his lands stretched to the sea from the distant mountains in the North, but he was just a man. Tonight Llianna needed a God.

Dark clouds gathered in the West, promising rain. Llianna gritted her teeth and climbed faster, scraping her fingers on the rock. *Pain is strength for a true warrior.* Or so Sigfinn taught the húskarlar, and a King's daughter must be at least as strong as his men at arms. Llianna reached the ground and ran into the shadows of the wildwood. The leaves whispered secrets and the moon shadows moved like warrior-dancers. Yes, tonight was a night for deep magic.

Llianna pulled barley bread from her belt-pouch and sprinkled crumbs on the ground for the Vaettir. Would the wood spirits come? Would they receive her offering? Faeoia said the Vaettir had lived in the wildwood since the beginning of Time and were inclined to be friendly to humans, but Faeoia said all sorts of things that others called crazy. Llianna waited, breathing in the smell of moist soil and moonbeams. She whispered the ritual words Faeoia had taught her.

"Hail to the Vaettir of the Land that holds me and weaves my path. I come to make offering and ask blessings."

The leaves whispered on, but the Vaettir did not come.

Llianna kicked at the ground. A blessing would have been welcome, but she could do without. She stroked the bark of Vardträd, the ancient yew tree that held the center of the wildwood. No one knew how long Vardträd had stood there, guarding the Land, protecting Gullhyrndr. Everyone knew it was forbidden to cut the wood or strip the leaves.

Llianna reached for a low-hanging branch. The leaves whispered more urgently. Llianna rested her hand on the branch. It was forbidden to take wood from Vardträd, but what else would do for the journey she must take that night?

The great tree murmured, and the branch trembled. Or was it

4

Llianna's own hand that shook? She bowed her head and sent the image of a staff to the heart of the tree, a staff to match her own height, a staff to hold the center while she summoned a God . . .

The tree sighed, and the branch came free to rest in Llianna's hand. She braced the branch on the ground, took the hunting knife from her belt pouch, and pressed the blade against the wood.

The wood resisted.

Llianna pushed harder on the knife. Sweat dampened her skin.

Then Sigfinn's voice in her mind: *hold lightly; let the knife do the cutting.* Sigfinn, who had taught a young girl how to hold a blade and slide it between a man's ribs. He had also taught her to shape wood: *hold lightly; let the knife do the cutting.* Llianna softened her grip and guided the knife over the wood. *Light but firm.* Yes, the sharp blade entered the wood as if invited, and she stripped the side branches, leaving a straight, clean staff.

Llianna bowed to Vardtrad. The great yew rustled its leaves, a blessing of sorts. Testing the weight of her new staff, Llianna walked out of the wildwood and took the moonlit path to the cliffs. She left the barley bread for the birds.

The Gullhyrndr cliffs had stood sentinel over the restless sea even longer than Vardtrad had guarded the Land. It was here the Kings and Queens of Gullhyrndr were sent on their final journey from the World of Life to the realms of the Gods. It was here that Llianna's mother's pyre had burned twelve years ago.

She made her way between the boat-shaped hollows where

Kings and warriors had rested on their funeral pyres, where the ritual words had been spoken to guide them through the crossing from life to death. Llianna shivered; *someone walking on her ashes* . . .

She stood close to the edge of the cliff and looked out over the sea. Moonlight etched a glowing pathway that rippled with the tide. The sea murmured below the cliffs, sighing like a huge creature. Llianna smiled. The fishermen said the sighing was the sound of the sea making love to the land, and making love was what had brought her out alone in the night.

Well, not exactly making love . . .

Llianna had only a vague notion of what happened when a man and woman came together like *that*. What she did know came from the serving women, who went on and on about the doings of the bedchamber when they thought she wasn't listening. But *little goats have big ears*, as the saying went, and Llianna had heard the women sighing and smacking their lips, laughing and whispering about desire and pleasure and the size of men's body parts. Interesting enough to be sure, but what she really wanted to know about was true love, the love that drew a man and woman together. Was it like the pull of the tides? Did it sweep everything away like a storm wind? Could it really move the moon and stars and make the great cycles go around, as the poets wrote? More than anything, Llianna wanted to know how to find her one true love. And the person she needed to ask was her mother.

Which is why she needed a God.

"It disturbs the Wyrd to disturb the dead, dear girl." Faeoia had said that at evening meal, as if she saw more with her milky eyes than all the clear-eyed people in the stronghold.

Llianna had nodded, and Faeoia had said nothing more. Perhaps the old nurse knew that Llianna was destined to disturb the Wyrd, or perhaps she couldn't hold a thought for more than a fleeting moment. Llianna shrugged. It didn't matter what Faeoia knew or what she saw with her second sight; Llianna was going to disturb the dead and disturb the Wyrd. Didn't the old tales say that the Threads woven by the Norns could be rewoven? Didn't they say that one with enough courage and daring could alter the course of Destiny as it flows through the Well beneath Yggdrasil?

Llianna climbed down the rocky path to the shore, holding her staff like a sword. She reached the sand and stood before the moonlight and waves, summoning all her courage and daring. With a silent prayer to the Winds, she planted the staff in the sand.

"Here is the center of the World."

Nothing happened.

When the Warrior Queens in the old tales planted their staffs, the whole World stopped to listen, caught between one breath and the next. But there had been no Warrior Queens in Gullhyrndr for a thousand years. Llianna stamped her foot; she might only be twelve years old but, if Faeoia told true, she came from a line of Queens who traced their descent from Freya. And why shouldn't it be true? Didn't birds alight on her shoulders when she called them? Didn't elk eat from her hand? Didn't storm clouds dissolve when she wished it?

Sometimes.

If only she could study the old ways with a real wisewoman like those who lived on Angan Eyeland, where Faeoia had been born, where Llianna's mother had been born, where women gathered under the stars to dance and sing and call on Frigg and Freya and the elements of Air, Fire, Water, Earth . . .

Llianna sighed impatiently. All she had were Faeoia's stories. How was she to know if her words were right? How was she to know if her staff needed magic runes like the ones Óðin had carved on Gungir? She shook her head, sending her golden plaits coiling around like snakes. Faeoia's stories would have to be enough . . .

"*Here is the center of the World!*" she cried.

A deep rumble echoed across the cliffs. Had the Earth decided to answer her summons after all? Llianna turned to face North and raised her hands above her head, palms facing towards the cliffs.

"Sentinels of Nordri, powers of Earth, I invoke you and call you. Three roots deepening. Stone. Mountain. Fertile field. Come! By the Earth that is Nerthus, our Mother, send forth your strength, and be here now."

She turned to the East, where the Sun would rise whatever happened this night.

"Sentinels of Austri, powers of Air, I invoke you and call you. Golden eagle of Yggdrasil who has knowledge of all things. Storm-pale hawk. Wind-witherer. Come! By the air that lifts your wings, send forth your grace, and be here now." A rushing sound filled the air, as if a thousand thousand birds flew overhead.

The hairs on Llianna's arms prickled with excitement. She turned to the South, towards the moonlit path on the water. "Sentinels of Sudri, powers of Fire, I invoke you and call you. Red flames of winter fires. Glowing sun of summer's warmth. Heat of passion. Courage burning. Come! By the fire that melts fear, send forth your flames, and be here now."

Llianna faced West. "Sentinels of Vestri, powers of water, I invoke you and call you. Aegir! Mighty one of the watery depths. Grey-green serpent of the salty abyss. Ancient one who controls the tides and shapes the land. Glorious father of change . . ."

The sea roiled, spitting up shining arcs of silvery fish.

"Aegir! Come! By the waters of the World, be here now!"

The water settled into glass smooth stillness. Nothing moved.

Llianna held her breath.

A single plume of water rose and rose from the sea, shimmering in the moonlight. Waves rolled into shore, breaking around her legs.

"Who calls me from the depths? Who dares?" asked a voice like thunder.

Llianna breathed again, trembling with fear and wild delight. "It is I, Freya's daughter, who calls."

The column of water swirled faster, hissing like giant serpents.

"That line was lost," roared the thunderous voice. "Wasted on human bondage. Denied by human folly. Who dares claim it now?"

"I am Llianna, daughter of Ronja, daughter of Eydis, daughter of Anniken, daughter of Naja, daughter of Sighrith, daughter of Marina, daughter of Aedel, daughter of Dagmar, daughter of . . ."

"Enough! That line was lost! Who dares claim it?" The God swirled closer.

"I am Llianna, daughter of Ronja, daughter of Eydis, daughter of Anniken, daughter of Naja, daughter of Sighrith, daughter of Marina, daughter of Aedel, daughter of Dagmar, daughter of . . ."

Aegir towered over her, dripping icy water onto her head. "You have power. I smell it."

Llianna held her ground. "I am Llianna, daughter of Ronja, daughter of Eydis, daughter of Anniken, daughter of Naja, daughter of Sighrith, daughter of Marina, daughter of Aedel, daughter of Dagmar, daughter of . . ."

"Stop!" roared the God.

Llianna gulped a breath and stood quietly.

Aegir moved even closer, spraying droplets of seawater like rain. Ozone filled the air, sharp as knives, clear as crystal.

"It is so," he said, thunder and hope together.

Llianna sucked in another deep breath, filling her lungs with ozone. "I ask a boon."

"Of course you do. You all come to ask a boon. None ever ask the cost."

"Cost?" Llianna's breath caught in her throat.

"Go now, Freya's daughter, lest the cost of this night's work be too great. You are young. Too young."

"Too young? They all tell me that! Am I too young to have called you here? Too young for you to answer?"

"Hmmph!" Less like thunder, more like a cold wind.

"I am young, but already I am betrothed, my life chosen by others. It is for this I come."

"I am no völva, scrying your love life in a pond! Begone!" The pillar of water swirled away towards the horizon.

"Stop!" commanded Llianna.

The God stopped.

"Summon my mother."

"You know not what you ask. Better you find a völva."

"Summon my mother!"

The water tower swelled and heaved, as if giant sea creatures fought within.

"You have the power," said the God.

The water stilled.

The air shimmered.

Through a veil of mist stepped a woman with grey-green eyes and flowing golden hair. Beautiful. She walked the moonlit path to stand before Llianna.

"Llianna. A name of power. A name of Fate." Cold. Hard.

Dead.

Llianna staggered back. What had she expected? A warm embrace? Glad tears? A mother's arms?

"Fear not, my child. I have no comfort for you, but I bring no harm. There is harm enough in your Fate."

"My Fate. Is it my Fate to marry Rothmar? Is it my Fate to live at Ravensborg? To do nothing but breed children and keep my husband happy?"

"Would that be such a poor Fate?" asked Llianna's mother. She sounded softer, almost warm.

"There is more. I know it!" cried Llianna. "What of true love? What of love that moves the moon and stars? What of happiness?"

"Ah. The dreams of the young. The dreams of innocence." She sounded wistful.

"Can I not dream?" asked Llianna. "Must I do the bidding of others all my life? Must I submit to the Fate chosen for me? Tell me, Mother, tell me!"

"What can I tell you? You are born to a story both glorious and dreadful. But sufficient unto the day is the evil thereof. You will have love that moves the moon and stars. I can promise that at least."

"I will? You promise?"

The beautiful woman reached out and gently stroked Llianna's cheek. Her touch was cold as death.

"I promise. Go now and walk your walk. True love will come."

"But I am betrothed to Rothmar. He is an old man. How can

true love come? Tell me, Mother!"

"Go now. The veil between the Worlds stretches thin. Walk your walk, and all your dreams will find you." Why did she sound so sad?

"Mother?"

The beautiful woman faded like mist in the morning sun.

The tower of water hissed and spiraled out to sea, creating whirlpools in its wake. Waves rushed in, chasing Llianna back to the cliffs.

She stood alone on the rocks, her tears mixing with the salt water dripping from her hair. Water surged against the rocks, hissing and spitting. The God was gone.

True love will come. Her mother had said that. She had promised. The rest of her words drifted away.

Whoosh. Two birds flew from down from the wildwood, wings brushing Llianna's hair. *Ravens.* Huginn and Muninn - Thought and Memory. Was it so close to dawn? Would they tell Óðin what they had seen? Would He care?

Llianna turned and climbed the path to the clifftop. She passed back through the wildwood, holding to her mother's promise: *true love will come.* She spared no thought for the Sea God's warnings as she climbed back up the tower to her bedchamber, dropped her wet clothes on the floor, burrowed beneath her bed furs, and drifted to sleep.

With Law shall or Land be settled, and with lawlessness wasted -
Með lögum skal land vort byggja en eigi með ólögum eyða.
- The Saga of Njál, 69

"Wake up, Lli. Wake up!" Marina tugged at the pile of furs on Llianna's bed.

Puffs of cold rushed into the cocoon of sleepy warmth where Llianna dreamed happily of true love.

"Lli! You have to get up!"

"Go away!" Llianna burrowed deeper under the furs.

Marina pulled the furs away and flung them to the floor. "Something's happened! Everyone's talking about it."

"Aargh!" Llianna opened one eye and wrinkled her nose. Why did her room smell like fish?

"Something in the sea!" cried Marina. "A huge creature that sank boats and flooded the storerooms! The harbor guards say it was a sea dragon but your father says there are no such things and Dagmar says it was probably a great blue whale but Falden thinks it must have been a sudden sea storm . . . and Rothmar came last night and he didn't even get wet so there wasn't a

14

storm on the Land . . . and the Keepers just rode in . . ."

Llianna sat up and opened both eyes. Most of Marina's habitual, non-stop chatter had rolled over her sleep-fuddled brain, but the mention of *Keepers* made her pay attention.

"The Keepers are here? The Testing is today?"

Marina stamped her foot impatiently. "Yes. Today! They are already gathering in the Hall. You have to get up!"

"Aargh!"

"Get dressed. Hurry!" Marina ran to the door. "And wear something nice."

Llianna slid off the bed and picked up her damp tunic. Ah, the dead fish smell. She threw the tunic, vest and leggings into the corner and rummaged in the clothes chest for something else to wear.

Marina hurried back in with a freshly laundered blue tunic and matching leggings.

"But those are yours," said Llianna. The soft cloth had been colored with precious blue dye brought by traders from far distant lands, a gift from Rothmar for Marina's last birthing day feast.

Marina smiled and pushed the clothes into Llianna's hands. "Yes, but I am already dressed and breakfasted. As you can see."

Llianna could see; Marina wore the Ravensborg colors - red tunic and black leggings - and her golden hair was neatly braided with matching ribbons. She looked like a princess.

Llianna sighed miserably and pulled on the borrowed clothes. Her skin felt scaly and dry from the soaking she had received in the night, and her legs ached as if she had been on the practice ground with Sigfinn for hours. She limped over to the washing bowl, splashed cool water on her face, and rubbed her cheeks dry with her hands.

Marina knelt on the floor to look under the bed. "Shoes? Where are your shoes?"

Llianna shook her head. "I left them somewhere."

Marina scrambled to her feet and ran to the door. "Hurry! Do your hair!"

Llianna untied her plaits and shook out her hair. She pulled the comb through the tangles, wincing as it stuck in clumps of dried sea spray. She tugged harder. The whalebone comb bent, but the tangles would not budge.

Marina ran back in with Llianna's soft, deer-hide boots. "When did you last visit the bathhouse? You look like you're in mourning!"

"I should be so lucky," said Llianna. If she were in mourning she wouldn't have to visit the bathhouse every day and keep her hair groomed and do all the other ridiculous things required of a King's daughter.

"Name not that well from which you would not drink." Marina sighed and shook her head, as if she were an elder instead of two months younger than Llianna.

Llianna scowled at her. "Stop that! You sound like a gothi." She turned away to pull on her boots.

Marina moved around to stand before Llianna. She crossed her arms over her chest, frowned meaningfully, and pursed her lips.

"Oh, don't do that!" said Llianna. "You always make that horrible face when you're cross with me. What's wrong now?"

"Where will I start? You run wild like a wayward child, your hair looks like the Vaettir have spelled it, and your room smells like a stagnant pond."

"Oh. When you say it like that . . ."

Marina touched her gently on the shoulder. "Here, let me help."

She untangled the comb, smoothed Llianna's hair, fitted a fine gold circlet on her head, and led the way down the tower stairs to the first level. They stopped at the railing. The yard teemed with men, horses, carts, and hoof-churned mud. The Keepers had arrived.

Llianna moved towards the stairs, but Marina pulled her away.

"We'll be filthy by the time we get through that," she said, pointing to the chaos in the yard.

Llianna sighed unhappily, but she followed Marina along the colonnade, taking the longer, cleaner way to the King's Hall on the opposite side of the stronghold.

They entered the Great Hall through a side door and slipped into their places by the King's chair. Llianna was there by right as King's daughter, but Marina had been fostered at Gullhyrndr since she was eight, and she was honored as the King's ward and sister of King Rothmar of Ravensborg.

At that moment King Rothmar was embracing Llianna's father

as an equal, although he was younger by thirty years. King for three years since his father's untimely death, Rothmar still looked like a boy with clear skin and bright eyes. Llianna frowned and bit the inside of her cheek. Rothmar's age was the crux of the problem: everyone thought him an eminently suitable match for her, but he was almost ancient - twenty-eight! And he had been married before. What did she want with an old, married man? Well, not really married because his first wife had died of the summer fever three years ago. Maybe it would help if Rothmar smiled more often; he was quite handsome when he smiled: clear grey eyes, generous mouth, strong chin . . .

Llianna shook herself. What was she thinking? Rothmar was a serious, old (married) man; even if he was handsome, he wasn't the true love her mother had promised . . .

Her thoughts rambled on through the formalities, until Marina nudged her to step forward to be presented. Llianna managed a proper curtsy, although she refused to take Rothmar's hand to rise. She was quite capable of standing on her own. And that was the other problem: a girl was expected to take the hand of her betrothed and lean on him for support. Why would she ever want to do that?

Rothmar frowned, let his hand drop, and turned to greet Marina. Who curtsied beautifully and allowed her brother to lift her elegantly to her feet and into an embrace.

"Dear sister. How are you?"

"Very well, dear brother. And you?"

Llianna wanted to vomit. *Dear sister. Dear brother.* They hardly knew each other! Rothmar was sixteen when Marina was born, already training at arms, and away when their mother had died and Marina was sent for fostering. He had visited Gullhyrndr for Council gatherings, but he hardly saw Marina when he was there. Who needed brothers, anyway? Llianna's own brothers were both grown men who never called her *dear sister.* Dagmar, who would be King one day, stood possessively behind the throne, looking down his nose at everyone; Falden, a year younger, stood at his brother's right hand - *to symbolize loyalty*, said Sigfinn. Llianna shrugged. Who needed them! Different mothers, different lives, and they showed no interest in her; according to them, girls were to be seen and not heard. Although she doubted that they even saw her.

Her brothers' wives, daughters from the neighboring strongholds of Vadsted and Aereskobing, sat at the far end of the high table, heads together, gossiping. They had arrived at Gullhyrndr the same year as Marina, but Aedel and Hillevi, seventeen and eighteen years old, had made it clear that they did not want *children* sitting with them at the table or stitching with them in the solar. Llianna and Marina had taken their revenge on the *andskoti*, as they called them: snakes in their beds, frogs in their shoes, mud on their clean clothes. *Andskoti* meant *enemy* in the old tongue.

Now Aedel and Hillevi both had babes, and Llianna and Marina had grown out of tormenting them, but they still called them *andskoti* . . .

Marina nudged Llianna in the ribs. "They're here."

Three men entered the Hall, strangers in somber, grey robes. Hard-faced. Hard-eyed. *Keepers.*

Marina dropped into a low curtsy. Llianna copied her, but she kept her eyes on the Keepers. Chosen of the Gods. Wise ones. Keepers of the Way.

Leeches, Faeoia had called them. *Sucking the lifeblood of the Land for their own ends.*

"Welcome to Gullhyrndr," said Llianna's father, stepping down from the dais to greet them.

The Keepers inclined their shaven heads to the King. It was not quite enough of a bow to signal true respect, yet it was sufficient to avoid insult. Llianna drummed her fingers against her thigh and narrowed her eyes at the men; did they learn that precise degree of disrespect at Keeper training? What did it mean? Was Faeoia right when she called them leeches?

"We come to serve." The middle Keeper would be the Questioner, the Truthseeker, come to test Llianna and Marina for their fitness to marry Kings and bear heirs for the fiefdoms.

They wouldn't know truth if it bit them on their nether regions. Faeoia again.

Llianna hoped Faeoia was right about that part of it. The Questioner made her skin crawl. He looked like a hawk with his hooked nose and hooded eyes. As if he had heard her thoughts, he turned his head and stared at her.

Llianna nodded respectfully, but inside her a small mouse scrambled to hide from the hawk. Not good. Not good at all.

The Questioner turned away and sat in the special high-backed chair made ready for him. His assistants unpacked leather panniers and placed scrolls, ledgers, quill pens, and ink on the table before him. The Questioner clasped his hands on the table and began.

"I call on the power vested in me to reveal the Truth in all things. I call on the Truth to guide me in upholding the Laws. Let the Ravensborg supplicant come forward."

Marina stood before the table and sank gracefully into a deep curtsy.

"You are daughter of Kings, betrothed to a son of Kings. Your worthiness must be confirmed and witnessed. You will demonstrate this by answering questions and performing the required tasks."

Marina rose, clasped her hands demurely, and bowed her golden head.

"Recite your father line."

Marina recited her father line back forty generations, voice clear and sure.

One of the assistants checked the list against a page in the ledger, tapping the paper at each name.

"Tell the founding of Nyrland."

Marina recounted the history, the conquest of the Land, and the settlement of the seven fiefdoms. She recited the names of the fiefdoms and spoke the words of the Sevenfold Pledge that bound them.

The Questioner looked at her intently.

"Tell what you know of herblore."

"Nothing," said Marina.

"Tell what you know of summoning."

"Nothing," said Marina.

"Tell what you know of preventing conception."

"Nothing," said Marina.

The questions and answers continued, the Questioner naming sixty-three wrong thoughts and ninety-four wrong actions, Marina answering with the same denial every time.

Llianna's palms grew damp with sweat. Marina could truthfully answer "No" to all the questions, but Llianna had already counted eighteen wrongs she could claim. Of course she would deny them when her turn came, but what if Faeoia was mistaken and the Questioner could see truth? What happened to someone who was not found worthy?

Two hours later the Questioner pronounced his findings.

"The daughter of Ravensborg bears no taint. She is a fitting Queen for Vadsted and suitable to bear sons for the seven fiefdoms."

Marina sagged with relief and sank into another deep curtsy.

The Questioner left the Hall, and Llianna looked for an opportunity to slip away to find Faeoia.

"No you don't," whispered her father, taking firm hold of her elbow. "You will come and sit beside Rothmar for morning invocation, and you will show him the respect due our neighbor and ally. And your betrothed."

Llianna groaned. Her father guided her to sit beside Rothmar, who greeted her solemnly. Why wouldn't he smile? He had kind eyes, the color of dove's wings or early morning mist . . .

The gothi stood and spoke the invocation. Rothmar made the ritual responses as seriously as he did everything. Llianna managed to join in, although her mind still scurried around like a mouse looking for a way to escape. Maybe if she were to become suddenly ill . . . a fever . . . a terrible headache . . . a fainting spell . . .

The gothi completed the invocation. Food and drink were served, but Llianna could only sip a little water. Maybe she could develop a stomach ache and say it was something she ate . . .

"Are you ready?" asked her father, offering his arm to accompany her to the front of the Hall.

Llianna held his arm and walked to her Testing.

King Bekkr watched uneasily as his only daughter was summoned by the Questioner.

"I call on the power invested in me to reveal the Truth in all things. I call on the Truth to guide me in upholding the Laws. Let the Gullhyrndr supplicant come forward."

Llianna stood before the table.

"You are daughter of Kings, betrothed to a son of Kings. Your worthiness must be confirmed and witnessed. You will demonstrate this by answering questions and performing the required tasks."

King Bekkr sighed. His bloodlines carried no taint, but he had defied the advice of his Councilors to marry Llianna's mother; sometimes right action had nothing to do with what was normal or expected. Strangely the Keepers had not objected at the time. Would they find fault now? Llianna looked so much like Ronja with her honey-colored hair and strong features. Too strong for a woman? The Gullhyrndr Councilors had said that about Ronja, but Bekkr already had sons, and he had insisted on Ronja for his second marriage. Now they would be putting Ronja's daughter to the Test, and Bekkr's defiance would be revealed as wisdom or folly depending on the Questioner's finding. King Bekkr clenched his jaw and prepared to endure his own trial as Llianna stepped forward.

Llianna dipped into a curtsy. Not as deep or as graceful as Marina's but respectful enough. She hoped.

"Recite your father line."

"I am Llianna, daughter of Bekkr, son of Haldr, son of Frenck, son of Rovmar, son of . . ." Llianna named her father's fathers for forty generations. Why did they never ask for the mothers?

"Tell the founding of Nyrland."

Llianna recounted the history, using the same words as Marina. The history was always told the same way: the conquest of the Land by the Seafarers, the allocation of Land to the original families, the settlement of the seven fiefdoms.

The Questioner beckoned Llianna closer.

Every instinct told her to run, but she stepper closer, hoping that none of her fear showed on her face. Hoping that the hawk could not sense the mouse . . .

"Tell what you know of herblore."

"Nothing," said Llianna. First untruth.

"Tell what you know of summoning."

"Nothing," said Llianna. Second untruth.

"Tell what you know of preventing conception."

"Nothing," said Llianna. Third untruth.

The questions and answers went on as before, the Questioner again naming sixty-three wrong thoughts and ninety-four wrong actions. Llianna answered with the same denial every time, although the count of untruths went beyond eighteen this time.

The questions stopped.

The Questioner looked at Llianna and narrowed his eyes. "The daughter of Gullhyrndr will be tested further. Prepare a private room."

Llianna's breath caught. Spots flickered before her eyes.

The Questioner stood and left the Hall in a swirl of robes. His assistants followed.

Llianna ran past her pale-faced father and out the side door, along the colonnade, down the stairs, along the hallway to Faeoia's room.

She flung the door open and burst like a storm wind into the small room.

Faeoia looked up from the cards spread before her on a low table. Her white hair was plaited and wrapped around her head like a crown, and her rheumy eyes twinkled as if Llianna had done something amusing.

"He did know!" said Llianna. "You said he wouldn't know, but he did."

"What does he know?" asked Faeoia mildly.

"He knows I'm lying," said Llianna.

"Did he say that?"

"No, not exactly."

"Then he does not know. He smells something, but he be unsure what it is. Stay calm. Stay clear. Repeat what you have already said."

"Stay calm? How would you like to be in a room with a hawk that smells something?"

"I would like it not at all if I be a mouse," said Faeoia. "It would trouble me not at all if I be a warrior."

"Well, I'm not a warrior! Sigfinn has taught me the Code, and I know how to fight, but I'm just a girl who has thirty-one wrong thoughts and twenty-two wrong actions." Llianna sat on Faeoia's bed and dropped her head into her hands.

Faeoia picked up a carved staff. Crack!

"Aargh! Why did you do that?" cried Llianna, rubbing her shins. "Now I'll be crippled as well."

Faeoia glared and shook the staff. Sparks flew from her eyes.

"The only thing that be unworthy about you be the way you be acting right now. You know better!"

"Do I?" Llianna scowled at her old nurse.

"You do," said Faeoia. "You know that ideas of worthy and unworthy be ways that Keepers control people and suck the lifeblood of the fiefdoms. You know that wrong thoughts and wrong actions be only those that intentionally harm yourself or others."

Llianna sighed miserably and nodded. She did know those things. Then why was she so scared?

"Fear be a warning of danger," said Faeoia, answering the unspoken question in the uncanny way she had of reading Llianna's thoughts. "The Questioner be dangerous. He be a greedy, little man who believes he be powerful. Dangerous."

"He has power to decide my Fate," said Llianna.

"No! He has power to decide if you will wed Rothmar and be queen of Ravensborg. Beyond that, he has no power to decide anything about your Fate. That be in better hands than his."

"Oh. Well that's not so bad. I don't want to marry Rothmar, anyway."

Faeoia rolled her eyes and sighed. "It be your Fate."

"But I won't marry Rothmar if the Questioner finds me unworthy."

"Then you will be found worthy," said Faeoia.

"Aaargh!" Llianna limped out of Faeoia's room.

"There you are!" Marina hurried down the hallway and grabbed

Llianna's arm. "They are ready for you."

"What? Are you working as messenger for the Keepers now?"

"Don't be stupid. I just don't want you to keep them waiting and get into more trouble." She tugged Llianna along towards the meeting room.

"More trouble? More trouble than what?" asked Llianna.

"Than you are already in! You glared at the Questioner like he was going to take a bite out of you, and you barely curtsied. Do you want to fail?"

Llianna gasped. "Ah! Thank you, Marina. You are the best friend anyone could have."

Marina nodded knowingly and made sure Llianna reached the door of the meeting room.

Llianna let go of Marina's hand and gathered her courage to walk in by herself. The Questioner sat at a table, his assistants to either side. Aedel and Hillevi sat on a bench by the door, present for the sake of propriety. Llianna nodded to the *andskoti*. What were they thinking? Were they hoping she would fail? A good reason to succeed . . .

She smiled demurely at the Questioner and curtsied low enough to make Marina proud. "Please excuse my previous behavior. I was nervous in the presence of someone so powerful, and I acted badly."

The Questioner nodded in acknowledgement, and the rest was easy. Llianna answered the questions in a soft voice, eyes downcast. She acted confused about the meaning of some of the wrong thoughts and actions, and she thanked the Questioner profusely when he explained anything to her.

An hour later, they returned to the Hall.

"The daughter of Gullhyrndr bears no taint. She is a fitting Queen for Ravensborg and suitable to bear sons for the seven fiefdoms."

Marina ran over and hugged Llianna.

King Bekkr relaxed his jaw and smiled as if he had known the outcome all along.

"The Pledge Ride will commence at dawn," said the Questioner.

Llianna didn't know whether to laugh or cry. The Questioner had determined that she carried none of the taint of the old ways, and her suitability as Queen of Ravensborg had been officially confirmed. She could laugh because it had been so easy in the end, and she could cry because the Questioner's endorsement sounded more like a curse than a blessing.

She endured the celebration that followed and escaped to her room as soon as she could, disgusted with herself and angry with everyone. The courtiers had offered congratulations, but a talking bird could have given the answers required by the Testing. The bird might even have done better; a bird would not have been silly enough to glare at a hawk. Llianna sighed miserably. What was her father thinking to subject her to the Keepers? He had always said that Gullhyrndr and Ravensborg had resisted the Keepers' tyranny, but the Testing had been a blatant display of the Questioner's power. Faeoia was right; *most men are fools, too caught up in their own importance to see what's standing right in front of them.*

As if conjured by Llianna's thought, Faeoia bustled in, cackling like an old raven. "You fooled them good and proper, my girl. Wouldn't know the old ways if they up and bit them on their . . ."

"Hush, Faeoia. I nearly forgot everything you've taught me, and the Keepers are still here. They'll be watching me on the Ride."

"Watching perhaps, but not with eyes that see," said Faeoia.

"I hope you're right," said Llianna. "The Questioner makes my skin crawl."

"Sensible skin," said Faeoia, folding Llianna's clothes for the journey.

‡

Faeoia folded the clothes, but her mind roamed East across the sea to Angan Eyeland, where her sisters gathered on full moon nights to dance and sing praises to Freya and Frigg and the older Goddesses whose names no one remembered. Tending Ronja's child was Faeoia's sacred task, and she did it willingly, but she missed her home and the circle of women who had taken a quiet girl from the fishing village and taught her to walk with the Goddess. The women had been loving and fierce, tender and strong, alive with the rhythms and cycles of Nature and the seasons; they had laughed and cried and raged and danced their way into Faeoia's heart, and still her heart beat in time with the women's chanting, still her blood moved with tides of Angan Eyeland . . .

‡

Solvaldr stood naked at the window of the tower room in the Keepers' Sanctuary a league outside Aereskobing. It was here he came to remember that he was mortal. The cool, mountain air moved softly over his skin, stirring the fine hairs on his body, giving pleasure. He sighed deeply and stroked his body in forbidden places. No one could see him here. No one could deny him the release he sought. These stolen moments were his only deviation from the Law, and he guarded them well. Not for him the risk of a woman's caresses, although he had watched men and women together, and he could understand the temptation. But his was a life of service to the Law.

The air cooled the sweat on his skin, and Solvaldr moved from the window to kneel before the Book of Law resting on a chest against the wall. The Book was old and precious and the cornerstone of Keeper tradition. Written by Devilan after the First Battle, it always rested in the room of the First Keeper in the Aereskobing Sanctuary. The Sanctuary was the heart and mind of the Land, located at the center of the string of pearls that made up the seven fiefdoms of Nyrland. Here the Book of Law was held. Here the Laws were interpreted. From here they were upheld.

Solvaldr spoke the First Law, as he did every morning:

"Though the mills of Law grind slowly;

Yet they grind exceeding small;

Though with patience Law stands waiting,

With exactness Law grinds all."[i]

He rose and dressed in the purple robe that signified his role as First Keeper. Solvaldr rarely smiled, but today he allowed a slight softening at the corner of his mouth. Today his plan to secure Ravensborg had been advanced. The misbegotten Gullhyrndr princess had been Tested and found worthy. A travesty, but a necessary one.

Oh, the Second and Third had raised objections.

"She is the daughter of a sorceress. Never can she be Ravensborg's Queen!"

"Her bloodline is tainted. King Bekkr must have been mad or ensorceled to have sired a child on that woman."

Solvaldr had let them talk, and then he had explained.

"You are right, and therein lies our victory over Ravensborg. The balance between Kings and Keepers is delicate. We cannot challenge the Ravensborg King openly without risking uprisings in the other fiefdoms, but we can seed corruption from within. We turned a blind eye to Bekkr's marriage to that whore from Angan Eyeland. If she had born a son, he would not have seen his first year. But a daughter, married to one of the last withholding Kings, is exactly what we need. She will hand Ravensborg to us on a platter."

"How so?" asked the Second.

"She is tainted, and the taint will show."

"King Rothmar was well schooled by his father. He will be watching for us to move on Ravensborg," said the Third.

"King Rothmar does not have his father's cunning," said Solvaldr. "He came to the throne too young, and he is an idealistic fool. The Gullhyrndr princess will give us the chink we need to open Ravensborg."

The Second and Third had bowed their heads to his superior understanding, and Solvaldr had begun planning how the Keepers would profit from Ravensborg's iron mines and weapon forges. No matter that it would be years before the noose tightened; Ravensborg had just been given enough rope to hang itself.

"Is there anything more beautiful than gold?" - Freya's question. Plain-thoughted Thor spoke. "A farm at first light is more beautiful than gold, or a ship's sails in the mist. Many ordinary things are far more beautiful." - Norse Tales

"Are you ready?" asked Marina at dinner.

Llianna shrugged. "Everyone asks me that! I'm as ready as I can be. Faeoia fussed around in my room all afternoon, so I suppose she's decided what I should take. No need to ask you if you're ready . . ."

Marina laughed, her blue eyes sparkling. She looked beautiful in a blue skirt and beaded bodice, matching ribbons in her hair. Just for a moment, Llianna wished she had agreed to have new clothes made for the Testing; she still wore the borrowed tunic and leggings.

Marina clapped her hands with excitement. "We're going to see the rest of Nyrland at last! Once we marry, all we'll see are the insides of strongholds."

"I want to see the fiefdoms," said Llianna. "I just wish we had better companions."

"What? Are you worried the Questioner will catch you collecting herbs or summoning the dead?" asked Marina.

Llianna bit her lip. Marina had an uncanny ability to unknowingly name the very thing that must not be named. It made Llianna want to strangle her.

‡

Llianna and Marina assembled for the Pledge Ride the next morning, resplendent in new riding clothes that even Llianna had not been able to refuse. Gullhyrndr and Ravensborg, the westernmost fiefdoms of Nyrland, were equally proud of their warriors and their beautiful women. Llianna wore green and gold for Gullhyrndr, and Marina wore the red and black of Ravensborg.

King Rothmar and King Bekkr entrusted them to the Keepers' care, as was proper for the Pledge Ride.

"You are symbols of Gullhyrndr and Ravensborg. Make us proud," said Llianna's father.

Llianna smiled sweetly, careful to show nothing of what she really thought about being called a symbol. Her father may defy the Keepers to keep Gullhyrndr's harbor free of their control, but he truly believed in the Sevenfold Pledge that bound the fiefdoms, and he expected her to honor it. King Bekkr would not welcome her thoughts about freedom and true love.

Llianna quieted the rebellious thoughts; it really was exciting to be visiting all the fiefdoms, the pearls in the strand of Nyrland, as the songs named them. The Ride would take her away from the endless, boring lessons expected of a Queen-in-waiting, yet a journey in the company of Keepers was not her idea of a real adventure. A real adventure would be leaving Gullhyrndr in the dark of night with her true love, a hero, handsome and brave, who promised undying devotion . . . She would climb down the tower wall and ride away with him, her hair flowing behind her like a golden banner as they galloped through the moonlight, whispering secrets . . .

" . . . do you think it will all be as beautiful as they say?" asked Marina. "I can't wait to see Naustrup's pearls! Rothmar said I will be asked to choose a strand. Do you think I should get white or pink?" She went on, happily anticipating their journey, while Llianna secretly dreamed of freedom and of love that moved the moon and stars . . .

Her dreams were rudely challenged by the reality of plodding along with three Keepers, twenty húskarlar, and a wagon in which Faeoia sat regally beside the driver. Llianna rode a pony suitable for a girl, a dappled grey mare with a round belly and an unlikely name: Vaskr. It meant 'brave' in the old tongue, and Llianna could only think that someone with sense of humor had named the slow, sweet-tempered creature.

If the strongholds were the pearls in the strand of Nyrland, the Keeper Sanctuaries were the filler beads, strung between the strongholds at regular intervals. Built from stone, the Sanctuaries resembled small strongholds, walled with ramparts and towers.

The differences became obvious once inside the austere halls - the nights spent at the Keeper Sanctuaries were quiet and solemn, with simple meals, hard beds, and silent men in grey robes gliding around like restless spirits.

"Do you think they cut their tongues out when they enter the order?" Llianna asked Marina, when they were in their room with the door closed. "They don't even whisper to each other."

"Discipline," said Marina. "I know you find it hard to believe, but some people actually do as they are told."

Faeoia chuckled and settled down to sleep on one of the narrow beds. Unfortunately the old nurse also snored like a pregnant sow, and Llianna seriously considered smothering her, except the Keepers provided no pillows.

In the end, she stuffed the tips of her plaits in her ears and covered her head with her arm. That reduced the snoring to a sound more like a swarm of angry bees, and Llianna managed to drift into a restless sleep to pursue her dreams of true love and adventure.

‡

They rode into Vadsted on market day. Farmers and merchants gathered in an open area by the stronghold gates, displaying their goods: goats and sheep milled in makeshift pens; carts served as stalls laden with fleeces, kiln-dried pots and platters, woven cloth, and casks of cider. Llianna looked eagerly at the market, but the

Keepers led them past the exciting bustle and into the stronghold.

King Vigmund greeted them and ushered them into the Hall, where his Queen and three sons waited. Llianna gave greetings from her father and from Aedel, who had sent a parcel for her mother. Aedel's brothers shared the Queen's thin lips and mean eyes, and Llianna worried for Marina, betrothed to the oldest brother, Fastulf, heir to Vadsted. Rothmar might be old, but at least he had a noble face and the bearing of a King! Fastulf stood as tall as his father, but he leaned like a sapling overshadowed by the parent tree, robbed of light and the space to grow into himself.

Marina didn't seem to notice. She blushed when she was presented to him, and later she talked incessantly about how handsome he looked and how kind his eyes were and whether he liked her and . . .

Llianna stopped listening. They had been served a midday meal outside under trees lining the practice yard, and now the Vadsted húskarlar were displaying their famous fighting skills. Llianna was especially interested in a short staff used to good effect by the men. At Gullhyrndr, staffs were used for hand-to-hand fighting, but the shorter Vadsted staffs could also be used on horseback or in confined spaces. She watched intently as the men fought, her hands moving in time with theirs. Sigfinn's training in staff, sword, and shield had strengthened her body and taught her to observe others, the way they moved, the way they thought; the Vadsted fighters were strong, but one favored his left side, and another gave away his moves with the tilt of his head. Llianna itched to join them and exploit their weaknesses. It would make Sigfinn proud.

"You admire our warriors," said King Vigmund. "Do you have training in self defense?"

Llianna nodded. Sigfinn had explained the necessity of calling their work *self defense*. After all, what would a Queen-in-waiting want with warrior training?

It had been nine years since Raiders had last come in longships to test the Nyrland defenses - most of Llianna's life - but all seven strongholds retained standing troops of húskarlar strong enough to fight off the fiercest Raiders.

Sigfinn spoke of the peaceful years as a strange circumstance. *It be a peculiar thing to train men to fight the fiercest foe, yet to pray every day that they never need their training.*

Vadsted certainly boasted skilled warriors, but the stronghold was especially renowned for producing the finest woolen cloth, woven from fleece taken from the longhaired sheep grazing the sloping land between the stronghold and the mountains. Vadsted was blessed with natural pastures and safe grazing for the flocks, just as Gullhyrndr was blessed with a natural harbor that made it a center of trade. *Pearls in the strand.*

South of the stronghold, Vadsted farmers planted the fertile, undulating ground all the way to the sea cliffs with crops of flax and corn and rows of kal, the green-leafed vegetable used in everything from soup to Vadsted's famous elk pie.

"This will be my home one day," said Marina, looking out over the fields. "I will miss the harbor and the constant coming and going at Gullhyrndr, but this is so peaceful."

"And you'll never run short of kal," said Llianna, who hated the bitter greens, no matter how healthful they were said to be.

Marina laughed. "I'll be sure to send some to Ravensborg every summer!"

Llianna screwed up her face and made a disgusted sound. Marina giggled, and soon they were both laughing loudly, forgetting the Keepers.

The serious part of the visit, the real reason they were there, came on the last evening. Llianna and Marina were required to confirm the Sevenfold Pledge in front of the whole population of Vadsted, or as many as could fit into the Hall. The Keepers read the preliminaries, and Llianna stepped forward.

"I, Llianna, daughter of Bekkr, confirm by oath upon this covenant that I desire to preserve peace and perfect amity with each of the seven fiefdoms and to uphold the Law, until the end of the Nine Worlds. But if I fail in the observance of the aforesaid, may I be accursed of all the Gods. Regard as truth what I have now covenanted, as it is inscribed upon this parchment and sealed with my blood." Llianna pricked her finger with the pin offered by the Questioner and smeared blood on the bottom of the parchment.

Marina repeated the confirmation, and they stepped back, congratulating each other on remembering the words and managing the bloodletting with dignity. The people of Vadsted cheered and clapped and happily joined in the feasting. The celebration filled the Hall and flowed out into the square.

The next morning they left Vadsted for Aereskobing, where Marina had a cousin married to a Master in the King Rodigr's household. Llianna also bore greetings from Hillevi, her brother Falden's wife, oldest daughter of King Rodigr. There would be kin and close connections in all the fiefdoms . . .

The seven strongholds had been exchanging children for so long the bloodlines were interwoven like a many-stranded braid. It ensured that they never fought amongst themselves, except for the mandatory wedding brawls and the occasional dispute over bride payments. It also meant that children were sometimes born cross-eyed or dim-witted, but there were enough healthy offspring to keep the fiefdoms' ruling families in Kings and Queens. So it had been since the beginning when the first settlers had arrived in their longships, seeking a Land where they could build strongholds and live in peace. Other Seafarers still lived by raiding and warring, but Llianna's ancestors had chosen to settle and become farmers and traders and Law Keepers.

Thinking of the Keepers made Llianna shiver. Why did they scare her so? Sigfinn and Faeoia had both taught her that fear was the true enemy, not anything that might come from outside. She had learned to slow her breath and find an inner place of balance in the face of danger; she had learned to fight with knife, staff, sword and shield. Yet the Keepers disturbed her balance and left her feeling as if spiders were crawling over her neck, her arms, her skin . . .

What had Faeoia said? *Sensible skin.*

Was it her mother's blood warning her?

Not for the first time, Llianna wondered why her father had chosen his second wife from outside the ruling families. Ronja had come from Angan Eyeland, a small island off the coast of Eskerris, a wife chosen for love rather than duty. Of course Llianna had asked him, but King Bekkr just said that the bloodlines of Angan Eyeland were as pure as any, descended from the ruling families of Eskerris. With two strong sons born from his first marriage, he had chosen to marry for love.

Love was something Llianna could understand, especially love that moved the moon and stars. Yet it was not the way of Kings to marry for love, and it was not the way of the Keepers to allow it. Strange.

Maybe true love was always mysterious and strange . . .

"Was she beautiful?" Llianna had asked her father when she was younger.

"As beautiful as sunrise on the water," he had said.

Now that Llianna had seen her mother with her own eyes, she knew it was true; Ronja had been beautiful, and she had carried herself with the dignity of a Queen. Yet all the so-called *wrong* thoughts and actions must have come from Ronja's line along with the honey-colored hair and grey-green eyes. What would happen if the Keepers discovered the wrongness? What would they do if they knew that Faeoia had been teaching Llianna the old ways of her mother's mothers? What would they do if they knew that Sigfinn had taught her to fight like a warrior?

At least Sigfinn had been a part of Gullhyrndr since Llianna's father was a boy, but Faeoia had arrived from Angan Eyeland with Ronja, and she had stayed to care for Ronja's child. Why had the Keepers allowed a King's daughter to be nursed by an Eyelander? The Keepers would condemn Faeoia's teachings, yet the old nurse had somehow stayed on after Ronja's death and become a permanent part of Gullhyrndr. However it had happened, Llianna was glad of it; how could it be wrong to know the names of healing plants and to feed birds from your hands? How could it be against the Laws to ask blessings of the Moon as She moved through Her cycles?

The only problem with Faeoia was her refusal to answer direct questions, and Llianna had a thousand questions. Faeoia had taken Llianna into the wildwood and taught her forbidden herblore, and she had told her the old tales by the fire on long winter nights, but she stubbornly ignored most of Llianna's questions.

"The best learning comes through your own living," said Faeoia over and over again, but Llianna suspected that there was some terrible truth that the old nurse feared to reveal, something so wrong that it could not be named. She ground her teeth in frustration and vowed to uncover all the truths and all the lies, even if she had to tie Faeoia to a chair and threaten her with . . .

well, with whatever would make her reveal the secrets she held.

Llianna's whirling thoughts plagued her as they rode into the Keeper's Sanctuary on the road to Aereskobing. The walls of the Sanctuary loomed high above the road, watching, waiting to close in . . .

"This here be the center of Keeper power," said the worker who carried their bags to their small room. "The Book of Law be here with the First Keeper." He sounded as proud of the Sanctuary as King Vigmund had been of Vadsted.

"The Laws be made here," said the worker, leaning close to whisper it.

Llianna shivered. Would the Lawmakers all be hard-eyed and make her feel like a mouse scurrying around for a place to hide?

Their stay at Aereskobing Sanctuary did not reveal any Lawmakers. As always, the travelers ate separately from the Keepers, retired to their bare room, and left the Sanctuary early the next morning.

Llianna swayed in the saddle, bleary-eyed and drooping with tiredness; she had not slept at all the night before, skin prickling with warning. The walls were solid stone, but Llianna had been sure they were watching her. She had told herself she was being foolish and settled down to sleep, but the prickling hairs on her arms and neck had made her sit up to watch the shadows. The Aereskobing Sanctuary hummed with menace, yet nothing untoward had happened, and Llianna rode away wondering if she had imagined it all and kept herself awake for nothing.

She rode close to the wagon. "Did you feel it?" she asked Faeoia.

Faeoia spat over the side of the wagon. "That be the center of the Keeper's power. The First Keeper sits there like a spider, watching for movement in the threads of his web so he can be feeding on whoever be caught."

Llianna shivered again and gave thanks to be leaving the walls and shadows behind.

They rode into Aereskobing an hour later, and the richness of the city soon distracted Llianna from her fears. The stronghold proudly displayed the wealth earned from the mines for which it was renowned in the seven fiefdoms and beyond: colorful banners flew from the towers, stone blocks paved the road, and a huge fountain played in the forecourt of the stronghold, water droplets rising in arcs.

King Rodigr greeted them warmly. Llianna delivered Hillevi's greeting to the King, and he pulled her into a great bear hug and kissed her on the lips. Llianna gritted her teeth, smiled politely, and stepped back beside Marina.

"See. It could have been worse. What if your father had chosen Rodigr instead of Rothmar?" Marina shook with suppressed laughter.

Llianna elbowed her in the ribs, and turned to greet the King's daughters, Hillevi's younger sisters. The Queen had died birthing the youngest, and Rodigr had not remarried, so Marina's jest was more likely to make Llianna shudder than laugh.

Hillevi had sent fond messages for her younger sisters, both of whom looked like their father. Marilla and Handlar happily showed Llianna and Marina around the stronghold, sharing the latest gossip about the scandalous behavior of the kitchen girl with the married horsemaster. Llianna liked them immediately; if only Hillevi back at Gullhyrndr had been half as friendly as her sisters.

After visiting the rest of the stronghold, they stood on the top walkway of the northern tower and looked out towards the distant mountains.

"The mines are there," said Marilla, pointing to a massive hand of five ridges, extending from the mountains towards the sea.

Llianna remembered her lessons – the mines brought wealth to Aereskobing: gold and silver, emeralds and rubies, black diamonds and sapphires.

They rode to the mines the next day, and Llianna eagerly ventured into the tunnels while Marina waited in the shade of an ancient grove of elm trees with Marilla and Handlar. The mines stretched deep into the ridges, and Llianna admired the strength and determination of the strong-armed miners who chipped away at the rock, patiently unearthing the riches that had made Aereskobing the wealthiest of the fiefdoms. She also decided that mining was not one of her dreams, unable to imagine spending so many hours away from sunshine and fresh air.

King Rodigr spoke proudly of the mines and strutted around as if Aereskobing was the biggest pearl in the strand of the seven fiefdoms. More than once Llianna wanted to remind him that he needed Gullhyrndr's harbor, Eskerris's shipbuilders, and Naustrup's seamen to trade his gold and precious stones. Instead she smiled politely and thanked him for showing her Aereskobing's splendid mines.

Llianna forgave the King his pride when he gifted her a rough piece of uncut emerald the size of her thumb. The smoky green reminded her of the sea off Gullhyrndr's cliffs, and the royal goldsmith mounted it to hang on a gold chain near her heart.

"It matches your eyes," said Marina.

"Then sapphires match yours, too. Sort of!" said Llianna.

Marina smiled and stroked her own gift of seven sapphires set in a gold necklace to signify the seven fiefdoms.

The Keepers also tucked away rich gifts, and Llianna wondered about the wealth accumulating in the Sanctuary coffers.

Llianna and Marina confirmed the Pledge for Aereskobing and sat with Marilla and Handlar for the feasting. They all drank too much mead and gossiped mercilessly about the courtiers. Llianna laughed as loudly as the others and rested well in the safety of the stronghold.

‡

Vigley, the next fiefdom in the strand, was not as prosperous as Aereskobing.

"The fiefdoms might have different degrees of wealth, but they all have an equal share of pride," said Faeoia, and she was right.

Llianna began to understand that Nyrland might stand as a single Land, but the fiefdoms operated as separate kingdoms with their own identities and allegiances. She also began to understand her father's investment in the Sevenfold Pledge; it bound the fiefdoms together when pride and competition might tear them apart.

The coast curved southward at Vigley, and the landholders had taken advantage of the milder winds to plant grape vines on the south-facing walls of their farms. The vintners turned the summer grapes into eikvin, a honey-colored wine aged in oak barrels and sought after by traders far and wide.

The Keepers so praised the wine served at the evening meal that Llianna took a quick sip from her neighbor's cup when he had turned to speak with someone else.

"Uggh!" Llianna wrinkled her nose and gulped a mouthful of water to clear the tart taste. The eikvin was nearly as bad as the tonic Faeoia brewed for winter fevers.

Llianna looked up to see Mennin, youngest son of King Lund, watching her. He smiled, lifted his wine cup, and saluted her. Llianna laughed out loud, and everyone turned to stare. The Questioner frowned.

Llianna stopped laughing and stared at the far wall. Had the Keepers been making marks against her name in their ledger? Was laughter at the dining table one of the wrong actions?

‡

The Pledge Ride reached Eskerris late in the day, riding along a coastline lined with fishermen's cottages. The stronghold sat on high ground above the shallow bay, but water was the lifeblood of Eskerris. The first evening, Llianna stood on the parapet of the stronghold to watch the floti of fishing boats return to shore, the fishermen's songs carrying over the water. She added Eskerris to her dream of eloping with her beloved; they would live among the fisherfolk, and he would take his boat out each day and return singing. She would mend nets and make red currant syrup and pick herbs and summon sea Gods . . .

"Lli?" Marina shook her arm. "Whatever are you thinking? You were muttering to yourself like a gothi!"

Llianna shook off the dream and smiled at Marina. "I was thinking that I might like to be a fisherman's wife instead of a Queen."

"Don't say things like that! Those Keepers follow us like shadows and write down everything we say." Marina looked around nervously. "It's unnatural."

"I wonder what they fear so much," said Llianna. "A girl dreaming of true love is hardly a threat to the seven fiefdoms. I'm sure all girls have dreams."

"The future Queens must be without taint," said Marina, quoting from the Keepers. "Is dreaming a taint?"

"I wonder who decides whether something is a taint or not. Do you think I should ask the Questioner?"

Marina squealed in fright. "Don't you dare!"

One by one, the fishing boats cleared the reef and surged up onto the beach like sea creatures coming ashore to sleep. The fishermen unloaded their catch into baskets held by women and children, who welcomed the men home with songs and laughter. A good life . . .

Faeoia walked with Llianna and Marina down the wide road to the shore, where the fishermen's wives sat on a low wall with the day's catch displayed in baskets.

"They be hoping the stronghold will need fresh fish for the visitors," said Faeoia.

"Fine mackerel today," called a woman from the sea wall. "Just out of the water."

Faeoia pointed to one of the silvery fish. "Always look at the eyes. They need be bright and clear; dull eyes mean stale fish. The scales should shine, and a fresh caught fish always smells like clean water. And make sure you check the gills." Faeoia pointed to the lump of soft, red tissue under a flap behind the fish's head. "The color should be strong."

"You be buying?" asked the woman.

Faeoia said something in a language Llianna had never heard, and the woman smiled.

"Does this remind you of Angan Eyeland?" asked Llianna.

Faeoia nodded, a faraway look in her eyes.

"What happens to the fish they don't sell?" asked Marina.

"They be dried and salted and carted to Gullhyrndr to the trade ships. Eskerris mackerel fetches a good price."

Llianna had seen the barrels of Eskerris fish at the harbor, marked with the characteristic double fish symbol, and she had tasted it before, but it would never be the same after seeing the fishing boats and hearing the fishermen singing.

The baked fish at dinner that night was cooked with chestnuts and shallots.

"This is delicious," said Llianna.

King Ardfiskr nodded happily and spoke proudly of the Eskerris fishing fleet.

"If there were time I would take you to the forests where the boats are built; the trees are as old as the Land, and the air is so clear you feel like you can fly."

"Is it far?" asked Llianna.

"Two leagues as the raven flies, but it is not a trip to do in a day. There is a new boat rolling in tomorrow, so you can see it launched."

Next morning Llianna and Marina stood with King Ardfiskr and the Keepers on the top level of the stronghold, an open space ringed with a low wall of stone. People lined the road from the mountains, waiting for the boat.

"Launching a new boat is celebrated by everyone," said the King. "From the Eskerris pines come the boats, and from the boats comes the livelihood of Eskerris."

Marina nudged Llianna and pointed. A boat appeared in the distance, as if floating on air. The people on the road cheered.

The boat moved closer, balanced on the curved bed of a big-wheeled cart pulled by four sturdy horses.

"It is the mystery of Eskerris," said King Ardfiskr. "The Land gives us the boats for the Sea, but we must work to bring the boats and the sea together!"

The horse pulled the boat-cart to a stream that had been deepened to make a channel to the sea. Eskerris had no harbor, just a long, narrow stretch of pebbly beach with shallow water fringed by a reef. Picturesque, but not exactly a harbor for launching boats.

The teamsters unhitched the horses and led them away, leaving the boat suspended on the cart by the channel. A young man climbed up into the boat, waved to the crowd, and braced himself against the rear of the curved hull. Was he going to ride it into the water?

The young man signaled. Men surrounded the cart on three sides and rocked it back and forth until the boat tipped towards the canal. There it hovered like a giant wingless bird, the man on top holding fast. The boat tilted further and slid off the cart to land in the water with a great splash. Loud cheers erupted from the crowd. The young man threw down ropes, and the other men pulled the new boat slowly towards the open water through break in the reef.

Llianna cheered along with the crowd and added another chapter to her book of dreams . . .

‡

As they were preparing to leave Eskerris, Llianna asked Faeoia to show her where Angan Eyeland lay. They walked to the top of the stronghold and looked out to the horizon.

"It be a lonely place," said Faeoia, pointing to a distant speck in the ocean. "But it be beautiful. The winds and sea currents keep it warmer than the mainland, and fresh water flows all year. There be groves and places to swim. Beautiful."

"Do you miss it?" asked Llianna.

Faeoia shook her head. "I would like to see it again, but it be the daughters of Angan Eyeland I miss more than anything."

Llianna stared at the distant island, blaming the stinging in her eyes on the glare from the water.

"Tell me about them," she said softly.

"Listen," said Faeoia. "You can hear them on the wind. You can hear them in the water."

Llianna heard the whoosh of the waves; was that what Faeoia meant? She heard the wind whispering across the stronghold walls. Was that it? She pushed her hearing further, out over the water to the island where her mother had been born . . .

A song, soft as a summer breeze, strong as a storm wind:

The Mother shares Her love in the falling rain
The Mother shares Her love in the corn and grain
The Mother shares Her love in the warm hearth fire
The Mother shares Her love in the breeze that flies

Great Mother may we share with you our gift of song
We raise our voices joyfully, we raise them strong
Oh, Mother we are grateful for all you do
And we have come together now in praise of you . . .[ii]

"I hear them," said Llianna softly.

‡

In a stone cottage in a glade at the heart of Angan Eyeland a young woman stared into the flames of a fire. Her golden hair hung in ringlets to her waist, and her eyes watered with the smoke. She saw her sisters' song take wing and fly across the water to the girl on the mainland. *Llianna, daughter of Queens.*

Meera turned from the flames to speak with the old woman carding wool in the corner. Amara carded by feel, her eyes white with age.

"She hears us," said Meera.

Amara nodded. "Of course she does."

"Will she come?" asked Meera.

"Not yet," said Amara. "She has some growing and some learning and some loving and losing to do before she can cross the water."

"Will she come in time?" asked Meera.

Amara laughed, a sound like the murmuring of the sea. "In time to see me in this old body, you mean?"

Meera nodded. "You be her kin. It be right that she finds you here when she comes."

The old woman rubbed her hands together, working the oil from the wool into the swollen joints of her thumbs. "She will come in the right time, and I will be here if the Norns have woven it so."

‡

The women's song stayed with Llianna as they rode along the coast road from Eskerris to Naustrup. She savored the sea breezes and the messages carried across the water. Gulls skirted the shore, crying raucously, and silvery shoals of fish flashed in the waves. The land sloped gently to the shore, with no towering cliffs like those at Gullhyrndr.

As they neared Naustrup, boats came to shore with the tide.

"Pearl divers," said Faeoia.

"Look! They're women!" Llianna pointed to four pearl divers pulling a boat from the water. "How wonderful."

King Ralvr's daughter, Avenr, explained that the pearl divers lived along the coast in summer, working the oyster beds from dawn to dusk, and it was the women who did most of the diving, more able to withstand the cold than men. Llianna looked triumphantly at the Keepers, but their attention was on the tray of pearls presented by the King: white pearls, pink pearls, and one black pearl, large and lustrous.

Marina found a strand of luminous white pearls that the King was pleased to give her, and Llianna pointed to the black pearl that shone with lustrous depth. No doubt the Keepers would note her choice in their ledger.

Llianna and Marina successfully confirmed the Pledge on their last night in Naustrup, and Llianna began to long for home. What a relief it would be to see the last of the Keepers . . .

‡

They rode home as the season turned, summer's warmth giving way to crisp mornings and breezes that whispered of cold and snow. They bypassed the strongholds this time, stopping only at Keeper Sanctuaries.

"Why do you think the seven fiefdoms are spread all along the coast?" asked Marina, as they rode past Vadsted for the last part of their journey.

"Where else would they be?" asked Llianna, distracted from a daydream about a handsome, young warrior who saved her from certain death at the hands of bearded Raiders . . .

"Well, they could go further inland, over the mountains."

"That's the Wastelands. No one would want to live there."

"But the Wastelands must end, mustn't they? I wonder if anyone has even been there to see."

Llianna looked at Marina thoughtfully. There she was doing it again - naming one of the unnamable things that niggled at Llianna: why didn't anyone ever talk about the land beyond the mountains? Even Sigfinn had brushed off her questions about it.

Llianna looked over her shoulder to check the whereabouts of the Keepers. It would not be safe for them to hear Marina thinking aloud like that. The three Keepers rode at the rear, like shepherds herding recalcitrant sheep. Llianna pulled a face that was not at all queenly, but she made sure the Keepers did not see it.

True to form, Marina forgot about the Wastelands and went on to talk about what she would wear to the welcome dinner at Gullhyrndr.

Óðin asked for one drink from the well, but he did not get this until he gave one of his eyes as a pledge. - The Edda

They rode into Gullhyrndr late in the day, the sea shining like the gold for which the stronghold had been named. Llianna's father met them in the forecourt and swept her up in a hug as soon as she dismounted.

"It is good to see you safe! Did you have any trouble on the road?"

"Why would we have trouble? You always say travelling the seven fiefdoms is as safe as dining in our own Hall."

Her father just grunted, placed her back on the ground, and turned to speak with Sigfinn and the húskarlar chiefs.

Rothmar and Marina were doing the *dear sister/dear brother* thing, so Llianna left for the solitude of her room. She happily anticipated sleeping in her own bed - without anyone snoring beside her - and being free to think her own thoughts for as long as she wanted. And, best of all, no more Keepers!

But the Keepers were still there at dinner, muttering to each other and looking suspiciously around the room. Llianna sat with Marina, too tired to do much but lean on her elbows and watch people eat. A movement caught her eye - her father signaling the gothi. Was there going to be some kind of ceremony?

The gothi stood and held his arms up for silence.

"Óðin, far-wanderer, grant us wisdom,

Courage, and victory.

Friend Thor, grant us your strength.

And both be with us."

Llianna tensed. Why was the gothi invoking the prayer for danger? What risk was there? She had confirmed the Pledge, and The Keepers would be gone tomorrow. She looked to her father. Frown lines creased his forehead and his jaw clenched. What was happening?

"May we be feasting and drinking

In Valhalla for a full night

Before the Krakenstar

Knows that we art dead.

May we livest to be a hundred and ten.

And may Óðin's be the last voice

That we hearest."

The gothi bowed to the kings and stepped back.

"We have heard the invocation for protection and parting," said King Bekkr. "Enemies have risen in our land, and we leave on the morrow to defeat them." He raised his cup high.

The húskarlar stood and raised their cups. In one voice they cried: "I make this oath: that I shall be in the forefront of fierce battle, forging ahead with my lord and friend, coming to the war-call carrying my weapons. And though I had rather lay down my life than see harm come to my lord, still should the poisoned point or aged edge strike him down, then I shall not flee a single footlength from the field, but rather shall advance into the enemy army, slaying as I might, to avenge the protector of the people. And by Freyr, and by Njordr, and the Almighty Ase, may the sword smite me upon which my hand has rested, may my own edge twist and turn against me should I fail to keep this oath."

Llianna whispered the words with them, as Sigfinn had taught her when she was six years old and dreaming of being a sworn warrior and standing beside her father in battle. Battle! If only she could fight as the sword-maidens of old had done, living by the Warrior Code: "I live with courage, I walk with truth, I fight with honor, I love with fidelity, I train with discipline, I work with industriousness, I maintain self-reliance, I persevere."

"What did you say?" asked Marina.

"Nothing," said Llianna, realizing she had been speaking the Code aloud.

The men strode from the hall in a flurry of excited talk and urgent plans. The wives of the húskarlar bustled out after their men, squawking like the giant gulls that flew in from the sea to scavenge for kitchen scraps. Marina and Llianna were left alone at the table.

"At least they have something to do," muttered Llianna,

scowling after the women. "Preparing the banners, oiling the hauberks . . ."

"What did you say?" asked Marina again.

Llianna shook her head. "Who could we possibly be fighting? Have the Raiders returned? Isn't it too late in the season for longships? Where would they have landed?"

Marina shrugged. "I'll find out." She set off through the door to the kitchen.

Llianna left the Hall and hurried after the chiefs to the practice ground. Sigfinn was more likely than the serving women to know what was happening. Who could they be fighting? The last of the sea Raiders had been defeated before she was four years old. Who would dare attack Gullhyrndr and Ravensborg, the strongest of the seven fiefdoms, with húskarlar trained to fight on land and water?

Sigfinn stood with the húskarlar chiefs on the far side of the circular training area. Torches cast shadows on the raked sand, and the men's voices disappeared in to the night. Llianna strained to hear Sigfinn, but a lone raven called from the wall, distracting her. Was there only one?

A second raven flew past Llianna's head, stirring her hair with its passing, just as the ravens had the morning she had summoned Aegir. Harbingers of doom, the common folk called the ravens. Were they flying at night to bring warning?

Sigfinn finished with the men and waited for them to leave

before beckoning Llianna to join him in the arms room. He always knew when she was there, even when she hid in the shadows behind the bales. She hurried across the yard, through the door, and down the three steps that led into the long room.

A single torch cast flickering light on the walls. The heavy smell of clove oil tickled Llianna's nose; Sigfinn had been cleaning the swords. Racks of them lined the walls, the whole history of swords over the centuries: single-edged with no guards, double-edged with low guards or with massive pommels made for Giants. Thick pommels, thin pommels, five-sided hilts, pommels ornamented with bronze, copper and silver . . .

"Are you planning to stand there staring at the wall, or do you want to know what be brewing?" Sigfinn sat on a bench, chin in his hands, looking even more glum than usual.

Llianna sat opposite the arms master and mirrored his dejected pose. The imitation was automatic, something she had learned to do as a small child, drawn by Sigfinn's authority - and his availability. Unlike the King, Sigfinn had always found time for her. Early in the morning, or after the men left, he had welcomed a lonely girl and taught her how to fight.

"It be the Förnir , the old folk," he said, still staring at the floor.

"Förnir ? Are they still here?"

"Where else would they be, Kio? Those that survived fled into the mountains after the First Battle a thousand years ago, but they did not go far, and they have never stopped mourning their loss and feeding their hate."

Spider legs of fear crawled across Llianna's skin. "And now?"

"And now they be back." Sigfinn stood and swept an arm through the air to take in the weapons lining the walls. "We be needing all this and more."

Llianna frowned up at Sigfinn. "But our men are the strongest fighters in the seven fiefdoms! Surely they can defeat an old tribe."

"Ah, Kio, that be where we have all been wrong, thinking of them as a broken people. There be forces in these lands older than Time, older than Memory and Sorrow. The Förnir always had power, but I fear they have may have found a darker power in their exile, though their souls be forfeit for doing so. The forces of darkness be stronger than the mightiest warrior."

Sigfinn still called her Kio - little goat - but he spoke to her like an equal. Llianna loved him for that, but she hated to hear him speak so grimly of defeat.

"No! Do not say it! Our warriors are like the heroes in the old tales. They cannot be defeated. Do not despair!"

Sigfinn shook his head and sighed deeply. "It is not for the warriors that I despair, Kio. It be for you."

"Me? But I am safe here, aren't I? You have taught me to fight and the húskarlar are strong . . ." The spider's legs were crawling all over her now.

"No one is safe if the Förnir have joined with the Noctimagi."

Llianna had heard tales of the Noctimagi, the dark twins of the fabled Ljósálfar, but the stories were all of far distant evil in far distant times and places. Weren't they?

"The Noctimagi? Are they real? Where are they? In the Rondveggr?" They called the mountains Rondvegger - Shieldwall - but what good was a shield if the danger was already inside?

Sigfinn nodded. "The Noctimagi be real enough. They have always been there, in the deepest caverns of the mountains. Rumor says they be stirring."

"What rumors? What can we do? Can I fight?" asked Llianna.

"Always questions, Kio. You must go to Ravensborg with Marina. It be furthest from the fighting, and your time has not yet come."

"What do you mean, my time? What time? To fight alongside my father like my brothers? To strike the enemy in battle?"

"Ah, Kio, dear Kio, I may live to regret teaching you to fight. You dream of glory, but battle be pain and blood and death."

"Not if we win!"

"Yes, even if we win," said Sigfinn, ruffling Llianna's hair like he had done when she was three years old. "Go now and see what your father has decided."

Llianna threw her arms around Sigfinn and squeezed as hard as she could. His body was strong and lean like a true warrior, so why did he speak of defeat like an old man?

He returned her hug and then turned her towards the door. "Go, Kio. There be work to do."

She left to find her father.

Sigfinn watched her go and sat alone with the swords and shadows, contemplating the threat to Gullhyrndr. It had all been simpler when old king Haldr was alive, when he and Bekkr had been lads together, beating back the Raiders who came in their longships to plunder Nyrland's coastal settlements. They had made a good team, training húskarlar to watch the coast, setting up beacon fires to signal an attack, mounting defenses that sent the Raiders scurrying away to other shores with easier pickings. Nothing mysterious about Raiders, no dark magic or thirst for revenge, just big men with big beards, strong sword arms, and a hunger for plunder. Simple.

Sigfinn shivered; *someone walking on his ashes*. The threat from the mountains smelled of dark magic and old grievances, and the Förnir would not be repelled like the Raiders; there was nowhere else for them to go. Nyrland had been theirs before Sigfinn's forebears had come in their longships to claim the land, and now they wanted it back.

Sigfinn sighed deeply. That he should have lived to see the days of the old prophecy come to life! He mumbled a prayer to Óðin, asking that there be time to complete Llianna's training, time for her to grow into what would be asked of her . . .time for her to become strong enough to face the dark magic of the Noctimagi . . .

‡

Deep beneath the mountains in tunnels and caverns carved by Time, the ones the Nyrlanders called Noctimagi observed the eternal cycles. Sun and Moon did not shine in the deepest places, yet still the rhythms of light and dark could be sensed in the air, in the rock, in the blood flowing through bodies that had never known the Upper Worlds.

Halidor carried the oil lamp to Sanctuary, walking in the footsteps of his father's fathers to light the watchlights at the center of the Nine Worlds. Seven watchlights for seven thresholds; seven Watchers standing vigil.

Six adepts followed Halidor, moving their feet in time with his, obeying the Law of silence. Sanctuary was the center of the Nine Worlds, the watchlights the beacons that called the Warriors home. Or so Halidor had been taught by the Elders; no one had walked the Way of the Warriors in a thousand years, yet the Watchers still tended the lights and waited . . .

Halidor held the flame to the watchlights until each oil-soaked wick flared. Sanctuary filled with a soft glow even as the Moon returned from three nights of darkness in the World above. Halidor had never seen the Moon but, like all Watchers, he could sense the cycles through the changing rhythms of his body. His uncle Ariorn, who defied the Laws to visit the Upper World, had described the Moon as a huge, golden watchlight in the domed vault of the Nine Worlds. Halidor sighed silently; he would sacrifice all the privileges of his position in Sanctuary to accompany his uncle in the Upper World, see the Moon, smell the air, let the wind take him wherever it blew . . .

Impossible. Forbidden. Dangerous.

It might be tolerated in one as powerful as Ariorn, but never in an adept of Sanctuary. The Laws must be served . . .

You will reach your destination even though you travel slowly - Kemst þó hægt fari - Icelandic proverb.

Llianna scowled at the untidy pile of crumpled travelling clothes on her bed. It was true; she and Marina were being sent to Ravensborg.

"For your own good," her father had said. Why did adults always say that when they were making you do something you didn't want to do? The Förnir had not been seen West of Vadsted, but there was no doubt that Ravensborg would be safer. Nevertheless, Llianna just wanted to stay at Gullhyrndr and be part of what was happening.

Her father had also said something about it not being her time yet, just as Sigfinn had. What did they mean? When she had asked her father about it, he had just shrugged and told her to go and prepare for another journey.

Llianna kicked the bed post in frustration.

"Aargh!" Pain throbbed in her foot, and she hobbled over to the window. The sky still arced above the World, and the sun had risen as usual. How could her life be changing so quickly? Was this what came from disturbing the Wyrd?

Wispy clouds raced each other across the sky, and Llianna's thoughts raced with them . . .

Marina hurried in, looking pleased with herself. Of course she would already have sorted and packed her travelling clothes while Llianna was still sitting on the windowsill wondering about Fate . . .

"I knew you'd be dreaming instead of packing." Marina began busily folding Llianna's tunics and leggings. "We need to take all our tunics and leggings, and of course we'll need dresses . . ."

"Stop!" Llianna jumped down from the windowsill and snatched a tunic from Marina's hands. "I'm sick of everyone telling me what to do." She shoved the tunic untidily into the big leather pack at the foot of the bed.

Marina touched Llianna's back. "I'm sorry, Lli. I'm just excited about seeing Ravensborg again, and I'm scared . . ."

Llianna turned and held her friend's hand. "We'll be safe. I promise."

"I'm not scared for me," said Marina. "I'm scared for you!"

"But why? We'll be going to Ravensborg together, and we'll look after each other."

Marina shook her head and turned back to the pile of garments on the bed.

Llianna frowned at her friend's back. What was going on? Why did people keep saying they were scared for her? Did they know something that she didn't?

"Why are you scared for *me*?" she asked, moving around to look Marina in the eyes. "What do you mean? What's all this about?"

"I don't know what you're talking about," said Marina, not meeting Llianna's eyes.

"Marina! Don't do this. We're sisters in all but blood, and I know you know something. Tell me!"

Marina put down the clothes and sat on the bed. "If you spent more time with the women and less time with Sigfinn, you'd know about the . . ."

Llianna didn't let her finish. "Huh! I didn't even know about the Förnir , that's how much time I've spent with Sigfinn lately. If I spent any less time with him, I'd . . .I'd . . ."

"Be like me?" asked Marina.

"That's not what I meant. It's just that nothing ever happens in the kitchens or the women's rooms except burned bread, pricked fingers, and gossip."

Marina rolled her eyes and crossed her arms over her chest. It was her waiting look, and it always worked; Llianna could only keep up her outrage so long . . .

"Well, what exactly would I know if I spent more time with the women? What amazing secrets do they share when I'm not there?"

"The prophecy," said Marina quietly.

"What prophecy?" asked Llianna.

"That's what I mean! The mountains could be moving and you

wouldn't notice unless they moved directly across your path."

Llianna threw her hands up in the air. She had no idea what Marina was talking about. Moving mountains?

"Just tell me. Please."

Marina sighed. "There's a prophecy, and everyone says it's about you, and it says you aren't to know your Fate until it finds you, so no one can tell you, and everyone talks about it, but no one knows what it means, except maybe Faeoia, and she doesn't make any sense, and everyone creeps around as if the next thing they do might lure you to do something to disturb the Wyrd, and no one wanted the Keepers to know about it, and . ."

"Stop!" Llianna held up her hands as if to ward off a blow. "What is this stupid prophecy? Do you know the words?"

Marina sat up straight and closed her eyes. She had the most amazing memory, but it only worked with her eyes closed.

"When darkness comes from mountain halls
Covering land and scaling walls
A child will come from Freya's line
Born in death, lost in time.

Strong and wild, swift and free
Her fate is carved in Life's tree
But guard it well, lest she be lured
To tamper and disturb the Wyrd.

Her power will come in anger born

Fired by Freya and the Norn

To vanquish darkness and despair

For all that moves in Earth, Water, Fire, and Air."

"*Paska*!" Llianna cursed in the old tongue, slumped down beside Marina on the bed, and dropped her head into her hands.

"What?" asked Marina, looking nervously around the room.

"*Helvete*!" Llianna thumped the bed. "I think I already did it."

"Did what?" asked Marina.

"Disturbed the Wyrd," said Llianna.

"What are you talking about? How does someone disturb the Wyrd? How could a girl disturb the Wyrd?" Marina stood and stomped around the room. "I'm sick of this silly prophecy! It makes everyone talk nonsense, and now you sound like Ketilfrith when she's had too much to drink, and . . ."

"Stop!" said Llianna again. "Who's Ketilfrith?"

"What?"

"Ketilfrith? You just said I sound like her."

"Oh. She works in the kitchen, but I just meant that you're cursing and talking nonsense, and I can't bear how everyone goes around looking over their shoulders all the time as if some awful Fate is just waiting to pounce, and . . ."

Llianna held up her hands.

"I talked with my mother."

"Yes, but dreams don't disturb the Wyrd. Don't you start jumping at shadows like the rest of them! No one even knows if the prophecy is really about you. Just because your mother's mothers were shield-maidens all the way back to Freya, that doesn't mean . . ."

"My mother's mothers were shield-maidens?"

"Well, that was before. And . . ."

"Marina! How do you know all this? How do I not know it?"

"That's what I mean! It's the prophecy, that bit about *guard it well lest she be lured*. Everyone thinks you need to be protected from knowing about it, or something awful will happen. It just doesn't make sense. I mean, if you don't know about it, you could just go and do something without knowing . . ."

Llianna rolled into a ball, covered her head with her hands, and groaned.

"What?" asked Marina.

Llianna burrowed under the bed furs.

Marina sat down on the bed and pulled at the furs. "What? Have you really done something? What is it? What did you do?"

Llianna uncovered her head and took a deep breath. "I really did talk with my mother. Down at the sea. With Aegir. Before the Pledge Ride. The night before the Testing."

"*Paska*! That thing in the sea was you? You did that?"

Llianna sat up. "That's the first time I've ever heard you curse." She laughed, and then she couldn't stop, the laughter drowning out the dread curdling her stomach.

Marina stood with her hands on her hips, scowling. "It's not funny, Lli! What if the prophecy's true? What if you really have disturbed the Wyrd?"

Llianna stopped laughing and stood, crossing her arms over her chest. "If I have, then I suppose that's my weaving. There's nothing I can do about it now. At least I wasn't 'lured' by anyone to go and talk to my mother." Even as she said it, she wondered about the burning desire for true love that had taken her to the sea to summon a God.

Marina shook her head. "Just don't tell anyone I told you about the prophecy."

"I promise," said Llianna, picking up a tunic and throwing it into her travel bag. "And don't you tell anyone about me summoning Aegir." Her hands were busy with packing, but her mind roamed far along strange pathways . . .

‡

The Kings and their men gathered noisily at daybreak to leave Gullhyrndr. The yard filled with shouting men, stomping horses, and workers running to and fro with water bags and supplies. The Keepers were there, obviously intending to ride with the Kings.

"No happening without a Keeper," said Llianna softly. She stood on the steps with Marina in the pale morning light, praying for the safety of the men.

Rothmar fussed over Marina and was courteous to Llianna. Dagmar and Falden strode around giving orders and offered no farewells. Llianna's father held her close and whispered into her hair.

"Be safe, little one. Be strong."

Llianna hugged him, breathing in the smells of battle: oiled leather, cold metal, and sweat.

"You, too," she said, making him laugh the deep belly laugh she loved.

The Kings and their chiefs rode out, and their warriors followed on foot, leaving horses enough for Sigfinn and the ten húskarlar who were to ride with Llianna and Marina to Ravensborg.

"My voice goes with them," said Sigfinn, watching the fighters march out. "They have heard it often enough in training that it lives in them now."

"Are you sorry to stay behind?" asked Llianna. Silly question! Of course he wanted to be with the húskarlar, marching alongside the men he had trained and the King he had served all his life. *She* wanted to march with the men, so how much more must Sigfinn want to be there.

"They don't need an old man along on a fight like this," said Sigfinn. Brave words.

"Not true," said Llianna. "But I'm glad you're coming with us. You'll see us safe to Ravensborg."

"That I will, Kio. That I will."

Faeoia hobbled outside to hug Llianna and fasten a pendant around her neck. Malachite for protection, twisted around with silver wire and hung on a plaited cord to rest next to the emerald.

"Wear it close to your heart and never take it off, dear child,"

Faeoia said, patting the pendant through Llianna's tunic.

Llianna hugged Faeoia fiercely. "I'll miss you."

The old nurse laughed. It sounded like the crackling of dry leaves. "Not true, dear child. Your time be upon you, and there be no more need for nursing."

"My time? What does that mean?" She almost asked about the prophecy but remembered her promise to Marina.

"The answers be yours to find," said Faeoia. "Go! They be waiting for you."

"But. . ."

Sigfinn called for them to mount.

"Go!" said Faeoia, waving her hands as if shooing away a stray cat. "I be keeping the dead company until you be returning."

Llianna mounted Vaskr and rode away from Gullhyrndr, Marina at her side, Sigfinn leading the way. Where would she find the answers Faeoia said were waiting? Would they be at Ravensborg? She still had to confirm the Pledge there, as Marina had done at Gullhyrndr. Would that complete something? Or was Faeoia talking about something completely different?

‡

Sigfinn took them through Midli Pass to the Western road, a different way from the Kings and their men, who had taken the road North towards the high mountains. The Western road snaked though the foothills, rising and falling gently enough to make it easy work for the horses and a pleasant ride for Llianna and Marina.

"What will you miss the most?" asked Marina.

"I'll miss the harbor and the sunlight on the water. The sound of the masts in the wind," said Llianna. "The excitement when a trade ship comes in. The wildwood. Climbing the tower."

"It's sad to be leaving," said Marina. "I wonder what Ravensborg will be like after all these years. Do you think anyone will remember me?"

"Of course they will," said Llianna. "And don't be sad. One phase of our lives has ended and another is beginning."

"You sound like a gothi! Next you'll be spouting prophecy," said Marina.

"No, I won't! I don't believe in stupid prophecies, remember! We can reweave the threads of the Norn, change the path of Destiny, decide for ourselves . . ."

Marina scowled. "So says the daughter of a line of daughters descended from Freya. Or don't you believe in that either?"

"I may be of Freya's line, but I can choose my own Destiny!" said Llianna. "Why can't that be true?"

"Because there are Laws, and they may not be broken," said Marina, making the sign to ward off harm.

"Now *you* sound like a gothi!" said Llianna, urging her horse into a canter.

They slept under the stars that night, sheltering in a small wood near a stream running down from the mountains. Birds settled in the trees, warbling about the day's adventures until the deepening shadows made them fall silent and tuck their heads beneath their wings. Llianna lay awake, watching the two men on guard walk the perimeter of the camp. Marina slept soundly alongside her, untroubled by thoughts of Fate and Destiny. Llianna could not forget so easily.

The mountains loomed, a dark shadow against the night sky. Where were the Förnir waiting with their dark magic? Would her father find them and defeat them? What if the prophecy were true, and the fate of the seven fiefdoms rested with her? What could one girl do to change the World?

She remembered Sigfinn's words about the Noctimagi. What power did they have that even Sigfinn feared them? A breeze whispered through the trees, and Llianna shivered.

"Someone walking on your ashes," Faeoia would have said.

Llianna knew where her pyre would burn and where her ashes would lie; all in her line were honored with funeral pyres on the cliffs overlooking the sea. Who might be walking there? And when would her pyre burn?

She drifted to sleep wondering how long her life would be and who would mourn her when she was gone . . .

Where you recognize evil, speak out against it, and give no truces to your enemies. - Hávamál, st. 127

By the middle of the next morning, Llianna was deathly afraid that her funeral pyre was going to be lit much sooner than she had thought. A rough-looking band of about twelve men had ridden out from behind a ridge and surrounded them, aiming arrows at their hearts before Sigfinn could give the order to fight or flee. Now the arms master sat rigidly, clenching his fists and scowling at the swarthy man who declared himself the leader of the band.

"Your names and purpose," said the man in an accent Llianna had never heard.

"No business of yours," said Sigfinn gruffly.

The man moved his hand.

An arrow flew straight.

Sigfinn fell.

"No!" Llianna leaped from her horse to crouch over Sigfinn, shielding him. He lay terribly still.

"Your names and purpose," said the man again.

"We are from Gullhyrndr, traveling to Ravensborg," said Marina quickly, holding up her hands to ward off another attack.

The man moved his hand again.

Arrows flew.

The Gullhyrndr men fell.

"*Hruga uskit'r!*" Llianna surged to her feet, yelling curses. "*Hrafneultir!*"

She hurled herself at the leader, fighting to reach him, to tear him to pieces. His horse screamed and reared.

Llianna stumbled and fell backwards. She hit the ground hard and air rushed from her lungs, leaving her gasping.

"Bind her!" ordered the leader. "And gag her. She curses in the old tongue."

Two of the men grabbed her and a hand covered her mouth. She bit down hard.

"Aargh! The bitch bites."

"Wash yourself, Horgen. She might have mad-dog disease!" called another of the men, laughing.

They all joined in, laughing and calling crude advice.

Llianna wished them dead.

Fire filled her body.

The men holding her fell, writhing on the ground as if pierced by arrows. Then two more fell screaming from their horses.

"Stop!" A young man rode forward, fingers forming horns to avert magic.

The screaming turned into groans and sobs, and Llianna stood alone, warded, wrapped in stony silence, shaking with rage and fear.

A force like a storm wind hit her, and she fell.

Marina sat unmoving on her horse, too shocked to think. Two of the attackers pressed close on either side, holding her reins. She took small breaths through her mouth and tried to make the men, the bodies on the ground, the awful silence, go away. If she moved, it would all be real, and it couldn't be real. Hadn't they just been riding peacefully to Ravensborg? Weren't they protected by Sigfinn himself? Hadn't he survived countless battles? Wasn't the danger the other way, in the mountains?

"You!" The young man who had stopped Llianna edged his horse close enough to touch Marina's shoulder.

She flinched, and it all became horribly real: the men surrounding her, the bodies on the ground, Llianna . . .

Marina sucked in a deep breath and let it out in a wail.

"Not her, too!" said one of the men, reaching for his knife.

The young man shook his head. "She has no power."

Marina glared at him.

"If looks could kill . . ." said one of the men.

"But hers cannot," said the young man.

The leader signaled for them to leave. "Get the other one. Leave the rest for the wolves."

The men hesitated, muttering about magic and power.

The leader gestured impatiently towards where Llianna lay as if asleep. "She is warded. Give her to Gravnir if you fear to ride with her."

The men lifted Llianna to sit limply in front of the young man, who fumbled uncertainly until he worked out how to hold her with one arm and control the reins with the other.

Marina reached for Llianna, but one of the men pulled her arm back.

"She will live," said the man who held Llianna.

They rode out then, leaving Sigfinn and the others to ignoble death. No pyres, no prayers . . .

Marina raised her right hand and recited the needed words in a whisper: "May Óðin give you knowledge on your path, May Thor grant you strength and courage on your way, And may Loki give you laughter as you go." It was the best she could do.

They left the road and followed unmarked trails into the mountains until the sun dropped low in the sky. Marina clung to her horse, desperately afraid for Llianna. The leader finally called a stop in a clearing between giant boulders. Birds sang warnings through the treetops, and shadows moved as if alive. The young man dismounted and lifted Llianna down to lie on the ground.

Marina slid off her horse and ran to kneel by Llianna's side. Llianna's chest moved with her breath, but that was the only sign of life. Had the man harmed her?

"She is not harmed. I have her warded," said the man. He mumbled some more words, and Llianna's eyes opened.

Llianna looked up into Marina's anxious face and the face of a stranger. She gasped. The stranger's eyes were the color of the earth - rich, dark brown. Never before had she seen such eyes; her own and those of everyone she knew were shades of blue or grey or green. Light eyes. The stranger's eyes were dark as night.

"Who are you?" asked Llianna.

"Ah, that was going to be my question," said the young man.

"I am Llianna, daughter of . . ."

Marina nudged her and shook her head.

Llianna looked at her friend, blinking to clear her vision. "Where are we? Where's Sigfinn?"

Marina shook her head again. Tears filled her eyes.

Llianna sat up. "What? What's happened?"

Marina pointed to the other men. "They killed them. Sigfinn. The men. They took us."

Llianna struggled to stand.

The man mumbled something again. Llianna closed her eyes, slumped back, and resumed the slow, steady breathing as if asleep.

Marina stood. Fear filled her body. *Fear is strength to the true warrior.* How many times had she heard Llianna say that?

"What do you want with us?" she asked, stepping between Llianna and the man.

"I will tell you that when I know who you are." He left to tend the horses.

Marina's momentary strength drained away, and she sat with

Llianna's head on her lap, wondering what would become of them.

The men lit a fire and brought food from their packs. The young man sprinkled a few crumbs of bread on the ground and shook out some drops of water from the flask.

"Hail Earth Mother of All!

May your fields increase and flourish,

Your forests grow and spread,

And your waters run pure and free.

Accept my offering, O Earth Mother.

Bring forth that which is good, and sustaining

For every living thing."

Marina sighed. The words were beautiful, but how could he say them after what his companions had done to Sigfinn and the men? Who were these people who called to the Earth Mother yet killed so easily? And what would Llianna do when she finally woke to the awful truth of what had happened? For that matter, what had she done to make those men fall like that?

Marina's mind skittered from thought to thought, like a wild horse trapped in a yard. Sleep did not come.

‡

The next morning Llianna stirred and woke as if from a night's sleep. She sat up slowly, body aching as if she had been on the practice ground all day with Sigfinn. *Sigfinn!*

"What happened? Where's Sigfinn?"

Marina just shrugged and handed her a waterskin.

Llianna drank and looked warily around the encampment.

"I had dark dreams," she said to Marina. "Ambush. Attack. Sigfinn."

"Oh, Lli. They killed him. And the others."

Llianna closed her eyes. "*Paska!* I feared my dreams told true."

"You tried to fight them," said Marina. "You called power. Do you remember? What was it?"

"I just wanted them dead, and they fell. It felt like fire, like wind, like lightning. It's gone now." What had it been? Would it return?

"One of the men spelled you," said Marina. "He called you völva."

"He has brown eyes," said Llianna.

"What?" Marina felt Llianna's head. "You must have a fever."

"No, I'm all right. But how could Sigfinn be gone? He's been there forever." She wrapped her arms around her knees and said the words Marina had recited the day before.

"All who are born die," said the brown-eyed man, standing close, looking down at Llianna.

She wiped tears from her cheeks. Who was this man? He had been there in the strange dreaming, hovering like a dark cloud.

"I am sorry for your loss," he said.

"You're sorry?" said Marina. "Your friends killed him!"

"Nevertheless. Killing and sorrow can exist together," he said quietly.

"Not in our world," said Marina.

"Then your world must be very predictable and very safe," replied the man. "My world is neither."

And now they were in his world. And in his power. Llianna tested for the current that had filled her when they were attacked. Nothing. Had he really blocked it? Or had she just imagined it? It didn't matter; she still had the fighting skills Sigfinn had taught her . . .

She lunged at the man, pulled his belt knife free, and thrust upwards. "*Hrafneultir!*" she cried.

He twisted impossibly fast and grabbed her knife hand. The bones of her wrist scraped together, making her yell in pain and drop the knife.

"Powerful, weapon-trained, and cursing in the old tongue," said the man, pulling her closer. "Who are you?"

Llianna met the brown eyes and held his gaze.

"Who are you?" she asked back at him.

"My name is Gravnir, and I am Landvördr."

Llianna pulled against his hold. "What is that? I don't know that word."

"Ah, you call us Förnir. Have you heard of the Förnir?" asked Gravnir. He still held her wrist, although more gently.

Llianna nodded.

Marina muttered something too quietly for Llianna to hear. A prayer, perhaps.

"And now you," said Gravnir. "Who are you?"

Llianna took a deep breath, squared her shoulders, and answered. "I am Llianna, daughter of Ronja, daughter of Eydis, daughter of Anniken, daughter of Naja, daughter of Sighrith, daughter of Marina, daughter of Aedel, daughter of Dagmar, daughter of . . ."

"Stop!" It was the same place Aegir had stopped her.

"You name the mothers like the old folk, yet you are from Gullhyrndr. Explain."

This Gravnir was young, but he spoke with authority.

"She is no one. We are no one," said Marina, pulling Llianna away. "We were just on our way to Ravensborg. We have family there."

"Yes, but which family?" said Gravnir. "I do not harm women, but some of my people might do so. Unless you can be traded for something we need."

"What do you need?" asked Llianna.

"Lli!" Marina pulled her further away.

Llianna shook her off. "What do you need?" she asked again.

Gravnir sighed. "What do I need? No one has ever asked me that."

Llianna waited.

"I need freedom for my people. I need land for us to build homes and live in peace. I need to see the stars at night and the sunrise in the morning, instead of seeing only the shadows of mountain caverns. I need my ancestors to go to their rest and stop clamoring for vengeance . . ."

Llianna shook her head. This man was one of the enemies her father had set out to destroy. His fellows had killed Sigfinn. He was Förnir, or whatever he called himself. And yet he spoke of freedom just as she might, just as anyone might.

"I do not expect you to understand," said Gravnir. "Long have our people been enemies. Long have the Landvördr been exiled." He turned away and gave orders for feeding the prisoners and guarding them.

"Well, I didn't expect that," said Llianna quietly.

"Expect what?" asked Marina, biting into the hard bread left by one of the men.

"That one of the Förnir would speak like that. That they want the same things we want. That they are not just shadow-ridden monsters."

"They killed Sigfinn," said Marina.

‡

They rode on into the mountains, and Gravnir did not approach them again. The way became steeper, and the horses moved more carefully, picking their way over broken rocks. Llianna and Marina held tight to the manes and prayed the horses were sure-footed enough to keep to the trail. The sky seemed closer up so high, and the clouds moved faster. Once an eagle circled down to hover above the line of riders, as if counting their number. Llianna strained to reach the eagle in the way she had always reached birds and animals, but her power remained blocked by whatever Gravnir had done. Was it gone forever?

The sun dropped behind the peaks, ending the day abruptly. The leader called out orders, and the men dismounted along the trail. Llianna and Marina sat by their horses, Förnir ahead and behind them. Someone handed along more bread and flasks of water.

"I need to pass water," said Marina quietly, looking around for somewhere that offered some privacy.

"Wait until it's dark and we'll do it over the edge like the men," said Llianna, who had practiced pissing like a boy when she was younger.

Marina sighed miserably, but she managed well enough when it came to it.

They settled down together to rest. Night birds called forlornly from the rocks, and the moon rose slowly over the tallest peak.

"It's beautiful," whispered Llianna.

Marina groaned. "If you like sleeping out in the mountains with a band of killers."

"We don't have much choice," said Llianna. "Yet."

They moved on before sunrise the next day and rode until the sun was high in the sky. The leader ordered them to dismount by a sheer cliff and led them through a narrow crevice hidden behind fallen rocks. They entered a cave, and Llianna sent her senses into the rock of the mountain. Nothing; her power still lay dormant.

Torches were lit and the horses led away. The leader ordered Gravnir and three men to take Llianna and Marina deeper into the mountain. The air was still and cool, smelling of soil and damp. How deep did the tunnels go?

Deep. They walked a long way before the tunnel opened into a cavern, high and wide as the Great Hall at Gullhyrndr. In the center milled twenty or more Förnir, talking loudly. The language was unknown to Llianna, but she recognized the gathering as a council of chiefs. How many had she watched at home, stealing into the Council room and listening from behind a curtain or pillar? The same strutting and hand waving, the same voices vying to be heard, the same tone of authority from the leader . . .

Gravnir called a greeting, and the others all turned to stare at Llianna and Mariana.

"What have you found, Gravnir?" asked a man at the center of the group. He stood head and shoulders above the rest and spoke with command.

"Lowlanders, Fangar. From Gullhyrndr."

"Ah! Even as the men march to fight us, the women come calling." He beckoned them closer.

Despite her blocked sensing, Llianna's skin crawled at the menace in the man's voice. She held Marina's hand tightly and walked slowly to the middle of the cavern.

"Two fine doves a long way from their nest." Fangar leaned close, eyes stripping their clothes. His breath smelled like rotting meat, and he had the look of a raptor with his dark eyes and thin lips.

He reached out, hand moving like a snake striking.

Llianna yelped and stumbled back. Her breast throbbed, and her rage beat against the warding, but the spell held her as surely as if she really were a dove in a trap.

"Ripe and ready for plucking." The man called Fangar laughed, but it did not reach his raptor's eyes.

Llianna struggled harder against the ward, but Gravnir put a hand on her arm and shook his head.

"They have value beyond their bodies," he said, moving to stand between them and Fangar. "They can be traded."

"For what? What do we need but vengeance and victory?" Fangar laughed and lunged past Gravnir to pinch Llianna again. "This one is mine."

"And the other?" asked one of the men.

"Take her."

Marina screamed as they dragged her away. Llianna fought to reach her, but Fangar pulled her across the cavern and hurled her against the wall.

Llianna threw out a hand to save herself.

Her wrist broke with a sound like wood snapping.

She had a moment's thought of the staff she had cut to summon Aegir, then searing pain brought her to her knees.

"Begging for it already," said Fangar, grabbing her hair.

Marina screamed again, and the sound thrust Llianna past pain and killing rage to an eerie sense of deep calm. Time slowed.

In the endless space between one moment and the next, Llianna reached with her good hand, pulled the blade from Fangar's belt, and slashed it across his neck.

He screamed.

Time stopped.

Fangar's blood blossomed and floated onto Llianna's face.

The moment passed, and time snapped back into its regular rhythm.

Fangar growled like a wounded bear. Crazed with pain and rage, one eye showed through the blood on his face.

Never leave a wounded enemy. Kill him. Always. Sigfinn.

Llianna circled Fangar, angling for a direct thrust to his heart.

Up under the ribs, at least until you grow into your height. Sigfinn again.

Llianna dropped into a crouch, tensing her legs to push off the ground for extra strength.

A horn sounded, loud and strident.

"They come!" cried one of the men. "To the pass."

Fangar rushed her, bloody hands reaching for her throat.

Llianna pushed off with her legs.

The knife skidded off a rib and tore through his tunic. If only she had two strong hands. . .

"Fangar! Leave her!" The other Förnir ran to the sound of the horn, grabbing shields and helmets.

Still Fangar came forward.

Llianna braced for another thrust, pushing her broken arm against her chest to grip the knife with both hands. *Pain is strength . . .*

"Fangar!" One of the men grabbed him and pulled him away. "We need you!"

Fangar turned a wild eye towards Llianna. "I'll finish this later!"

He ran after the others, yelling orders, blood still dripping from his face.

Llianna dropped the knife and curled around the pain in her arm, cursing.

The cries of the men faded. Marina stumbled over, face streaked with tears.

"Lli, Lli! Did he hurt you?"

Llianna cradled her arm, but she shook her head. *Pain is strength for a true warrior.* "We have to get out of here."

Marina pointed to the shadows by the entrance. Two men stood guard, swords in hand. Big men. Big swords.

"Can you . . .?" Marina asked.

"I don't think so. I don't even know what I did." Llianna reached for the memory of fire and wind, for the sense of calm, but she found only pain and trembling exhaustion.

They edged closer to the entrance. The guards stepped out of the shadows to block their way, dark eyes cold.

"What now?" whispered Marina.

Llianna shrugged. The movement sent stabbing pain up her arm. She muttered another curse; even with Sigfinn's training, she could not defeat two grown men with only one hand. She felt as helpless as a dove caught in an eagle's talons, and she hated the feeling. Sigfinn's words echoed in her memory: *No one is safe if the Förnir have joined with the Noctimagi.* It seemed the Förnir were dangerous enough on their own . . .

Time passed. No sound reached the cavern, and the guards still blocked the way out. Llianna and Marina sat close together, backs resting against the wall.

"We could run past them," whispered Llianna when the waiting became unbearable. "Take them by surprise."

Marina shook her head. "You're hurt."

Llianna urged Marina to try; at least she might escape, even if Llianna's arm made her too slow.

Footsteps sounded in the tunnel. The guards turned and raised their swords. Had the Kings won through already? Llianna and Marina stood and crept towards the door.

Gravnir strode into the cavern, dismissed the guards, and ushered Llianna and Marina out into the tunnel.

"Where are we going?" asked Llianna.

No response. Gravnir marched ahead, forcing them to run to keep him in sight. Llianna's arm punished her with every step, but it was better to be moving than to be waiting for the raptor to return and feed. She bit down on her lip and ran along the tunnel. Dark spots flickered in her vision, and the air grew thick as wool . . .

Keep moving.

Left foot.

Right foot.

Keep moving . . .

Gravnir hurried along the tunnel, heart drumming in his chest like thunder. What he was doing was more than dangerous; it was betrayal and would warrant death if he were caught. But he had seen something back in the cavern, something he could not deny: the girl had power, and her Thread crossed his. Not unusual in an enemy, but her Thread went on after the crossing, twisting and turning, crossing and recrossing his. What did it mean? Could she be the one named in the prophecy? Her Destiny shone in the Tapestry like a strand of starlight, and Fangar could not be allowed to kill that light. As he surely would, slowly and painfully, for the wound she had given him. Gravnir walked faster.

When Gravnir finally stopped, Llianna ran straight into his back. She slid to her knees, cradling her arm and moaning.

Gravnir squatted before her and gently lifted her chin. "Where are you hurt?"

Llianna lifted the broken arm with her good hand. Bruises mottled the skin, and a lump the size of a goose egg covered the break.

"Ah! Powerful, weapon-trained, and brave. If we had time I would like to hear your story." Gravnir helped her to her feet and bound her arm against her chest with the leather strap that had held his sword.

"There is no time for stories. You must leave now." He pointed to a glow of light in the tunnel ahead. "That way leads to the far side of the mountain, away from the battle. And away from your road, I fear."

Llianna gasped. He was letting them go . . .

She turned to ask him why, but he was already striding back the way they had come.

"Come on," said Marina, stumbling towards the light.

They came out into bright sunlight and a completely unfamiliar landscape. The mountains ended abruptly, giving way to a vast plain stretching to the horizon. Small clusters of twisted trees dotted the plain. Nothing moved except the wind, blowing hot and fierce from the North.

Out of Ymir's flesh was fashioned the earth,
And the mountains were made of his bones;
The sky from the frost-cold giant's skull,
And the ocean out of his blood. - Vafþrúðnismál: 21

"What a horrible place!" Marina scowled at the tortured trees.

"They look like people," said Llianna.

"Like people in terrible pain," said Marina, shivering. "What is this place?"

"The Wastelands." Llianna pictured the huge maps lining the wall of the King's meeting room. The land North of the mountains was not part of the seven fiefdoms stretching along the coast like pearls on a string.

"Wyrdstrup." That was the name on the map for the land beyond the mountains.

"Fate at the end of the World," said Marina, translating the old naming.

"A strange name for a strange place," said Llianna. "He may have done us no favors bringing us here."

"I wonder why he did it," said Marina, looking back towards the mountain.

Llianna shrugged.

"*Paska!* Everything hurts." She cradled her broken wrist against her chest.

"Can you walk? Where will we go?" asked Marina.

Llianna pointed West. "The Rondveggr runs all the way from Ravensborg to Naustrup. If we follow it, we must come to Ravensborg."

Marina looked from the wasted land before them to the sheer cliffs behind them. "Not much of a shield wall if the Förnir live inside it," she said, echoing Llianna's thought from days ago.

The mention of Förnir was enough to make them start walking. They stayed close to the cliff face, wary of the strange trees and barren plain. The sun walked with them, scorching their faces and drying their throats.

"Do you think there's water here?" Marina looked around doubtfully.

Llianna shook her head and pointed to a clump of the twisted trees. "Over there. Maybe."

They crossed the open ground to the trees, Marina looking fearfully over her shoulder for any sign of Förnir. Llianna knelt at the foot of the largest tree, picked up a rock with her good hand, and scraped at the soil. Her arm hurt horribly, but without water they would die.

"Here. Let me do it." Marina took the rock and dug more vigorously. Sweat ran down her face, stinging her eyes.

"There's nothing here," she said, wiping her face.

Llianna took the rock and scraped at the dirt.

The hole deepened.

"Look!"

The soil in the bottom of the hole had turned dark. Moisture!

Marina took over the digging until a layer of gritty water seeped into the bottom of the hole. She dropped the stone and scooped up a handful.

"Erck! It's like eating eggshell."

Llianna took some. "Suck out the water and spit out the grit. It's not so bad."

"How do you know? You haven't even tried it." Marina took another mouthful.

"Sigfinn showed me," said Llianna softly.

They sucked and spat until their thirst subsided and their jaws ached. Grit stuck in their teeth and scratched their throats.

"Is it far to Ravensborg?" asked Marina, looking miserably at the soggy hole.

"Far enough," said Llianna. "Let's go."

They walked to the next group of trees and rested in the patchy shade until the sun dropped low enough for the branches to cast ghostly shadows.

"We need food," said Llianna. "Look for plants. Anything green. Or brown, I suppose."

It took six days to reach the end of the mountains and the road to Ravensborg, days of sucking water from dirt, eating the roots of spindly plants, and sheltering from the hottest sun. Nights of stumbling along in the moonlight or sleeping fitfully against one of the twisted trees. Once they found a nest and ate the eggs straight from the shells. Despite their aching hunger, Llianna insisted they leave one egg to hatch.

The last three days they rode with eight goats in a cart, delighted to be off their feet and grateful for the bread and goat's milk offered by the farmer Brod, a red-cheeked man of middle years and large heart. He tended Llianna's arm with herbs and clean wrappings, and he insisted they ride in the cart even though it slowed his progress to market.

"If it was my own daughters wandering like this, I'd want them cared for and no mistake," he said, and proceeded to care for them as if they were his own. He mentioned their wandering a few times.

"Strange for two young ones like yourselves to be wandering alone," said while milking the goats.

"Must be hard being out and about on your own," said while cooking fish he had caught.

"Wouldn't like my daughters wandering around on their own," said while herding the goats back into the cart after grazing them for the night.

Llianna and Marina just repeated their story about leaving their farm to find their father who hadn't returned from Ravensborg the previous market day. Clearly Brod did not believe them.

"But it's almost true," said Marina, as they were alone gathering wood for the night's fire.

"Except we're obviously not from a farm! Look what happened when he asked you to milk Hildigard!"

"What about when you said 'My father likes to hunt wild boar!' Since when do farmers 'like to hunt'?"

"Exactly! He knows we're lying, but he's too kind to say it directly."

"Does it matter?" asked Marina.

Llianna shrugged. "Only that he deserves the truth."

"But it's not safe," said Marina.

"No. And it might not just be Förnir who would take advantage of *drengskapr* on the road."

"*Nobility?* Not looking like this," said Marina, picking at her filthy clothes.

Their hair hung in rough braids, their clothes had taken on the grey-brown tones of farmers' garments, and their skin was almost as dirty.

"I wonder who Brod thinks we are?" said Marina.

"I think he just sees his own daughters and wants to do right by us," said Llianna. "Bless him for it."

Brod's kindness made her weep for Sigfinn as she lay awake at night, wondering if her father was safe, if they had won the battle . . . if the brown-eyed Förnir was still alive. She even thought of her brothers once or twice.

Brod had heard rumors of a battle in the mountains to the

East, but he could not tell them who had won; if it did not affect his family or his goats, it did not trouble him who won and who lost the battles.

Llianna and Marina entered Ravensborg somewhat restored. At least their feet had stopped aching and they were well fed. Llianna's arm still hurt horribly, but she kept it strapped and prayed that it would heal well.

"It's like a dream, what happened," said Marina.

"A nightmare," said Llianna, frowning at the crowd at the gates: people, carts, and animals on their way to and from market. Noisy. Smelly. Not home.

Brod left them by the stronghold, with good wishes and a soggy hessian bag of goat's cheese. They still hadn't told him who they were, for his own safety as much as theirs, and Llianna blessed him again for his kindness, given with no thought of reward.

Marina pulled the bell cord at the side gate of the stronghold.

The guard opened the top gate, wrinkled his nose at their unwashed smell, and told them to go around to the supplicant's door.

Marina stamped her foot. "We're not here for kitchen scraps. We're here to see the King. Open the gate!"

The guard poked his head out and spat at their feet.

Marina punched the man's face so hard he staggered back, holding his nose and yelling. Blood welled between his fingers.

Llianna reached through and unlatched the gate. They ran into the stronghold and past the guard, who yelled and chased after them, still holding his bloody nose.

"The kitchens," called Marina, leading the way across the yard to an arched doorway.

The guard followed, yelling as if the stronghold were under attack by Raiders.

Marina and Llianna ran through the archway and along an open corridor that ended in another yard. A huge cauldron steamed in the middle of the square, and women stood on benches stirring the contents with large wooden paddles. Llianna sniffed: lye and lavender. Washing day.

Marina ran across and stood before a tall, grey-haired woman who was directing the washerwomen like a warrior chief, waving her arms around and yelling instructions. The woman looked down over her ample breasts and made flicking movements with her fingers, waving Marina away like she was a stray cat.

The guard ran up and grabbed Marina's arm. "Got you!" He turned to the tall woman. "I tried to stop them, but they forced their way in." Blood still seeped from his nose.

Marina tugged at the woman's skirt. "Thyvri? It's me. Marina."

The guard pulled Marina away. Marina clung to Thyvri's skirt, forcing the tall woman to stumble after them. The three of them - irate guard, desperate Marina, bewildered Thyvri - staggered across the yard. The washerwomen stopped to stare, mouths hanging open at the sight of their mistress pulled along like a goose-girl.

"Thyvri!" cried Marina again.

"Stop!" yelled Thyvri.

The guard stopped.

Marina skidded into him.

Thyvri swayed like a great tree, caught her balance, and bent down to peer at Marina's face.

"Mari?"

"Mari!" She pulled Marina away from the guard and whirled her around as if she were two instead of twelve. "Oh, barn, how I have missed you!"

The guard backed away, sniffing noisily and wiping his nose on his sleeve.

Thyvri put Marina down and looked around. "Where is your brother? You look like an urchin! Whatever has happened to you?"

The guard hurried away, muttering to himself.

Marina beckoned Llianna over and briefly told their tale. Thyvri rolled her eyes, hugged Marina again, and bustled them off to the kitchen where she ordered tubs of hot water, plates of steaming food and pitchers of milk. While they washed, Brod's goat's cheese was mixed with eggs, flour, grated potatoes and onions, and fried into delicious potato cakes.

Clean, fed, and safe, dressed in clothes salvaged from the storeroom, Llianna sat at the huge kitchen table as Marina told Thyvri their story in more detail. Marina spoke in her usual non-stop way, with barely a pause for breath. When she reached the part about punching the guard, Llianna stopped her.

"I can't believe you did that!" she said.

"This is my home," said Marina, launching straight back into the story.

Llianna thought of the small, grey birds that nested in the tower in Spring – gentle honey-eaters that turned into a frenzy of beaks and claws when the ravens came too close to their nests. Who would have known that Marina could be that fierce and strong? She sat there now looking none the worse for their ordeals.

Llianna was even feeling better herself; her arm had been expertly poulticed with boneset and wrapped again, soothing the savage pain that had been with her since the caverns. The storytelling became a constant drone in the background, Thyvri's voice merging with Marina's. Llianna's thoughts drifted. She shuddered at the memory of the Förnir and Fangar's ravenous eyes, yet her heart secretly hoarded the memory of Gravnir's kindness . . .

"Lli. Lli!" Marina called her attention back to the kitchen. "They think Rothmar has defeated the Förnir. A rider came this morning. The húskarlar are coming home."

Llianna sighed. "My father?"

"He must be well. They would have heard if he fell. They won, Lli. It's over."

"I hope so." Llianna shivered. If it was over why was dread spreading through her body like black ice?

Thyvri saw Marina and her friend settled in the big bed that had belonged to Marina's mother. The girls fell asleep, and Thyvri sat by the fireplace, watching over them as they rested. Fancy the young things walking all they way from the mountains like that! Who would have thought that Carlar's daughter would have such strength? Marina's mother had been sweet and pretty, but she had not been strong. Thyvri did not doubt for a moment that it had been Llianna who had seen them through the worst of it, broken arm or not. She had a touch of the old folk about her, that one, a touch of magic.

Thyvri tucked the furs around the sleeping girls and went to stand by the window. What would that touch of old magic bring to Ravensborg? Would Llianna be the wife Rothmar needed to hold his own against the Keepers as his father had done? Or would she be the weak link through which the Keepers tightened their hold on Ravensborg?

Thyvri shivered. *Someone walking on her ashes . . .*

‡

Llianna and Marina woke to the softness and warmth of a real bed. They rose and dressed in the clothes Thyvri had found for them, grey dresses with wide sleeves and long skirts.

"How does anyone do anything dressed like this?" asked Llianna, tugging at the tight neckline.

"They have people to do things for them," said Marina. "You

are a Queen-in-waiting, not a farm girl!"

They ate in the kitchen, Thyvri hovering to make sure their plates were emptied before she went off to gather baskets and capes for a trip to market.

"Thyvri reminds me a bit of a Keeper," said Llianna, who was more accustomed to Faeoia's odd ways.

Marina frowned at her.

"Well not exactly like a Keeper, but she watches everything and seems to know what you're thinking before you know yourself."

"That's why the stronghold runs so well," said Marina. "Just like Klaudina manages the kitchen at Gullhyrndr."

Llianna remembered Klaudina standing in the kitchen, overseeing preparations for a feasting; the Gullhyrndr cook could supervise at least eight different dishes and still know what the kitchen boys were doing behind her back. It was like watching Sigfinn teaching the men a complex battle strategy. *Sigfinn* . . .

Llianna and Marina accompanied Thyvri to market, and Llianna looked for Brod, but the goat farmer must have gone home to his wife and daughters. Thyvri selected fabric for new clothes for Marina and Llianna, arranging for it to be delivered to the stronghold. Marina and Llianna chose some ribbons and visited the shoemaker.

"You will be mistress of all this one day," said Marina. Did she sound wistful?

Llianna tried to imagine living at Ravensborg, married to Rothmar, ordering goods at market, running the household. None of it seemed real.

‡

Rothmar rode in with his chiefs late on the fourth day. They carried the Ravensborg flag - three black ravens against a red sky - and people lined the road, cheering to welcome them home.

Llianna stood behind the parapet above the main gate, Marina by her side. Thyvri had dressed them in new green skirts and bodices befitting Kings' daughters. Llianna's hair was braided with matching ribbons, and she felt like a fool. Why did everyone think it desirable to dress a girl up in ribbons and lace like a wishing tree? Even with people to help her dress, it was still too much bother.

Llianna pulled at the stiff bodice, longing for the freedom of tunic and leggings. How could anyone climb or run in a dress? And why did men like to see women dressed like wishing trees anyway? She shuddered, thinking of Fangar's grasping hands.

Marina pointed excitedly at the cavalcade, but Llianna scowled at the sight of Rothmar riding at the head of his men. She might only be able to wish men dead when her anger took her to that deep place of calm power, but she wasn't about to let Rothmar treat her like a fool!

"Lli? What's the matter? Is it your arm?" asked Marina.

Llianna shook her head. "It's nothing. Let's go down and find out what's happened."

Rothmar did the *sister/brother* thing with Marina, and he greeted Llianna courteously, assuring her that her father and brothers fared well. Later that day he sat with them to hear their story.

Marina spoke, and Rothmar listened attentively, asking questions about the Förnir caverns.

"There is much we do not know about the Förnir. Enough for now that you are safe and that we have won this battle. You did well to survive in the Wastelands. Perhaps they are not as bleak as we have heard."

Marina shuddered. "They are horribly bleak, and the trees look tortured and there's no food or water unless you know how to find it and the sun is too hot and the nights too cold and we wouldn't have survived except Lli knew how to find water and what to eat but we were starving and . . ."

Llianna put her hand on Marina's arm. "Enough that we are safe," she said, echoing Rothmar's words. She turned to him. "You speak as if there might be more battles."

Rothmar nodded. "The Förnir will rise again. It is an old story, and the end is not yet written."

"Will you tell us?" asked Llianna. "I have never heard the full story."

Rothmar was silent for a while, looking from Llianna to Marina, as if making up his mind about something. He nodded. "It is needful that you know the story. It seems the time has come again for the Förnir to rise, and you will both wed men who are sworn to fight them." Did he blush a little when he looked at Llianna?

"The Förnir lived here before our people came from over the sea. They are an old race, as old as the Land, and they did not give it up willingly. Many were killed, and not always cleanly. They were dark days, and much was set in place then that still shapes our lives today. Perhaps it could have been done differently, but that chance has long since passed. In the end there was a great battle, and the Förnir were defeated. Our people won the land, although great harm was done to the Lands beyond the mountains."

Llianna remembered the twisted trees and shook her head - so much pain.

"What happened?" asked Marina. "What made it look like that? How could a battle do that? And it was so long ago!"

"It was strong magic," said Rothmar. "Magic called forth to stand against the dark forces of the Förnir and their allies. It won us the Land, but the price for the victory was high." He glanced at Llianna and looked quickly away. "We live well enough between the mountains and the sea, but much was lost to us in the First Battle."

"For the Förnir as well," said Llianna quietly.

Rothmar frowned at her and then nodded. "They lost everything."

"And now they are in the mountains, inside the Shieldwall," said Llianna.

"And it is said they have found the dark magic again," said Rothmar. "It is the return that was prophesied, but it has been so long we thought it would never happen."

"Prophesied?" asked Llianna.

"But you won the battle," said Marina, talking over the top of Llianna. "Doesn't that mean we're safe?"

Rothmar sighed like an old man. "No one is safe if the Förnir have joined with the Noctimagi."

"That's what Sigfinn said before we left Gullhyrndr." Llianna wiped a tear from her cheek.

"Sigfinn remembered the old tales," said Rothmar. "He will be missed."

"You speak of prophecy and of a return. What is this?" asked Llianna, her heart racing. Was it the same prophecy that Marina had told her at Gullhyrndr?

Rothmar closed his eyes and sighed deeply. "There is a prophecy that names a darkness arising from the mountains. It seems that time has come."

Llianna crossed her arms over her chest. "Not all the Förnir are dark. The one who let us go seemed to care about us, and not just for what he could take."

"Care about *you*, Lli," said Marina. "It was you he called brave. It was you who blazed with power."

"What is this?" asked Rothmar, staring at Llianna. "Tell me about this power."

Marina blushed; she had agreed not to mention the strange

force that had filled Llianna.

Llianna sighed. "When they killed Sigfinn and the men, I was filled with a force of wind and fire, and I would have killed them all."

"Would have? What stopped you?" asked Rothmar.

"The one who saved us did something that blocked the power," said Llianna. "I don't know what he did, and I don't even know what it was in me that he stopped."

"Has this happened before?" asked Rothmar, worry lines creasing his forehead.

"Never," said Llianna, shaking her head as if to deny the power that had filled her.

Rothmar stood and paced to the window and back, glancing at Llianna like she might suddenly change shape.

Llianna stood and met Rothmar's eyes. "People at Gullhyrndr say the prophecy is about me. They speak about my time coming. If that's true, I think my time might be here, although I'm not sure what that means." Tentacles of fear ran across her skin.

Rothmar came and held her hands. "This strange power does point to the prophecy, but that will unfold with or without our thoughts about it. You are safe here, and I will send a messenger to Gullhyrndr."

Llianna was grateful for Rothmar's kindness, but she waited impatiently for the messengers to go and return. She longed to return home, to ask Faeoia about the prophecy, make her tell all the secrets . . .

"I wish you would stay safe here at Ravensborg," said Marina, shuddering at the thought of riding back to Gullhyrndr.

"It is your home, and it is right that you stay here," said Llianna. "But I have to know more about this prophecy and about my mother's mothers. Who were they? What am I meant to do?"

"You are changing," said Marina, stroking Llianna's hair. "You're like a spark that lands on dry grass and becomes a blazing fire. I hope it doesn't burn everything up."

Llianna thought of the twisted trees and shuddered. Was that her legacy? A power that could destroy the World?

She banished the dark thoughts and hugged Marina close.

"You're right, dear Mari. I am changing. But I will always love you."

"I love you, too," whispered Marina.

Later that night, Llianna sat alone by the fire while Marina slept. It was true; she was changing. Ever since the power had filled her like a storm wind, it was as if she belonged in a bigger story than the one she had lived in before, and she very much feared that she might never quite fit anywhere again.

‡

First Keeper Solvaldr slapped the messenger. Twenty years of planning almost ruined by a Landvördr attack! If they had killed or ruined the girl, he would have had to start again, and he might not live to see the culmination of another plan.

. . . the mills of Law grind slowly . . .

Solvaldr dismissed the cringing messenger and strode to his tower room; he needed time to think. Why had the Landvördr risen now? Was it the wretched prophecy? *A child will come from Freya's line . . .*

Did the exiles really believe a child could save them? It showed how desperate they had become.

Solvaldr sat at his desk to write letters to the five Kings who had pledged húskarlar to serve the Keepers – all the strongholds except Gullhyrndr and Ravensborg. If the five Eastern fiefdoms could form a shield wall, the main force of the Landvördr attacks would move westwards to Gullhyrndr and Ravensborg.

There was more than one way to make a bear dance . . .

The man that walks his own road walks alone. - Hávamál st. 58

Gravnir endured prolonged questioning by the Elders about the prisoners' escape. The first battle had been fought and the next was being planned, but first they must deal with what had happened in the caverns that day. Gravnir told them that the girl's power had resurfaced while he was taking them deeper into the caverns to hide them from the Lowlander fighters. He described how she had overcome him and escaped . . .

The Elders looked skeptical, and Fangar glared at Gravnir with chilling menace. The knife cut inflicted by the Lowlander girl had left an angry red line running across his eyelid to his chin.

"The Lowlanders are strong," said Olafeur, the First Elder. "If they also have the power of the Warrior Queens, we must think carefully. The Land was destroyed by that power in the First Battle."

Gravnir stood quietly while the Elders argued about whether to pursue an alliance with the Noctimagi as their ancestors had done a thousand years earlier. He had questions he dare not ask: Had the Elders already opened negotiations with the Noctimagi? Did the dark cousins of the Ljósálfar still inhabit the deeper reaches of the mountains?

The warriors argued for gathering as much power as possible to defeat the Seafarers' descendants, and Fangar continued to watch Gravnir with eyes of death. Gravnir sighed miserably, wondering if he could slip away and lie low until the prisoners' disappearance was forgotten, or until the Landvördr had all been killed in this insane war they seemed determined to have.

After another interminable discussion, Olafeur called for silence. He looked intently at Gravnir.

"We cannot know the truth of this matter with the prisoners. Your story will be taken as truth this time, but you will be watched. And you are not welcome at Council until all becomes clear."

Gravnir sighed with relief and left the cavern, Fangar still scowling at him with malignant hatred.

"And no harm is to come to Gravnir in our caverns," said Olafeur, loud enough for Gravnir to hear.

Gravnir shivered; he hoped the warriors had heard Olafeur's command as clearly as he had.

Thence come the maidens, mighty in wisdom,
Three from the dwelling, down 'neath the tree;
Urth is one named, Verthandi the next,
On the wood they scored, and Skuld the third.
Laws they made there, and life allotted
To the sons of men, and set their fates. - Völuspá: 20

Llianna spoke the words of the Sevenfold Pledge in a quiet ceremony with Rothmar, Marina, and the Ravensborg gothi, completing the terms of the Pledge Ride and moving one step closer to the day she would marry Rothmar and become Queen of Ravensborg. The thought of marrying Rothmar no longer filled her with despair, but she still dreamed of the true love promised by her mother. She also dreamed of darkness coming from mountain halls, waves and waves of darkness covering the seven fiefdoms.

The messenger returned from Gullhyrndr with Falden leading fifty húskarlar to take Llianna home. Falden greeted her politely, but he addressed his questions to Rothmar and ignored Llianna for the rest of the journey. They rode in tight formation, scouts ahead and behind, alert for attack by the Förnir. Llianna was guarded day and night, with five húskarlar assigned to stand with their backs turned while she attended to personal business in the bushes or washed in the icy streams that flowed down from the mountains. Falden had barely spoken with her, but his men watched her as if their lives depended on it. By the time Gullhyrndr came in sight, she felt like a precious relic from a sacred grove – valuable, but only for the meaning she held for others, with no life of her own. A peculiar experience, but better than being taken by the Förnir again; just the thought made her wrist ache and her stomach clench.

Her father rode out to meet her, head still on his shoulders and all four limbs working. Llianna breathed a sigh of relief to see him safe. *Seeing is believing,* Sigfinn always said. Always *had* said.

"Let us sit a while so I can hear your story," said the King, dismounting. He beckoned Falden to join them.

Llianna followed her father to a fallen log, where she sat between him and Falden. The húskarlar and chiefs kept watch from a respectful distance, but Llianna didn't care if they saw her cry when she spoke about the ambush and Sigfinn's death. He had been friend to her and her father both.

King Bekkr raised his hand and said the blessing for the dead.

"May Óðin give you knowledge on your path, May Thor grant you strength and courage on your way, And may Loki give you laughter as you go."

Llianna doubted that Sigfinn had laughed as he went, but it was good to hear the words spoken in her father's strong voice.

"I have sent men to find the place and honor the dead," he

said. "They will bring Sigfinn home, and we will light his pyre on the cliffs."

Llianna nodded; Sigfinn would have liked that.

She told the rest of her story, hugging herself as she described Fangar and the walk across the Wastelands. Her father listened carefully, and then he spoke of the battle and the fierceness of the Förnir.

"They are fighting for somewhere to live," she said, remembering Gravnir's words.

Falden made a choking noise but stopped at a look from his father.

King Bekkr frowned. "We, too, fight for somewhere to live, Llianna. But there is more to the Förnir's fighting, something dark and vengeful. They may want Land, but they want it strewn with the dead of the seven fiefdoms. There have been battles near Vadsted, though not as fierce as here in the West. It is beginning."

"What is beginning?" asked Llianna, her throat suddenly tight.

"The prophecy," said her father, quietly. He raised an eyebrow in question.

Llianna nodded.

Falden stood and paced restlessly. King Bekkr waved him away, and Falden stalked over to sit with his men.

"Marina told me," said Llianna quietly. She almost didn't say the next thing, but it was time, and she had to know . . .

"Do you think it's about me?" she asked, not knowing if she

wanted him to say yes or no.

Her father shook his head. "I am not a seer to know these things. Someone I trust told me to take your mother to wife and to cherish her daughter as if the Fate of the World depended on it."

"*Paska!*" said Llianna. "Why didn't you tell me?"

He ignored the curse, which told Llianna how troubled he must be.

"I didn't tell you because the prophecy counseled against it."

Llianna scowled.

"And you needed time to grow into that fierce temper of yours!" He pulled her close and hugged her against his chest. "I'm sorry this has come in our time."

Llianna wiggled free. "Tell me what you know. Please."

"Not enough, I'm afraid," said King Bekkr. "I was never told much, and I only half believed what I was told, anyway. I would have married your mother without the advice, and cherishing you has been as easy as drawing breath. Now I just want to be able to keep you safe."

"If the prophecy is about me, I need to know what it means," said Llianna.

"Ask Faeoia," said her father. "She came with your mother, and she stayed to tend you. Ask her."

"Faeoia," said Llianna, hearing something in the way her father said the name. "You knew what she was teaching me all this time! And Sigfinn. You knew, didn't you?"

Her father nodded. "If the prophecy was about you, it seemed important for you to learn more than embroidery and poetry."

"Thank you," said Llianna, hugging him tightly.

They rode on to Gullhyrndr, arriving late in the morning. Llianna's father smiled tiredly. "Enough of battles and prophecy, Llianna. You are safe. Rest now, and we will feast tonight to welcome you home."

Llianna dropped her riding cloak in her room and ran to find Faeoia.

The old nurse was sitting by the kitchen hearth, warming her toes and bundling herbs for drying – rosemary, thistle, tansy, sage. She patted the bench beside her, and Llianna sat close enough to give her a hug and whisper, "Tell me about the prophecy."

Faeoia nodded. "Ah. It be time then. In my room." She stood, wafting the smell of the herbs over Llianna. *Rosemary for remembrance . . .*

Llianna walked with Faeoia to her small room off the kitchen corridor. The back wall of the room drew heat from the kitchen hearth, and Faeoia hobbled across to a bench to sit with her back against the warm stone. Llianna pulled up a stool and sat facing her.

"Ah. It has been cold here with the dead," said Faeoia. She closed her eyes and sighed deeply.

Llianna waved her hands impatiently. "The prophecy, Faeoia. Tell me."

"Ah. It be yours," said Faeoia. "Child of Golden light, child to heal the Earth."

"That's not part of it," said Llianna, frowning.

Faeoia chuckled. "The prophecy be longer than your arm, golden child. There be verses within verses, and the whole tangle be like a skein of wool after the kitchen cats have been at it."

Llianna leaned forward and held Faeoia's gnarled hands. "Please just tell me."

Faeoia shook her head. "Ah! Come."

She hobbled to the door, beckoning Llianna to follow. Llianna stood and kicked at the stool in frustration. Why wouldn't Faeoia just tell her what it all meant?

Faeoia took a grey cloak down from the hooks on the back of the door, settled it over her shoulders, and pointed to the other cloaks.

"Take one."

Llianna frowned at the cloaks and chose a green one with a hood of white bear's fur. Where did they all come from?

Faeoia chuckled again. "Ah! You wonder how an old woman like me comes by such richness." She stroked the fox fur on another cloak. "I was not always old. Some of these I made when I was younger. Some are gifts. Some have been with me so long I no longer remember who gave them to me." She turned from the cloaks and selected a stout walking stick from a stack against the wall.

"Where are we going?" asked Llianna

"Come," said Faeoia, leading the way out into the corridor and along to the side door.

Llianna followed her across the yard to an overgrown corner behind the herb garden. Was the old nurse walking more easily? Was she standing straighter?

Faeoia pulled back a thick fall of ivy to reveal a small postern gate. She took a loose rock from the wall and handed Llianna a key. Llianna turned the key in the lock and handed it back. Faeoia replaced it in its niche, and they crossed through. She repeated the sequence on the other side, locking the gate with a key hidden in the outer wall.

Llianna shook her head in wonder; all these years she had been climbing the tower wall when she could have been using the secret gate!

Faeoia led her along the path that skirted the stronghold wall, heading north towards the wildwood, taking the same track Llianna had used the night she called Aegir. Had that only been two moon cycles ago?

They came to Vardträd. The great yew tree still stood sentinel at the center of the wildwood – did the affairs of men and women affect it at all?

Faeoia reached into the deep pocket of her cloak and brought out a handful of breadcrumbs to sprinkle on the ground for the Vaettir. Would they accept her offering?

The leaves rustled, and a soft breeze brought the smell of the sea to the wildwood. Bright eyes watched from the leaves as

Faeoia led the way through into the old forest, following deer paths and moving between the trees like shadows. Llianna's heart raced; never had she ventured so far into the old forest. She had defied Sigfinn's warnings to explore the edges of the forest, but even she had hesitated to go further.

"Bears, wolves, and old things best left alone," Sigfinn had said. Of course that had intrigued Llianna, and she had spent days at the edge of the forest, stalking shadows between the trees, heart leaping at any sound. Then Marina had come, and her life had changed: lessons in the library; trips to market to learn about buying supplies, planning banquets, and choosing fabric for formal gowns and cloaks; embroidery in the sewing room; music lessons in the solar.

Her father had sat her down and explained the new regime. "You are eight years old, and it is time to learn the ways of women rather than running around like an un-mothered filly."

Llianna had been astonished. It had never occurred to her that girls would want to do anything except climb walls, practice sword fighting and shield-binding, and explore the edges of the old forest, but Marina actually enjoyed the library lessons, market trips, and embroidery. Llianna had tried to learn the poetry, stitch the samplers, and play the harp, but none of it came easily to her. Marina, on the other hand, recited whole sagas by memory, embroidered tapestries, and sang like a nightingale. Llianna had hated her for a while, but it wasn't really Marina's fault, and it had been good to have someone her own age to sit with in the Great

Hall, making up stories about the young, handsome húskarlar . . .

Llianna stumbled over a fallen branch and brought her thoughts back to the present. Where were they going? Amazing enough that Faeoia could walk so far, let alone that she knew the paths through the old forest. Had everyone been hiding things from her?

They walked between more huge trees standing like sentinels guarding ancient secrets. The shadows deepened and birds called warnings from the branches. A lizard ran across Llianna's foot. She shrieked, but Faeoia did not even turn around.

Just when Llianna had decided that Faeoia was leading them in circles, they stepped into a round clearing. The trees stopped abruptly, as if forbidden to grow there. Opposite them stood one of the rocky outcrops that dotted the forest like abandoned offspring of the mountains. Faeoia walked straight up to the rockface and shook the bushes.

"At last!" said someone from behind the bushes. "I have been waiting."

A cave!

The bushes parted, and a woman emerged, small and stooped, even older than Faeoia. She wore tunic and leggings made from scraped hide. Vines twined through her white braids, and she held a tall staff hung with feathers and beads. Lines etched her face, but her green eyes sparkled like a child's.

"Well come, Freya's daughter." She looked intently at Llianna.

Llianna froze, like a deer hiding in a thicket. Images swirled before her: *a battlefield strewn with bodies; a sad procession of húskarlar bearing a body wrapped in furs; a funeral pyre on the cliffs at Gullhyrndr . . .*

She shivered; *someone walking on her ashes . . .*

"Ah!" The old woman looked from Llianna to Faeoia. A question passed between them, and Faeoia nodded.

"What?" asked Llianna. "What do you see?"

"Seidr cannot be compelled," said the old woman. "Come." She held the bushes aside.

Llianna sidled past the bushes to stand before a narrow opening in the rock. The crevice tapered at top and bottom, so she had to squeeze through sideways, grunting with the effort. She straightened and opened her eyes onto a candlelit dream. The cave glowed with light and warmth and smelled of summer: flowers and berries and sun-warmed grass. Soft piles of fur rugs surrounded a table set with four candles. The walls hummed.

"Sit," said the old woman.

Llianna sat. Was she dreaming? Had Faeoia fed her sleeping herbs?

"Call it a dream if you will," said the old woman. "Dreaming is one way the story can be told."

"What story?" asked Llianna, hoping that at last it would be the story she needed to hear, the story that had been kept from her all her life. The old woman had named *seidr*, so she must be a völva, a seer, and seers knew all the stories . . .

"Not all," said the old woman. "Not all stories have been

written, so they cannot be known."

"Do you know my story?" asked Llianna. "Do you know the prophecy?" She thought of the question she had asked her mother, and a wave of shame turned her cheeks red. What had she been thinking? Why had she only asked about love? Why hadn't she asked her mother about Fate, about her Destiny? Her mother had even named it, but Llianna had been too preoccupied with the idea of true love to understand what she was hearing. What of the power that rose up from her anger? What of the deep, still place within? What of the Förnir who wanted to destroy her world? Love would not stop their dark magic . . .

"Love is no small power," said the old woman. "Do not dismiss it so easily."

Llianna frowned at the völva. Was she reading her thoughts? Was that part of being a seer? But enough of useless questions; she needed answers. She needed to understand the strange power that had come to her.

"What of the other, the killing power that comes with anger? Is it the opposite of love? Is it hate? Is that my Destiny? What of the prophecy?"

"Prophecy is a double-edged blade," said the old woman. "Tell it and it leads one way. Keep it secret and it leads another way. Once it is written it will have its way with us."

"Oh!" Llianna reached into the bag she carried on her belt and pulled out a scroll. "I wrote the prophecy down after Marina told it to me." She unrolled the scroll.

"When darkness comes from mountain halls
Covering land and scaling walls
A child will come from Freya's line
Born in death, lost in time.
Strong and wild, swift and free
Her Fate is carved in Life's tree . . ."

The old woman held up her hands. "Say no more!"

"But . . ."

"They are words of power, and words of power must be used wisely."

Llianna stood and glared at the völva. "How can I use them wisely when I don't even know what they mean? What's the use of a prophecy if no one can understand it?" She crossed her arms and hmmphed with as much force as she could muster.

The völva watched her, unblinking, like an old wood owl . . .

Llianna rolled up the scroll and returned it to her bag, sighing miserably. "Now that I've written it down, will it have its way with me, like you said?"

The völva shook her head. "It is not your writing, child, that determines Fate. It is the writing of the Norns on the Tapestry of Life. Your scroll is not long enough to hold their writing, nor is a lifetime long enough to unroll the scroll on which they write it."

Llianna put the scroll back in her bag. Why did everything just get more complicated every time she tried to make sense of it?

"The Norns are the most powerful forces in the Nine Worlds. It is they who have written you into the Tapestry, and you must find your Thread and follow it." The völva spoke like a wisewoman, but did she really know anything about the prophecy?

Llianna looked around for Faeoia. Why had the old nurse brought her here?

"My sister waits outside," said the völva. "This is not her path to walk."

"Please tell me what you know," said Llianna. "Is the prophecy about me? What must I do?"

The völva smiled and motioned for Llianna to sit.

"It is not mine to tell," said the völva. "You come and you ask, 'What is my Destiny?' This is a hard question because Destiny is not a small thing. Destiny arises from the Tapestry and is woven through with Life. Life is in our actions, in our stories, our songs, our ceremonies; all of these arise from the Tapestry. It was woven by the Norns and by our ancestors: men, women, elk, ravens, serpents, fish, air, fire, water, earth, wind, sun, rain. Life makes the weaving and the weaving makes Life."

"But I need to know . . ."

"You must see for yourself. It is the only way," said the völva, sounding frustratingly like Faeoia.

The old woman reached into her belt bag and sprinkled a pinch of herbs onto the nearest candle. A smell like mulled wine filled the cave.

The smell took Llianna to memories of the Great Hall at Gullhyrndr, memories of music and laughter and safety. She sighed and closed her eyes.

"That's right," said the völva in a voice like a soft breeze. "Being there in that known place, seeing what there is to see, hearing what there is to hear, feeling what there is to feel."

Llianna saw the flames in the hearth of the Great Hall, the ruddy glow on the faces of the húskarlar. She heard the men laughing and singing their raucous songs. With the sights and sounds came a sense of wellbeing, warmth in her body and peace in her heart.

"Now look around this place once more and notice what you have never seen before. There is a door where no door has been, and this door is open. Even as you rise and walk through the door, you can look back and know this place of warmth and peace waits for your return. And now your journey takes you through the door, and as you move deeper and deeper, you can see what there is to see, hear what there is to hear, and feel what there is to feel here in this place . . ."

Llianna moved as if in a dream. She walked through a door into a tunnel of moonlight and shadows. The stone beneath her feet was worn smooth, as if countless others had passed this way before. The way stretched ahead. A memory of the Förnir tunnels came and went in the space of a breath; this tunnel offered promise rather than threat. She walked on. Shapes emerged from the shadows: women with braids of writhing snakes; húskarlar in hauberks etched with runes; a valkyrie shield glowing with golden fire; a great tree with many branches, and in the green branches all the living things of the World. She heard the susurration of wind in the leaves, and she felt her Destiny waiting . . .

"And now you stand before water, water as far as the eye can see. And your way continues on the other side of this water . . ."

Was this a test? How was she to cross?

"Even while you wonder how it is that you can cross, your deeper wisdom knows . . ."

Llianna closed her eyes and reached her senses into the water. A shining creature rose from the depths to carry her across, and she laughed with delight to see other creatures swimming below. The whistling song of the creatures spoke of cool depths and limitless joy.

Then Llianna reached the far shore and stepped into a land she had never seen. The völva's voice followed her.

"And however it is you cross the water, you come to this new shore knowing that anything can happen at any time. There ahead of you is a dwelling, and the door is open. As you move inside, you notice that no matter what it looked like from the outside, this place is ever so much bigger on the inside. Moving now, along hallways, though doorways and arches, past rooms, seeing what you can see, hearing what you can hear, feeling what you can feel . . ."

Llianna walked slowly through the door into this new place. Was it a stronghold?

A castle?

A palace of dreams?

People wandered there, oblivious to her presence, people living and dying in their own times and places. She heard them talking, laughing, weeping, singing, whispering, moaning in pain and pleasure, praying. She felt small as a pinch of soil and big as the night sky, humble and grand all at once.

"And right in the center of this place is someone who has been waiting ever so long for you to come. That's right, finding your way now to the center where someone waits for you to come."

Llianna followed the voice through more arches, along a hallway, down a flight of narrow stairs. The air grew cooler. The way ended at a wooden door. Llianna knocked three times. The door opened. She walked through . . .

. . . into a room like a cave. Smoke rose from a smoldering fire, turning everything to shadow. Three women sat on low stools around the fire. Were they singing? Chanting?

Llianna moved closer and the words came clear.

"Her time is coming. Nearer. Nearer. Her time is coming. Nearer. Nearer . . ."

Llianna sat on the ground in the fourth place around the fire. And suddenly she was falling, falling . . .

. . . falling from a great height towards the Tapestry that covered the Nine Worlds. She knew it as the work of the Norns, but she had never imagined anything as wondrous. Threads twined and turned, crossing and recrossing to form patterns that swirled and changed like water flowing over rocks in the sunlight. One Thread caught her attention, and she floated towards it, enthralled by the colors, the textures, overcome with wonder. She hovered for a long time, entranced by the swirling colors, wondering if this were another test . . .

She reached out and touched the Thread. A vibration shivered through the surrounding Threads, like the signal that tells a spider that a fly has landed in its web. Llianna had a vision of being stuck there forever, as in the old story of the farm boy who took hold of a golden goose. She pulled her hand away.

What had she said about changing what the Norns had woven? Surely if that were her Thread . . .

She focused her attention back on the Thread, touching it with her senses rather than her hands. Along one strand a knot had formed, like the messy knots that tangled her embroidery threads. She mentally tugged at the knot. The Tapestry screamed, a sound like rocks in terrible pain; the sound went on and on, as if the ground, the trees, the air were screaming.

Llianna released the mental image of the Thread and covered her ears, moaning. The sound died, but it echoed in her body, warning her to leave the knots alone.

But what if they were the knots and tangles of her own life? Shouldn't she be able to undo them and smooth the Thread?

She returned her attention to the Thread. This time she delicately settled her awareness on the surface and ever so gently entered into the weaving. She stayed there, softly present, listening, sensing, not trying to make anything happen . . .

. . . an image arose, as if from within the Thread, of a shield-maiden standing on a cliff overlooking the sea. The shield-maiden faced away, so Llianna could only see the back of her leather hauberk and the golden, honey color of her thick braids. The woman stood tall and strong, but there was something sad in the way she gazed over the waves as if waiting for someone . . .

Llianna longed to touch her, but that would surely set the Tapestry off again. With a silent blessing for the shield-maiden, Llianna slipped out of the Tapestry. The völva's voice reached her as if from a great distance.

"Giving and receiving whatever there is to be given and received, and turning now to retrace your way from this place to the place where you started. Moving back now along the hallways, through the doorways and arches, past the rooms, out the door, over the water, along the passages, and back to the place where you began, seeing what there is to see, hearing what there is to hear, and feeling what there is to feel . . .

Despite her desire to stay with the Tapestry, Llianna found herself back in the Great Hall, seeing the flames in the hearth, hearing the men singing, feeling warm and peaceful.

She shook herself and was back in the völva's cave.

"And so it begins," said the völva, handing Llianna a cup of sweet marshmallow tea.

‡

Llianna walked slowly back from the völva's cave to the

stronghold, noting the path through the forest. She and Faeoia did not speak and, when they reached the kitchen corridor, Faeoia simply took the borrowed cape and disappeared into her room, leaving Llianna wondering if it had all been a dream. Had she really walked through the old forest and met a seer? What exactly had been given and received as she sat with the Norns?

Llianna went to her room and stood at the wide sill to look out to sea. She retraced the inner journey she had taken in the völva's cave, feeling the places within that had been touched by the mystery. *And so it begins . . .*

Loki tricked Idunn into leaving Asgard and going into the forest with him. He told her that he had found apples that she would find to be of great worth and asked her to bring along her apples so that she might compare them . . . - Skáldskaparmál: 1

Iduna walked softly through the wildwood, gathering berries from the bushes and trees growing beside the stream. She filled her basket with cranberries, blackberries, raspberries, lingonberries, blueberries, and strawberries, a feast for the Gods and Goddesses of Asgard.

The sun moved past the mid-point of the sky, and Iduna sat for a while with her feet in the deliciously cold water. Birds flew down from the trees to rest near her, and from the forest strutted an elk, crowned with six-tined antlers. Iduna offered the elk a palm full of lingonberries and threw blackberries to the birds. Her allotted task was to feed the Gods and Goddesses, but what were the birds and animals if not Gods of the forest?

Iduna left the stream and walked slowly back to Asgard, singing the spells that filled the berries with the spirit of Nature, the life force that kept the Gods and Goddesses young and strong.

She had learned the spells from her mother, who had them from her mother, words of power passed down from mother to daughter since the beginning. Iduna's long hair coiled around her body like golden snakes as she sang, and flowers bloomed where her feet touched the ground. So it had been since the dawn of Time, and so it might have continued except for the heedless greed and anger of three Gods.

Óðin, Loki, and Hoenir left Asgard and traveled far in search of adventure and riches. Their journey took them into a barren mountain range where Iduna had never walked.

"My life force is weakening," said Óðin. "We must return to Iduna and her life-giving berries."

"Just a little further," said Hoenir. "I want more to show for our travels." His bag already bulged with gold and precious gems, but Hoenir always lusted for the next treasure.

"We can slaughter an ox for our next meal," said Loki, who never troubled with matters of property or ownership of herds.

Óðin let it be, so they killed an ox, prepared the meat for cooking, and sat around the fire waiting to eat. Strangely the meat did not crisp and sizzle; no succulent smells arose from the fire.

"It must be spelled," said Hoenir, looking around warily.

"It is I who, by my magic, prevent your meat from cooking!"

They looked up. Perched in the tree was a huge eagle. Óðin muttered something about Loki and his thieving ways.

"Give me my fill of your meat, and I shall release the rest for

you," said the eagle.

Loki objected, but Óðin invited the eagle to eat his fill. The great bird glided down and took the choicest parts of the ox with his sharp talons and fierce beak.

"That is enough!" cried Loki. "All the best meat is gone!" He grabbed a fallen branch and lunged at the eagle.

The eagle moved faster than light and took the branch in its talons, carrying Loki into the sky. Loki screamed and cursed, but the eagle spiraled higher and higher.

Loki threatened and begged, and finally the eagle offered Loki a choice.

"Bring me the life-giving service of Iduna, or I will carry you to my children who will strip the flesh from your bones."

Loki agreed.

The three travelers returned to Asgard, inventing glorious songs and stories about their journey. The longest story was about Loki's encounter with the eagle and his escape, but only he knew the bargain he had made with the creature; only he knew that the eagle was the giant Thjazi in his bird form.

When the travelers had been welcomed home, all the songs sung, the stories told, and the mead drunk, Loki crept away to the wildwood to find Iduna. He knew the way to her bower; her mother's mothers had always welcomed him, feeding him the ripest berries, the sweetest nuts, the most succulent fruits.

"Ah, Loki, you are returned safely. I dreamt of a giant who carried you away. I am glad to see you well." Iduna smiled, and

the World grew brighter.

Loki ate some berries and spoke of his travels, offering to show Iduna a place he had found where cloudberries grew all year round.

They left Asgard the next day, Iduna carrying her basket to fetch cloudberries for the Gods and Goddesses. They journeyed for three days and came to a barren mountain range.

"Where is this place?" Iduna asked, but Loki had disappeared.

A rush of wings, and Iduna was snatched up in Thjazi's talons and carried to the giant's lair; Thrymheim, he called it - Thunder Home - for the sound of the wind in the mountain peaks and the pounding avalanches that covered the World below with snow.

"Feed me the elixir of Life," demanded Thjazi.

Iduna offered Thjazi berries from her basket, but he flung them away.

"I can gather berries myself," he growled. "I want the magic you give the Gods! I want to live forever!"

Iduna spoke of the life-giving power she carried, but Thjazi was bellowing too loudly to hear. He locked her in a stone cell and left her alone on the mountain.

Asgard was quiet. Without Iduna's life-giving berries, nuts, and fruits, Time moved through the halls of the Gods, wrinkling skin, bending backs, turning hair grey. The Gods and Goddesses grew frail and old.

"What is this?" asked Freya, her once golden hair hanging limp and grey, her breasts sagging.

"Ask Loki," said Óðin. "Ask him how he escaped from Thjazi."

Loki was summoned. He arrived without his usual jauntiness; even he had become old and bent.

"What have you done with Iduna?" asked Óðin.

"Why does everyone always think it's me?" asked Loki.

"You were seen leaving with Iduna," said Óðin. "Where is she?"

Loki denied his guilt until the other Gods and Goddesses threatened him with all the combined pain and torment they could muster.

He confessed.

"Bring her back," said Óðin. "Or you will be the first of us to die."

Loki crept away, wondering how in the Nine Worlds an aging God could stand against a giant in the peak of his strength. Then he thought of Freya's hawk feathers and did what came naturally to him; he stole one. The feather allowed him to become a hawk, and he flew to Jotunheim, the land of the giants. He crept into Thrymheim.

Loki being Loki, he was lucky enough to find Thjazi away from home, and he turned Iduna into a nut and carried her away in his talons.

From behind them came a great, thundering cry.

"Fee-fi-fo-fod, I smell the blood of a lying God, Be he live, or be he dead, I'll grind his bones to make my bread."

Thjazi was coming.

The deafening beats of massive eagle wings filled the air.

Loki flew faster, the Iduna nut clasped in his talons.

Thjazi's eagle form filled the sky, blocking the sun.

Loki sped towards Asgard.

A ring of fire burst to life around Asgard.

Loki crossed the flames.

Thjazi followed.

The flames exploded upwards like the violent birth of a volcano.

"Thjazi is dead," said Óðin. Charred eagle feathers spiraled to the ground.

Loki limped in with Iduna, whose basket overflowed with berries. The Gods and Goddesses ate the life-giving fruit and rejoiced.

"Blessed be Iduna, the life-giving power of Nature."

Iduna carried her empty basket back to the wildwood and bathed her feet in the stream . . .

The Goddesses are no less sacred, nor are they less powerful.

- Gylfaginning: 20

The night after Llianna's first visit to the völva, the Great Hall glowed just as it had in her vision, and she was welcomed home with food and music and laughter. She looked for Sigfinn at the head of the húskarlar table and flinched to see one of his chiefs in his place. The húskarlar families lined tables further down the Hall. Llianna frowned - where were the wives and children of the men who had been killed with Sigfinn?

She turned to her father. "What provision is made for the families of the men who die in service?"

He raised his eyebrows. "Ah, a question fit for a Queen! You will do well by Ravensborg with thoughts like that."

"The families?" prompted Llianna, ignoring her father's reference to Rothmar.

"The families are as well as can be. They receive the man's stipend until the woman remarries or the sons are old enough to work. It does not make up for their loss, but they get by."

"And what of the daughters?" asked Llianna. "Can they not work to support the family?"

"Women's work will not support a family," said her father.

"Why not?" asked Llianna. "Why should women work for less than men?"

"It is the way of things," said her father. "Would you change the World and turn everything on its head?"

"Perhaps," said Llianna.

‡

The next morning Llianna dressed quickly, ate in the kitchen, and retraced her steps to the völva's cave. This time she brought an offering of freshly-baked bread and a flask of cider. Her body hummed with excitement. Hadn't she had wished for a wisewoman to teach her?

She found the path to the clearing, and the seer waited in the shadows. Not a dream.

The völva took the gifts and invited Llianna into her cave. "Good instincts. Bringing gifts. Good instincts."

Well, that was something; if nothing else, she had good instincts. Llianna sat in the same place and opened her senses to receive the völva's teaching.

And so began a time of learning and testing, a time of deepening, with many days spent in the völva's cave and many more spent wandering the old forest, learning the völva's way of seeing and sensing the plants, the animals, and the seasons. Llianna's father let her know that he accepted her absences from the stronghold, although he never mentioned the völva directly. Did he know about the völva's lessons as he had known about Faeoia and Sigfinn, or had it gone beyond him now that the prophecy was coming to life? Whatever the reason, Llianna eagerly embraced the chance to follow the thread of her Destiny.

The völva offered no name, and she made no attempt to befriend Llianna. She did offer wisdom different from Faeoia's practical lessons, and Llianna took it up as if were food. She learned to settle deep within, to move between the Worlds, to find her Thread and follow it. The fiery anger that had felled the Förnir appeared as a glowing strand twisting through Llianna's Thread on the Tapestry. It could not be touched directly without the surrounding strands vibrating and screaming, so she worked to extend her senses into the Tapestry and waited for the Thread to reveal itself . . .

Most useful, she wrote to Marina of her time with the völva. *And much more interesting than needlework.*

Their letters were carried by messengers riding between Ravensborg and Gullhyrndr with reports and battle plans for defeating the Förnir. Llianna saved Marina's letters to read by candlelight in her room at night, and she smiled as Marina's thoughts and stories tumbled off the page as if she were there, speaking in the breathless, non-stop cascade of words that was so familiar . . .

Life here is full. Rothmar has brought in more men for training as he thinks there will be a big battle maybe not right now or he hopes that's true so the men can be trained but in the coming years and he's worried about the dark magic. I've been overseeing the sewing of banners and saddlecloths and all the other things I'll need to do when I go to Vadsted - at least it's not Naustrup so we can visit more often. Unless we can't because it's too dangerous with the Förnir and I can't even go to Vadsted myself and I'll have to stay at Ravensborg until I'm an old woman and I'll never marry . . . Oh, what do you think will happen? Will there be battles all our lives? Does your seer say anything about it?

The völva said nothing at all about the World beyond the forest and the Tapestry of the Norns, and she never again mentioned the prophecy, ignoring Llianna's questions as stubbornly as Faeoia ever had. Nevertheless Llianna returned again and again to the cave. She learned more about the healing power of plants and minerals, and she deepened her calling of the elements, honoring the living relationship with Air, Fire, Water and Earth. She memorized the names of all the plants, birds, and animals in the old forest, and she drank twenty-three different kinds of herbal tea brewed in the völva's cave. Most importantly, she learned how little she could really do to change the warp and weft of the great Tapestry.

"Thought and Desire at the service of personal advantage poses a danger to the Tapestry," said the völva.

Llianna absorbed the lessons, and she dreamed. Her nighttime dreams were different from the trance-like dreaming in the völva's cave. The dreams that came while she slept took Llianna back to other times, other lives. She dreamed of shield-maidens and wise women, of mothers and daughters in an unbroken line from the beginning of Time. Some of the women looked like her: tall, dark blonde hair, strong faces, and far-seeing grey-green eyes. Were these her mother's mothers?

Llianna waited eagerly for the dreams, hungry to know more of her motherline. What had they been like? Why did so many appear as shield-maidens, fighting to protect the land?

The dreams continued, but there were still no real answers to her questions. If only Sigfinn were there!

Thinking of Sigfinn reminded Llianna of the húskarlar who had died in service to Gullhyrndr. Who were those men, and what of their families?

Driven by her curiosity and a need to do something useful, Llianna ventured beyond the practice grounds to the sprawling settlement where the húskarlar lived. She had a list with the names of the men who had ridden with Sigfinn that fateful day, and she was determined to speak with their women and see that their children were cared for.

Two men stood at the gate, as if they guarded a separate stronghold.

"Your business?" asked the younger one.

"I wish to visit some of the women who live here." Llianna

wondered if she should have brought Klaudina, the formidable woman who ran the kitchen. Klaudina had lived in the húskarlar settlement as a girl and had talked at length about her childhood as Llianna had sat in the kitchen, warming her toes at the huge fireplace on long winter days.

"It be a lively place," Klaudina had said. "What with back to back houses and children everywhere. No shortage of friends there when I was a girl. Course most of them married into the settlement, didn't they. We all had our eye on the handsomest, bravest boys . . ."

"How did you know?" Llianna had asked. Maybe Klaudina would be more forthcoming about true love than Faeoia had been . . .

"Know what, dearie?"

"Which boys were bravest?"

"Oh, that was easy! They bragged about themselves something wicked, strutting around like roosters, crowing and fluffing their feathers."

Llianna had laughed at that, and the fierce, armed húskarlar had never looked quite the same to her.

"Did you set your eye on anyone?" *Did he love you? Was it true love? How did you know?*

"Oh, well. I did fancy one of the lads, but he got himself into a spot of bother and had to marry Unfridd."

"Oh, I'm sorry," said Llianna. "Was that some sort of punishment? What did he do?"

Klaudina had looked helplessly at Faeoia, who had just chuckled and moved closer to the fire.

"What?" asked Llianna.

"Nothing to worry about," said Klaudina. "I left the settlement after that and came to work here, and this has been a good life."

Llianna had looked at Klaudina's ruddy face and chapped hands and had revised her ideas about what made up a good life.

"I married, you know. Adeko was master of horse, a fine, strong man who never beat me."

Another revelation about the nature of a good life . . .

And now Llianna stood at the gate of the húskarlar settlement with only the fragments of Klaudina's revelations to guide her.

"I am Llianna, daughter of King Bekkr. I wish to visit the families of the húskarlar who rode with Sigfinn that last time."

The guards gaped at her. Who had they thought she was?

"Er, pleased be to enter," said the young one, pushing open the gate.

Llianna entered the world Klaudina had described: houses pressed together in crooked rows, children everywhere, and men strutting around like roosters. She stifled a smile and asked the guards where she might find the women.

"Down at the river most like, or out at market," said the young guard, pointing in opposite directions.

Llianna decided to go to the river. She walked slowly along a cobbled lane winding between the small houses. Who had built the houses and cobbled the lanes? Were the húskarlar builders, too?

Children ran up to follow her, laughing and goading each other to speak to the strange visitor. The children seemed well enough, if a little wild, and Llianna began to think her visit wasted. The húskarlar families took care of their own.

She spotted the women as she left the last of the houses and crossed a pasture where cows grazed and chickens scratched. The outer wall of the stronghold snaked across the hill beyond the river, enclosing the húskarlar world inside the bigger world of Gullhyrndr. Llianna thought of the nesting dolls Faeoia had gifted her; eight dolls, each small enough to sit inside the next. She had arranged them on her windowsill, wanting them all to be free.

One of the women saw her, and they all stood to stare at the stranger. Llianna gathered her courage and walked up to them. Fifteen women with ruddy faces and chapped hands.

"Greetings," said Llianna. "I am Llianna, daughter to King Bekkr."

Most of the women bobbed respectfully. Two or three didn't.

"I wish to speak with those whose men rode with Sigfinn that last time."

"And what would you wish to say to them?" asked one of the women who had not bent her knee.

"I wish to know if they are well, or well as can be, and if they have what is needed for their children." Why were they staring at her as if she were speaking in tongues?

"You're naught but a girl. What can a girl bring to the likes of us?" Grief and pride and something else . . . anger?

"I have my father's word that they will be cared for. Please let me speak with them. I was there when the men died."

A young woman stepped forward. She held a bundle of washing over her rounded belly, as if protecting the babe.

"My husband rode with Sigfinn and did not return. I would hear how he died."

The other women mumbled and shuffled until two more stepped forward.

"Let us sit," said Llianna, pointing to a low rise.

The women followed her and sat together facing her like children waiting for a tale. The young one sat in the middle, an older woman on her left, and a tall girl on her right. Had the girl been married, or was she there for her brother or father?

Llianna cleared her throat. "I am sorry for your loss. Sigfinn was dear to me, and I mourn him every day. But you have lost men from your families. I cannot change that, but I do not want you to suffer hardship because of it. Please tell me what you need."

The young woman clasped her hands over her belly and leaned forward.

"Tell me how he died. Was he brave? Did he suffer?"

Llianna took a deep breath. "It happened so fast. We were surrounded by Förnir. Their archers killed Sigfinn and the men. All our men held steady, and they did not suffer. The suffering is for those of us left behind."

The young woman wiped tears from her cheeks.

"What is your name?" asked Llianna.

"Raakel. My husband was Osten. This is our first babe."

The other women spoke then, naming themselves, their men and children. The girl, Lunet, had lost a brother - Eiolf - who had been her guardian since their mother died of fever and their father died a year later, thrown from a horse. There was something about Lunet that reminded Llianna of Marina, a lightness in the face of grief and loss, a sort of innocence.

The similarity prompted Llianna to ask Lunet if she would consider living in the main stronghold. The girl's face lit with excitement.

"Oh, yes. Eiolf was trying to find me a place, but . . ." Grief moved across her face like a dark cloud.

The other women took heart and asked for help with food for their children. There had been no provision from the King.

Llianna made a list of their needs and returned to the gate with Lunet, who carried a small bundle of belongings and a new hope in her heart.

"I wish to see your chief," said Llianna to the guards. "Now!"

The young guard ran off. He returned with an older man, whose swagger said *chief rooster* loud and clear.

Llianna wasted no time on niceties. "My father sent provision for the families of the men who rode with Sigfinn. See that they receive it."

The chief's face darkened. He puffed out his chest and opened his mouth to object.

"Stop!" Llianna held up her hand. "If you utter a lie here, I will know it, and my father will know it. Better you attend to the King's behest before he hears of the delay."

The man spluttered and nodded his understanding, but his eyes said something else.

Llianna turned to leave, congratulating herself on handling that just as she had seen her father do a hundred times. Then she remembered that she had not asked for the man's name.

She walked on, head high, showing no sign of the sudden doubt that gripped her. As much as she wanted to prove that she could manage the man herself, she resolved to tell her father. After all, the women's wellbeing was more important than her pride.

Lunet hurried along after Llianna. "He had that coming," she said. "Takes more than his share and steals when he thinks he can get away with it."

"His name?" asked Llianna.

"Aaaviag. He is a bad one."

"*Was* a bad one," said Llianna.

‡

Lunet made herself a bed in the small room near Llianna's, exclaiming all the while over the linen and furs.

"So soft!"

"So warm!"

She unpacked her belongings - a spare tunic, a winter cloak, a sewing bundle, a broken comb, and a small stone statue, woman-shaped, with large breasts and tapered legs. This she placed under her pillow.

Next day Llianna returned to the húskarlar settlement and met again with the women. The first two brought friends who had also lost men in the blighted expedition. The King's provision had miraculously appeared after her visit, and the women gained confidence in Llianna's promises.

Lunet walked beside Llianna and explained the way of things in the settlement.

"Children run free until they get their work. For the boys it be arms or horses, unless they be maimed or weak. For the girls it be marriage and babes and work from dawn to dusk. Some few move on to the stronghold proper, like Klaudina. Like me."

"Can the children read?" asked Llianna.

Lunet shrugged. "There be no need. The need be for counting." She lifted her hands to demonstrate counting. "There be stones for more than ten."

Llianna nodded. She had seen Sigfinn's stones, small rounded pebbles he carried in a bag on his belt. Another bag hung alongside, empty until he added stones for multiples of ten. He had taught her to count using the stones. It had made more sense than numbers on a slate in the learning room.

"I can do stone counting, milk a cow, do buttering and

cheesing, card wool and spin yarn, weave a pattern, and cook food for twenty or more," said Lunet proudly.

"Good. Now you can learn to read and write and help me with my hair."

"Oh, I can plait and braid well enough. Everyone knows how to do that."

Llianna shrugged. She could plait her hair to start the day, but by midday it had worked itself into a mess of tangles and knots. Marina had patiently untangled and rebraided it, but Marina was in Ravensborg, and Llianna needed help.

Lunet happily helped with plaits and braids and anything Llianna needed. In exchange she had a bed, ample food, and new clothes and boots. Not to mention lessons in reading and writing and the manners of a stronghold.

Lunet accompanied Llianna to her meetings with the völva, but she waited outside in the glade, carding wool or practicing her letters with a stick on the ground.

"It be magic," she said when Llianna first introduced her to the völva. "Best I stay outside."

"Why?" asked Llianna. "There is no harm in it."

"There be harm if it is not your path," said Lunet, and the völva agreed.

So Llianna continued her lessons, Lunet accompanying her as far as the clearing or wandering with her through the forest. Lunet easily learned the names of herbs and could find them as if she had some magic after all.

"Just a feeling for the Land," Lunet called it.

Llianna wondered what magic was if not that, but she let it be. Lunet had left the settlement, and she was changing her way of speaking and moving through the World, but settlement ways would always be a part of her.

‡

A whole year passed, and Llianna still hungered for the stories she most needed to hear, the stories of her mother's mothers, of the time before. She gathered honey cakes from the kitchen, and went alone to Faeoia's room.

"It is time for me to know," she said, handing Faeoia the plate of cakes. "Everything."

"That be a lot of knowing," said Faeoia, taking a bite of cake.

Llianna snatched the plate away. "No more until you tell me."

"Hah! Give them back and sit down."

Llianna handed back the plate and sat on a stool before Faeoia's chair.

"Ah. It be needful that you be ready," said Faeoia. "It violates the Tapestry to awaken someone before their time."

Llianna sighed. Was that what they had all meant when they said her time had not yet come?

"I'm ready."

Faeoia nodded. "Yes, you be ready now. I will tell you of your mother's mothers, as the story was told to me, and your Thread will tighten." She took a bite of honey cake and chewed slowly.

Llianna waited. How much tighter could her Thread be?

"Once, long, long ago, at the beginning of time, Sky and Earth were one, moving together in the Void. There they would have remained for all time, but for the Chance that lives in Chaos. From Chaos comes the night, from the boundless empty space comes the power of Nature. From Chance came a spark that gave rise to a wind that blew between Sky and Earth, driving them apart."

Faeoia's arms rose in a graceful arc, and her hands came together, leading her body forward into a crouch, impossibly supple for old bones.

"Curling into a sphere, Earth formed the solid matter on which we stand." Her arms moved gracefully, arcing upwards. "Spreading wide, Sky arched into the vault of the Heavens above."

Llianna listened, entranced.

"The space between they filled with their children. As their children came forth, Sky and Earth bestowed gifts on them. To men they gave strong bodies, for digging the soil and holding their loved ones. To women they gave strong hearts, for they be the life-givers."

"Women are the life-givers," whispered Llianna.

"We honor the Earth as our Mother. Her hills be like breasts. She feeds us. She was there at the beginning and will be there at the end."

Llianna sighed. Here was the missing part of the story . . .

"Listen now, and I will tell you the true reason that women be the life-givers. It happened like this. The first men and women came forth into a garden between two rivers. In this place was food and water enough for them to live forever. They swam in clear pools, slept in the Sun, and supped on ripe fruits. All was well."

"What happened?" asked Llianna.

"Time passed," said Faeoia. "Earth and Sky began to grow sleepy. No more did they dance as they had when they were young. No more did they bring forth children. A great and wise power came to women in the form of a Serpent." Faeoia's hands moved in front of her in gentle undulations, leaving tracks in the air like the curving pathways of snakes.

"The Serpent spoke to the women and told them the secrets of bringing forth life from within their bodies."

"Why didn't the Serpent speak to the men?" asked Llianna.

"Because men cannot hear Serpents speak," said Faeoia, as if that explained everything.

"Why?" asked Llianna. "Why can't men hear the Serpent speak?"

Faeoia smiled.

"Before the first men and women lived in the garden between the rivers, there was another. Long has she has been forgotten. This is her story."

"But how can she be *before* the first ones?" asked Llianna.

Faeoia smiled again. "What comes first, the bird or the egg?

The time of Sun or the time of Rain? So it is, and so it has always been. There is no beginning, and no end. The green shoots be nourished by all that has gone before. They grow and, when the season is done, they return to the Earth."

Llianna nodded. She had seen the Tapestry, and she knew the truth of Faeoia's words.

Faeoia raised her hands to her shoulders, elbows held close to her sides. Her fingers curled outwards, forming the shape of claws.

"The very first woman was strong and wild. She knew the true names of every living thing. She even knew the true name of Chaos. When the first man came to the garden, he wanted to be with the woman like the lion was with the lioness, like the horned elk was with the cow."

Her hands moved again, drawing horns and graceful leaps in the air. "The fierce one knew that men and women could come together in a different way, a way filled with love and joy, but the man turned his back and refused to listen to her wisdom. One night, as frogs called from the rivers and crickets sang, the man tried to force the woman to do what he wanted. She rose up and uttered the name of Chaos, and the World changed."

Llianna held her breath, waiting.

"Where she had stood was a Serpent, scales shimmering in the Moon's light. When the first women came, the Serpent was waiting."

"What did the Serpent say to them?" asked Llianna.

"Ah!" said Faeoia. "That is the secret. Come closer, and I will whisper it to you."

Llianna moved closer.

"Name for me the powers of Nature," whispered Faeoia.

"Earth, Air, Water, Fire," said Llianna.

Faeoia nodded. "First the Serpent spoke of Earth: *I am the womb of life. From me you come and to me you shall return. Nothing be wasted. Do not fear.*" Her voice sounded like the hissing of snakes.

"Next the Serpent spoke of Air: *I am the breath of life. From me come the winds of change. Nothing remains the same. Do not fear. To live you must leave the safety of the womb. To eat you must crush the wheat. Nothing remains the same.*

"Then Water: *I am the beginning of life. From me all things come forth. Nothing be forgotten. Do not fear. The primal vortex of destruction be also the central wellspring of creation. Nothing is forgotten.*

"Finally the Serpent spoke of the golden light of the Sun, and the glowing flames of Fire: *I am the heart of life. From me comes the searing heat of desire. Nothing be unknown. Do not fear. The barley and the rye agree to live in the Sun and die in the flames to give you food. Nothing be unknown.*"

Llianna, mesmerized by Faeoia's sibilant whispers, swayed from side to side.

"And that is what the Serpent said to the women."

Llianna sighed deeply. "That is what they teach on Angan

Eyeland?" she asked.

Faeoia nodded. "So it has been taught since the beginning. Iduna has been, Iduna be, Iduna will always be."

"Iduna. A name from the old tales," said Llianna.

"Yes," said Faeoia. "Iduna be the life-giver. But the Law Keepers banished the old ways. They wanted the Mother's power for themselves."

"Is that why my mother's people left Eskerris?" asked Llianna.

"Your mother's mothers left so they could live as life-givers and lovers, priestesses and warriors. The Keepers had renamed them *völur* and shield-maidens, but they wished to live as priestesses and warriors. Warrior Queens."

Llianna knelt on the floor and laid her head on Faeoia's lap.

Faeoia stroked Llianna's hair. "All your mother's mothers back though Time carried power."

"Why do I not know this? Why has it been hidden from me?"

"With the power came great responsibility, and something happened in the time of the First Battle that changed everything."

"What happened?" asked Llianna, desperate to hear, yet dreading that this was the terrible thing that had been hidden from her. Why else would it have been kept secret for so long?

Faeoia's eyes became even more clouded, as if she were looking though mist to a far distant time.

"You have seen the Wastelands beyond the mountains."

Llianna nodded. How could she ever forget the twisted trees and dry, rocky ground?

"Once that was fertile land, sheltered by the mountains, warmed by the northern sun. As often happens, it was in this rich land that the battle was fought. The Förnir were strong, and they were desperate enough to call on dark powers to aid them. Towards the end of the day, the battle went in their favor, and they rallied their strength to push back the ones they called Seafarers. Usurpers. The Förnir would have won then but for the Warrior Queens. There were three - Anniken, Sighfrith, Ronja - and they carried Freya's power."

"Those names. They are in my mother line," said Llianna.

Faeoia nodded. "They were sisters, and your mother was from that line. The Warrior Queens ended the battle and saved the seven fiefdoms."

"But?" asked Llianna.

"But the Land beyond the mountains was destroyed, and the Kings came to fear the power of the Warrior Queens. Ronja and Sighfrith did not survive the battle, but Anniken lived to have children - your mother's mothers. The Kings gathered to decide the Fate of the daughters born to this line. From that gathering came the Law Keepers."

"The Keepers arose to control the Queen and her daughters? But hadn't she saved them?"

"Yes, but men easily come to fear women's power. Women bring forth life from their bodies, which a man can never do. Women ride the waves of pleasure through a whole night, while men grow tired and need sleep. And some women have the power to kill with a look, with a thought, with a wish."

"Oh! That's what I did."

Faeoia nodded again. "Yes, you carry Freya's power. You be a true daughter of the Warrior Queens of old, and your power be needed in this time. But men fear the power, and what they fear they need to control."

"Wishing trees," said Llianna quietly. "They dress us like wishing trees and expect us to sit quietly all day stitching stupid patterns on stupid samplers!"

"As if that will stop true power!" said Faeoia, spitting to the side. "Foolish men."

"I still don't know how the power came to me," said Llianna. "Can you tell me?"

"The prophecy - a child will come from Freya's line . . ." Faeoia sighed. "There have been many mothers and daughters since the First Battle, but you be the one named in the prophecy."

"How do you know? What will I have to do? And what happened to all the others?"

"I do not know," said Faeoia. "Anniken birthed daughters, but her daughters were called 'shield-maidens' rather than warriors, and never again has a woman wielded the power of the Warrior Queens."

"But why did Anniken let that happen? Why didn't she use her power to protect her daughters?"

"It is not known. The stories be old, and much has been lost in the telling over time. Perhaps she found the cost of power too great and did not want her daughters to pay the price. And remember, the Förnir had been defeated, so there be less need for Warrior Queens to stand against the dark."

"So the daughters were called shield-maidens, and then even that was taken from them. Women have been sorely punished for that long ago victory of the Warrior Queens." Llianna moved restlessly around the small room. "I always knew something was missing!"

"Yes, and now it be found. It be needed," said Faeoia.

Llianna sat back on the stool and dropped her head into her hands. "My mother said there was harm in my Fate . . ."

‡

For two moon cycles after talking with Faeoia, Llianna left Lunet behind and roamed the old forest, reaching for the power to split wood and crush rock. Nothing happened. She could sense the force that had filled her the day Sigfinn died, but no matter what she did, it remained elusive. The weather grew colder, and Llianna returned to the völva's cave and the slow lessons in following her Thread. She also resumed training in the yard as she had with Sigfinn, Lunet a reluctant partner.

"You would be better hitting the pole," said Lunet, nursing another bruise where the training sword had hit her arm.

Llianna scowled and swung her sword at the fixed target, a pole wound around with ship's rope. It withstood her thrust with considerably more strength than Lunet could muster, but it offered no challenge.

She released Lunet and worked alone to strengthen solitary moves like sword thrusts and duckwalk cutting, but she needed someone to partner her in the shield bind and the stepping exercises; the pole and the wall were just too . . . too still. She imagined a partner as she pushed her shield against the wall, whirling to step in intricate patterns all over the yard. Lunet clapped and praised her skill, but what Llianna really needed was someone to push back, someone to test her speed and her reflexes. What she really needed was Sigfinn back from the dead.

Lunet was able to throw apples as moving targets for sword practice, an exercise they both enjoyed. Afterwards they collected the apple pieces and took them to the stables, returning to the stronghold chatting happily and smelling of horse.

Llianna's arms grew stronger and her movements became more fluid, but she still had no idea what to do about the power inherited from her ancestors. Could she find it again to use it against her enemies? What if it rose up like a flood and destroyed the Land as her long ago ancestors had done?

She attacked the rope pole with renewed strength to dispel the thoughts, and she fiercely sliced apples from the air as if they were the unanswerable questions that plagued her . . .

Then the Förnir resumed their attacks on the roads between the fiefdoms, lying in wait and leaving death in their wake. Visitors came to Gullhyrndr by road less often, and many farmers stopped coming to market. Llianna's brothers led húskarlar out to guard the roads, and the stronghold prepared for battle. Would this be the time when she was called to use her power?

The skirmishes continued, but the Förnir proved elusive; two years passed and still no decisive battle. Two years, and Llianna began to fear that the prophecy was just a tale told by old women who dreamed of times long gone . . .

He flees no fire who jumps over it. - The Saga of King Hrólfr Kraki

Wedding feasts . . .

Marina's letters, once full of details about life at Ravensborg, became filled with thoughts about her betrothal. Her husband to be was Fastulf, the sapling they had met at Vadsted, an important ally for both Gullhyrndr and Ravensborg.

. . . Do you think Aedel has said mean things about me to her brother? Do you remember how we put the snakes in Aedel's bed just before the Gathering when we were eleven? Do you think she told him? At least you've seen Rothmar more often so you know him and I have never said awful things to him about you. Oh, what will it be like to be married? We're having two feasts one here and one at Vadsted. I wish we could wait until you came for your wedding but they say we will miss Frigga's timing if I don't leave before you come. At least I will see you on my way to Vadsted and we can share your feast there but I won't be here for your wedding and you won't be in Vadsted for my wedding feast . . .

Wedding feasts. The time had come for Llianna to honor her father's arrangement for her to marry Rothmar. She still dreamed of *inn mátki munr,* the mighty passion, but her betrothal to Rothmar had been settled when she was eight years old. It was duty, and Sigfinn had taught her to honor duty when he had taught her to ride as a child. Even the völva insisted on the necessity of duty.

Rothmar was kind and good and handsome, but what of passion? What of love? Had her mother lied when she had promised that true love would come? Llianna wished she could ask her again. The desire that had taken her to summon Aegir simmered in the background, a flame that still flared into a longing so fierce it made her tremble. Surely there must be a matching flame somewhere in the Nine Worlds . . .

She shook off the longing and the thoughts. Passion and desire might exist somewhere, but she had been traded to Ravensborg as a reward in a long line of gifts, promises, and commitments between the two fiefdoms, just as Marina had been traded to Vadsted. And that meant a wedding, with two feasts, one at Gullhyrndr to farewell her, and one at Ravensborg after the ceremony. And it also meant a new dress . . .

"No lace," said Llianna, using the voice of persuasion she had learned from the völva.

"But it be a wedding dress!" said Helgha, head weaver and sempstress for Gullhyrndr.

"Nevertheless," said Llianna firmly. "No lace!" She shook her head, tossing her braids around. What good was the völva's voice training if she couldn't persuade a sempstress to make a dress that didn't look like a wishing tree?

She found the right voice of authority, and they settled for a whalebone-ribbed bodice with thirty-eight satin covered buttons and no lace.

"As long as someone is there to do it up and then unbutton it afterwards," said Llianna.

Helgha smiled knowingly.

Llianna scowled at her and stalked out of the room. Would it be Rothmar helping her out of the dress after the wedding? Or would the women prepare her for him, like a platter of delicacies?

She went to ask Faeoia, but the old nurse ignored the question and started talking about the weather.

"Smells like rain. Like hope. Like something needful about to happen . . ."

Llianna left Faeoia babbling about the weather and went to her room to think about buttons and what comes after a wedding. She sat on the windowsill, knees drawn up to her chin, and watched the rain - the needful rain - fall over the sea like a grey shroud.

It was out of the question to ask any of the other women about the buttons and the rest of it; they would giggle and gossip, and soon everyone in Gullhyrndr would be looking at her knowingly. And it wasn't the sort of thing you could ask a völva . . .

She did ask Lunet, but weddings in the settlement had been simple affairs with more ale than romance. The women wore their best clothes, but buttons were a luxury rarely seen; most of the clothing was tied with laces that came undone easily enough.

What Llianna did know was that the wedding would take place on a Friday - Frigga's day - at the beginning of Summer, a month after she turned sixteen.

"The roads will be passable," said the stablehands.

"There will be new honey for the bridal-ale," said Faeoia.

"You will look beautiful," said Lunet.

Llianna sighed miserably. Bridal-ale! She had seen the barrels made for weddings before, enough to last a full moon cycle after the wedding: honey mead for a moon cycle to sweeten the marriage.

"Does the groom swallow the mead before or after he nibbles the girl?" wondered Llianna, talking to herself.

"Huh?" Lunet shook her head, puzzled by Llianna's strange thoughts.

‡

Marina arrived at Gullhyrndr the morning of Llianna's farewell feast, accompanied by Rothmar, fifty húskarlar, and a troop of serving women. Llianna joined in the formal greetings and was courteous to Rothmar, but as soon as possible she whisked Marina off to their special seat on the colonnade overlooking the yard.

"I've missed you," she said, hugging Marina close.

"Oh, Lli. It's so good to see you! You look the same but more so, if you know what I mean. I don't think you'll ever look old, like you never looked really young either. Sort of everlasting. Is that the right word? No, it's eternal. Eternal and so beautiful. Rothmar thinks so, I know. Do you think Fastulf finds me beautiful? Do you think he's beautiful? Oh, what will it be like being married? Can I see your dress? Mine has so much lace I feel like a wishing tree! The farewell feast at Ravensborg was beautiful under the stars with a huge fire and everyone came and I have a whole wagon of gifts. And . . ."

"Who's that?"

"What?"

"Who's that man?" Llianna pointed down to a tall man dressed in the Ravensborg red and black. He moved with the lithe strength of a trained warrior, but he was no ordinary húskarlar. He crossed the yard as if he owned it, and everything - men, horses, dogs - rearranged themselves around him.

"That's Hugo. He's our cousin from Brodrup. Father's sister's son. He's . . ."

". . . beautiful." Llianna sighed, and a part of her left to fly down to the tall stranger.

He looked up.

Time slowed.

Llianna smiled and raised her hand.

Hugo bowed, sweeping his arm before him in a grand gesture. His black hair fell forward over eyes the color of the sea, the color of summer skies, the color of . . .

Llianna sighed, and time moved forward. Hugo disappeared into the Hall.

"Lli? That was odd. It was like you knew each other, but that's not possible. Hugo has only just come to Ravensborg and he's never been to Gullhyrndr. Rothmar trained with Hugo's father at Brodrup so he's known him all his life and now Hugo has come to Ravensborg and Rothmar says he's the best at everything. You should see him at swords. He moves so fast he's just a blur. And he sings like a minstrel and . . ."

"Oh, dear." Llianna shivered. The part of her that had flown down to Hugo had left an aching hollow in her chest.

"What? Are you ill?" Marina felt Llianna's forehead and peered into her eyes.

"Perhaps." Llianna hugged herself to still the trembling that had stormed through her at the sight of him. Him. *Hugo.* Even the name felt right, as if she had known it all her life.

Marina rubbed Llianna's back. "You're shaking! Of course you are! You're worried about leaving Gullhyrndr again and living at Ravensborg. I was so scared on the road, thinking of last time." She shuddered but managed to keep talking. "Oh, I wish I was going to be there to welcome you. But, come, we are together for your farewell feast and Rothmar is here. How often does that happen? A betrothed at a farewell feast!" Marina went on, telling stories from her own farewell feast and acting as if nothing remarkable had just happened.

But what had happened? Llianna shook her head. Nothing had happened, and Marina was here for just one night, so she pulled herself back from the storm and smiled at her friend.

"Come, dear one, let's get some food and have our own feast in the wildwood, like we did when you first came to live here. We can tie ribbons on the wishing tree and make wishes for long, happy lives."

"Dear one?" Marina rolled her eyes. "Who have you been spending time with? Come, show me your dress and then we can go to the wildwood."

Llianna let herself be carried along by Marina's excitement. Nothing seemed to dampen Marina's spirits or stop the flow of words for long, not even leaving her home to wed a stranger.

They slipped quietly into the weaving rooms, deserted as everyone prepared for the night's feasting. Llianna's wedding dress hung suspended on a rod tied to the rafters. It moved gently, as if filled with life.

Marina gasped. "Oh, Lli, it's beautiful! It's a gown for a Queen. How ever did you talk them out of having lace?" Marina walked around the dress, admiring the embroidery. "So many buttons! How will you get them all undone?"

Llianna sighed. "I don't know. I've been wondering that myself, but I didn't want to ask anyone for fear of them laughing."

"You're so strange! You've been climbing the tower since you could walk. You go off at night - alone - to summon a God and you've been visiting a völva in the old forest but you won't risk a few silly women laughing at you. How will you ever run a stronghold and manage all the workers?"

Llianna shrugged. She had been hoping the stronghold at Ravensborg would continue to run itself. After all, it had done quite well without her, so there was no reason it couldn't just go on like that after she arrived . . .

Marina stood with her hands on her hips and proceeded to lecture Llianna on her duty as Rothmar's wife. "You have to take your place as Queen alongside Rothmar. Everyone will expect you to oversee the household and the storerooms and order the clothing for Rothmar and your children and there are the banners for the húskarlar. The women stitch them but the Queen designs them. I have some drawings ready for the Vadsted banners. Do you want to see them?"

Llianna followed Marina to the wagon carrying her possessions from Ravensborg to Vadsted. Marina showed her the drawings and unfolded the wedding dress from the chest where it had been neatly packed away. She twirled with it held against her, laughing in delight as the lace and ribbons flared out like swan wings.

"It's lovely, and so are you, dear Mari. Fastulf will be enchanted."

"Is that a true seeing? Did the völva teach you to tell the future? Will I have lots of children? Will I live to be a grandmother, surrounded by a huge family? And will Fastulf be good to me? And will I see you more often than I have these last years?"

Llianna shook her head. "The first thing the völva said to me was that the seeing cannot be compelled, and that seems to be true. I wish you all those things with all my heart, but I really can't see into the future."

"It's all right," said Marina, placing the dress back in the chest. "I wouldn't want to know if none of that's going to happen and I'm going to die in my first childbed or fall from my horse on the way there or . . ."

Llianna shivered and made the sign to avert, a fist with two fingers pointing forward like horns.

Marina shrugged off the fey mood. "Now let's find your Lunet so I can meet her and then we can all go to the wildwood and talk the day away."

Lunet greeted Marina shyly. She knew of her from Llianna's stories and knew the love they shared. She offered to leave them alone for the day, but Marina insisted she accompany them to the wildwood.

They shared a feast prepared by Klaudina - barley bread, cheese, herring, honey cakes and sweet cider. Llianna and Marina talked of their years together at Gullhyrndr, happy to have Lunet there to hear it all for the first time. They shied away from talk of the future, except for tying ribbons to the branches of the wishing tree that drooped over the still, deep pond at the heart of the wildwood.

"I wish you many children," said Marina, tying a blue ribbon to the tree for Llianna.

Llianna scowled at her. "I wish you joy in all you do," she said, tying a white ribbon securely to a high branch.

They both wished Lunet long life and happiness, but she refused to speak her wishes aloud.

"It undoes the wishing," she said, tying ribbons for both of them to the tree.

When they had one ribbon left each, they decided to tie them on together and wish for peace from battles and killing.

"Do you think the wishes always come true?" asked Marina.

"Only if they are not spoken," mumbled Lunet.

Llianna sighed deeply. "We can but tie our ribbons and make our wishes. Our Fates will still unfold as they were written."

"Now you sound like an old woman again! Remember when you were going to write your own Fate?" said Marina.

Llianna nodded. "I haven't given up on that, but I have seen the Tapestry since then, and there are some Threads that can't be touched."

"The Laws that cannot be changed," said Marina, shivering.

The shadows had grown long, and they ran back to the stronghold to dress for the farewell feast.

‡

The Great Hall was resplendent with hanging boughs and

hundreds of candles, the tables laden with platters of meat, bread and delicacies reserved for high feasts: boiled beef, roast pork with honey gravy, roast beef with mustard gravy, herring, suckling pig, roast goose, boiled leeks, sprouted peas, walnuts, barley bread in the shape of interlocking circles, bowls of frumenty, honey cakes, and tubs of butter and honey. Mead flowed as if from a bottomless well, and there were many loud speeches and raucous songs of well-wishing and farewell.

Llianna sat at the high table between Marina and Rothmar, nibbling her food and trying not to look around the Hall for Hugo. *Hugo.* She said his name to herself with guilty delight. How could a name make you hot and cold and shivery all at once? If this was *inn mátki munr*, then no wonder the bards wrote songs about it and the storytellers wove whole sagas about star-crossed lovers. It really was a force to move the moon and stars!

Rothmar seemed not to notice her distraction. King Bekkr sat on the other side of Rothmar, engaging him in conversation and frowning at Llianna when he caught her eye. Llianna took his meaning and tried to do the right thing by her betrothed, commenting on the food and asking politely about Ravensborg. Rothmar was charming, listening attentively to her, offering her the choicest cuts of meat, filling her cup with mead. His breath was sweet and his hands looked gentle. He had even smiled once or twice. Llianna had to admit that he would make a fine husband . . .

. . . but her thoughts wandered back to Hugo. Hugo, who was

nowhere to be seen. Where was he?

Óðin gives riches to some, word skill to wights, breezes to sailors, song-craft to skalds, and gives manfulness to warriors.
- Hyndluljóð

Hugo stalked the northern walkways of the stronghold alone, eyes on the distant mountains. This was the closest he had ever come to the Förnir caverns, but his thoughts were not with his sworn enemies. He was remembering the strange encounter with Rothmar's betrothed. *Llianna.* Even the name made his heart beat faster. He could still feel the shock of that first sight of her, looking down from the walkway like a Goddess. What had happened? What had passed between them like an arrow aimed straight for his heart?

Hugo was no stranger to women; they found his dark hair, blue eyes, and edge of danger attractive enough to offer him anything from flirtatious smiles to much, much more. But this was different. That first sight of Llianna had ignited a fire that burned with the passion of *inn mátki munr,* a fire that had shone from her as well. Hugo slapped his hands on the rampart. Could Fate be so cruel? She was Rothmar's betrothed, and Hugo's Destiny did not include true love; his Destiny lay with fighting the Förnir. Simple as that. He had known it for as long as he could remember, a shimmering power in his solar plexus. It had started with the Warrior Code his father had him repeat every day on rising and every night before sleeping: "I live with courage, I walk with truth, I fight with honor, I love with fidelity, I train with discipline, I work with industriousness, I maintain self-reliance, I persevere."

The Code fuelled his fearlessness, his excellence at combat, his brilliance at sword fighting, and his Gods-given certainty about the rightness of his actions - he was born to defeat the Förnir. Images of them had filled his dreams and driven him to train for hours longer than any others, developing skills beyond the best, seasoned warriors. The Code had honed his strength and fighting skills, but it had earned him no friends. The others called him *Svartr Valdyr* - Black Wolf - for his aloofness and for his black hair. Most people in the seven fiefdoms were fair-haired, and the occasional children born with dark hair were considered either blessed or cursed, depending on where they were born. In Brodrup, the westernmost stronghold of Ravensborg, black hair was taken as a sign of Óðin's favor: weren't his familiars the black ravens, Huginn and Muninn? Hence the name Hugo and the certainty that he would grow into a hero worthy of the old tales.

Now *inn mátki munr* eclipsed the shimmering power of battle and the Gods-given certainty with a feeling Hugo could not name; it set his heart beating faster and made his hands tremble. Was he afraid? He, the consummate warrior, afraid? Of a woman?

Hugo banished the thought and reached for the certainty that defined him.

Instead he heard a name. *Llianna.*

A beautiful name, yet it was not beauty that had called him. He had glimpsed her glorious hair and bright smile, but what called him was her life force, a stream of molten gold that glowed like the Sun . . . and something else, an echo that reached back to the old tales.

Hugo pulled his thoughts away from Llianna and the forbidden fire. Here at Gullhyrndr he could sense the Förnir close, planning their revenge. So far Ravensborg and Brodrup had been spared direct attacks, but Rothmar had warned Hugo and the húskarlar that they might encounter Förnir on the road to Gullhyrndr. Yet the road had been quiet, beautiful even in the summer light, alive with birdsong and the droning of bees. Hard to imagine that the dark magic of the Förnir could intrude on that. Hard to imagine that anything could intrude on the bond of fire that had arced between him and Llianna . . .

No! That was not where his thoughts belonged. Hugo squared his shoulders and used his warrior-trained will to turn his attention back to the Förnir, back to his Destiny.

How much simpler life would be if he had lived in the old days of fire and blood, magic and sacrifice! In the old days he would have been a bloodsworn warrior, fighting in the spirit realms when the veils between the Worlds grew thin, vanquishing evil before it took shape in the World. He had dreamed his initiation a thousand times:

Standing at the edge of the world, calling a prayer into the wind.

"Golden Eagle of the dawn, Windmaker, rising Sun. By the Air that is the Breath of the Nine Worlds, send forth your Light."

Ravens dipping and soaring in the first light, skimming close enough to stroke his cheeks with their wingtips. Spreading his arms. Could he fly with them?

The holy men climbing the mountain, calling their own prayers that the Great Ones might grant the power to see with other eyes, hear with other ears.

He turning as they cross the ridge, the Elders of all seven tribes, gathered for this most sacred ritual; feathered masks, scarred chests, incense coiling around their heads like air snakes. He walking forth to meet them, arms outstretched in welcome. At last his time had come.

They absorbing him into their midst like a beast swallowing prey. Sweat, sharp and musky, stinging his nostrils. The lingering scent of smokeweed making his head swim, stirring sickness in his belly. Breathing in. Out. In again. His heart beating in time to the drums echoing from the valley.

Crossing to the rocky ledge where it would be done, his stomach roiling like storm clouds. He turning once more to the East and repeating his prayer. The ravens hovering in the air. The masked men repeating his words, nodding their over-sized heads. He laying on the stone and closing his eyes.

They holding him with calloused hands, tethering his body to the Earth that his soul might fly free to swoop and soar in ever-widening gyres until he could see all of the Nine Worlds.

If the sacrifice was accepted.

If he was found worthy.

Cold and sharp, the point of the knife blade pressing against skin. Skin parting. Pain flaring like fire, burning, burning. Breath stopping. Screams bursting forth, wild, desperate, shattering. They taking his eyes with the sacred knife, sharpened and honed, used once in a lifetime.

And it was done.

They releasing him and stepping back, silent as the darkness that fills him, the deep, impenetrable blackness of a mid-winter night.

Blind.

Not worthy.

He curling around the pain and weeping tears of blood.

A wing tip brushing his hair.

Colors dancing and whirling like wind-tossed leaves: the blue distance of air, fire's rosy glow, endless green depths of water, Earth's ochre hills.

Shapes emerging from the darkness: birds and beasts and his own kind, moving through their lives unseeing.

He standing and walking to the edge of the World.

The old men sucking in their breaths, waiting for him to fall.

He knowing exactly where to place his feet. Two ravens

spiraling from the clouds, paying homage. The rush of air from their wings ruffling his hair. He laughing and laughing and laughing.

Flying.

Soaring.

Higher and higher . . .

‡

In the stone cottage in the glade at the heart of Angan Eyeland, a young woman stared into the flames, watching the smoky image of the girl on the mainland. Llianna, daughter of Queens.

Meera turned from the flames, and Amara nodded knowingly, licking her lips. "*Inn mátki munr.* The ancient Threads pulling together. The line of Queens and the line of Bloodsworn Warriors."

"She is betrothed to another," said Meera.

Amara smiled toothlessly. "The Black Wolf has some growing to do before it be his time. He must step beyond his father's shadow and the shadow of his father's father."

"So must all men," said Meera.

"That be true, but some shadows be darker than others," said Amara. "And the Old Ways be weaker across the water."

Meera turned back to the fire. "He denies her. He denies *inn mátki munr.* Be he flawed?"

"No more or less than any bright soul born in shadow. He be not trained in the Ways. His time will come."

‡

Llianna slept late the morning after the feast; too much mead and too much trembling excitement coursing through her body. Marina woke her, dressed already in her riding clothes, ready to leave for Vadsted.

"Come quickly," said Marina. "We're leaving soon." She ran off, leaving Llianna to struggle awake from dreams filled with longing for something she could never quite reach: eagles and ravens, and women glowing with the power of Earth, Air, Fire, Water . . .

She banished the dreams and dressed quickly. Lunet hurried in and braided Llianna's hair into one long plait that hung over her shoulder like a golden cord.

Lunet was unusually quiet, but Llianna had no time to ask her about it. She left her and ran down to the yard. Marina and Rothmar were taking their leave of Llianna's father, but all Llianna saw was Hugo, standing stiffly at Rothmar's side, glowering like the God of Thunder. Whatever was wrong with him?

Her father beckoned her to his side. "Llianna, our guests are leaving for Vadsted, but Rothmar has assigned húskarlar to join our men to escort you safely to Ravensborg. It is better you ride now with the wagons before the rains come, and Rothmar will make faster time back from Vadsted if he does not stop in at

Gullhyrndr to escort you."

Llianna thanked Rothmar for his care and allowed him to take her hand.

"I look forward to seeing you at Ravensborg," he said, bending to kiss her hand.

Llianna flushed and looked up to see Hugo watching intently. Heat pulsed though her body, making her gasp.

"Is something wrong?" asked Rothmar. "Do you fear the ride to Ravensborg?"

Llianna looked down and shook her head.

"Do not fear. I am sending my best warrior with you," said Rothmar gently.

Llianna sensed her Thread tightening, one of the skeins pulled firmly into place by Fate.

"Hugo will see you safe to Ravensborg."

Hugo stepped forward and bowed. No flourish, his blue eyes shadowed like storm-tossed water, his face set like a wooden mask.

Llianna stammered her thanks and backed away to stand beside her father. King Bekkr looked at her strangely.

Marina ran up and hugged Llianna, and they walked together to the horses.

"Handsome, isn't he?" said Marina.

"Who?" Llianna's cheeks flushed red.

"Oh, don't pretend you haven't noticed. I saw you yesterday when he was in the yard. That black hair and blue eyes like robin's eggs, what girl wouldn't be moved? But don't be fooled; they call him *Svartr Valdyr* at Ravensborg. He's dangerous."

"Which must be why Rothmar is sending him to see me safe," said Llianna abruptly, wanting to stop Marina's talk of Hugo. "After what happened last time, I'm glad of it."

"So am I," said Marina. "I just wanted you to know, that's all."

Llianna nodded. Did she need to know more than her heart already told her? Her heart that fluttered like a captive bird, even while Marina's words played over and over in her mind: *He's dangerous.*

Never a whit should one blame another
for a folly which many befalls;
the might of love makes sons of men
into fools who once were wise. - Hávamál: 92

Llianna watched Marina until she rode out of sight, and then she found Lunet and hurried through the wildwood to the old forest, a path she knew so well she could walk it in the dark. The völva waited in the clearing, sitting on a log in the dappled light at the edge of the trees. She beckoned Llianna over to sit beside her. Lunet wandered around the clearing, picking wildflowers and grasses from beneath the trees.

"So, the Thread of *inn mátki munr* has tightened," said the völva, reading Llianna in the uncanny way she had.

"He's dangerous," said Llianna, the words tumbling out before she had even thought what to say.

The völva frowned. "Most things of value come with risk. Double-edged, like the axes of the Valkyries. Besides, only the ignorant have fear of wolves."

"But wolves are dangerous," said Llianna. "Aren't they?"

The völva shrugged. "Wolves be hungry like all creatures, but they be no more evil than you or me."

"So it's not wrong to feel like I do?" asked Llianna.

"Love be no small power," said the old woman, just as she had on Llianna's first visit three years ago. "Do not dismiss it so easily."

"Oh, what will I do without you?" Llianna handed the völva a small leather bag containing precious granules of frankincense resin. "Thank you. Thank you for everything."

"Good instincts," said the völva, tucking the bag away inside her tunic.

Lunet handed the flowers to the völva, bobbing her head as a sign of respect. The völva patted Lunet's cheek and whispered something Llianna couldn't hear.

They walked back slowly to the stronghold, savoring the peace of the forest.

The next farewell was to Faeoia, and Llianna put it off until the candles were lit for the night and everyone was gathering in the Hall. She walked slowly down to Faeoia's room and hesitated at the door. For some reason Sigfinn came to mind, and she sighed sadly with the old familiar pain of his loss. Llianna brushed away a tear and entered the room.

"Faeoia?"

Cupboards and chests hung open, their contents strewn on the floor and over the bed. Faeoia's robes were heaped untidily on a chair, and the place smelled overpoweringly of . . .

Llianna sneezed.

Clove oil? Had someone been there with a sword? Had someone done this? Had they hurt her?

"Faeoia!" Llianna knelt down to look under the bed and climbed up to hang out the window. "Faeoia!"

"Llianna?"

Llianna tumbled down from the windowsill. "Oh, Faeoia! I'm so glad to see you. Are you hurt?"

"Why would I be hurt, dear child? I am old, but I can still manage a little sorting and packing."

"Packing? You made this mess packing?"

"You cannot expect me to leave everything behind, dear child. Now move aside so I can get on with it."

"Oh! You're coming with me!" said Llianna.

"Of course I be coming," said Faeoia. "Who else should be there when your time comes?"

Llianna sat in the bed and surprised herself by sobbing like a baby. All her life it had been Sigfinn who had been there for her, Sigfinn who had listened to her woes and bandaged her cuts, Sigfinn whom she now missed with a deep ache. But of course Faeoia had always been there, too. Teaching the old ways and waiting, as she said, with the dead. Waiting with Llianna's mother's mothers for the return of the Warrior Queen . . .

The cavalcade that left Gullhyrndr for Ravensborg consisted of sixty húskarlar, four wagons, and Llianna and Hugo, riding as far apart as courtesy permitted. Faeoia rode in a wagon, wrapped in a green cloak, Lunet beside her, eyes wide at the prospect of leaving Gullhyrndr. Llianna rode a black mare whose steady gait promised an enjoyable ride to Ravensborg. She had a moment's thought of Vaskr, the oddly-named pony lost along with so much else on her previous trip to Ravensborg. A shiver rippled up her back: *someone walking on her ashes.*

The first night they camped close to the road, húskarlar forming a solid ring around the wagon where Llianna slept next to Lunet and Faeoia. The old nurse still snored like a pregnant sow, and Llianna tossed on the blanket bed, sleep chased away by the snoring and by the longing in her heart and body. Would marrying and bedding Rothmar cure this? Or would she be afflicted forever, cursed by Fate to love one she could never have?

Late the next morning, they approached the place where the Förnir had attacked last time. Llianna shuddered at the memory, senses alert for any sign of danger. The sun shone through wispy clouds, and a light breeze freshened the air with the distant ozone of the sea. Birds trilled from the treetops. Surely no evil could be lurking this time . . .

Snap! Something moved in the trees. Llianna jerked her hands so hard her horse tossed its head and snorted in protest. She tightened the reins, pulling the horse around in a circle.

"Only a fallen branch," said Hugo, who had ridden over to investigate the disturbance. "It happens at this time of year when the wood dries and the leaves are heavy." He reached for Llianna's reins to calm her horse.

Llianna slapped the loose reins down on his hand. "*Paska!* Let go!"

Hugo pulled back, eyes wide with surprise. A lock of black hair had fallen over his forehead, and his face was flushed. He looked like a God.

Llianna calmed herself and steadied her horse. "Forgive me," she mumbled. "I was startled."

Hugo nodded curtly and rode back to his place at the front.

What had she just done? The one person she wanted to see her, smile at her, think well of her, and she had cursed and struck him! It was going to be a long trip to Ravensborg . . .

Two days and nights passed in easy riding and restless sleeps. Hugo kept his distance from Llianna, although húskarlar still shadowed her every move. Lunet seemed to have found an affinity with Faeoia, the two of them sharing stories and giggling like children. Llianna had ample time to think about the future and what it would mean to be wife to Rothmar. Despite the talk of prophecy and Destiny, despite the stories of the Warrior Queens, she feared that her Fate would be the same as her mother's: marriage and the travails of womanhood, running a stronghold, doing her duty as Queen, bearing children, perhaps dying in childbed. Every cell in her body rebelled. Many times she was tempted to turn her horse and ride back to Gullhyrndr to walk the trails of the old forest and sit with the völva, to find her shining Thread and follow it through the Tapestry . . .

It was so much easier to believe in a glorious Destiny in the seer's cave, easier than plodding along with a surly guard and silent húskarlar. Even Faeoia had nothing to say to reassure her; she rode in the wagon, talking with Lunet, humming to herself, as if they were headed for some happy event.

On the fourth morning, Llianna woke very early. She made her way in the dim light to the stream to wash away the echo of the dark, elusive dreams that troubled her sleep. The everpresent húskarlar stopped at the edge of the trees to allow her some privacy. The two men settled to sit with their backs against trees, talking quietly to each other, complaining no doubt about having to escort a spoiled princess to her morning ablutions

The ground sloped down to the stream, and the men's voices faded, so there was no one to see Llianna step out of the cover of the trees. No one to see her walk slowly down to the water. No one to see her stop and raise her hand to her mouth, going as still as a deer in the presence of a hunter.

Before her in the dawn light stood Hugo, waist deep in the water, back turned, rubbing his body with fine grit from the streambed.

He was beautiful, long limbed and strong, with the arms of a warrior and the grace of a . . .

Llianna flushed. What was she doing? Staring at a naked man, admiring his body . . .

His body.

Hugo raised his head, graceful and powerful as a stag sensing something on the wind. His eyes blazed.

Llianna raised her hand, to deny the moment.

Then Hugo smiled, and Llianna surrendered to the inevitability of standing there alone with a man whose presence made her soul shimmer.

"The water is like swansdown," he said. An invitation.

Llianna walked to the edge of the stream and knelt to run her hands through the silken water.

Hugo waited, still as a statue. Llianna rose and walked into the stream to stand before him. The water came up to her breasts, rubbing the wet wool of her tunic against her skin. Fire pulsed through her body.

"I shouldn't be here," she said.

Hugo said nothing, but heat rippled from his chest, as if a fire burned there instead of a human heart.

Llianna stepped into the fire . . .

They were not together long, not like lovers who lie together for a whole, stolen night, or even for a few precious hours. They did not lie together as lovers at all, but that is not what their hearts and souls remembered. Their hearts and souls remembered love that moves the moon and stars . . .

They stepped from the water together. Llianna's clothes hung heavy and wet, yet she felt light as a feather. Hugo shone naked in the dawn light. Llianna turned away, but it no longer mattered; she did not know him as a woman might know a man with her body, yet he was already a part of her . . .

Hugo moved away to dress, and Llianna stood quietly,

watching the sun rise over the trees. She glanced to where the guards waited; had they seen her enter the water? What would they think? She looked around for Óðin's ravens; did they report such things to the God?

Hugo came to stand before her, clothed now, damp hair falling over his eyes. He bowed his head and sank gracefully to his knees.

"Forgive me," he said, raising his remarkable eyes to meet hers. "Sometimes I am a fool. Never would I wish to betray you or my King. This force that flows between us . . . I do not understand it. It compels me beyond reason, beyond duty, and I would turn it to good. I pledge myself to you, to my Queen, to the betrothed of my King, as warrior and protector. I pledge my life to protect you and all you hold dear, in courage and truth, honor and fidelity. If you will have me as your sworn warrior." He lifted a knife from his belt pouch and sliced the blade across his palm. Blood dripped onto the shale.

Two ravens flew from the trees, calling loudly. A warning?

Llianna trembled. She wanted to take his beautiful face in her hands, kiss his lips, his cheeks, his neck . . .

"My Queen?" Hugo bowed his head again, waiting for her to accept or reject his pledge.

"I accept your pledge as warrior and protector," said Llianna, although she wanted to say other words, to speak of love and longing and . . .

She lifted his bleeding hand and pressed her lips to the cut. He tasted of mountains and starlight.

Hugo stepped away, and Llianna wiped her lips with the back of her hand. Still his blood coursed through her body, sealing the warrior's pledge.

Hugo turned towards the camp and Llianna chastely followed him back to the waiting húskarlar. The guards' sleepy faces suggested that they had not seen the sacred marriage or the warrior's pledge that had taken place in the half light.

Llianna walked ahead of the men and smiled to herself. How could she keep secret the fire that flowed between her and Hugo? Wouldn't it show on her face every time she looked at him? Wouldn't it sound in her voice when she said his name? Wouldn't it blaze forth like the fire between them to burn away the pretense of her union with Rothmar? So ran Llianna's thoughts as they walked back to the wagons. Hugo had become distant again, but now Llianna knew it for what it was: a shield to cloak his fire. How would she cloak her own?

Yet cloak it she must. It would break the trust between Gullhyrndr and Ravensborg to reveal the truth of the love that shone between her and Hugo, but how could Fate be so cruel? Why wed her to one man and have her love another? Was that why her mother had looked so sad when she had promised true love? Llianna turned the questions over and over, but the threads remained twisted and tangled. She would accept Hugo as her sworn protector, but in her secret dreams he would always be more . . .

They rode on towards Ravensborg, and Hugo remained distant. Llianna caught glimpses of him scouting ahead or cantering past to check behind them. He rode with the same grace with which he did everything, like a young God. He would meet her gaze for a moment and then move on. The moment opened into a long, moonlit night, into a lifetime, into eternity . . .

Faeoia nodded knowingly every time Llianna looked her way. The old nurse said nothing, but she probably knew some obscure verse of some obscure prophecy that predicted exactly what was happening! Lunet also let Llianna know with smiles and gestures that she understood and would keep her secret.

Sleep became elusive, and Llianna used the time to enter the deep inner states she had learned with the völva. She missed the quiet and holding of the seer's cave, but the völva's teachings traveled with her as part of the Tapestry, offering solace. Llianna found her Thread and was reassured to see that it continued to shine brightly despite the disruption in the pattern that came with Hugo's Thread. *Hugo's Thread!* It glowed in the Tapestry with the same inner fire Llianna felt every time she saw him . . .

Late on the fifth night Llianna lay still, traveling deep in the Tapestry. Faeoia snored loudly, and Lunet snuffled beside her, a familiar, reassuring chorus. Then something changed, pulling Llianna fully awake. The snoring and snuffling continued, but the glade had become strangely quiet. The night birds no longer called, and even the leaves had stopped their whispering, as if the World were holding its breath. Llianna shivered.

Someone moved. Footsteps coming her way.

A shadow loomed from the darkness.

Llianna sprang up, arms braced to fight.

Hugo.

"Quiet," he whispered. "There is danger. Dress quickly and come."

Llianna woke the others, pulled on her boots, and followed Hugo, crouching low in the shadows, heart racing wildly. He was her sworn protector, her pledged warrior . . .

Behind them someone yelled, and Hugo pulled Llianna behind a tree. More yells and the sound of weapons.

"Faeoia!" cried Llianna, pulling away. "Lunet!" Where were they?

Something bumped against Llianna's arm. She whirled around, fists clenched.

Faeoia frowned at her and walked on into the forest, as if escaping armed men was something she did every night. Lunet followed, eyes wide as a spooked horse.

"What happened? Is it the Förnir?" asked Llianna, hurrying after Faeoia.

No answer. They kept moving, leaving the sounds of battle behind. Hugo followed behind, guarding them.

Hours later, he signaled for them to stop in the lee of a rocky outcrop.

Llianna sagged against the stone. "Where are we going?" she asked.

"Ravensborg," said Hugo.

"But the horses. The men?"

"The men are doing the task for which they came, and we will have to do without horses. The Förnir force was large, and we were outnumbered. It was as if they knew we guarded someone special." He shook his head, staring off in to the dark as if he could see through the shadows.

Llianna shivered again; *someone walking on her ashes . . .*

"There is a tale told at Ravensborg of you walking with Marina from the Wastelands," said Hugo. "This is not so far."

"It is not that," said Llianna. "I was thinking of their safety; the men, the horses."

Hugo nodded. "Of course. You are a Queen." He turned and led them on through the dark.

They walked until dawn restored color to the leaves, and birds began chattering about the new day. Llianna breathed a sigh of relief; the night was over.

A flash of color.

Men leaped from the trees to block their path.

Hugo drew his sword.

Llianna braced to fight.

A wave of darkness took her, swamping her senses, stealing her breath. Darkness took her, and she fell.

‡

Hugo?

Lunet?

Faeoia?

Llianna's frantic thoughts scrabbled for purchase, but everything slipped away.

What . . .?

She opened her eyes.

"Oh, no!"

Brown eyes. *Gravnir.*

"Our threads seem destined to cross," he said. His eyes shone with power, and he really was very handsome . . .

Llianna shook off the strange thoughts. "What happened to the others? Where are they?" She struggled to her feet. She felt sick, and her head hurt horribly.

"Your man was faster this time," said Gravnir. "He fights like a Landvördr warrior."

Hugo's fire still burned, Llianna was sure of it; she would know if it went out.

"Where is he?" She rose to a crouch and lunged towards Gravnir, fists clenched.

Gravnir stepped back, holding his hands up to block her fists. "So, he is more than a húskarlar. I can see you have grown into a woman since we last met."

"Stop it!" said Llianna, turning away. "This is not a game. Your people killed someone dear to me last time, and I don't know why you let us go, but . . ." She gathered her intention to fight him again.

"Stop!" He held up a hand.

The strength drained from Llianna's arms.

"How do you do that?" asked Llianna.

"Old magic," said Gravnir. "That is why the Seafarers fought us. They feared it, and so they killed it. Is that not the way it works?"

"I don't know. Just tell me what's happened to the others."

He shrugged. "Your man fought like someone who could defeat four Landvördr warriors, so he and the women are probably looking for you already."

"Where are we?" asked Llianna, looking around. "And what are these Landvördr you keep talking about?"

"The Landvördr are my people. You call us Förnir."

Llianna remembered him saying something like that last time. It had made no sense then, either. *Landvördr? Guards of the Land?*

"We are not Förnir. The Förn were here before even the Landvördr; they are the Ljósálfar, the true Old Ones. We are the Guardians."

"Guardians?"

"Of the Land."

Well, she had the meaning almost right, but it still made no sense.

"What do you want with me?" asked Llianna.

"That depends."

"On what?"

"On what you decide when you have heard my story."

Llianna sat down on a rock and pinched herself to make sure she wasn't dreaming. Gravnir was the oddest person! He was the enemy, but he wanted to talk instead of fight. He was Förnir, or whatever he called himself, but he spoke like a young gothi. He had gone to the trouble of stealing her away from the others, yet he didn't seem at all concerned about Hugo finding them. Llianna looked around; surely they couldn't have come far. How long had she been spelled? Had he carried her?

"They will find us here soon," said Gravnir, sitting on the ground in front of her. "But not just yet."

"You are so odd!"

"Yes. I am an oddity. My own people say that, too. I have the old power. I ask too many questions. I break the rules. They do not trust me, but they need me to see the future, to read the signs."

Llianna felt the same strange attraction to Gravnir that she had years earlier. It was nothing like the fire and glory and starlight of Hugo, but it was . . . something.

"Don't all the Förnir - er, Landvördr - have the old power like you?" asked Llianna.

Gravnir frowned. "That is not the right question. The question is why do you have the old power?"

"Me?"

"What do you call it then? What you did when we first met?

The way you felled the men?"

Llianna sighed. "I don't know. That was the first time it happened. I think it came because someone I care for was in danger, but I can't make it happen. There was something else, too, like a deep calm, but I can't make that happen either. It just came." She shook herself; why was it so easy to talk with him when he was her enemy?

"Ah! You can also reach *djuplogn*. Of course!" Gravnir stood and paced around the rock where Llianna sat.

She refused to turn and watch him.

He came to stand near her. "You are the one who is Förn."

"An Old One? I don't think so. My mother's mothers were Warrior Queens, but their power was taken by the Keepers."

"It is the old blood that gave rise to the Landvördr. It runs in my veins, but in you it is a torrent." His brown eyes softened. "You are a true child of Munstrond. You are the one named in prophecy."

All Llianna heard was the word *prophecy*. She stood and climbed up on the rock to look down at Gravnir. "I will not live my life according to some line or another in an old prophecy!"

Gravnir laughed. And kept laughing until tears poured down his cheeks.

"What's so funny?" asked Llianna, glaring down at him.

He wiped eyes and took some deep breaths. "Only someone named in prophecy could say that! . . . *some line or another in an old prophecy*. How many lines of prophecy do most people have written about them?"

Llianna crossed her arms. "Well, I still won't be told what to do by a prophecy."

"Of course not, but Fate will have its way regardless."

Llianna shook her head. Now he sounded like the völva!

"And you?" she asked, jumping down from the rock. "If you have this old blood, what does that mean?"

"I was born to fight for my people's freedom and for the Land. My power serves them, as yours must serve your people, but I would not have us be enemies." He came close and held her hands. His eyes were as deep as she remembered, as she had dreamed about for many cycles: brown and rich as the soil after welcome rain.

"Llianna?" Hugo stepped out of the trees, sword drawn. The look on his face made Llianna drop Gravnir's hands, but Gravnir pulled her close, a shield between him and the black-haired warrior.

"Hugo. Er . . . this is Gravnir. He's a . . . er . . . he's not an enemy."

"His men are dead," said Hugo, still holding his sword ready.

"Where's Lunet? Is she safe? Faeoia?"

"No thanks to him," said Hugo, pointing his sword at Gravnir.

Faeoia and Lunet stepped out from the trees to stand beside Hugo. Llianna breathed more easily to see them safe.

"What does your *not enemy* want with us?" asked Hugo. His eyes glittered dangerously.

"I want nothing with you," said Gravnir. "Your kind have killed my people and poisoned our Land. My business is with your woman."

"I am not his woman." Oh! Why did she say that?

The cold look on Hugo's face set like forged metal.

Gravnir raised his eyebrows. "Then we can continue our conversation? I have much to tell you about your mother's mothers, and there is something you must see . . ."

And that was it. Nothing else would have stopped her from crossing to Hugo, touching him, taking that look from his face.

Hugo watched her with steely eyes.

Llianna sighed.

"All of us?" she asked.

Gravnir smiled thinly. "With your man waiting for a chance to kill me? I think not."

"He is not . . ." She looked down at her feet, took a deep breath, and looked up to meet Hugo's eyes. "I need to hear what he has to tell me about my mother's mothers. It is important. Please."

Hugo lowered his sword. The muscle along his jaw clenched. "On your word he is safe for now, but if you are harmed in any way . . ." His words were forced and clipped.

Faeoia reached up and placed her hand on Hugo's shoulder. She whispered something too softly for Llianna to hear. Hugo shook his head and crossed his arms over his chest.

Gravnir pulled Llianna towards the horses. "I have no time for threats or star-crossed lovers; your man can come, but he says nothing and does not interfere. Come, we must be gone if I am to show you what you need to see."

Llianna looked from Gravnir to Hugo. She shrugged helplessly. A sharp pain in her chest made her gasp. Had her denial of Hugo broken a Thread?

"How long will it take?" she asked Gravnir.

"Two days. I will return you here in two days." He turned and walked away towards the mountains.

"I must do this," Llianna said to Hugo.

Hugo stood by the rock, as still as if he were carved from stone. Llianna wanted to run to him, to rest her head on his chest, to whisper to his heart, but Gravnir was striding away, and he held the answers she had been seeking all her life.

Lunet ran to Llianna's side. She looked frightened, but her hand was steady as she reached for Llianna.

Gravnir did not look back.

Llianna held Lunet's hand and hurried after him. "Two days. Just two days," she whispered to herself. It did not occur to her until much later just how much courage it had taken for Lunet to join her like that. Hugo stalked after them like a wounded bear.

Gravnir led them to the horses he and his men had left hobbled near a stream. The horses had water and grass, yet they milled restlessly, ears pricked, showing the whites of their eyes.

"Something has frightened them," said Llianna, looking around uneasily. She sniffed for the musk of a mountain lion, but the air smelled only of horse and trampled grass.

Gravnir did not seem worried, so she took the reins he offered and mounted a dappled grey mare with a broad back and strong neck. Lunet clambered up onto a tall, solid bay and looked around anxiously. Hugo offered to help Faeoia mount, but the old nurse shook her head and settled herself under a tree to wait for them.

"This be your time," she said to Llianna.

They left Faeoia with food and water and followed Gravnir through the trees and out into the foothills leading to the mountains. When the peaks loomed on the horizon, Gravnir stopped.

"Where are we going?" asked Llianna. "Surely we can talk here."

"There is something I must show you," said Gravnir.

"As long as it's not Fangar!" said Llianna, shuddering.

Hugo scowled, and Lunet looked terrified; she had heard from both Llianna and Marina about the awful events of the previous trip to Ravensborg.

Gravnir snorted. "I did not risk my life to free you from him just to take you back. The others are all on the other side of the mountains."

A shiver skittered up Llianna's spine. What trouble were the Landvördr causing over there?

Gravnir led them through a defile into a narrow valley running between two peaks. The valley took them through the mountains to the Wastelands beyond. They came to a track too steep for horses, so they left them tied to one of the tortured trees and climbed up to a natural landing carved into the rock. It was about the height of the sea cliffs at Gullhyrndr and looked out over the ravaged land that stretched to the horizon.

"It was here your mother's mothers stood in the First battle," said Gravnir.

"Ronja and Sighfrith and Anniken," said Llianna. "Anniken is my foremother."

"As Sighfrith is mine," said Gravnir.

"That's not possible," said Llianna.

Gravnir beckoned her to the rear wall of the platform. Inscribed there in the softer rock were words, cut roughly with a dagger or a sword. Hugo stood with arms crossed over his chest, looking uneasily over the plains. Llianna read the words, speaking slowly as she made out the carved letters.

"Three queens stand here to face the foe

Holding in their hands both hope and woe.

Power to kill that some may live

Lives and futures theirs to give.

Know this as true:

We choose death at this place

That there be children of our race."

He looked intently at Llianna.

"What does that mean?" Lunet asked, tracing the letters with a finger

"They meant to die," said Llianna. "Their sacrifice won the

battle, but that doesn't prove anything."

Gravnir sighed. "Their sacrifice stopped the battle, but they did not win."

"What do you mean? Of course they won!"

"That depends on who tells the story."

"No matter who tells the story, my people defeated your people and claimed the seven fiefdoms."

"Are you so sure the Warrior Queens were fighting for your people, as you call them?"

Llianna's head reeled. What was he saying? She ran her hands over the words carved into the rock.

"Ronja died here, but the other two lived to bear children," said Gravnir. "You and I are descended from those children."

"But how could that have happened? You call yourself Landvördr, and I am of the seven fiefdoms. I can trace my mother line back to . . ."

Gravnir nodded. "Yes, you can trace your line back to Anniken, even as I can trace mine back to Sighfrith. At first I thought it might have been an accident of war, a woman taken as plunder and forced to bear a child, but these were Warrior Queens. They could not have been forced."

Lunet still traced the carved words with her finger. *We choose death at this place, that there be children of our race.*

"We are those children," said Gravnir.

Hugo growled, raising the hairs on Llianna's neck. What threat did he sense in Gravnir's claims?

"Children of which race?" asked Llianna. "Anniken was the first mother of my mother line. She came to this land from over the sea."

"And I was told Sighfrith was Landvördr, but I think we were both deceived."

"But that would mean . . ."

"Yes. The Warrior Queens were not fighting for the Landvördr or the Seafarers. They were fighting for the Land."

"They destroyed the Land," said Llianna, looking out at the Wastelands.

Lunet walked to the edge, her arms crossed over her chest. "The Land weeps. It is in great pain."

Llianna groaned in frustration. What was she meant to do with all this pain and power and death?

"*We choose death*," said Gravnir, repeating the words carved on the stone. "I do not pretend to understand what that means, but there is more I must show you. Perhaps you can help make sense of all this."

Llianna doubted that she could make much sense of anything at all. What if the stories she had been told were lies? What if her mother's mothers did not come from across the sea as she had been told? What if she and Gravnir were cousins?

His words rang true, but could he be trusted? He had been there when the Landvördr killed Sigfinn and the húskarlar, and the death of his own men at Hugo's hand had not even caused a ripple of feeling.

"Death was their lot," said Gravnir, as if reading her thoughts. "Our people choose their path at birth, or it is chosen for them. They were warriors, and the way of the warrior is death." He glanced at Hugo, who still stood with arms crossed over his chest, staring at Gravnir as if he wanted to tear him apart.

"Not all your people fight?" asked Llianna.

Gravnir shook his head. "There are warriors and workers and breeders and teachers and . . ."

"Like the húskarlar settlement," said Lunet quietly.

Llianna had only heard one word. "Breeders? Is that what Sighfrith was? A breeder?"

"I was not there," said Gravnir. "If that is what she was, I think she did so willingly. My forefathers may have wanted her for her power, but she wanted something as well."

"If you are right, she wanted you to be born," said Llianna.

"Both of us," said Gravnir.

Llianna rubbed her hands over her face and held her head. Had her long ago ancestor made a terrible sacrifice to ensure she was born? If Anniken could see her now, would she find her worth the sacrifice?

"Perhaps Anniken and Sighfrith foresaw us standing here together, weaving something new," said Gravnir.

"Now you sound like a gothi!" said Llianna.

Hugo scowled like the God of Thunder, but Lunet looked curiously at Gravnir.

"Yes, I am the seer of the Landvördr. Wise one. Odd one.

Untrusted one." Gravnir spoke in the self-deprecating tone he had used earlier, but Llianna heard the pain in his voice.

Gravnir shrugged off her concern. "It is my walk to walk."

Hugo turned away and looked out over the Wastelands. "We are exposed here. What is it you would show her?"

Gravnir pointed to the far end of the platform. Llianna walked there with him, leaving the other two behind.

"Oh!" Embedded in the rock at the far end of the platform was a wooden shield. The painted decoration had faded, but the gold and silver runes inlaid around the rim glowed with light. At the center of the iron boss a blue crystal gleamed like a sea serpent's eye.

Drawn by a power that burned through her veins, Llianna reached to touch the crystal.

Gravnir held his breath.

Her fingers brushed the stone.

A sound like an arrow moving through air, and the crystal came to life, pulsing with inner light. All else disappeared, and Llianna stood alone with the shield. No, not alone. Beside her stood three Queens.

"Take it," said one.

"It is yours," said another.

"You are the one," said the third, reaching to stroke Llianna's cheek with icy fingers.

Llianna covered the pulsing stone with her hand and the shield fell away from the rock. She caught it and held it close to her chest. It was surprisingly light.

With a sound like a summer breeze, the Warrior Queens faded away.

Gravnir whistled low though his teeth. "I knew you were the one!"

"This is why you saved me? Saved us. Back in the caverns?"

He nodded. "It is written that our people will be saved by a Warrior Queen, like the Queens of old. It had to be you."

Llianna looked down at the shield. It was very old, and it rested lightly in her arms, but already she sensed that it would not always be easy to bear. She frowned. "And my people believe the same, that a Warrior Queen will rise to save them. How can both be true?" she asked.

"That is the question I have asked since I found you," said Gravnir. "I stand here, seeing what the ancient Queens saw, hearing the sounds of long ago battle, and feeling the terrible price they paid that day. How can one person save us all?" He walked to the edge of the platform and stared out over the desolation.

A movement caught Llianna's eye - three eagles spiraling down from the peaks. Lower and lower they came, carried on invisible winds, using their great wings to circle overhead like messengers.

"They come for you," said Gravnir. "The old tales are true."

"They come for the Warrior Queens," said Llianna, bowing her head.

When the eagles rose again, Gravnir led the climb back down.

Lunet followed close behind Gravnir, but Llianna paused at the top of the rough trail. Hugo stood quietly beside her as she searched the sky for the eagles. They were almost back to the peaks now, three dark specks in the sky. The platform was empty again. Did the Queens keep vigil in that lonely place?

The wooden shield hummed, vibrating in her hands like a horse bunching its muscles to surge into a gallop. The Queens walked with her now.

Hugo just nodded when Llianna met his eyes, acknowledging the power that had found her. He said nothing, but what was there to say?

They found the others at the base of the cliff. The horses stamped restlessly, rolling their eyes at the barren plains.

"They smell something," said Lunet.

"What happened here lingers," said Gravnir. "It is in the trees, in the air, in the soil."

Hugo produced rope from his saddlebag and helped Llianna strap the shield to her back; the original leather sling had long since rotted away, but the handgrip still held strong. The Valkyrie shield bounced against Llianna's back as they followed Gravnir into the Wastelands along a path visible only to him. The Queens might be riding with her, but Llianna wished she knew more about the forces she would be called to stand against.

They slept that first night beside one of the trees, after drinking sparingly from the flasks tied to the saddles and eating cheese and apples Gravnir offered them from the sack he carried.

They watered the horses by digging holes as Llianna and Marina had done three years ago, although the digging was considerably easier with the shovel Gravnir had strapped to his saddle. Llianna had a hundred questions, but the Land did not encourage talking, so she lay on her cloak, one hand on the shield by her side, watching the stars and wondering about the strange Fate that had her sleeping in the wilderness, with Hugo at once so close and yet so far from her. Lunet lay awake beside Llianna, thinking her own thoughts about Warrior Queens and Fate and the paths one may be called to walk. Hugo sat silhouetted against the night sky, sleepless and watchful.

They rode on at dawn, moving deeper into the Wastelands, the mountains becoming small behind them. Llianna looked back often, reassuring herself that the path remained clear.

The first sign that Gravnir really was leading them somewhere was a large rock shaped like a foot. A foot?

They passed more broken, carved body parts and sections of pillars, strewn around as if thrown by Giants. Gravnir said nothing, and Llianna began to wonder about all she did not know of the Land and what had gone before. A great stronghold must have stood there once, more magnificent than the Great Hall of Gullhyrndr. Where had the stone come from to build such a place, to carve statues and pillars?

They stopped at the edge of a deep, winding channel that crossed their path and cut the plain like a wound. A riverbed?

"A thousand thousand years the Blarskaut flowed," said

Gravnir. "Until the First Battle."

"Blue border," said Llianna, translating the old name.

"The southern boundary of Munstrond." Gravnir sounded wistful.

"I have never heard of this place," said Llianna. "Munstrond means *breast* in the old tongue. What stood here?" Beyond the dry riverbed lay broken walls and tumbled pillars.

Lunet sighed. "The Mother's sanctuary. It is said to have been beautiful."

"How do you know this?" asked Llianna. "It is not mentioned in our histories."

Lunet shrugged. "The old women tell stories that no one believes. I like their stories."

"You are wise to do so," said Gravnir. "I see Munstrond in my dreams. The thread was severed from the Tapestry, and it yearns to be rewoven."

Llianna closed her eyes and entered the Tapestry, seeking the truth of Gravnir's words. Surely such a severing would show itself as a fraying of the Tapestry, a scar in the weaving.

"You will not find it," said Gravnir.

"Why not?" asked Llianna, opening her eyes.

"It was in the keeping of the Old Ones, and their power was fading, even at the time of the First Battle. I think that is why they sent the three Queens forth to do what they did." Gravnir smiled sadly. "The true Guardians were here before the Landvördr, before the Seafarers. Their blood flows in our veins, but I do not understand what they want from us. I once thought my task was to free my people. They are not all like Fangar, and they lost much in the First Battle."

"And now?" prompted Llianna. "What is your task now?" She still didn't understand all Gravnir was saying, but she agreed with his wish that they not be enemies.

"I have brought you to Munstrond so the way forward can be revealed to the daughter of Queens." Gravnir looked longingly at the ruins across the riverbed.

Hugo moved his horse restlessly along the ancient riverbank, but Llianna followed Gravnir's gaze, wondering if his trust in her was misplaced. How could she find anything in a place that had been laid waste a thousand years ago? She turned to say that and saw Gravnir look over her shoulder, his expression changing to one of horror.

Llianna looked behind her.

Paska! Fangar rode towards them with a band of Landvördr armed with bows.

Gravnir went still. Lunet whimpered and crouched low on her horse. Hugo urged his horse between Llianna and the Landvördr and reached for his sword.

Llianna felt for her elusive power. Would it come?

Gravnir nodded slightly. He had freed her to try . . .

"Think carefully before you do anything rash," called Fangar, closer now. He signaled to riders behind him. Something in his manner made Llianna hesitate.

"Wait," she said to Hugo.

Two riders came forward, dragging something between them.

Gravnir made a choking sound, and Llianna looked more closely at what the men held.

"Oh! No. . . no . . . no!"

"She lives, but they will kill her if any of you move at all." Fangar waved an arm towards the archers.

Llianna gasped in shock. What had they done to her? Marina hung limply between the horses, legs bare, hair matted.

Marina groaned and lifted her bloody face to meet Llianna's gaze with pain-filled eyes.

Kill them all, said Marina's eyes. *I am already dead.*

Llianna reached within. The deep calm came to meet her, and she drew up a thunderstorm.

The Landvördr men fell as if a giant hand had struck them down. When the storm passed, Fangar was alone.

Llianna whirled towards Gravnir, grabbed his sword, and rode to confront Fangar.

"For what you did to me, you lose a hand. For what you did to my friend, you lose your life."

Fangar laughed, drew his sword, and spat at her face. "A girl cannot fight a warrior." He raised his sword.

Llianna lunged, faster than thought and memory. Fangar's hand spun through the air to land on the ground with a thud like a bowshot bird. The hand twitched, reaching for the sword that had dropped from lifeless fingers.

"Now your life." Hugo rode past Llianna, sword flashing like lightning. Fangar died before he took another breath, stabbed cleanly through the heart.

Llianna leaped from her horse, and ran to Marina.

Marina! She lay so terribly still.

"Oh, my beautiful, beautiful one. I'm here now. They can't hurt you any more." Weeping, she dropped Gravnir's sword and slid the shield from her back. She sat and gently lifted Marina's head onto her lap, stroking blood-matted hair from her face.

What she saw made her want Fangar to die again. Slowly. But her power to kill arose from necessity, and necessity was swift and clean. Too clean for what had been done to someone so beloved.

She reached in to find Marina's Thread, to reweave the torn strands. And was denied. The völva had taught her what that meant.

"Lli?" Marina's voice was a whisper.

"I'm here, dear one."

"Rothmar. He's alive."

"Shhh. Later. Let me look after you."

Marina opened her eyes. "Find him. He's alive."

Her eyes closed.

Llianna held Marina close, felt her friend's heart stop, and slipped into the Tapestry to find her.

There she was, soft and lovely, moving away towards the great river. Llianna walked by Marina's side, guiding her past the temptations that snared unwary souls: calls of loved ones; pleas for help; promises of pleasure. They reached the final river.

"Thank you, dear Lli. I love you." And Marina crossed over without looking back.

Llianna sat for a long time, holding Marina's body, holding off movement and the pain it would bring . . .

A noise called her back. Voices?

She opened her eyes to see Gravnir and Hugo circling each other like rabid dogs. Was she dreaming?

No. Of course Hugo would blame Gravnir for the attack, and he would be looking for more enemies to kill.

The two men were of a height, dark and light, night and day, and they both looked murderous.

Llianna lifted Marina's head and placed it softly on the ground. She stood slowly, bowed low with grief and exhausted from walking between the Worlds.

"Stop!" she commanded. "Enough of death."

The men turned to look at her. For a moment she wondered what she would do if they ignored her. Fall at their feet and play dead? Throw the shield at them?

"Call your man off," said Gravnir. "Please."

"He's not my . . ." Llianna bit her lip and looked at Hugo. His face was set in the cold mask of pain and loss, yet he had stayed with her, holding to the pledge at the river.

She crossed to him. "That is a lie. Hugo is my man in every way that matters." The steel became molten and flowed between them.

Hugo held her hands and bowed his head.

"You stood with me," she said.

"I have sworn it. I will always stand with you," he said. "Although it seems you need little in the way of protection." His mouth curled in a wry smile.

Llianna raised Hugo's hands to her lips and kissed his knuckles. What had it cost him to admit that?

Lunet walked over, tears streaking her cheeks. "You killed them," she said to Llianna, looking around in wonder. "You saved us."

Llianna nodded tiredly. Yes, she had saved them, and she had avenged Marina. Yet something hard and ugly had settled in her, a heavy knot in her chest and a bitter taste in her mouth. Was that how it had been for the Warrior Queens?

Gravnir walked away from the bodies and sat with his head on his knees. Llianna left Lunet and Hugo with Marina and walked slowly over to him.

"You didn't know, did you?"

He shook his head, eyes closed. "The warriors have never trusted me."

"What will you do now?" she asked.

"I would still take you to the place where all this began," he said. "Your man can come."

"We have to take Marina home," said Llianna, wiping away tears with the back of her hand.

Hugo came to stand with Llianna. "A King's daughter must be laid to rest on the land of her birth."

Gravnir stood and paced restlessly, waving his arms. "We are so close! You must see Munstrond before we leave."

Llianna reached out to stop Gravnir. "What do your people do with their beloved dead?" she asked.

Gravnir sighed deeply. "Since our exile, we have we buried them, waiting for the day when we can light their pyres on our own land."

Llianna nodded. "Let us do that then and mark the spot well. We can send men from Ravensborg to bring her home, and she can be laid to rest as she deserves."

Hugo and Gravnir dug Marina's grave, taking turns to use Gravnir's shovel. Llianna and Lunet tended Marina's body, washing away the blood with their drinking water. Llianna gently smoothed Marina's hair, as Marina had so often done for her. Gravnir offered a blanket as a shroud.

They gathered to lift Marina's body

Llianna gasped. "Rothmar," she said, remembering what Marina had been saying as she held her.

Gravnir and Hugo frowned at her.

"Marina last words. *Rothmar's alive.* We have to go and find him." Llianna gestured to the horses.

"But . . ." Gravnir pointed across the riverbed towards the ruins of Munstrond.

"We can come back," said Llianna. "I have to go. For Marina."

Gravnir sighed. "Where was the attack? Where were they traveling?"

A knot released in Llianna's chest; he really hadn't known what Fangar planned.

"They were riding from Gullhyrndr to Vadsted. She was to be married."

"Then, come. I can take you through a pass to that road."

"Marina?" asked Llianna, looking at the sad, shrouded form of her friend. If they were not going to Munstrond, surely they did not have to leave Marina's body in the Wastelands.

Gravnir looked back the way they had come. "We can carry her to the mountains. There are caves where she can rest until she is returned to Ravensborg. It will be closer for your people, but we must hurry if you hope to find your friend alive."

They rode back to the mountains, Hugo holding Marina's shrouded body as if she were sleeping. Llianna remembered his words: *to protect you and all you hold dear.*

Gravnir led them to a narrow defile close to the ledge where the Warrior Queens had stood in the First Battle. The defile led to a shallow cave carved from the mountain in ages past. Around the cave grew calendula, the golden flowers glowing in the soft light.

"It is dry and cool here. I will ward the entrance so she is safe," said Gravnir.

Hugo placed Marina's body on a natural ledge at the back of the cave and turned to Llianna with sad eyes. "I am sorry for your loss," he said, head bowed.

"Thank you for bringing her here," said Llianna, wondering at Hugo's grief. Did his pledge bind him to her so fully that harm to those she held dear would wound him, too?

She called to Lunet, and together they gathered calendula flowers to lay around Marina's body, a golden bier fit for a princess. The flowers smelled of growing things, of life, but they were the color of sunset, the color of endings. Llianna kissed the last flower and placed it on the shroud.

"May Óðin give you knowledge on your path, May Thor grant you strength and courage on your way, And may Loki give you laughter as you go." Llianna spoke softly, her tears turning the calendula bier into a shimmering golden boat that would carry Marina home . . .

"She was brave," said Gravnir. "I remember her fighting to help you in the caverns."

"Thank you," said Llianna. She hadn't known that.

"She loved you so much," said Lunet.

Llianna smiled sadly. She had known that, but it was good to hear it said aloud.

They left the cave, and Gravnir moved his hands and muttered an incantation to seal the entrance. They rode away in silence to collect Faeoia.

Llianna was too sad and weary to be amazed by the sight of her old nurse mounting a horse; Gravnir commented on it and received a haughty dismissal from Faeoia.

"Old folk have had a lifetime to learn things. Never

underestimate us, young man."

Faeoia rode close to Llianna, humming the cradlesong that had been her favorite as a child. The song made its way in, soothing the raw grief, but it did nothing to soften the taint left by the killing. Did Faeoia know? Was that why she sang?

Gravnir led them through a pass to the road that led to the way Marina and Rothmar had taken from Gullhyrndr to Vadsted, to where the Landvördr had attacked, to where Rothmar may still be alive . . .

‡

Rothmar was alive, although he was beginning to wish for death. The attack had happened quickly, with noise and chaos and killing, and his horse had bolted, carrying him away from the fighting. Like a coward.

The horse was dead, which was fair and right, given that it was the horse that had run like a coward. It was also a blessing, as the poor beast had fallen and broken something that had made it scream like a demon. A screaming horse was enough to make a man wish he was dead, but the screaming had stopped when he had smashed the horse over the head with a rock. It was thirst that was killing him now. And the horse. When it fell, it had landed on him, pinning him firmly to the ground. Fortunately it was sandy ground, the remnant of some long lost sea perhaps. So he was trapped but not broken, although he could not really tell because there was no feeling at all from the waist down. He was also raving in his thoughts, but he was unable to stop. The raving seemed to be keeping him alive . . .

‡

Gravnir took them along tracks skirting the main road, using the concealment of the trees. Hugo sat his horse like a guard, back stiff, alert for danger. Llianna trusted that Gravnir truly wanted to help them, but who knew what lay ahead?

‡

Rothmar walked in summer fields with beautiful, naked women playing harps and flutes and singing like nightingales. Flowers bloomed and bees flitted across the grass, collecting honey and bringing life. Strangely the flowers smelled like rotting horse, but who was he to complain about that? The World worked in mysterious ways . . .

‡

Marina's dying words echoed in Llianna's mind, and they stopped only to rest the horses from the fast pace she demanded. They reached the turnoff to Gullhyrndr, and Hugo hesitated. He wanted Llianna to return to the stronghold with Lunet and Faeoia, but there were no guards to send with them.

"No," said Llianna. "I will not be treated like a sack of precious goods to be carried from one place to another as if I cannot fend for myself! The Warrior Queens did not sacrifice everything so their daughters could be dressed like wishing trees and treated like helpless bundles of treasure!"

Hugo scowled at her, and Gravnir looked amused. Lunet and Faeoia made it clear they would go wherever Llianna went.

Two days later they found the ambush site. It smelled like rotting meat, and a cloud of vultures flew up screeching as they rode in. Llianna breathed through her mouth and swallowed the urge to shriek with grief and rage. If Rothmar had been alive when Marina was carried off, it seemed impossible that he had survived this horror.

Hugo dismounted and walked among the dead like a strange sort of Valkyrie, searching for the chosen. The vultures gathered in the trees, making raspy, hissing sounds at having their feast disturbed.

"He is not here." Hugo stood by her stirrup, face pale, eyes shadowed.

Llianna could almost hear him saying, "I have failed you," but it was not his doing that Marina lay dead and Rothmar could not be found. How could Hugo survive this warrior's pledge if he made himself responsible for every blow struck by others?

"The Landvördr did this, not you," said Llianna.

"The what?" asked Hugo.

"Landvördr. It's the true name for those we call Förnir," said Llianna.

Hugo shrugged. "They may have done this, but now it is my task to find him." He waved his arm in an arc.

They left the bodies to the vultures and rode in different directions, keeping each other in sight. The smell faded, but the feeling of dread grew heavier in Llianna's chest.

Then a cry went up, and Llianna urged her horse over to where Lunet was struggling with something on the ground. Rothmar!

It took all of them to move the dead horse and pull Rothmar free. He was covered in dried blood and ants, but he was alive. Barely.

Rothmar was dancing with the beautiful women when the ground shifted beneath him. There was one in particular, a fine-boned woman with golden eyes and large, round breasts . . .The field of flowers faded, and indescribable pain flooded his body. Ah! Now the punishment for cowardice, even if it was the horse that ran away. He steeled himself to be scoured and flayed and exiled forever from the music and sweetness. It did not seem fair, but he was in no position to argue about it. With whom did one argue matters of Fate anyway? The Norn? Óðin? There had only been the women, and now they were gone . . .

Llianna dripped water into Rothmar's mouth, stroking his throat to make him swallow. They had washed off the ants and most of the blood, but he still looked like a corpse and smelled like death.

Nothing appeared to be broken except the Thread that connected him to life. He moaned and his hands twitched as if reaching for something, but he wandered a long way from his body.

"We need to take him to the healers at Gullhyrndr," said Hugo.

Faeoia squatted by Llianna's side and held a cloth to Rothmar's lips. She squeezed the cloth, dripping dark, herbal medicine onto his parched lips and into his mouth.

Llianna gently stroked his throat.

He moaned.

Faeoia rubbed the liquid onto Rothmar's chest and then cupped his head, one hand behind and one on his forehead. She stilled herself to drop into the Tapestry.

Llianna held her breath. Would Faeoia be denied as she had been when she sought to heal Marina?

Rothmar's eyes flickered open. "How long must I be punished?" he asked, voice raw. "It was the horse that ran."

Llianna leaned close. "You live," she said softly.

He looked past her to Lunet. "Marina?" He tried to move his head, but only managed to roll his eyes.

Llianna looked to Hugo, who shrugged helplessly. Rothmar subsided into merciful unconsciousness.

They rode slowly back to Gullhyrndr, Rothmar on the horse in front of Hugo, his limp body held close against Hugo's chest, as if he could lend his life force to keep Rothmar's Thread attached to the Tapestry. Faeoia continued to drip life into Rothmar with her herb tea whenever they stopped to rest. Halfway home he began to swallow water more easily. Perhaps he would live.

Llianna rode beside Hugo, painfully aware of the improbable circumstance that had her true beloved carrying her betrothed back towards life. Would the skeins of her Thread always be so twisted? Would they never run straight and true?

Hugo kept his thoughts to himself.

The Valkyrie shield rode with Llianna, its power dormant for now. She wanted time to study the runes, to decipher the message from her long ago ancestor, to make sense of the terrible Fate that delivered such a great a gift at the same time as bringing such terrible grief.

These women are called Valkyries. They are sent by Óðin to every battle, where they choose which men are to die and they determine who has the victory. - Gylfaginning: 36, The Prose Edda

They arrived at Gullhyrndr late in the day, Hugo calling to the guards to open the gate and summon the healers. Llianna's father came striding into the yard with the healers, face like thunder.

"What is this? Rothmar!" His eyes took in Llianna, Lunet, Hugo, Faeoia. Then he saw Gravnir and went still.

"Who is this?"

"He helped us," said Llianna.

Hugo nodded. "It is so."

"Marina?" asked King Bekkr, looking at Llianna.

She shook her head, and tears welled for the first time since finding Rothmar. She told her father where Marina's body lay, and he gave orders that she be brought to Gullhyrndr. He also sent orders to the húskarlar chiefs to gather the men to ride the next day to hunt the Förnir.

King Bekkr turned to face Gravnir. "You helped my daughter, and I am in your debt. I would hear the whole of this tale." He motioned for Gravnir and Hugo to follow him back in to the stronghold.

Llianna whispered to Lunet, pushed past the healers bustling around Rothmar, and strode after her father.

He stopped and held her hands. "I am glad to see you safe."

"I will meet with you."

"Better you rest."

Llianna pulled away, took the shield from her back, and held it before her. The King's eyes widened and his face grew pale.

"Ah!"

"It is my time," she said. "At least I think it is."

Llianna's father nodded and led the way to the Council room. Her brothers looked confused when she entered the room; women did not sit in Council. Llianna ignored them and placed the shield in the middle of the table. The blue serpent-eye crystal caught the light, and Dagmar and Falden stared at it as if it might bite them.

King Bekkr turned to Gravnir.

"You pose a dilemma."

"So say my people as well," said Gravnir. If he feared the King's decision about his future, he did not show it.

"Your people? The same people who attacked Rothmar and killed Marina? The same people who took my daughter captive four years ago?" Bekkr's voice rose in outrage.

Llianna caught Gravnir's eye and shook her head slightly. *Don't tell him you were there!*

Hugo scowled, but he remained silent.

Gravnir leaned forward to answer. "The people who did those things were warriors. Not all Landvördr are warriors."

"Landvördr. I have not heard that name," said the King. "We call you *old ones*, but you call yourself *guardians*. What is it that you guard?"

"We guard the Land," said Gravnir. "At least that is what we did before the First Battle. Much has changed, but not all Landvördr are your enemies. We live and die according to our function, like an ant colony. The warriors who attack and kill your people are bred and trained to do that and only that. They do not have families. They do not ever build anything or gather food or even hunt. They destroy."

Llianna shivered, remembering Fangar. Remembering Marina.

"It makes them formidable," said Gravnir. "And unreasonable."

"Unreasonable?"

"Their intention to kill and destroy cannot be changed. But not all Landvördr want this war."

King Bekkr looked thoughtful. Llianna's brothers tensed, moving their hands towards their swords.

"And the other functions?" asked the King.

"Breeders. Food providers. Healers. All that is needed for a colony to survive. All those who do not live for fighting, death, and revenge."

"And you?"

"I am an oddity," said Gravnir, just as he had said to Llianna.

"Why are you here?"

"I follow the prophecy of the Warrior Queen." He bowed his head to Llianna.

"Prophecy, be damned!" said Dagmar.

Llianna laughed; it sounded more like a sob. Being a child of prophecy seemed to involve tragedy and absurdity in equal measure.

Hugo stood and moved restlessly to the window, as if the room had suddenly become too small.

The others all turned to stare at her.

"I've been saying be damned to the prophecy for years, but it seems that prophecies have a way of catching up with us." Llianna lifted the shield off the table and held it before her. "This belonged to Anniken or one of her sisters, and now it has come to me. We can deny our Fate all we like, but it will find us. It seems the time of the Warrior Queens is returning, although I don't know exactly what that means."

"What does that mean?" asked Dagmar. "What does the shield do?"

Hugo crossed to the table and told them about Llianna killing Fangar and his men.

"Are you sure there is no other explanation?" asked Dagmar. "Such power is unheard of."

"Dangerous," said Falden, scowling at Llianna.

"Not unheard of," said Llianna's father. "Just not seen for a long time. Your sister comes from a line of mothers that goes back to Anniken and the First Battle. The prophecy foretold her birth."

"Prophecy? I thought that was just some old story!" said Dagmar, mirroring Falden's scowl.

The King gestured to the gothi. The old man stood and cleared his throat.

"When darkness comes from mountain halls
Covering land and scaling walls
A child will come from Freya's line
Born in death, lost in time.

Strong and wild, swift and free
Her Fate is carved in Life's tree
But guard it well, lest she be lured
To tamper and disturb the Wyrd.

Her power will come in anger born
Fired by Freya and the Norn
To vanquish darkness and despair
For all that moves in Earth, Water, Fire, and Air."

"That's you?" Falden asked, gaping at Llianna. He looked like a boy whose hunting dog had suddenly transformed into a mythical dragon.

"Seems so," said Llianna. "Although I'm not sure about vanquishing darkness and despair. I'm not sure of much at all."

"Ridiculous," said Dagmar. "How could a prophecy come to life right here without anyone knowing about it? You must all have drunk stagnant water, and it has gone to your brains."

Llianna was too exhausted to argue with Dagmar, and she wasn't sure she could. Perhaps it was just tiredness and grief, but it did all seem somewhat ridiculous. If she hadn't been there, she wouldn't believe that she had killed all those men either, and she had no idea how to do it again, or even if she wanted to do it again. Hugo returned to his seat, looking sad and troubled, and Gravnir looked like he wanted to punch Dagmar, but suddenly all Llianna wanted to do was climb into her bed and sleep.

The talk veered away towards fighting the Landvördr, and Gravnir was dismissed, accompanied by two húskarlar. The others went on to plan a response to the attack, but Llianna could no longer stifle her yawns. She excused herself, picked up the shield, and climbed the tower stairs to her old room. The bed was made up and a tub of warm water waited by the fireplace. Lunet helped her undress and gently washed her clean of sweat, blood and fear.

Llianna staggered to her bed and fell into a restless sleep. She woke in the dark, sobbing and retching, her body sick with grief for Marina and with the weight of the Landvördr deaths she had caused.

She slipped out of bed and went to sit on the windowsill, the shield on her knees. A dark moon night. Dark night for dark deeds. Dark thoughts . . .

Would the Warrior Queens' power always destroy? Was that her Destiny?

Llianna wished she could ask Sigfinn how a warrior came to terms with dealing death in battle. Had it troubled him to kill the Raiders? Was that what he meant when he had said, "You dream of glory, but battle be pain and blood and death"?

Llianna sighed miserably. What use was there in power that just killed? What about the life-giving power that Faeoia called on when they lit candles to honor the cycles of the moon? What of the power that brought forth new growth in Spring? What of Iduna?

Llianna propped the shield against the wall and dragged a fur blanket from the bed. She sat on the windowsill all night. When the first light of dawn showed on the horizon, she stood and made a vow to the rising sun: "I pledge what power is granted me to Life, to saving and restoring, to healing the Land and the people."

There! Now she had her own pledge . . .

‡

Dagmar led a hundred húskarlar out the next morning to clear the roads between Gullhyrndr and Vadsted. Falden took a hundred more towards Ravensborg, and the King led two hundred towards the mountains. Hugo rode with Falden, taking the grim tale of Marina's death and Rothmar's injury to Ravensborg. Llianna longed to ride with him, but her duty lay with Rothmar, who could barely swallow broth let alone sit a horse or ride in a wagon. She also needed to make preparations for the pyre that would burn on the cliffs when Marina's body was brought home.

Hugo had found her in the kitchen to say farewell, and it had been a formal leave-taking with so many eyes and ears surrounding them. He had lifted her hand chastely to his lips, but the inner fire still burned, and she felt the thin scar etched on his palm. As he strode away, Llianna rubbed her hand; the skin showed no sign at all of the fire. Would it always be like that now? Formal and impersonal; he her sworn protector, and she his Queen, nothing to show but a fading scar . . .

Llianna slapped her hand against her thigh and scowled at the departing men. Gravnir looked at her enquiringly, but she just shook her head and kept scowling.

"It is disappointing to be left behind," he said softly. His request to accompany the King had been firmly refused.

"We value your counsel but ask that you remain our honored guest at Gullhyrndr," had been King Bekkr's response. Everyone knew that *honored guest* meant *carefully watched*.

Llianna sympathized with Gravnir, but he was Landvördr. She was excluded because she was a woman, and that was a different thing altogether. Gravnir consoled himself by walking in the wildwood and visiting Rothmar, to whom he had become strangely attached. Llianna found no consolation; she grieved for Marina, she missed Hugo, and she chafed at the role assigned to her by duty and custom. How did one go so quickly from killing Landvördr to stitching linen and spooning broth?

Lunet stayed by her side, quietly supportive. Llianna spoke with her about Marina and about her fears for the future, but Lunet could only listen and commiserate; she could not change Llianna's Fate.

As usual, Faeoia ignored Llianna's questions, settling happily back into her small room and professing not to miss her belongings lost on the journey. "What are a few cloaks when I have walked with prophecy and seen the coming of the Warrior Queen!"

Llianna wished she could be as pleased by it all as Faeoia. The prophecy might be unfolding just as it was meant to, but it was deeply unsettling to be holding a Valkyrie shield and listening to all the talk about Warrior Queens. No one could read the runes on the rim of the shield, and her only reliable warrior skills were those she had developed with Sigfinn. Custom said she couldn't use the fighting skills in the usual way, riding out with the húskarlar and defending the Land, but the other power came and went like a fey wind, with nothing of the grace or precision of Hugo's sword fighting or the discipline Sigfinn had taught her. And what if the killing force was the same force that had destroyed the Land beyond the mountains in the First Battle? What if the Warrior Queen's legacy was death and destruction?

Llianna took her questions to the völva, but the old seer just directed her to the Tapestry, and that led her in circles. Finally Llianna sought out Gravnir.

She found him sitting by Rothmar's bed, spooning broth into his mouth and wiping his chin, more patient with Rothmar than she ever could be.

Gravnir put the bowl down and looked at her enquiringly. Llianna asked Lunet to take over Gravnir's task and beckoned him outside to the walkway.

"How is he today?" she asked.

Gravnir sat on a bench against the wall and gestured for Llianna to join him.

"He lives," he said quietly, looking towards the door of Rothmar's room. "But it will take time for him to come all the way back. He was wandering between the Worlds when we found him."

"Why do you care so much? You don't even know him."

Gravnir sighed deeply and dropped his head into his hands. "My people did this out of desperation and a desire for revenge. Your people have marched out to avenge this attack, and so it goes on. I want to save my people, bring them back to the light. If this King can live, then perhaps there is hope for something other than death and destruction." He shook his head. "Foolish, I know."

"That may be the least foolish thing I have heard since we returned," said Llianna. "All I can think about is how to use my elusive powers, and the men have gone off to kill or be killed. Who is more foolish?"

Gravnir shrugged. "At least you all have a purpose. I'm just watching over a poor, broken man, willing him to live, as if that will miraculously give me something I want."

"Can I ask you something?" said Llianna.

"What is it?"

She unslung the shield from her back and pointed to the runes. "Can you read these?"

Gravnir shook his head. "They are ancient, from before the First Battle."

Disappointed, Llianna rested the shield against the wall. "That word you used - *djupor*? What does it mean?"

"*Djuplogn*. It is the inner state of perfect balance that gives rise to true power. It cannot be taught. It is a gift of the old blood."

"How do you know that?" asked Llianna,

Gravnir looked down and scuffed his boots on the ground. "I just do."

"Not good enough!" said Llianna, jumping up to pace before the bench. "How do you know these things about the old blood, about the Warrior Queens, about everything?"

A cry from Rothmar interrupted Gravnir's answer. He hurried into the room, and Llianna followed more slowly. Rothmar still seemed like a stranger, but it hurt to see him lying there so weak and pale. Marina's memory hovered in the room, making Llianna want to run and keep running. When Rothmar had first roused enough to ask how Marina had died, Llianna had actually run from the room, leaving others to answer. Not exactly the courageous action of a child of prophecy!

Now Rothmar tossed on the bed, moaning and crying out as if in great pain or great fear. Where did he roam in his nightmares?

Gravnir lifted Rothmar and smoothed his bedding, humming as a mother would to a babe. Rothmar settled, and Gravnir returned outside to the bench. Lunet stayed by Rothmar's side, humming the soothing tune.

"What do you want to know about *djuplogn*?" he asked.

"Everything," said Llianna. "You said I had it, but it's more like it has me. Something just rises up, and I can't control it. How do I know it comes from this *djuplogn*? How do you know? How do we know it won't just rise up and destroy everything?"

"Like the Warrior Queens?" asked Gravnir. "The strength of their combined power was greater than anything I can imagine. I can weave shifts in the flow of the elements and make a decent warding. You can call up fire and death, but they could move Worlds."

Llianna clenched her fists. "And what good did it do them? They stopped the battle, but now it has to be fought again, and more people will die, and I have no idea what to do about it. I need to know more about the prophecy and the powers I'm meant to have. I don't want to call up fire and death!"

Gravnir held up his hands in surrender. "I learned about

djuplogn from my dreams and from a man I met in the Wastelands. He is a wanderer, and he is wise beyond anyone I know. He swore me to secrecy."

"An oath you have just broken," said Llianna.

Gravnir shrugged. "Some things are more important than oaths."

He told her all he knew, which was not enough to fully answer her questions. The power that came to her was frustratingly elusive and easily blocked by someone like Gravnir. Llianna very much doubted that Warrior Queens would have been so easily stopped, and she longed to ride off in search of Gravnir's mysterious wanderer, to take action instead of waiting . . .

‡

The húskarlar returned with Marina's body wrapped in a shroud packed with honey, aloe and garlic. They laid her to rest on the cliffs of Gullhyrndr, surrounded by jewelry, books of sagas and song, and all the foods she had loved in life. The flames of her pyre glowed golden like the flowers they had laid on her bier in the mountains, the smoke rising high to signify her royal blood.

Rothmar, still too weak to climb the cliffs, stood on the parapet of the stronghold to add his blessings to his sister's journey. Llianna kept vigil on the clifftop until the coals died down and all that was left were ashes.

‡

Solvaldr heard the reports of Rothmar's injuries and cursed the Fate that had seen the Ravensborg King rescued. His death would have moved the Keepers' plans forward, but an ailing King was a vulnerable King. Perhaps it was time to help Fate along . . .

Ever with grief and all too long
Are men and women born in the world;
But yet we shall live our lives together . . . - Brynhild's Ride to Hel

The first Frigga's day of summer came and went, and Llianna wept for the wedding that would not be taking place at Vadsted. She spent the day in the wildwood, sharing food with the Vaettir and looking sadly at the ribbons hanging limply on the wishing tree.

In the evening she visited Rothmar. This would have been their wedding day, too. He was alone, leaning against the doorpost, staring at the clouds.

"The ravens are loud today," he said.

Llianna looked towards the turrets of the tower, where the big, black birds gathered at dusk. They did seem noisier than usual.

"You are stronger," said Llianna.

Rothmar nodded. "I can truly thank you for my life now that I have stopped wishing I was dead."

"You were very ill."

"I had almost crossed over when you found me. It was hard to come back."

Llianna was thinking of what to say to that when she heard horses moving fast towards the gate. She ran to the walkway wall and climbed up to stand on the edge, holding a pillar for support.

"What is it?" asked Rothmar.

"I think it's Hugo!" she cried, fire flaring in her body. "He's back!"

Rothmar looked at her thoughtfully and a little sadly. "He made good time," he said mildly.

"I'm just glad to see that the roads are safe," said Llianna.

"Of course," said Rothmar, agreeing to the lie. "Perhaps you should go and bring him here when he has eaten." He walked slowly back to bed.

Llianna hesitated, but the fire burning in her veins urged her to run down the stairs to the forecourt.

She found Hugo striding across the yard from the stables to the kitchen. He looked leaner, face pale, dark circles under his eyes; like a wolf who hasn't yet realized he has survived a long winter.

He nodded in greeting and kept walking.

"Hugo?"

He stopped and turned to face her.

"Has something happened?"

"I have made my report to Ravensborg. They mourn, and they await the safe return of their King and his betrothed." Voice like ice.

"Are you unwell?" asked Llianna, reaching to touch his arm.

He stepped back. Her hand dropped uselessly to her side.

"I am tired and hungry," said Hugo. "If I may have your leave to refresh myself before reporting to Rothmar?"

"Of course," said Llianna.

Hugo spun around and strode to the kitchen.

Llianna hugged her arms tight around her chest and walked unseeing to the stairs. What was wrong? Why did he scorn her like that? After all they had shared, she had thought they might at least be friends . . .

She waited on the landing leading to Rothmar's room, inventing stories to explain Hugo's strange mood.

"Do you think he's fallen in love with an innkeeper's daughter, or someone at Ravensborg?" she asked Lunet.

Lunet snorted and busied herself with mending a torn tunic.

"Or perhaps he's ill. He might be dying of a terrible illness . . ."

Lunet rolled her eyes.

"Or perhaps a gothi has cast a spell, and he is constrained by magic . . ."

"I will see Rothmar now." Hugo stood before her, face and hands washed, hair tied back, eyes dull. He looked a little better, but he still smelled of horse and sweat and distance.

"Of course," said Llianna. Would that be it from now on? Would that be all she would ever say to him?

He moved past them and entered the room. Llianna followed. Where else could she go?

"Rothmar!" Hugo knelt before his King.

"Come, cousin, what sort of greeting is this for one returned from the dead?" Rothmar held out his arms, and Hugo rose to embrace him like a brother.

"Ravensborg is well, although they mourn for Marina," said Hugo. "The road was clear, but there are reports of more attacks on merchants and farmers in the East."

Rothmar nodded. "We will join the fight as soon as I can ride."

Hugo asked leave to rest, and he walked away without looking at Llianna.

She sat down heavily on the chair by Rothmar's bed. He moved to sit on the edge of the bed facing her.

"Duty and honor are strong in Hugo," said Rothmar softly. "He is enduring a great struggle."

"Why do you tell me this?" asked Llianna, wondering if he taunted her.

"Marriage is made by our families to suit the needs of strongholds, Kings, and treaties," he said sadly. "It is not made by our hearts. We cannot will our hearts to obey our families."

Llianna sighed. Did Rothmar love another as well? Was this marriage hard for him, too? Who was his beloved? Would she be at Ravensborg for him to see every day? Her thoughts must have shown on her face . . .

"Let it be, Llianna. I owe you my life. I will not force you to love me. I cannot. But we must do our duty to our families."

She nodded, but her heart clenched like a fist.

Lunet was waiting for her when she left, eyes troubled.

"Oh, what is the matter with me?" cried Llianna.

"It is lovesickness," said Lunet, shaking her head.

"Lovesickness? Is that a real thing?"

Lunet stopped walking and looked intently at Llianna. "Looks real to me."

"Is there a cure?"

"The girls in settlement say you need a hair from the dog that bit you, but that might not do here."

"What are you talking about? A hair?"

"You know, a night with the one you want. To cure the itch."

Llianna couldn't help but smile. It did feel like an itch, a huge, unreachable itch that kept her awake at night and distracted her during the day . . .

"Does it work?" she asked.

Lunet shrugged. "Sometimes. Sometimes it just makes it worse."

"That's what I thought," said Llianna.

‡

True to his pledge of protection, it was Hugo who saved Rothmar from the assassin's blade. Hugo had been pacing the ramparts, wrestling the demon of *inn mátki munr* with all the strength of a trained warrior, when a dark figure had appeared atop the far wall, outlined against the night sky. Hugo had followed soundlessly as the intruder crept towards Rothmar's room. He had surprised the man, but this was no untrained hireling; Hugo found himself fighting for his life with a *drapverr*, a trained killer. That explained why he was unable to disarm the man and take him alive, and why he took a painful cut to his chest.

The assassin's body was removed, and a healer called to tend Hugo's wound.

"Who sent him?" asked Rothmar, frowning at the bloodstain where the killer's body had fallen.

Hugo grimaced as the healer stitched the cut along his rib. "Work out who benefits from your death, and you can answer for yourself."

"You benefit from my death," said Rothmar. "But that doesn't answer my question."

Hugo snorted. "Well, who would want you dead?"

"I have no idea. Perhaps the Landvördr want to finish what they started, but it does not seem likely. Besides, they want us all dead."

Hugo stood to test the stitches. He winced, but claimed he was strong enough to stand guard.

"Thank you again for my life," said Rothmar. "I am not sure I warrant all this saving, but I am grateful."

Hugo nodded and left to speak with King Bekkr about extra guards, although even the guards would bear watching; the assassin had known exactly where to find Rothmar . . .

‡

They left for Ravensborg fifteen days later, with no further sign of threat to Rothmar. King Bekkr had suggested that the attack may have been intended for him, a response to one of the many judgments he had handed down to settle disputes; such judgments usually involved aggrieved parties who bore no love for the King. The room in which Rothmar recovered was one of Bekkr's private rooms.

Hugo was not convinced, bearing first-hand evidence of the intruder's fighting skills and having seen the certainty with which the assassin approached Rothmar's room. He resolved to keep close watch as they rode to Ravensborg.

Rothmar had declared himself able to ride at least three leagues a day, three times the distance a healthy person could walk in an hour. Four full lines of húskarlar accompanied them, riding in formation, surrounding Rothmar, Llianna, Lunet, Gravnir, and Faeoia's wagon. Hugo rode on the outer, scouting the way forward. He spoke with Rothmar, but not once did he talk to Llianna or even meet her gaze.

Gravnir traveled with them at Rothmar's request, and Llianna wondered if that had been part of his intention in spending so long at Rothmar's side. What had he said? *. . . as if that will miraculously give me something I want.*

What Gravnir wanted was to be part of the unfolding prophecy, just as Faeoia did, and that meant staying close to her. Llianna shook her head; would she end up with a whole troop of followers waiting for the next miracle?

"Who are you arguing with?" asked Rothmar.

Llianna looked at him blankly.

He smiled. "You were shaking your head so hard your hair was whipping around."

"Oh. I was arguing with myself."

"Who won?" asked Rothmar.

Llianna smiled at him. He had a sweet sense of humor for someone so serious, and she could see why Marina had adored him. Thinking of Marina wiped away the smile. Death was painful enough, but violent death, brutal death, brought with it shock, horror, helplessness, a range of feelings that twisted the strands of grief into ugly knots. Would Marina always hover between them like a dark cloud?

Rothmar settled into his usual state of serious silence, and Llianna went back to pondering the odd circumstance of being a child of prophecy.

The ramparts of Ravensborg appeared late on the eighth day. Rothmar had maintained his three leagues a day, a leisurely pace for the rest of the cavalcade, and he looked healthier than when they started from Gullhyrndr. Llianna was glad of that when the whole stronghold turned out to welcome their King home. What would they have made of the near corpse Rothmar had been when they had dragged him out from under the rotting horse?

People lined the road, cheering, throwing flowers at the horses' hooves, singing and laughing. Rothmar was certainly well loved.

Lunet's eyes shone with delight. "This is for you! They are welcoming their Queen."

"Really?" Llianna waved more graciously to the sea of faces, but she still breathed a sigh of relief when they reached the walls of the stronghold.

"They are glad to have a Queen again," said Rothmar. "It brings balance to the Land."

‡

The wedding took place on the last Frigga's day of summer. Not as auspicious as the first Frigga's day, it nevertheless met the ritual timing for a royal wedding, and the harvest food was abundant. Llianna wore a gown of grey-green silk and felted wool, with strands of silver and gold rippling through the cloth. Her original dress had been ruined, and it seemed like a relic of another time anyway. The Ravensborg sempstress had not even suggested lace, forewarned perhaps by Lunet, or maybe reluctant to replicate the wedding gown that had been sent off with Marina on her ill-fated journey to Vadsted. Llianna was grateful for the restrained beauty of her dress, and for the artistic symbolism of the threads that twined so compellingly though her life.

She stood beside Rothmar and pledged herself to be Queen of Ravensborg. Rothmar's chiefs formed an honor line behind them, and Llianna tried not to look for Hugo. He had not spoken with her, and she had not sought him out. What was there to say?

The forged bond still shone between them like a beacon in the Tapestry, but Llianna tried not to look for that either. If Hugo could retreat behind his precious honor, fidelity and the rest of the Warrior Code, then so could she!

The wedding feast was boisterous, the people of Ravensborg grateful for a reason to celebrate rather than mourn. Llianna's face ached with the effort of smiling and receiving well wishes. She ate little and drank far too much bridal-ale, so that the final blessings seemed to come from far away and not be meant for her at all. She was surprised when Rothmar helped her stand to make the procession from the hall to the bedchamber. Had it come so soon?

Rothmar's married chiefs and their wives formed a passage of blessing for the bedding to come. Their ribald suggestions and hearty good wishes brought Llianna to the bedchamber dizzy and overheated. Buttons came to mind, and her long ago question about undoing them. Had it been another lifetime that buttons had seemed so important? This dress had no buttons, and Llianna had spared no thought for who would be undoing the ties out of reach at the back of the bodice. A child of prophecy had other things to worry about . . .

"Are you going to be sick?" asked Rothmar, eyeing her warily.

The bridal-ale churned in her belly.

Oh, no!

With a desperate groan, she bent over and vomited on the marriage quilt, a frothy mix of mead and the bites of food she had sampled at the feast. When she could move again, she wiped her mouth on her sleeve and burst into tears.

Rothmar approached her slowly, like he would a skittish horse. He lifted her to her feet, pulled the quilt off the bed and rolled it up for the washerwomen.

"Come, there is water for washing." He led her over to the bowl of scented water thoughtfully left by the attendants.

Face and hands washed, Llianna felt somewhat restored, if still a little strange.

"I'm sorry," she mumbled, looking at her feet.

"You need never apologize to me for making a mess," said Rothmar gently. "You pulled me raving from under that rotting horse, and I can only imagine how awful that must have been. You have seen me at my worst, my dear."

Llianna managed a weak smile.

"Can I help with the laces?" he asked.

And there it was. Simple really. He untied the laces, and Llianna let the dress fall to the floor. She stood before him in her undershift.

"I didn't know how that would happen, undoing the laces. It troubled me for a long time, especially when the laces were buttons, but then it seemed less important compared with other things, and now it just seems silly that I even worried about it." She stopped herself. "Oh, I sound like Marina!"

Rothmar smiled sadly. "We both miss her. At least we have that in common."

Llianna looked at him in surprise. Was he as uneasy about this marriage as she was? Had he spent time wondering what they had in common?

"Will we sit for a while?" asked Rothmar, indicating the cushion-covered bench at the foot of the bed.

Llianna sat at one end, Rothmar at the other, a gap between them.

"There are things expected of us now we are married," said Rothmar. "Have your women talked with you about this?"

Llianna nodded. Of course they had told her what was expected, but talk wasn't the same as being alone in a bedchamber with a man. The wrong man. She kept her eyes on the floor, tracing patterns in the tiles.

Rothmar slid across the bench until his thigh touched hers. "I will not force you to be my wife," he said. "But there are ways a man and woman can find comfort in each other, even if true love lies elsewhere."

Llianna met his eyes. Grey eyes. Sad eyes.

"How do you know?" she asked.

Rothmar sighed. "I loved my wife, and I wept at her pyre, but that was many years ago, and I have taken comfort since then."

Oh, he spoke of his true love, not hers . . .

"We are of the line of Kings, Llianna. Comfort and friendship may be the best we can hope for in marriage."

"And Queens," said Llianna. "The line of Queens."

"Even so," said Rothmar. "Will you come to bed that we may start to know each other and find what comfort we may?"

Llianna stood and lifted his hands to her heart. She looked into his eyes and thought that this moment could have been worse.

He guided her hands to untie his laces and, when he stood naked before her, he lifted her shift over her head. He smiled at her and drew her into his arms. His body was surprisingly warm, and Llianna remembered the fire that had run between her and Hugo in the stream. She tucked that memory away and smiled shyly at her husband.

"You are beautiful," he said softly.

Am I? wondered Llianna. It had never occurred to her. She was so accustomed to knowing herself from within - her strong will, her deep sense of self, the power of her life force - that she seldom thought of herself from the outside.

"Your eyes are the softest grey with a hint of green, like the promise of Spring. You are very lovely."

He was gentle and patient with her, coaxing her to open to him. She was surprised again when her body responded, softening and warming to his touch. Perhaps he was right about the comfort.

The biggest surprise was the pleasure Llianna found in their lovemaking. Who would have thought that duty would include such delight and release? She lay awake for some time after Rothmar slept, thinking of the morning she had stood with Hugo in the stream; she had thought that moment complete, but now she knew there was so much more.

Rothmar and Llianna emerged the next morning to a raucous welcome from bleary-eyed wedding guests. They shared a cup of bridal-ale, sipping in turns until it was empty. Thus did they announce to the gathering that the wedding had been consummated and all was well.

Llianna looked for Hugo. What would it mean to him to see her accept Rothmar like this? Did he understand about comfort and friendship?

‡

Hugo stood at the back of the gathering of cheering wedding guests. Unable to wholeheartedly join the celebration, he felt a strange mix of relief and deep regret: relief that Llianna was beyond temptation, safely married as was required; regret that it was Rothmar and not he who stood beside her sipping bridal-ale.

A small voice asked him if she really were beyond temptation, but Hugo refused to listen to it. The voice went on mumbling to itself, like a spring-fed brook running over rocks . . .

Hugo left five days later, leading Ravensborg's forces sent to fight the Landvördr, as the enemy were now called. Did it make any difference to give them another name? Probably not, but Rothmar had insisted. He was much recovered but not robust enough for the constant movement and battle-readiness required by the random attacks.

"Be my right hand while mine regains strength enough to join the fight," said Rothmar. Llianna stood by Rothmar's side, giving the Queen's blessing to the departing húskarlar.

Hugo bowed low. "I will lead Ravensborg's men in your name, Rothmar. I await the day you return to lead us all."

He lifted Llianna's hand and kissed it chastely. The skin did not burn, and Llianna sighed. How could he be so distant with the fire streaming between them?

She repeated the Queen's blessing for him as serenely as possible. How could she do that instead of taking him in her arms and holding him close?

He left, taking the warmth with him.

Llianna returned to her room to find a midnight-blue cloak spread on her bed as a gift. She recognized the motif on the back of the winter cloak: a stream at dawn, with stars fading and a magical light shining on the water.

She also found Lunet, sitting miserably by the window, her sewing forgotten in her lap.

"How are you?" asked Llianna, sitting beside her.

"Well enough," said Lunet, although she didn't sound it. "At least you are properly wed."

Llianna nodded. "It isn't as bad as I feared."

"Rothmar is kind," said Lunet. "It is something."

"More than something, I think," said Llianna. "Now tell me what is troubling you. Are you missing Gullhyrndr?"

Lunet shook her head. "It is nothing."

Llianna took her gently by the shoulders. "You have been by my side long enough for me to know when you are troubled. Please tell me."

"I have nothing to give you," Lunet said softly.

"Nothing? What more could you give? You have given me your companionship, your loyalty, your bravery, your cure for lovesickness." Llianna tried to bring a smile to Lunet's face.

"That's not what I mean. I mean that I have nothing to gift you for your wedding, no goods, no coin, no way of making a gift even."

A shock passed through Llianna's body, a cold wave of shame that made her gasp. How could she not have seen that? How could she have had this bright soul as a companion and never think about what she needed? Hadn't she even asked Gravnir what he needed that long ago day when they first met?

"Oh, Lunet! Forgive me. I didn't know." Llianna cringed; how could she not have known?

Lunet wiped tears from her eyes. "It is just the way of it, but I would like to have had a gift for you."

"What do you mean, just the way of it?"

"Women in service can expect a bed and food and some cloth for tunics if they are fortunate. I am fortunate; I have new tunics and solid boots, and you do not ask more of me than is right."

"More of you? Was it right to take you into danger on the road here? To put you at risk?"

"That was no more than you asked of yourself. That is not wrong."

"What would be wrong?" asked Llianna, a dull ache gripping her stomach.

Lunet sighed miserably. "Some of the women are expected to sleep with men they don't want, and with women if that's the way of it. And worse in the eastern fiefdoms, I've heard."

Llianna surged to her feet, fists clenched. "No! Not at Gullhyrndr. Not at Ravensborg!"

"Not your father perhaps, but it was not beyond Falden to take women to bed, like it or not. I have not heard tales from Ravensborg, but many things happen in a stronghold this big."

Llianna put that aside for the moment. "What you say about having nothing. Is that the same everywhere? For everyone?"

"The húskarlar receive coin and sometimes land. If they live long enough. Horsemasters and stablemen, too. But women receive only bed and food. It is the way of it."

"And the provisions when men die, like back at Gullhyrndr?"

"Some Kings are good, but there are many hands between the King's coffers and the widow's need. It is rare for the King's bounty to land where it should."

"What happens to the widows then? The children?"

"They may be fortunate and have family to take them in, but most don't. The children can be sold, or the widow herself."

Llianna didn't even want to know what that meant.

"Thank you for telling me. I have much to think about." Llianna opened a chest and handed Lunet a purse full of coins.

"This is too much," said Lunet quietly.

"Then buy me an expensive gift," said Llianna. "It is yours to do with as you will. We will talk about how much you should receive from now on for your service to me."

She found Rothmar in his solar, meeting with councilors and petitioners. He raised an eyebrow when she sat beside him, but he continued with the business of running the stronghold. When the others left, Llianna spoke of what she had learned from Lunet.

Rothmar looked thoughtful. "You are Queen. The Queen oversees the running of the stronghold. If you wish there to be changes, you can command that it is done."

Llianna absorbed that. "Does every Queen have that power?" she asked.

Rothmar shrugged and smiled. "Not every Queen knows how to use power wisely."

Llianna reached for parchment to begin writing her commands.

"Just try not to beggar me, will you?" The smile reached Rothmar's eyes, and Llianna wondered if it was possible to love two men for completely different reasons.

One's back is vulnerable, unless one has a brother -
Ber er hver að baki nema sér bróður eigi. - The Saga of Grettir

Llianna set aside one set of dreams and took up another, bringing changes to the stronghold with the help of Thyvri. It proved less difficult and more interesting than she had expected: decreeing payment in coin for women's work, organizing the never ending need for food, clothing, cooking, serving, cleaning, and all the other tasks that went into managing a stronghold full of people. Most interesting of all were the women's responses to receiving payment for their work.

"They think there's something you want," said Thyvri.

"There is," said Llianna. "I want women to be treated fairly, to have enough to feed and clothe their children, and to never have to sleep with someone out of fear or dire need."

Thyvri blinked back tears and patted Llianna's hand. "You're a match for him, and no mistake. Never a kinder pair in all Nine Worlds."

The women gradually came to accept their Queen's

beneficence and to bless her for her kindness. There were men who tried to take advantage of the new system, but Llianna's justice was swift and effective. More men left Ravensborg in the first month after the changes than in the previous five years, but Llianna said good riddance to them and set about building the sort of stronghold she wanted.

The Keepers heard of the changes and sent a delegation of five grey-clad men to investigate. Llianna and Rothmar met with them in the King's private rooms. The senior Keeper, a stern man called Bramer, was not the Questioner from Llianna's Testing, but he watched her with the same hawk-like menace. She, however, felt much less like a mouse.

"We have received tidings of changes at Ravensborg," said Bramer, directing his words to Rothmar. "A new Queen must be guided in the traditions of the stronghold, encouraged to follow the Law." He spoke slowly, as if instructing a child.

"What tidings would they be?" asked Rothmar mildly.

The Keeper consulted a leather-bound book. "Changes to the employment of women. Men put out of the stronghold for questioning the changes. Reports of a Queen who does not know her place."

Llianna tensed, but Rothmar placed a soothing hand on her arm.

"My Queen and I have discussed the management of Ravensborg. There is nothing I have not overseen. Perhaps your enquiry should be directed at me."

Bramer scowled but, as Rothmar predicted, he could not directly accuse a King of overstepping his authority. "I will consult my superiors. Deviation from the Laws must be addressed."

The Keepers politely refused Rothmar's offer to stay for the evening meal.

"You should have told me it would bring so much trouble," said Llianna, as they watched the Keepers ride away.

"Trouble enough when trouble comes," said Rothmar, although the worry lines on his face had deepened during the meeting.

"What will they do now?" asked Llianna.

"Go back to their masters, discuss Ravensborg in secret meetings, gnash their teeth. There is not much they can do if I put my name to things."

"So it is women they watch. Women they fear." Llianna crossed her arms over her chest.

Rothmar nodded. "Queens. They watch Queens."

"Because of the First Battle," said Llianna, thinking of the words carved in rock on a ledge overlooking the Wastelands. She shivered; *someone walking on her ashes* . . .

Rothmar put an arm around her shoulders. "There is nothing to fear while I speak for you. Long have Ravensborg and Gullhyrndr kept our own counsel and resisted the domination of the Keepers. They want the trade rights of Gullhyrndr harbor and the riches of the Ravensborg mines – iron and copper are as sought after as emeralds. Yet they dare not make open challenge lest the other fiefdoms rise up to stand with us. The other Kings have ceded more power to the Keepers, but it is an uneasy arrangement."

"But why tolerate them at all?" asked Llianna. "I don't understand why my father sent me on the Pledge Ride, or even why he let the Keepers into Gullhyrndr. He obviously doesn't like them!"

Rothmar shook his head. "There you have it. Your father and I walk a fine line between independence and open defiance of the Law of Nyrland. The Keepers have been a power in Nyrland since the beginning, but they dare not challenge the fiefdoms directly, and we dare not defy them directly."

"Hmmph."

"Hmmph indeed. If anything should happen to me, you must be wary of them. Call on your father or brothers, and I will name a Regent so you are protected. Then they dare not attack you directly."

"What would they do?" asked Llianna, tendrils of dread snaking through her body.

"Nothing if we manage them as we always have," said Rothmar. "I just mention it so you are prepared. They are narrow-minded bigots, but they were given power at the beginning, and they hold onto it tenaciously. They will pounce on anything that deviates from the Law, but it is not the Law they truly value; it is power. Your changes do not break any Laws, although they do seem to have stirred interest in high places."

"I'm sorry to bring trouble to Ravensborg," said Llianna.

"You have done nothing wrong. The Keepers will have to

accept that you have my protection." Rothmar pulled her close and kissed the top of her head.

‡

"The rope tightens," said Solvaldr, standing at the window of his tower room. He smiled; if one listened carefully, it was possible to hear the mill grinding . . .

‡

Llianna's fears of the Keepers faded into the background as she met the everpresent demands of managing the stronghold. Thyvri praised her work for the women, but she was not happy about Llianna's refusal to take up a needle and stitch the stronghold's banners with the other women.

"It's all very well to improve the lot of women, and you're doing that right enough, but a Queen has other responsibilities, too. Take these banners that need making . . ."

"Design them yourself," said Llianna, preoccupied with organizing reading lessons for the Settlement children.

"That would never do," said Thyvri, as if Llianna had suggested she sleep with Rothmar.

Llianna remembered Marina's pride about her banner designs for Vadsted, and she wondered if she could come up with something to satisfy Thyvri. As long as she did not have to sew the wretched things herself . . .

In the end it was Lunet who saved her. "Of course I can design a banner. I've seen enough of them now. There be nothing to it: ravens, red and black, cloudberries . . ."

"Cloudberries?"

"They only grow in the West, so they belong on Ravensborg banners. Like crested ravens and red-breasted songbirds."

"How do you know all this?" asked Llianna.

"I listen to the women," said Lunet, reminding Llianna of Marina.

"Please go and talk to Thyvri. Say I sent you."

Lunet nodded. "I'll tell her the designs are yours."

"Bless you!"

Thyvri was forced to accept that the only sharp objects Llianna would be using were knives and swords.

"But you cannot do sword fighting in the sewing room!" said Thyvri.

"Of course not," said Llianna patiently. "I will be training with the men at arms in the yard."

"Oh, no! That will never do. Hallmund would have an apoplexy."

"A what?"

Ravensborg, like the other fiefdoms, had imposed a strict division between men's and women's business. Llianna gave thanks again for Sigfinn's willingness to welcome a girl into his domain. She wished she could ask him about that now that she knew more of her own story and what might be required of her. Of course he had known about the prophecy - he and her father had defied custom to train her as a warrior, but how much had they known about what she would need when she grew into her power?

There had been no one to offer Marina warrior training, and she had grown into the roles and duties expected of a King's daughter. No wonder Llianna had been so surprised when Marina first came to Gullhyrndr: a girl who preferred needlework to sword fighting. With silent blessings to Sigfinn, Llianna left Thyvri to her mutterings, tied back her hair, slung the Valkyrie shield over her back, and went to find Hallmund.

Hallmund stood in the practice yard, surrounded by new recruits. He stood like a warrior, feet apart, legs strong, body poised for action. He looked nothing like Sigfinn - shorter and stockier - yet Llianna recognized the same discipline and attention to detail in the way he watched the two recruits bashing at each other with staffs. She selected a sturdy staff from the barrel and waited for the outcome.

The taller boy prevailed, and Hallmund signaled for the next pair.

Llianna strode into the center of the yard.

No one else moved.

"Is this some kind of joke?" asked Hallmund, in a voice like thunder. "Get out of the yard!"

Llianna held her ground.

"Whose is she?" bellowed Hallmund. "I will not have your night trysts interfering with training! Get her out of here!" Clearly he did not recognize his Queen.

The recruits looked guiltily at each other. There had been many night trysts, but none of them recognized the staff-wielding girl. What was she thinking? To catch someone's eye? Who would want a girl who didn't know her place, no matter how feisty she might be? They started to whisper and snigger, and a few of the bolder among them called out suggestions that had nothing to do with combat training.

"Enough!" commanded Hallmund, striding up to Llianna.

She raised the staff so that her wedding ring met his furious gaze. The ruby eyes of the gold double-headed raven glittered in the autumn sun.

"Oh!" He stood glowering like a bear that had suddenly forgotten what it was about to do.

"I am accustomed to training at arms," said Llianna. "I wish to do so here."

"Dismissed!" growled Hallmund, waving at the recruits. They hurried away, looking back over their shoulders and muttering.

"I need to train with someone," said Llianna.

"Show me," said Hallmund, raising his staff.

Llianna moved in fast, cutting low with the staff. Hallmund jumped over the sweep and lunged his staff straight at Llianna's chest, fast and lithe despite his solid build. She pivoted and swung her staff at his head. He blocked it, and the staffs met with a resounding thud.

Hallmund lowered his staff and nodded. "You can fight, but I cannot pair you with any of the lads. They would cripple themselves trying not to harm you."

"I'd like to see them try," said Llianna.

"Be that as it may, it cannot be done. But if you will accept an old man as a sparring partner, we might be able to arrange something."

"Accepted!" said Llianna, swinging the staff at Hallmund's legs.

He laughed and parried the swing.

Llianna met with Hallmund in the early morning, and they sparred as the ravens announced the day and the cows ambled out to the paddocks after milking. The days grew shorter and the mornings colder, but still they met to hone her skill with sword, knife, shield and staff. At the first meeting, he studied the Valkyrie shield for a long time, turning it over and over in his hands.

"Handgrip needs replacing," he said finally, as if he saw a thousand-year-old shield every day.

He fashioned the handgrip himself, carving it from lindenwood for strength and securing it to the frame with iron nails.

"You will need to learn the weight of it and the way it moves with your body," said Hallmund when he handed her the restored shield. He selected a shield of his own to engage the dance of the shield bind with her.

Llianna stood almost as tall as Hallmund, and the shields locked at the same height. The Valkyrie shield hummed at the contact, the wood so aged and so finely wrought that it resonated like a drum. Llianna learned to use the sound as a guide: more pressure this way; step back and release now; move in; and so on. The shield hummed, but it no longer shimmered with power as it had on the clifftop.

"You have some strength in your shield arm," said Hallmund, rare praise from the arms master.

"May it be enough for what is needed," said Llianna. *Whatever that would be . . .*

‡

The weeks at Ravensborg became months, and winter brought more snow and less time outdoors. Gravnir still hovered near Rothmar, although some days he stood on the parapets, wrapped in borrowed furs, looking out towards the distant mountains. Llianna waited restlessly for summer, when they might return to the Wastelands and Munstrond, when they could seek Gravnir's mysterious wanderer and the secrets he held. When Hugo would return from patrolling the roads . . .

She wrapped herself in the midnight-blue cloak and waited as patiently as her nature allowed. She longed to know how the húskarlar fared with the Landvördr, concerned for the men from Gullhyrndr as well as Ravensborg. Had they fought a battle yet, or had the skirmishes gone on until the passes were closed for the season? Was her father safe? Hugo? Her brothers? When would she be called to fulfill the place promised by the prophecy?

Rothmar's strength slowly returned and he, too, chafed to join the other Kings in protecting their lands. Gravnir seemed the least restless, as if he were waiting for a signal that had not yet come.

Rothmar took to sitting with Faeoia after the midday meal, listening to her tales. The quiet conversation seemed to soothe his melancholy, and Llianna's heart lightened to see them together. Faeoia was so uncharacteristically talkative that Llianna became curious, venturing close enough to listen more than once, but they always fell suspiciously silent in her presence. What could Faeoia possibly be telling Rothmar, and why didn't they want her hearing it? When she asked Rothmar about it, he just looked vague and said it was nothing.

That mystery was still unsolved when the first birds returned from their winter homes and new life rippled through the stronghold: winter bedding airing from every turret, children running wild in the sunshine, new foals in the stables.

Then Gravnir disappeared.

He was there at supper and gone by breakfast, taking only his horse and enough information to risk exposing Ravensborg to the enemy.

"It is strange," said Rothmar. "I should be terrified by this, yet I do not fear treachery. I think he has left for some purpose that serves his people but does not threaten us."

Llianna was relieved to hear Rothmar's words, and she hoped

he spoke truly. Had she brought ruin upon Ravensborg by bringing Gravnir out of the Wastelands? As he said himself, he was an oddity, and who knew what he would do next . . .

A long-awaited messenger from Gullhyrndr rode in ten days after the spring rites, and Llianna sat with Rothmar to hear his report.

"Gullhyrndr is well. King Bekkr sends his assurance that the Landvördr have been pushed back to the mountains. The roads are safe to travel."

"And Ravensborg? What of our men?" asked Llianna. Did she sound too eager?

"They have fought well with few losses. Your chief outwitted the enemy more than once. He is patrolling the foothills to keep watch on the passes."

"My brothers?" asked Llianna, giving silent thanks that Hugo was safe.

"Dagmar is well, and Aedel carries their third child. Falden took a wound to his leg last season, and it heals slowly. He is being tended by the best healers, and they hope to have him riding again by the middle of summer."

Llianna nodded her thanks and turned to brooding about Aedel's pregnancy. Aedel was providing heirs for Gullhyrndr, and it was time for Llianna to do that for Ravensborg. The völva had taught her the way of women's power, and her body could choose when to allow a babe a home and when to refuse it. So far her body had refused, and she knew people were whispering about it.

It reflected poorly on the King. It reflected poorly on the Land.

What was wrong with her? Hadn't she accepted Rothmar as husband? Hadn't she accepted his body as well as his marriage troth? Why was she refusing to accept a child of his body?

Hugo.

Her body knew Hugo as the father of her children, as the true resting place of her heart. And the body must agree to bear a child . . .

‡

Messengers arrived from Hugo, but he did not return to Ravensborg. He reported that the western settlements had wintered well, and he asked leave to continue leading the húskarlar on the summer patrols. Rothmar agreed, planning his return to active leadership for later in the season. Llianna listened to it all, pretending interest and hiding her frustration. Would Hugo never return?

A wise man's heart is seldom cheerful. - Hávamál st. 55

The first Frigga's day of summer approached, bringing thoughts of Marina. Llianna lingered over the memories of that last visit to Gullhyrndr: their escape to the wildwood; the ribbons tied to the wishing tree; Marina's delight in her lacy wedding dress; her breathless chatter about what she would find at Vadsted; her laughter at the wedding feast that night. The memories of the awful events that followed also flooded in, stirred by a sound or a smell or a glimpse of something from the corner of her eye.

Rothmar grew somber and thoughtful, and Llianna could guess where his memories took him. His mood lightened when she shared fond memories of Marina, but his spirit had been marked by the ordeals of last summer. They lent strength to each other in the companionable rhythm of working together, sitting close through the morning meetings. Llianna absorbed herself in attending to the business that directly affected the running of the stronghold: summer hunting and crop tithes, shipments of silk from the south and wool from the eastern fiefdoms, setting the dates for weddings . . .

‡

Summer passed and the last Frigga's day approached. Llianna's time was taken up with preparations for the one-year feast for their wedding. One morning she sat with Thyvri ordering extra provisions, organizing the washing and airing of linens for the guest rooms, arranging seating in the dining hall . . .

"Llianna."

Was she dreaming? She looked up from the seating list.

Hugo.

Llianna sighed, releasing a fear she hadn't known was there. He was safe!

"Well come, dear cousin. When did you arrive?" Did she sound calm enough? She clasped her trembling hands in her lap and willed her heart to stop leaping in her chest like a spring foal.

"Just this morning. They told me to bring these straight to you." He lifted a sack onto the table.

Thyvri exclaimed happily.

"What is it?" asked Llianna.

"Cloudberries," said Thyvri. "They grow in the marshes between here and the mountains." She signaled for a girl to take them through to the kitchen.

"Yes, I have heard of them. What do you do with them?" asked

Llianna.

"Cloudberry cream," said Thyvri, licking her lips and smiling happily. "I thank you, Hugo."

He bowed to her, graceful as ever.

Llianna stood. "Have you seen Rothmar?"

Hugo shook his head. That stray lock of hair fell over his eyes, and Llianna was back by the stream, the sun rising over the trees . . .

Thyvri stood and bumped the table, pulling Llianna back from the brink of *inn mátki munr.*

"Come, I will take you to him," said Llianna quickly. Of course Hugo did not need her to show him the way, but she was not about to have him disappear with nothing exchanged but a bag of cloudberries.

Thyvri narrowed her eyes at Llianna, but she said nothing and went off to supervise the making of cloudberry cream.

"I have missed you," said Llianna.

Hugo nodded. "It was a long winter."

"And spring and almost all of summer! Will you always be gone so long?"

"I will do what is needed," said Hugo. "You are safe here, and the Landvördr threaten the fiefdoms."

Needed by whom? wondered Llianna, although she took his meaning. It was just that the longing in her body was shouting ever so loudly, making it hard to hear the smaller voice of reason that spoke of duty and honor and other sensible things.

They found Rothmar alone in his meeting room, the morning's business done.

Hugo bowed to Rothmar. "Greetings, cousin, and blessings for this year feast. I trust all is well here."

Rothmar stood and embraced him. "Well come, dear cousin."

Llianna wanted to strangle them both. It reminded her of that long ago day when Rothmar came to Gullhyrndr, and he and Marina had been *dear brothering* and *dear sistering* all over each other. Now it was all *dear cousin* this and *dear cousin* that, when all she wanted to do was rest her head against Hugo's chest and feel his heart beat.

They started talking intently about the Landvördr, and Llianna slipped away to return to her lists.

Ever would Ódin
on earth wander
weighed with wisdom
woe foreknowing,
the Lord of lords
and leaguered Gods,
his seed sowing,
sire of heroes. - The Legend of Sigurd and Gudrún

Gravnir struggled up a low rise, wishing he had taken more from Ravensborg. At the time it had seemed like enough: a loaf of bread, a quarter wheel of cheese, ten onions, and twelve shriveled apples from the kitchen stores. One horse had also seemed enough, but now the sorry creature limped behind him, reluctant to place any weight on its damaged foreleg. It had happened eight days out of Ravensborg; the horse had landed in a hole up to the right knee joint, and it was only luck that had seen the leg sprained rather than snapped through. Luck for the horse, but not for Gravnir, who still had to walk. At least his meager stores of food and his cooking pot, flint, and water bottle were still tied to the saddle, and the horse provided some warmth during the cool nights.

It might also have helped if he knew where he was going, but the Wanderer had earned his name because he wandered, and Gravnir trudged up yet another hill, hoping to see his friend's mule ambling along on the other side. He did not have a specific destination in mind, but he did have a specific intention: find the Wanderer and work out exactly how Llianna's thread interwove with his, and whether it was going to save his people or bring further destruction. If the outcome was destruction, then Gravnir faced a terrible choice.

His single-minded devotion to saving his people had grown more desperate the longer he spent with the Seafarers' descendants. They were not the ruthless invaders their ancestors had been, but they were formidable fighters, and they posed a deadly threat to the future of the Landvördr. The threat lay not just in their skill at fighting but also in the blind hatred the people of the seven fiefdoms directed at the Landvördr. Oh, Llianna and Rothmar had accepted him, befriended him even, but they saw him as an anomaly, a strange exception to the general vileness of his people. Gravnir wished they could meet young Abigahil, whose eyes shone with the trust of a reindeer calf, or Hinric, who snuck out of the caverns at night to count stars. The Landvördr were not all killers, but how could he explain that to a King whose beloved sister had died so horribly? How could he save Abigahil and Hinric and others like them from the dark path of those seeking vengeance and destruction?

Gravnir knew that Llianna was part of the answer to that, and the Wanderer another part, but he did not know how all the pieces came together, or if he could find them all before it was too late . . .

And what about the warriors like Fangar? They carried the old blood as surely as the children, but they could never be persuaded to another path, even if Gravnir could find one. Would he just end up bludgeoned to death for his efforts after all? The warriors truly believed it was their Destiny to destroy the Seafarers and avenge the travesty of the First Battle, and a thousand years of true belief formed a dark enough power without the talk of dark magic and alliances with the Noctimagi.

Gravnir's thoughts wandered down all the paths of Landvördr life and lore, and his feet wandered the invisible paths of the Wastelands, seeking something that would change the darkness towards which his people were hurtling . . .

Each man must at one time die. No one may escape dying that once, and it is my counsel that we not flee, but for our own part act the bravest. - The Saga of the Völsungs

Llianna spoke again of returning to Munstrond, but Rothmar persuaded her to postpone her journey until they could be sure the roads were safe. She had cause to be grateful when messengers reached Ravensborg with reports of renewed attacks on the roads west of Gullhyrndr. The Landvördr seemed to be directing their attacks to the western strongholds, as if there was something there that they wanted . . .

Hugo rode out again with Rothmar beside him this time, and Llianna turned away from the complexities of marriage and *inn mátki munr* to continue managing Ravensborg.

The dream started a month later, waking Llianna from a sleep so deep she had no idea at first who she was or where she lay. The nights grew longer, and the first snows covered the ground, but the dream took her beyond Ravensborg, beyond the seven fiefdoms. It was always the same: Llianna was engaged in one of the everyday stronghold tasks when she heard a strange noise behind her. She turned to catch a glimpse of something, but it moved with her, so it remained behind her no matter how fast she turned. She turned faster and faster, like a wooden spinning top, her hair flying out like wings. The spinning opened a tunnel, and Llianna was drawn into the tunnel and out of the stronghold into a world of caverns and tunnels and golden light. She wandered through a labyrinth of tunnels and walkways, pulled by a mysterious force to find something that would save the Land, save her people, save the Landvördr . . .

Save the Landvördr?

That woke her every time. Why would she be called to save the Landvördr?

That question kept her awake, and Llianna cursed Gravnir for deserting her; there was so much she did not understand, so much that had been lost or hidden. How had they forgotten so many stories of the past? Perhaps that was what happened when fear overcame wisdom, concealing things until no one knew the true stories any more. And without the true stories, how could anyone read the signs and portents - and the dreams?

Llianna took to rising early and breakfasting alone on fresh-baked bread and goat's milk, still warm from the morning milking. Thyvri was usually there in the kitchen, directing the day's baking and rousing sleepy kitchen workers, but she left Llianna alone, respecting her mistress's mood of distraction and rumination. Llianna took her bread and milk to the large corner room on the first level where the stronghold's collection of books and scrolls lay covered in dust. Perhaps the true stories lay hidden there . . .

She cleared a table, placed her breakfast there, and worked her way through the manuscripts, looking for something that did not refer to horse trading, making weapons, or King lists. Reading had not been high on her list of preferred activities at Gullhyrndr, but Marina's arrival had forced her to attend lessons regularly, so she could read and write enough to make sense of everyday writing. Yet some of the faded words on the old manuscripts baffled her, so she made three piles: one pile contained items irrelevant to her search (very large), one contained likely-looking manuscripts (very small), and one was made up of documents that she found indecipherable (too large for comfort). She feared it was a hopeless task, but it was better than losing herself in household tasks while the men were off fighting their battles.

Days became weeks, and Llianna had a stack of firewood brought to the room so she could sit close to the fireplace as she worked. Wind and snow swirled outside, and the pile of irrelevant manuscripts grew higher. The weather kept her away from the practice ground, and the Valkyrie shield rested idly against the wall.

Llianna worried for Rothmar and Hugo out in the winter storms. The Landvördr had not stopped their attacks with the snows this season, so the men had not returned home. Would the killing never end?

The pile of useless information finally grew so high the manuscripts toppled to the floor in a cloud of dust. Llianna sighed wearily, pushed back the stool, and stretched her cramped shoulders. Why had the scribes thought it so important to record lists of Kings, numbers of húskarlar, and the size of horses? It reminded her of the pissing contests the Gullhyrndr stableboys had held behind the horse yards. Admittedly, she had joined them when she was five years old, but surely Kings had better things to do than record the size of their holdings? What of the histories? What of the stories of the past that could inform the present? Surely there must be more than just prophecy and vague speculation?

Llianna kicked at the fallen manuscripts, disturbing more dust to float in the pale, winter sunlight that filtered through windows she had wiped clean of cobwebs and grime. The snow lent the light an otherworldly glow, and the beams lit up a small leather-bound book bulging with ragged, velum pages. Llianna took it down from the shelf. Another book of lists?

She carried the book to the table. It fell open to a drawing of a plant: feathery leaves and a single purple flower with a yellow center. A book of plants? Llianna read the words with interest; here was something different, even if it wasn't what she was seeking.

She picked out familiar words: *Fire; Air; Water; Earth.*

Faeoia and the völva had taught her to work with the elements of the Nine Worlds, and Llianna still called on the elements when she woke in the morning and before sleeping at night.

"*Sentinels of Nordri, powers of Earth, I invoke you and call you.*

Three roots deepening. Stone. Mountain. Fertile field. Come! By the earth that is Nerthus, our Mother, send forth your strength, and be here now."

"Sentinels of Austri, powers of Air, I invoke you and call you. Golden eagle of Yggdrasil who has knowledge of many things. Storm-pale hawk. Wind-witherer. Come! By the air that lifts your wings, send forth your grace, and be here now."

"Sentinels of Sudri, powers of Fire, I invoke you and call you. Red flames of winter fires. Glowing sun of summer's warmth. Heat of passion. Courage burning. Come! By the fire that melts fear, send forth your flames, and be here now."

"Sentinels of Vestri, powers of water, I invoke you and call you. Green waves from the watery depths. Grey-green serpent of the salty abyss. Come! By the water that brings life, send forth your flow, and be here now."

And, of course, the invocation that bound them together, bringing balance.

"I stand at the center, where Air, Fire, Water, Earth come together in balance, where night and day, birth and death, joy and sorrow meet as one."

Llianna sighed deeply. Was this a book of such teachings? How strange to see the old words in writing, when Faeoia and the völva insisted that such knowledge must always be passed on by word of mouth so the teaching stayed true. Who would have written it and illustrated it so carefully?

Llianna concentrated on the words . . .

. . . Here beginneth the Book of Memory
most diligently compiled
and brought into one volume.

Ah! Book of Memory. She read on . . .

They who desire to have the most true knowledge of the greater mysteries, let them diligently peruse this little book and often times read it over and they shall obtain their prosperous and wished desire. Listen to these things, you children of the Old Ones, I will speak in the loudest and highest voice I can, for I come unto you to open and declare the most secret treasure of all the secrets of the Nine Worlds. I will not do it feignedly and erroneously but altogether plainly and truly, wherefore use you towards me such devotion of hearing as I shall bring unto you magistery of doctrine and wisdom, for I will show you a true testimony of those things which I have seen with my own eyes and felt with my hands. I will speak plainly and manifestly so that the unskilful, as those that are expert and skilful, shall be able to understand the secret of this mystery. Neither shall any justly use slanderous and blasphemous words against me, for seeing that the Old Ones have not written of the mysteries, I will plainly set down the true story before your eyes, together with the wisdom of the Old Ones, serving well for our purpose that the matter whereof we entreat may be manifest and plainly understood.

Llianna closed her eyes and stroked the page. Could this be it at last? The words were strange and ponderous and difficult to read, but they promised much . . .

She turned the page.

What?

The vellum stared back, blank as a snowstorm.

Llianna turned more pages, careless of the old vellum.

No! Those grand words could not be followed by silence.

But every page was blank.

"*Paska!*" Llianna cried out in frustration. Were the Norns testing her? First the völva with her insistence that seidr cannot be compelled, then Gravnir with his elusive mysteries, and now this.

"Aargh!" She pushed the table away and stomped to the window. Maybe it was simpler to be like the Kings and write lists of horses and men and weapons, rather than trying to understand the meaning of things. Maybe she should just manage the stronghold, have ten children, and forget about trying to understand prophecy and answering unanswerable questions.

Llianna rested her elbows on the wide sill and followed the slow-moving clouds across the sky, tracking the changes wrought by the winds. Being a cloud would be so much easier than being a child of prophecy . . .

Movement beyond the gates caught her eye. Riders. Her heart leaped. Had the men returned?

Llianna ran down to the forecourt to see Rothmar ride in with a guard of twenty húskarlar, a string of tired-looking horses, and eight wounded men with a pile of broken weapons in cart. Rothmar saw her and waved a greeting.

Where were the others? *Hugo?*

Rothmar dismounted and strode over. "Are you well?"

Llianna nodded. She was well in body, despite the dreams and the restlessness of her spirit.

"And you? How has it gone? Where are the others?"

Rothmar rubbed his forehead. "They are watching the roads between here and Gullhyrndr. Hugo and I have fared well, but there have been losses among the men. The Landvördr fight fiercely, yet I fear we have not felt their true strength yet. It is as if they are waiting for something. We cannot afford to leave the passes unguarded."

Llianna walked with him to his rooms. Would he say more?

He seemed to catch her thought. "Hugo sends you greeting."

"I thank you," said Llianna, feeling again Rothmar's kindness and generosity of spirit. Here was a King who did not keep endless lists of property and conquests!

Llianna left Rothmar to soak in a tub of warm water, readied at Thyvri's orders as soon as she had seen the riders approaching. He had returned with dark rings under his eyes and lines of fatigue on his face, and she hoped he would stay long enough to restore himself.

"How has it been here at Ravensborg?" asked Rothmar at dinner.

Llianna recounted the events of the last four months, and Rothmar seemed to find solace in the mundane world of the day to day running of Ravensborg, smiling and nodding at the stories of escaped pigs and three days of burned loaves when the baker's wife left him to live with his brother.

Llianna ran out of stories, and Rothmar lapsed into seriousness again.

"Will this fighting never end?" asked Llianna.

Rothmar sighed. "We are winning the battles, but the Landvördr wear us down. It is tiring to be away from home so long, especially in winter, but there is no knowing where or when they will strike. It is a clever strategy, and one that will prove disastrous for us unless we can find a way to lure them out into the open for a pitched battle. We are winning the skirmishes, only to have to fight them again and again."

"Not like the First Battle," said Llianna. "It seems the Landvördr have learned from the past. I wonder if we have."

"What do you mean?" asked Rothmar.

Llianna told him of her search of the manuscripts, of her sense that there must be something in the histories that would help. She did not tell him of the dreams that asked her to save the Landvördr.

"We certainly need something," said Rothmar. He spoke softly, and the lines deepened on his face.

Rothmar stayed for ten days, time enough to repair the weapons, exchange the horses, and take some rest. Time enough for Llianna to sleep in his arms and feel the gentle love that moved between them.

"I will miss you," she said, the night before he was to leave again.

"I wish our time had not been one of absence and battle," said Rothmar. "I am glad for the comfort we have offered each other."

"More than comfort," said Llianna, stroking his hand. "It seems that love takes many forms."

Rothmar's smile lit his whole face.

He rode out the next morning with the húskarlar, a wagonload of restored weapons, a string of fresh horses, and two of the wounded men who had been restored by rest, good food, and Thyvri's healing remedies.

Llianna returned to her manuscripts and more months of waiting . . .

Rothmar returned to fighting, but he did not want to go. He hated sleeping on the ground, hated the dirt, hated the cold, hated the lack of privacy. He hated waiting for the enemy to strike, never knowing when and where the attack would come. He hated the fighting when it came: the noise, the chaos, the sweat and blood and shit, the smell of fear. He hated it all, and he was duty-bound to keep doing it.

He tried to remember if there had been a time when he was a better warrior, a time when he had not hated it, but his memories snagged on the attack on the road to Vadsted. Something had changed in him as he lay on the ground under the rotting horse. Sometimes he wondered if he had lost his reason and was forever impaired. If that were true, he should hand command to Hugo and return home to his soft, private bed and ignominy.

He could not do it.

The love that shone between Hugo and Llianna already gave his cousin too much of what Rothmar could rightfully call his, but that was as Fate willed it. The command of the Ravensborg forces must remain with the King. Even if it killed him.

The Landvördr continued the random attacks on the roads between strongholds, a strategy designed to wear down the defending forces. The strategy was working; Rothmar's men were making mistakes, and mistakes cost lives and morale. The first mistake had been an oversight: a scout sent out alone when standing orders were for two or more to ride together at all times. The problem arose when the scout was returned in pieces scattered on the road over the next three days. The second mistake was the failure to replace a lame horse, another standing order. The horse fell behind, and pieces of the man and horse had appeared along the road over the next days.

There were also the settlements and homesteads reached too late, where Landvördr forces had taken the bloody revenge they sought with no one to defend the householders and farmers. Rothmar had wept as they buried the women and children.

At least the actual fighting offered a chance to do something, and Rothmar rode into battle with ferocity befitting a King. He still hated it, but he had one huge advantage: he wasn't afraid to die. That made him a formidable fighter, attacking and blocking and parrying as if he had six swords and shields rather than just one of each. More of his blows landed than any other fighter except Hugo, who fought like a hero from the sagas. Fighting back to back, they were unstoppable, but Rothmar ended each encounter with an aching shoulder and fingers clenched into a claw that only eased by soaking his hand in warm water for hours.

And still the Landvördr kept coming.

Long is the way and wearisome, but longer man's love doth last; if thou winn'st what thou wishest 'tis well for thee, but the norns work natheless. - Gróa, Svipdagsmál

Gravnir sat beside his horse in a cave overlooking the Wastelands. The horse's leg had healed well, but the snow season had forced him to stop his search for the Wanderer. Now he and the horse rested together in companionable silence, sharing body heat and the warmth of a meager fire. The big bay mare was growing the winter coat that would see her through the cold times, but Gravnir had no such protection, and they were both hungry. He needed to brave the cold to forage branches for the horse and tubers for himself. And to collect snow to melt for water. It was time to retreat, but he had not yet decided where to go. Ravensborg was tempting, but how could he explain his sudden departure? Returning to the Landvördr caverns was less tempting, but probably more sensible. Gravnir gave himself one more day to decide.

He woke to the sound of footsteps crunching in snow, and he knew he had left the decision too late. His fire had burned to coals, but there was light enough to see the three men outlined in the mouth of the cave.

Gravnir acknowledged the Landvördr hunters with a nod. They all looked weary and ragged.

"Bendeir." Gravnir greeted the leader.

"Gravnir. Long did we hunt for you, until the Elders decreed you lost."

Gravnir nodded. "I was lost, and now I am on my way home."

Bendeir looked as if he might say more, but it was not his place to question the seer. That task would fall to the Elders, and they would demand the truth. Gravnir sighed and gathered up his belongings. What truth would he tell them?

The three hunters shared their food with Gravnir. The hard bread and cheese tasted like nectar after ten days of tubers, and Gravnir decided that facing the Elders might be preferable to starving. Just.

The hunters led Gravnir across the Wastelands towards Munstrond. Were the Landvördr wintering away from the caverns? Always before they had just moved deeper into the mountains, away from the freezing winds and closer to the hot springs that bubbled in the lower halls. What did it mean if the Landvördr were wintering at Munstrond? Had the disastrous encounter with Fangar been observed? Gravnir wondered how he could explain that.

They arrived three days later at the riverbed and crossed to the old city, now covered with new snowfall. At the ruined gates,

Bendeir whistled, three long, two short, three long, and warriors appeared to escort them in. Gravnir tensed. Was that normal practice, or was he even more suspect than before he disappeared?

They took him straight to Olafeur and the other Elders, not even allowing him time to clean his face or tend his horse. The ruins of Munstrond hummed with secrets, but Gravnir feared he had run out of time to uncover them.

"Well come, young one," said Olafeur, beginning the formal meeting. His wise, old eyes were troubled, and Gravnir missed the warmth that had once flowed between them.

"Take the stick and share your story. We listen with our hearts."

Gravnir bent his head. He knew the ritual words but never before had he hoped so fervently for them to be true. He lifted the antler from the table, holding it across his shoulder like a staff.

"This is my telling. I speak from my heart."

The six Elders settled back on their stools to hear his telling.

"I followed a vision of a girl, the daughter of Queens. The child of prophecy lives, but her way is not clear. She was born among the Seafarers, yet she dreams of saving our people. She is the promised one, and I have walked with her for many months."

"You have walked among our enemies?" asked Vaarnari, who sat beside Olafeur.

Gravnir nodded. "I was made welcome and treated with as

much trust as I am given here."

Olafeur shook his finger at Gravnir. "Bitterness does not become you. We have always treated you with fairness."

"That is true of the Elders, and especially of you, but the warriors do not share your sense of fairness," said Gravnir.

"Which brings us to Fangar. Did you see him die?"

Gravnir nodded. What use lying when they may have been watching?

"Did you try to defend him?"

Gravnir shook his head. "He was beyond defense for what he did to the Ravensborg girl."

"He was a warrior. Who are you to judge his actions?" Peivas was the youngest Elder and liable to nastiness.

"I do not judge, merely state the facts. The Ravensborg Queen could not let him live after what he did to her sister."

"Nevertheless, you did not defend him." Peivas again.

"I would be dead with him if I had tried," said Gravnir, knowing that for a truth.

"She is that powerful?" asked Olafeur.

Ah. Subtle question.

"I had loosed my warding for her to sense Munstrond. I have reason to believe she can unlock the mysteries we seek." No need to tell them that he had not known the Landvördr were there, that he had not been bringing Llianna to them.

"So Fangar died because you loosed the wards," said Vaarnari. "How do we know you were not aiding her?"

How indeed?

"Because I say so." Gravnir held Vaarnari's fierce glare.

Silence.

In that silence lived all the possibilities of Gravnir's life: either they would accept his words and take him in, or they would call him liar and kill him. Or try to.

Gravnir held his hands open by his side and waited.

"So be it," said Olafeur. "Gravnir has returned."

The Elders stood to leave, and Gravnir tried not to sigh with relief.

A tug on his arm. "Come, mother sent me to find you. You must be hungry and tired." Abigahil smiled up at him, reindeer eyes glowing.

Gravnir took her hand and followed her through the labyrinth of ancient halls to a cluster of smaller rooms where he found food and rest and welcome. Abigahil's mother heated water for him to wash and presented him with the bag of clothes he had left behind when he rode away from the mountains to find Llianna.

"Thank you, Adelgunde. I am blessed by your welcome."

"It be you who bless us, Gravnir. We know what it is you do."

Did they really know? He had spoken of it when he was younger, a boy with a head filled with dreams and visions and prophecy, but he doubted that anyone remembered the ramblings of a boy.

Others brought him food and ale, quietly taking him back as one of theirs. These were the people he worked to save. If only

Llianna and Rothmar and even Hugo, Llianna's man, could be there, seeing these people as he did . . .

Gravnir took the opportunity to thoroughly explore the ruins of Munstrond. Abigahil and Hinric and their friends scampered along with him, climbing into crevices too small for him, retrieving anything that caught their eye. His sack filled with crushed goblets, rusted knives, and strange stone statues that must have held a special place in old Munstrond, judging by the sheer quantity of them lying around.

The children did not know what he sought; he barely knew himself. He enjoyed their chatter and laughter as he scoured the old city for some sign of the Warrior Queens, the prophecy, and anything that would serve his cause. The Landvördr prophecy was something children sang, inventing games to match the words. How many times had he heard it as they explored the old city?

"When darkness comes from mountain halls
Covering land and scaling walls
A child will come from Freya's line
Born in death, lost in time.

Strong and wild, swift and free
Her Fate is carved in Life's tree.
Find her brother, staying near
To live in hope and banish fear.

Their power will come in duty born

Fired by Freya and the Norn

To vanquish darkness and despair

For all that moves in Earth, Water, Fire, and Air."

It was similar to the prophecy he had heard at Gullhyrndr, yet there were differences:

. . . Find her brother, staying near

To live in hope and banish fear.

Their power will come in duty born . . .

Was that his task, to stay near Llianna's brother? He shuddered at the memory of Dagmar's hostility. How could that dullard be part of the prophecy? Dagmar did not even recognize Llianna's power, let alone have any real power of his own.

Gravnir turned the possibilities over and over, like the children turned the relics in their hands, guessing at their use. If only he could go back in time to Munstrond before the First Battle . . .

He sighed in frustration. If he could truly go back in time, then he would not have to guess the meaning of words that might have been changed so many times the true message had been forgotten.

Gravnir also worried about Llianna. What would happen if she tried to reach Munstrond now? How could he let her know that the Landvördr had moved from the mountains?

Now that he had time to think about it, why had his people left the mountains? The caverns had stretched beneath the peaks in a vast labyrinth that could not be penetrated by armed forces, and there were as many ways out as from a snow vole's burrow. Surely the Landvördr had been safe there?

He asked Adelgunde, and she asked her bondmate, Gaurol, and he asked his brother, but no one knew why they had not wintered as usual in the deeper caverns. The Elders had decided, and that satisfied most people.

"It must have been for our safety," said Gaurol, and the others agreed.

Gravnir still did not know if the Elders had gone in search of the Noctimagi, awakening the old magic as the Seafarers feared, but that was not a question to ask Adelgunde and the others. He was careful in what he said and to whom he spoke. He had been in enough trouble in his younger years for questioning the Elders and encouraging people to think for themselves, and now was not the best time for him to draw attention to himself.

He tried to learn the Elders' plans, but he was forbidden entry to the Council, and none of the warriors would speak with him. Even if the Elders had absolved him, the warriors held him responsible for what happened to Fangar and his men. Gravnir came to understand that there must be strict orders about his safety, else he would have been stabbed or garroted the first night back. So much for trust!

The Elders may have lost trust in him, but the children continued to follow him as he paced restlessly through the old city, collecting trinkets and worrying about the future. Being with the children took Gravnir's thoughts back to his own childhood, roaming the caverns, discovering rock carvings and hidden places. There had been no fear of the deep caverns back then, no reason to keep children close and post guards on the deeper tunnels. He remembered when it had changed; it was the day he had lost both his parents.

There had been rumblings from the mountain for as long as he could remember, but the noises this day had sounded different. Old Fathir had said his ears were ringing, sure sign of a quake. And he had been right. The quake had opened a crevasse big enough to swallow three hearths, eighteen people, and Gravnir's parents. Adelgunde had lost her family, too, and she took Gravnir in and treated him like the younger brother who had disappeared that day. No matter that he had strange visions and spoke in tongues no one understood; he was bondbrother, and nothing could change that.

Gravnir shook off the memories and gave thanks for Adelgunde's stubborn loyalty and unwavering love. He prayed to whatever Gods would listen that he could save her and the others from the disaster he knew was coming.

Then he dreamed again of the Warrior Queens and knew what he must do.

Hail to you, gods! Hail, goddesses! Hail, earth that givest to all! Goodly spells and speech bespeak we from you, and healing hands, in this life. - Sigrdrífumál: 3

Llianna's dreaming became as real as her waking life, pulling her further and further into the strange labyrinthine world of tunnels and light and impossible demands. Twice now she had seen Gravnir there in the dreamworld, walking through tunnels and along passages, seeking, seeking . . .

Where was he? Had he gone to Munstrond? Had he found his wandering wise man? Was he safe?

Spring returned to Ravensborg with the usual flurry of noise and cleaning and new life. Sparring with Hallmund resumed, but Llianna's heart was not in it; what use warrior training when all she did was wait for the men?

Rothmar rode in every six weeks or so, but Hugo stayed away. Rothmar was unfailingly kind, yet he carried his sadness like a wound. He never spoke of the child Llianna was not carrying, or of his hopes for an heir. He spoke of the fighting and of the Landvördr.

"It is strange, but Gravnir's gift of his people's true name has changed the way I think about them."

"How so?" asked Llianna.

"If they are called *guardians*, and they truly guard the Land, as Gravnir says, then perhaps they are not all killers."

Llianna spoke the Landvördr blessing Marina had repeated to her as they crossed the Wastelands on their walk to Ravensborg:

"Hail Earth Mother of All!

May your fields increase and flourish,

Your forests grow and spread,

And your waters run pure and free.

Accept my offering, O Earth Mother.

Bring forth that which is good, and sustaining

For every living thing."

"Those are not the words of killers," said Rothmar.

"So I thought, too, but it seems there are enough Landvördr who want to cause us harm. Maybe it doesn't matter if there are good people among them, if there are enough who want only revenge."

"It matters," said Rothmar. "It has to matter."

Rothmar returned to the fighting, and Llianna returned to her dreaming.

There are many magnificent places in the heavens. One is called Alfheim. The people called the light elves live there. They are more beautiful than the sun . . . - Gylfaginning: 17

Gravnir walked his unsaddled horse out of the Munstrond settlement to find grazing, as he had done every day for weeks. He took nothing but his knife and flint tucked inside his boots. Anything more would have raised suspicion and thwarted his plan to keep walking this time, past the trees, across the Wasteland to the mountains his people had left. He had to know why they had left. He had to know what remained there now his people were gone . . .

His ruse worked. Now he just had to cross the Wastelands - alone, with no food or water, riding bareback on a scruffy horse that had nothing to eat. Or maybe the Elders would miss him and send warriors to take their revenge for Fangar's inglorious end. That would solve the food problem . . .

No warriors came on the first day or the second. Gravnir managed to find two tubers and three eggs to eat, while the horse stripped the bark from every tree where he stopped to dig for water. No harm done; the trees could hardly be more dead than they already were.

The mountains loomed larger, and Gravnir gave some serious thought to what he might find in the deserted caverns. Had his people delved too deep and woken the Noctimagi as Llianna's folk believed? Gravnir shook his head and gave the horse a lecture on the perils of believing everything you hear. The horse twitched its ears and snorted, as if to say it would never be taken in by a story made up to scare children.

"Me either," said Gravnir. "Then why do I feel so scared?"

The horse just snorted again and tossed its head.

They reached the mountains late in the fourth day, and Gravnir guided the horse through a narrow defile to one of the hunters' caches. Water jars, dried meat, and withered onions . . .

A feast! There were even two bundles of kiln-dried grass for the horse.

Evening slipped quietly down the slopes, bringing quiet darkness. Gravnir savored the solid stillness of rock and stone. Surely nothing too terrible could be lurking in the caverns?

He woke to a soft snorting from the horse, a friendly, snuffling noise that almost certainly meant there was someone there in the dark, someone the horse was pleased to see. Presuming it could see in the dark.

Gravnir reached for his knife and braced against the rock wall. Had the warriors found him, after all? He hoped not; he really did not want to die before solving the mystery of the prophecy. Or maybe not at all, come to think of it.

Nothing moved. No sound. No whisper of displaced air except for the silly creature snuffling beside him.

The silly creature jerked its head and snorted.

Gravnir jumped like a scalded cat. What was wrong with the beast?

He crouched down by the horse's foreleg, wishing he had made a fire before falling asleep. He had been so tired, and his belly so blissfully full, that he had drifted to sleep where he sat, a half-eaten onion in his hand.

Was that it? Had the smell of the onion attracted a night feeder? Gravnir looked for the glow of rodent eyes.

Nothing.

He took a deeper breath and called himself nine kinds of fool. Never had he feared the mountains or the dark. Had his time with the Seafarers made him soft? Did he believe their stories about the evil deep in the mountains?

Of course not.

Then why were his palms sweating and the hairs on his neck prickling?

He gathered the reins, swung himself up onto the horse, bent low over its neck, and urged it back the way they had come.

It splayed its legs and stubbornly refused to move.

Gravnir dug his boots into the horse's flank. He might as well have kicked the rock.

Spiders' legs of fear ran up his arms, making his jaw ache.

The horse turned its head and nudged his boot.

"What?" he cried. "What is it?"

The horse leaped forward and raced back down the defile, shaking Gravnir like a banner in a storm wind. He flung himself over the creature's neck and desperately gripped the mane. Could the mad horse even see where it was going?

They raced out onto the plain, shadows of all the nightmares from all the most terrifying stories chasing them . . .

A tree loomed out of the darkness.

The horse reared.

Gravnir fell.

The ground caught him, and pain gripped his chest as the air was shocked out of his lungs. He curled in a ball and moaned. The horse kept running.

Gravnir slowly remembered how to breathe, and the pain subsided. He rolled onto his knees.

The tree held out a hand.

"Can I help you stand?" it said.

Gravnir screamed.

"Oh dear, you have frightened it," said another tree.

Gravnir backed away, scrabbling on his hands and feet like an upside-down spider.

The trees followed.

One of them waved a hand. *A hand?*

Gravnir stopped scrabbling and lay on the ground. He closed his eyes and wished himself awake.

He opened his eyes.

"Aargh!"

One of the trees bent over him, eyes glowing like stars. *Eyes?*

Gravnir sat up.

The tree resolved into a tall figure with luminous eyes. A woman? Where had she come from? Her hair, long and thick, gleamed silver in the light, and her eyes shone the most amazing shade of violet, with long silvery lashes. Her skin was fair, and her hands . . . she offered her hand again. Gravnir took it, and she helped him stand. Her skin felt warm, and she smelled of starlight.

"Huh?" What was he thinking?

"You are thinking thoughts befitting a child of the prir," said the woman. "I do smell of starlight. And rain. And . . ."

"Enough, Amrin. We must take him home." The other tree had turned into a man with long hair and kind eyes.

Gravnir nodded. Home sounded good, warm and safe.

They took an arm each and led him back towards the mountains. Their touch was like warm sunlight after a long, cold night. Gravnir's body tingled with excitement. He knew who these tall ones must be, but he had thought they lived only in his dreams and in the Wanderer's stories. He stopped walking and bowed his head.

"I am deeply honored, Ljósálfar."

The Wanderer had given him their name - Ljósálfar, the Old Ones who had left the Land during the Dark Days, when woodland and forest glades were destroyed in the First Battle.

They had been the wisest race in the Nine Worlds, and they had taken their wisdom away with them a thousand years ago . . .

Now, remarkably, two Ljósálfar stood beside him, as real as the mountains. Gravnir had always imagined them as ethereal beings, yet these two looked quite substantial. But why were they in the Wastelands? Shouldn't they be in a green forest with running water and dappled light? Shouldn't they be building tree houses and talking with the woodland animals, singing songs like the birds, and dancing by the light of the moon?

His mad thoughts continued as the Ljósálfar led him along the base of the mountain range, skirting the passes that led to the Landvördr caverns. When the promise of dawn touched the plains, the Ljósálfar turned into a small cutting, picking their way around boulders and between sheer walls of rock to follow a narrow path into the mountains. Gravnir had never found this path in his solitary explorations, but even he had been discouraged from roaming too far east after the quake.

Were these gentle folk the true origin of the dark tales the Landvördr had used to scare children into obedience?

The Ljósálfar led him into the mountain, through crystal caves reflecting the light of a thousand candles, along passages carved by water over aeons, and into caverns where water still flowed in streams, or dripped slowly from the roof, leaving deposits that formed great spikes. Some of the spikes joined with pillars rising up from the floor, forming archways and other wondrous shapes. In all his time in the Landvördr caverns, Gravnir had never seen such strange beauty.

His guides left him in a large cavern with a domed roof, silent but for the slow burning of the wicks in the oil lamps on the walls and the soft footfalls of Ljósálfar walking through the adjoining passages. Gravnir looked around in awe; he was alone with a people who did not exist. What did they want with him?

"It has been many turnings since a Landvördr walked these halls," said someone behind him, speaking in the language of the Landvördr.

Gravnir whirled around. The Ljósálfr's eyes glowed violet.

"I am called Avitr," said the woman in a bell-like voice. "I bid you welcome to Cavernacaeli, the most recent home of the Avius Careo."

"I thank you for your welcome," said Gravnir. "I have never heard this name, Avius Careo. What language is this?

"It is the original language of our people. It means 'those who are lost and without a place', the Lost Ones. Your kind call us Förnir or Ljósálfar, if they remember us at all. None remember what we once were," Avitr said solemnly.

"I don't understand." Gravnir rubbed his eyes. Was he really having this conversation? "I thought the Ljósálfar left the Land after the First Battle."

"Many did leave, but some of us lingered after the First Battle, loath to leave this place we had loved." Avitr's voice echoed with loss and regret.

"Were you here at the First Battle?" asked Gravnir. "I mean

you, not your people, but you?" Was it possible? The Ljósálfar were said to live for thousands of years, but . . .

"Indeed. I saw the Dark Days come," said Avitr. "I saw the Land sundered. My sisters and brothers left for the West, and our Mother and Father. They took the road that runs straight, and never have we seen them or heard their songs again this side of the Mists."

Avitr gazed into the distance as she spoke, and Gravnir thought she might be crying, but there were no tears. He remembered the Wanderer saying that the Ljósálfar did not shed tears but turned their grief into songs, lamentations of anguish and loss. A song of grief echoed in Avitr's voice as she spoke of the Dark Days.

"I am sorry," said Gravnir quietly, not knowing what else to say.

"I thank you for your sorrow, but we wove our own Fate," said Avitr gravely. "Come and see what we have made of our exile."

Avitr led Gravnir through more archways and past smaller caverns, pointing out sleeping chambers and sitting rooms. The Ljósálfar had made a home in the rocky caverns in much the same way as the Landvördr had done, but they had shaped the stone with more grace and beauty, following the natural contours of rock, and the overall effect was quite different from the grim mountain refuge of Gravnir's people.

They walked until they came to a huge space filled with natural light. Gravnir looked around in wonder, blinking in the sudden brightness. One whole wall of the cavern opened to the sky.

"This is why we call it Cavernacaeli," said Avitr quietly. "It is the old language: the cavern in the vault of the heavens. It is even more beautiful at night."

Gravnir walked slowly across the chamber, past Ljósálfar sitting in groups, sipping from fine bowls and eating from delicately patterned platters. The cavern looked out across the ranges. Below stretched a broad ledge, open to the sky. Here there would be stars at night and fresh breezes . . .

Avitr left Gravnir looking out over the peaks. She returned with two bowls of crystal clear water. Gravnir drank gratefully and admired the craftsmanship of the bowl. It was made of some kind of dull silver metal, inlaid with metals of black, bronze, and gold in swirling patterns.

"They are phiala concentio, singing bowls, crafted from the ore gifted by the mountain," said Avitr, picking up the empty bowl and running a finger around the rim.

A sound grew from the bowl, yet not from the bowl, a deep ringing, like the echo of chimes on a clear day. Gravnir listened, entranced. Avitr handed him the bowl and showed him how to run his finger slowly but firmly around the rim to produce the haunting sound.

When the sound faded, Avitr motioned for Gravnir to sit on one of the rugs that covered the stone floor. Swirling patterns covered the soft weaving. How could all this have been hiding in the mountains?

Avitr left quietly and returned with a platter of food for them to share: bowls of some kind of watery soup, a round of flat bread, and two bowls of a green vegetable Gravnir had never seen. Avitr scooped the vegetable onto a piece of bread and alternated bites of this with sips straight from the soup bowl. Just for a moment, watching the silver-haired woman eating, Gravnir thought again of pinching himself to check if he was dreaming. Then his stomach rumbled and he turned his attention to the food.

"Our food comes from the mountain," said Avitr. "It is mostly made from the muscus almus that grows in the caverns. You might call it lichen, but to us it is bread and meat as well."

Gravnir, who had lived in the mountains all his life, had never eaten lichen before.

"There is a first time for everything," he said, taking a bite. Not bad.

That night, the Ljósálfar held a meeting, where all gathered in the large chamber to speak about the stranger. Oil lamps lined the walls, casting a soft glow, and the stars appeared in the darkening sky. Curious about the lamps, Gravnir learned that the oil came from deep within the mountain and, according to Avitr, was freely given by the mountain for their use. If only the Landvördr had known about that!

A man in long flowing robes entered, bringing silence to the room.

"Acristr," whispered Avitr, sitting close behind Gravnir. "He is the one who led us here, and he leads us still."

About three hundred Ljósálfar sat in the huge cavern, some

dressed in leggings and tunics and others in long, soft robes like Acristr. Most of them were silver-haired like Avitr, although here and there were golden locks, and even one or two darker heads. Acristr addressed them in the old language, and Avitr translated as best she could.

"We are here to decide the matter of the stranger who has come among us. His presence was foretold."

The Ljósálfar seemed to know what that meant, but Gravnir was confused. How could his presence have been foretold when he had not even known this place existed? Was he part of a prophecy now?

When Acristr finished, it was the turn of others to speak. Avitr translated the debate in a whisper. It seemed Gravnir's arrival held great significance for the Ljósálfar, but they could not agree what it actually meant. The voices took on the sound of music, and Gravnir stopped listening to Avitr's translation. He drifted into a restless sleep and dreamed of trust betrayed and hopes shattered, kin slain and scattered. Avitr nudged him awake.

The Ljósálfar were all looking at him.

"You must speak now," said Avitr.

Gravnir shook his head to clear the dreaming and stood to address the meeting. "I greet you," he said, bowing his head toward Acristr. "I have heard of the Ljósálfar since I was a child. Long have I dreamed of walking among you."

At this some of the Ljósálfar nodded and smiled. Others scowled or turned away.

"It seems that some here do not welcome me. I can only say that I did not come to do harm. I came to the mountains seeking answers to questions of prophecy."

Avitr translated.

Acristr spoke, and again Avitr translated.

"Perhaps I can explain the dark way some look at you."

Gravnir nodded. That might help!

"It is long and long since your kind dwelled freely with the Ljósálfar. It was in the time before, and even our long memories grow dim," said Acristr. "I will tell you of the time before . . .

Once, long, long ago, at the beginning of time, Sky and Earth were one. Together they moved in Ginnungagap, the Void. Together they would have remained for all time but for the Chance that lives in Chaos. From Chaos came the night, from the boundless empty space came Life, the power of Nature."

The story held Gravnir spellbound, yet he struggled to understand all that he was hearing. Older than the oldest tales, it was the story of the beginning of all things.

"From Ginnungagap came a spark that gave rise to a wind that blew between Sky and Earth, driving them apart. Curling into a sphere, Earth formed the solid matter on which we stand. Spreading wide, Sky formed the vault above. The space between they filled with their children, first the Ljósálfar, the beloved of the above and the below. But Chaos dwelt still in the formlessness, and so issued forth the Dökkálfar, dark twins of the Ljósálfar, the ones your people call Noctimagi. This was the dawn of time. From

Sky and Earth came forth Aetas Gentis, the tribe of the first Men and Women. So it happened at the beginning, the forming of Life."

Gravnir picked out strands of the story - the birth of life out of the formlessness of Chaos, the origin of the different peoples.

Acristr kept talking, the story now flowing as if telling itself.

"In the first days, in the very first days, the Dökkálfar sought out the dark places of the Land, making their homes in the deep caverns. The Ljósálfar, children of light, lived in the forests of the West, and the Aetas Gentis settled in the East. Ages passed, and generations of Aetas Gentis came and went. Some of the Ljósálfar left their forests and walked East, seeking knowledge. The Aetas Gentis welcomed them, and the children of Sky and Earth dwelt together by the great rivers and increased. There were some from each who chose to come together, even as Sky and Earth had come together, two parts of a whole, divided yet fruitful. From these joinings came the ones known as Landvördr."

Gravnir gasped. *Landvördr!* Children of the Ljósálfar and the first people? He shook his head in wonder. If that were true, these people were his kin. The Ljósálfar were the Old Ones from whom he was descended!

"But it has been long indeed since the Ljósálfar and the Aetas Gentis brought forth life in this way. The Landvördr prospered, and their line bred true. Time passed and Ages came and went. The three kinds went their own ways, although long did the Landvördr cross between. The final sundering came not long ago in the turning the Aetas Gentis call the First Battle."

Not long ago? These people thought of one thousand years ago as recent history . . .

"Seafarers came from afar to take the Land. The Landvördr fought to save the Land, but they were betrayed. The Dökkálfar, our own brethren, arose from the dark to aid the Seafarers for their own ends, and they have been cursed for the evil they wrought. The Aetas Gentis sided with the Seafarers and Dökkálfar, and the Landvördr were almost destroyed. *Halfbloods* the Landvördr were called and despised for it. They were the Dark Days, and many Ljósálfar fled to the West. Some of us remained this side of the Mists to right the great wrong done by our dark brethren. We planted seeds that have taken a thousand years to grow, and now the time has come for the Land to send forth green shoots."

Gravnir stirred uneasily. Acristr was saying things that made no sense. Aetas Gentis? People who were not Landvördr yet had been there before the Seafarers . . .

The Ljósálfar looked to Gravnir to speak. What could he say?

"I hear your story and my heart aches. I do not understand all you say, but I have walked the ground where the Warrior Queens stood, and I have spoken with the latest daughter in their line."

This was met with a wave of whispering.

"I do not know the Aetas Gentis of whom you speak," said Gravnir. "There are only the Landvördr and the people of the seven fiefdoms now, and they are locked again in battle."

Avitr had been translating Gravnir's words slowly, and she patted him reassuringly on the arm. There was another swell of talking, until Acristr called for quiet.

Taking a deep breath, Gravnir continued. "I grew up in the mountains not far from here, but long have I dreamed of a different life for my people. Like you, the Landvördr are the lost ones, hiding away in caverns, exiled from the Land. My people call the Seafarers' descendants their enemies, but it seems the truth is more complex."

Acristr nodded. "When all is lost and wooded glades turn to stone, One will come to lead them home, Through fire and death and fearsome wrath, Hearts hold true to ancient troth."

Gravnir had never heard that verse of the prophecy. What in Óðin's name was *an ancient troth*?

Avitr leaned forward to whisper in his ear. "The ancient pact between the Ljósálfar and the Landvördr, the pact of kinship. Blood of our blood, children of the Sky and Earth, hold the Balance, tend the Land, side by side, hand in hand."

Gravnir turned to stare at her. *Blood of our blood!* All his life he had dreamed of saving his people, reclaiming the Land, but never had he imagined that his dreams might be shared.

The room filled with noise, everyone talking at once, like the chiming of a hundred bells. Acristr walked over to Gravnir and held up his hands for silence. The voices died away like the tones of the singing bowl.

Acristr led Gravnir back to the place where he had been

standing on a slightly raised ledge of rock.

"Please," he said. "Tell us your story. All of it."

Gravnir hesitated. Could he trust these impossibly old beings?

Avitr looked at him hopefully. The others watched him with glowing eyes, whispering to each other.

Gravnir sighed. Why else had he come to the mountains?

He told them what he knew of the prophecy, and he spoke of Llianna and the shield and the Warrior Queens.

The Ljósálfar listened intently, until the mention of Warrior Queens set them talking again. Gravnir stepped down from the ledge and went to sit with Avitr.

"What now?" he asked.

"Now we wait."

To Óðin many a soul was driven,
To Óðin many a rich gift given." - Einar, Heimskringla

Trees made Algram nervous. Their roots reached down into the fathomless depths of the Well of Urd, and their upper branches cradled the Gods and Goddesses. Or at least that was what his Amma had told him, and he believed her.

Algram did not fear small trees, trees without high branches, trees where Gods and Goddesses could not make their home, trees where a man could not be left to hang for nine nights. He woke trembling from dreams in which the bark of a great ash tree had been cutting into his back, entering his body to become part of him. Dreams of burning thirst and gnawing hunger. Dreams of two ravens waiting to peck out his eyes . . .

The gothi said the dreams foreshadowed greatness, that Algram was blessed of the old Gods. His Amma made the sign of banishing and whispered that he dreamed of Grímnismál, the Wanderer who dies and is reborn, eternally returning to heal the Nine Worlds. Strange dreams for a boy to be having. She said it was dangerous to catch the eye of a God, and Algram believed her.

Algram had no desire to catch the eye of the Gods; he just wanted to grow strong enough to work alongside his father in the forge all day, marry Edelgunde, have six children, and live to see them have children of their own.

It might have happened that way; at thirteen Algram was stronger than most, and he had been learning the ways of working metal since he could walk. His father had promised to let him make his first sword that season, and Edelgunde had kissed him on the cheek when they met behind the cow shed after supper.

The morning after Edelgunde's kiss, Algram finished milking the family's cow and hurried to the forge. Would today be the day he started work on his first sword?

"Can you take the plowshare out to Vandlr's place?" asked Algram's father, not looking up from the strip of metal heating in the fire. He never gave a direct order, but no one ever said "No" to Brokkr. Named for the mythic dwarf who had forged Thor's hammer, Algram's father was the strongest man in Langsvinger.

Algram scowled and hefted the plowshare onto his shoulder. Vandlr's farm lay two leagues east, an hour there and an hour back if he ran some of the way. The sun was just clearing the pines as he left, the shadows reaching for him like giant's fingers. He shivered; someone walking on his ashes . . .

Algram shrugged away the shadows, squinted into the bright,

morning light, and set out determinedly for the farm. He passed no one on the road; no market this week to bring the farmers and traders to Langsvinger. At least there were no carts stirring up dust to sting his eyes as he jogged along in the middle the empty road.

Vandlr received the plowshare gratefully, and Algram turned to leave for home.

"Wife just made blueberry pie," said Vandlr. "Sit a while?"

Algram never had worked out how to say no to Vandlr. It wasn't the pie that made him stay; it was the look in Vandlr's eyes. His son, Gregor, ten years older than Algram, had gone to fight the Raiders two seasons ago and had not come back. Algram had liked Gregor, and what the Raiders had done to him had become part of Algram's nightmares.

"Just a while then," said Algram, following Vandlr to a bench under the ash tree. The tree was far too big and old for Algram's liking, but he bravely sat and listened to Vandlr talk about the weather.

Vandlr's wife brought them pie, and Algram ate quickly.

She brought him another slice.

"Good growing season," said Vandlr. "Best crop of potatoes in ten years. I'll send a bag home for your mother."

Algram groaned. Now he would be carrying a load back as well.

Vandlr went on talking about the farm, and Algram wondered if that was how he had spoken with Gregor. What did a man do *when he lost his only son?*

Algram finished the second piece of pie and waited for a break in Vandlr's talking.

"I'd better be heading back," he said quickly, picking up the sack of potatoes.

Vandlr walked him to the road, talking all the way. Algram left him there and hurried towards home.

The sun had climbed high enough to warm the top of his head, and Algram called himself nine kinds of fool for forgetting his hat. Half way home the pie in his belly and the sun on his head called for a rest. He sat by the side of the road, leaning back against the sack of potatoes, dreaming of the sword waiting to be made . . .

"It be a young one. All alone."

Algram opened his eyes. Raiders!

He scrabbled away, scraping his hands on the ground.

"He be afearing," said a giant of a man with a winged helm and a huge double-sided axe.

"You be afearsome," said the giant's companion, laughing. It sounded like thunder.

"We be needing a sacrifice," said the giant. "It be the time for it."

The other man nodded.

They pulled Algram to his feet and grabbed an arm each.

"Big tree back at the farm," said the giant.

They held him between them and dragged him back to

Vandlr's.

Vandlr was lying where Algram had last seen him, but now his dead eyes stared at the sky, and his chest was a mess of blood.

"On the tree," said the giant, ripping Algram's tunic down the back.

Algram screamed and kept screaming as they stripped him and dragged him to the tree. The giant held him up high against the trunk while the other one bound him tight against the bark with thick ship's rope.

"Nine nights, boy. Live for nine nights, and the wheel turns again."

"What wheel?" asked Algram, but they had gone.

The first night passed slowly, fear and pain keeping Algram awake. Everything hurt, like when he had been deathly sick with fever two summers ago. The fever dreams came, too – swirling shadows reaching for him; voices calling his name; a chasm so deep it swallowed the moon . . .

The sun rose, and he was still alive.

Then the thirst began. Like an itch that he tried to ignore, the thirst grew unbearable. His tongue swelled. His throat burned. His lips cracked.

The sun sailed into the West, and Algram wondered why no one had come looking for him. Surely they had missed him? He worried at that all night, and by morning it was obvious: they had not come because the Raiders had been to Langsvinger as well. A single tear ran down Algram's cheek. He caught it with his tongue.

Rain came in the night. He licked the blessed water from his cheeks and his shoulders and stuck his tongue out to catch the drops falling from the leaves. He slept.

He woke to pain like ants biting his arms and legs. He screamed, but it came out like a croak. The tree croaked back.

A bird landed on his shoulder and looked hungrily at his eye.

"Not dead yet," croaked Algram.

"Not dead yet," repeated the bird.

The third night passed with Algram and the bird refusing death together.

It was on the fourth night that Algram saw the well. One moment he hung suspended over leaf-strewn ground; the next moment the ground opened, and Algram stared into bottomless, black water. There was something about a well, something his Amma had told him . . .

Algram drifted on the threshold of death; like a broken branch on the tide, he washed to the shore and was pulled out again, washed in, pulled out, washed in, pulled out . . .

The writing came to him at the end, strange angular marks that held all the knowledge and wisdom of the Nine Worlds. Algram no longer knew his own name, yet he whispered chants that healed his body and freed him from the bindings. He walked West and used magic to overcome the Raiders who held Langsvinger, freeing his people.

"Algram! You live!" A big man with voice like thunder lifted him off his feet and hugged him close. Who was this man? Who

was this Algram he called for?

He left quietly in the night while the people slept.

He was Grímnismál, the Wanderer . . .

That must have been Óðin the Old. Certainly the man had but one eye. - The Saga of King Hrolf Kraki

Soon after a visit from Rothmar, Llianna dreamed of the end of the Nine Worlds, a nightmare of fire and blood and terror. In the dream she was still waiting for a sign while the Threads on the Tapestry frayed and unraveled. She woke and threw back the bed furs; the waiting was done. The völva had taught her that the opposite of waiting was to act from will, and the time had come for Llianna to use her will. The Keepers taught that a woman's will must serve her people, her husband, her children, her stronghold; Llianna renounced the last threads of those teachings and reclaimed her free will from the fear-based Laws of the Keepers.

"Where are we going?" asked Lunet, packing clothes and food and flints and shovels, things that suggested a long journey on which anything could happen . . .

"Munstrond."

"Oh." Lunet had seen Munstrond from a distance the day Marina died, and she could happily have lived her whole life without seeing it again. But if Llianna was going, then so was she, although she would have preferred to be going with a troop of armed húskarlar. It was not that Lunet doubted Llianna's power; had she not felled all the Landvördr that awful day? It was just that a fey mood had settled on Llianna lately, and fifty warriors might be helpful if anything went wrong.

"We can be there and back before Rothmar's next visit," said Llianna, studying the maps she had found in the reading room. "We can ride fast and sleep out. Maybe eight days or ten at the most . . ."

Lunet just nodded and kept packing. Llianna often spoke her thoughts aloud like that, and she did not really expect a response. Anyway, she wouldn't want to hear Lunet's response; it would sound something like, "What are you thinking? Two women alone in the Wastelands with Förnir . . . er, Landvördr roaming around! Remember what happened to Marina? Just because you killed them all that time doesn't mean you can do it again, and what if Gravnir's helping them, and . . ."

Llianna would not want to hear it, so Lunet kept quiet. She bit her fingernails and jumped at shadows, but she was committed to Llianna, and Llianna was committed to riding to Munstrond.

Lunet did speak up once to suggest that Llianna send a messenger to Rothmar, telling him of her expedition.

"No. He would just worry, and he has enough to worry about as it is."

Lunet sighed miserably. Of course he would worry! That was

the whole point.

"It's all right, Lunet. He will understand." Llianna wasn't sure that was true, but the dream had stirred a fierce determination in her. It was the same determination that had led a twelve year old to summon a God, a determination that did not ask for permission or understanding from anyone. It had been nearly seven years since she had summoned Aegir and spoken to her mother; Faeoia had once said that seven years marked a time of change.

Faeoia seemed to know exactly what Llianna was planning; she smiled knowingly and gave her two warm traveling cloaks. Faeoia's acceptance did not reassure Lunet; even if the journey to Munstrond was foretold, she had seen enough of Fate's strange weavings to know that something could be foretold and not turn out well for those involved. She just hoped Rothmar wouldn't blame *her* if she and Llianna ended up dead.

Llianna told Thyvri they were riding to meet Rothmar. Thyvri mumbled about Llianna's willfulness and stubbornness, but she packed enough food for ten people, including special treats for Rothmar.

Llianna hung the Valkyrie shield from her back and rode away from Ravensborg with Lunet.

‡

Lunet gratefully ate Thyvri's food after the first day's riding, but she refused to eat the sweetbread packed especially for Rothmar.

She did curl up in Faeoia's cloak to sleep and managed not to dream about the last time she had ridden to Munstrond.

Two days later they approached the mountain pass leading to the Wastelands.

"There must be a reason there's no one on the roads," said Lunet, looking around nervously. "It's completely deserted."

"Rothmar said it's quiet on all the roads now," said Llianna. "It's good for us; the Landvördr won't be raiding if there's no one to attack."

"No one except us," said Lunet quietly.

Another four days brought them close to Munstrond, and Lunet began to breathe more easily. Maybe Llianna had been right; they had seen no sign of Landvördr.

That night Llianna lit a small fire with dead wood from one of the twisted trees. They baked onions and apples in the coals and watched the stars. The fire died down and the night settled into the deep quiet of the plains. Lunet drifted towards sleep, head resting on her knees. She willed herself awake; someone had to unsaddle the horses and arrange the bags and cloaks for bedding . . .

She opened her eyes.

"Aaargh!"

Llianna leaped up, staring wildly around, arms braced to fight.

On the other side of the fire sat an old man who had not been there moments before. Thin and grey, he sat with his knees pulled up to his chin, arms wrapped around his long legs.

"I bring no harm," he said.

Llianna moved close to Lunet. "Who are you? Where did you come from?"

"No home. No name. Just me." He sounded like one of the traveling mummers who came for festivals. He even looked like the mummer who dressed as Death for the plays: grey clothes, grey hair and beard, grey eyes . . .

"What are you doing here?" asked Llianna.

"I was wandering along when I saw your fire. Very visible it was."

"Wandering? You were wandering in the dark? Out here? Are you lost?" Llianna stared across the coals at him. He looked lost: tattered clothes, long stringy hair, gaunt face . . .

"I am a wanderer. A wanderer wanders. That is what I do."

A wanderer.

"Oh. Are you Gravnir's Wanderer?" asked Llianna.

"Not that I know of," said the man. "Has he acquired a wanderer?"

"Don't be ridiculous! Do you know Gravnir?"

"It is a great presumption to claim to know another. There is something ineffable about everyone." He nodded slowly, as if impressed by his words.

"He's cracked," whispered Lunet, tapping her head. "What should we do with him?"

Llianna shrugged. "Feed him?"

She offered him the last of the baked apple.

"Ah, a homely offering in the middle of the night. I am blessed." He took the apple and nibbled it daintily.

Lunet rolled her eyes, decided the stranger was harmless, and sat back down to watch him eat.

Llianna turned and peered into the dark. If this wanderer had seen their fire, might it also bring others? Perhaps it was time to move on . . .

"Wise decision," said the man, standing in one fluid motion. "Time we were gone." He kicked dirt over the coals, covering the last of the glow.

"We? Are you coming with us?"

"I am already with you. I am saving you from the Landvördr who are even now coming from the ruins of Munstrond to find out who would be foolish enough to light a fire so close to their settlement."

"The Landvördr are in Munstrond?" Llianna swung into the saddle; if he was telling the truth, riding away seemed like a very good idea.

"Not all of them," said the man. "At least five of them are on their way here. It is time to be elsewhere."

Lunet collected the food bag and strapped it to her saddle. Were they really going to ride into the dark? She mounted quickly; riding in the dark at the behest of a madman was definitely preferable to waiting for five Landvördr to arrive.

"Let's go!" cried Lunet.

"Do you have a horse?" Llianna asked the man, but he ignored her question.

"Head that way," he said, pointing into the darkness.

Llianna hesitated. Could they trust him? He almost certainly was Gravnir's Wanderer, but who knew where his loyalties lay?

The horses snorted and looked towards Munstrond, ears pricked. They had heard something.

Llianna and Lunet rode close together, urging the horses as fast as they dared in the dark.

"How do we know where we're going?" whispered Lunet.

Llianna pointed to the sky. "Follow the Bear." The stars shone brightly, and Llianna prayed the Wanderer's way led to safety.

They rode until the sky began to lighten, both drooping over their horses' necks. Llianna was dreaming that she sailed on a boat, bobbing rhythmically on a gentle sea. The boat stopped abruptly, as if it had run aground. Llianna opened her eyes.

A figure appeared out of the morning mist.

"Oh, no!" Lunet hunched over her horse and whimpered.

"Am I so fearful in the morning light?" asked their visitor of the night before. "It is true I have not had time to wash and groom this fine morning, but I do have food to share."

The grey man sat astride a grey mule, his feet trailing on the ground. He swung a leg over the mule's neck and jumped down. With a flourish, he lifted a double pannier from the mule's back.

"Will you join me to break the fast of the night?"

"Here?" asked Lunet, looking over her shoulder.

"Where else?" he replied, unfolding a cloth and placing it on the ground for a table.

Llianna slid off her horse and leaned against its shoulder while her legs steadied. She felt as weak as a baby, and the horse was none too steady either. She offered it her water bottle and the horse let her pour water between its teeth, a trick Sigfinn had showed her; the memory seemed a lifetime away.

Lunet did the same, and the horses ambled away searching for tufts of brown grass.

"They won't go far," said Llianna. "They're as tired as we are."

Lunet looked around uncomfortably. "Er . . .it's quite open here."

"That is one characteristic of plains, my dear. Wide open space." The man lifted food from the panniers and arranged it on the cloth.

"Oh. Well, I need to use a bush, but there are no bushes," said Lunet.

"Just go over there, and we'll turn our backs," said Llianna. "Won't we?"

The man obediently turned his back on Lunet.

Llianna sat on the ground by the cloth. There was not enough moisture in her body for her to need a bush, so she lifted the water skin and drank her fill.

The food was simple and delicious: bread, cheese, apples, pears, and honey cakes.

"Where did you get this?" she asked, reaching for another honey cake.

"It is the provender of the Land, offered in exchange for my service."

"Of course. Silly of me to ask." Llianna shook her head at Lunet, who tapped her head again and rolled her eyes.

"You are the one Gravnir calls the Wanderer, aren't you?" Llianna phrased the question more carefully in the hope of a sensible answer.

"I am."

Lunet sighed with relief.

"Do you know where he is?"

"I do."

"Well, where is he?"

"In caverns of light with long forgotten ones."

Llianna shivered. He was describing her dream . . .

"Can we go there?" she asked.

"It is by invitation only," said the Wanderer. "And we have not been invited."

"I think I might have been invited," said Llianna. She told him about her dreams.

He nodded thoughtfully. "Then they will seek us out and take up the ones they want."

"What about us?" asked Lunet, assuming she would not be wanted.

"The rest of us wander as we must."

They ate more food, listened to the horses tearing at the tough grass, and watched the sun rise over the eastern peaks. The ravaged plain glowed, redeemed for a moment by the new light.

"It must have been beautiful here once," said Llianna.

The Wanderer sighed deeply. "Beautiful as life itself." The lines of his long face deepened, transforming it into a mask of grief.

Lunet frowned at him. "How do you know that? It was destroyed a thousand years ago."

The lines dissolved, and he smiled. "Ah, a student of history! It is a fine thing to study the past, but beware the lies of chroniclers and kings. They remake history for their own ends, and we are served a scant repast at their table of deceit."

"Were you really here at the First Battle?" Llianna asked, prepared to believe almost anything after her sleepless night.

"Not exactly here," said the Wanderer. "I was on yonder cliff with the Queens." He waved his hand to the south.

"Don't listen to him," whispered Lunet. "He's raving."

"Yes, I am raving. Would you not rave if you had wandered this ravaged land for a thousand years, listening to the dreary song of the wind and watching life fade from all you loved? Would you not rave if you had to wait a thousand years to complete a task assigned to you by the Gods? Would you not . . ."

"Please stop," said Llianna. "I'm sorry for your pain, but I came here to find something. Can you help?"

"Of course. That is the task for which I have waited a thousand years. Have I not saved you from the Landvördr, fed you fine food, and . . .?"

"And what?" asked Llianna.

The Wanderer looked intently over her shoulder, narrowing his eyes and scowling.

Llianna's skin crawled. "What is it?"

She turned to look.

A lone rider appeared like a wavering shadow in the distance.

"Who is it? Is it the Landvördr?" She stood, legs still weak from the ride.

The Wanderer shook his head.

"It is a man," he said with disgust.

Llianna squinted at the horseman. A warrior, riding like he was part of the horse . . .

It couldn't be. Could it?

No.

Yes . . .

Hugo rode up, eyes fixed on Llianna.

"What are you doing here?" asked Llianna. Not the most gracious greeting, but she did not feel gracious. Had Rothmar ordered her followed?

Hugo bowed his head. "I have pledged to protect you, but you seem to have saved yourself again."

"Oh, well. I had some help." Llianna introduced the Wanderer, who gave one of his cryptic replies when Hugo asked his name.

Lunet smiled, visibly relieved to see Hugo.

"We were going to Munstrond, but the Landvördr are there." Llianna pointed back the way they had ridden in the night.

"All of them?" asked Hugo urgently.

"I think so," said Llianna, looking enquiringly at the Wanderer.

The Wanderer stroked the mule's ears and ignored the conversation.

Hugo gestured for Llianna and Lunet to mount their horses. "We must bring the men! We can trap them in the ruins!"

Llianna shifted uneasily from foot to foot, biting her lip and shaking her head. Rothmar would have said she was arguing with herself, and he would have been right. Of course Hugo would see an opportunity to crush the Landvördr; that was what they were fighting for. But Llianna remembered Gravnir talking about the Landvördr who did not fight, the Landvördr who were his friends. And there was her dream: *save the Landvördr . . .*

"Hurry!" said Hugo, turning his horse in circles. "It is two day's ride. We could lose them."

"I'm not going with you," said Llianna. "I have come here because I have to save the Land. Destroying the Landvördr is not the way."

The Wanderer made a soft noise. A sigh of relief? Llianna moved closer to him. "We are waiting for something."

Hugo glowered at her. "Not again! Remember what happened the last time you took up with a stranger! Is this something to do with your Landvördr friend?"

Llianna shook her head sadly, took a deep breath, and said, "Hugo, I appreciate your concern for my safety, but I am not a child to be chastened like this. I am a Queen, and I will choose my companions and my way."

Lunet gasped.

Hugo's mouth fell open in surprise.

The Wanderer laughed softly.

Hugo jumped off his horse and stalked over to Llianna. He looked remarkably like a black wolf. Llianna's heart raced, but she held her ground.

"When Thyvri's man rode in, I knew where you would be," said Hugo, his lip peeling back like a wolf snarling. "I left my King fighting the bloodiest battle yet and rode to find you. I pledged to protect you, and I will always find you, but I wish it did not have to be in the Wastelands in the company of strange men!"

"I am sorry that the circumstances of finding me are not to your liking," said Llianna, not sure whether to laugh or cry.

He snarled at her again and stalked back to his horse. "I ride to Rothmar."

Llianna held up her hands in resignation.

"Now that had been settled, do you think we can leave?" asked the Wanderer.

Hugo mounted and turned his horse in circles again. His duty to Rothmar bade him ride back and bring húskarlar to rout the Landvördr. His bond with Llianna bade him ride with her to the gates of Death, or wherever she led him. His bones sang the litany of his childhood, the deep, habitual repetition of the Warrior Code: "I live with courage, I walk with truth, I fight with honor, I love with fidelity, I train with discipline, I work with industriousness, I maintain self-reliance, I persevere."

With a ragged sigh, he turned his back on Llianna and urged his horse away, returning the way he had come. It was his Destiny to fight the Landvördr, to live as a bloodsworn warrior, with or without the old rituals, with or without *inn mátki munr* . . .

Llianna shaded her eyes to watch Hugo ride away. She sighed miserably; how could two shining Threads be so twisted?

She turned back to the Wanderer. "What will happen to Gravnir's people if the húskarlar attack Munstrond?"

"They will fight or flee, as always happens in war."

"It is war, isn't it? Rothmar says the Landvördr are avoiding a pitched battle, but it's war all the same."

The Wanderer shrugged. "It has been war for a thousand years, whether or not there has been fighting."

He led them away from their brief resting place to follow invisible trails through the wasted land. Llianna and Lunet rode close together, silent as the broken trees.

‡

That night they sat in a close circle around more of the Wanderer's food. Lunet longed for sleep, and she thought it a dream when a tall figure drifted past the horses and came to rest behind Llianna. A spirit of the place, perhaps, or one of the Queens Llianna talked about. Then the Wanderer looked up and smiled, and Lunet knew something else had come.

Llianna followed the Wanderer's look, turning her head to gaze up into shining, violet eyes.

"Well come to our feast," said the Wanderer.

"I thank you, Vardmadr. It is strange company you keep." The violet-eyed person entered the circle and sat, gracefully folding into a cross-legged pose.

The Wanderer made the introductions.

"Llianna, daughter of Queens. Lunet, companion to Llianna. Avitr, esteemed Ljósálfar friend."

Llianna heard the word *Ljósálfar* and was filled with wonder.

"Landvördr scouts are moving closer. We must go," said Avitr.

"All of us?" asked Llianna, remembering the Wanderer's earlier words.

"You are all well come," said Avitr.

She led them across the plain to the mountains, and they entered the caverns of Llianna's dreams . . .

Gravnir sat on the outer ledge of the Cavernacaeli, practicing with a singing bowl. The sound echoed off the rock face behind him, wrapping him in sweet music. He smiled contentedly. If he were not desperately worried for his people, he would stay with the Ljósálfar and leave the troubles of the world behind.

A movement caught his eye.

He turned.

Ah! The troubles of the outer world had found him. He put the singing bowl down and stood to meet them.

"Gravnir!" Llianna ran up and clasped his hands.

"I am glad you have come," said Gravnir.

"It's so good to see you, Gravnir! We found the Wanderer, or he found us. But I have to tell you something."

He led her to a rug and they sat close together. Llianna told him of Hugo's urgency to lead the húskarlar against the Landvördr in Munstrond.

"Ah. It has come then." Gravnir turned to the Wanderer and bowed his head. "I looked for you, but I should have known you would find me if I stayed in one place long enough."

The Wanderer smiled.

Llianna touched Gravnir's shoulder. "What will you do now? Will you go to your people?"

"I will think on it," he said, shaking his head. "If I warn my people, they may set a trap for your men. Why have you trusted me with this?"

Llianna sighed miserably. "My dreams say I must save the Landvördr, as well as my own people. I can't do that if the Landvördr are slaughtered in their sleep. I thought they could just go somewhere else so Hugo can't find them."

Gravnir shook his head. "I may be able to take some of them to safety, but it is hard to see how we can save anyone while warriors on both sides are determined to kill each other."

Llianna mumbled something about prophecies and curses.

Gravnir patted her arm and walked away with the Wanderer,

talking quietly.

"What happens now?" asked Lunet, who had been hovering close by while Llianna spoke with Gravnir.

"I have seen this place in my dreams," said Llianna, looking around in wonder. "But I never thought to be here in waking life."

"No doubt it is a place of deep mystery," said Lunet, considerably less impressed than Llianna with the caverns. "But mystery doesn't supply food or water or somewhere to rest!"

"Perhaps I can help you," said Avitr, making them both jump. The Ljósálfar moved through the caverns as quietly as mist.

Avitr led Lunet and Llianna along a spiral of corridors to a small chamber where two bowls of steaming water sat beside soft cloths and clean Ljósálfar robes.

"Ah! I thank you," said Lunet.

Avitr bowed and left Lunet and Llianna to shed their sweat-stained clothes, wash, and dress in the soft grey robes.

"We look like the Wanderer," said Lunet, stroking the fabric.

"Cleaner," said Llianna.

"Less hairy," said Lunet.

"Prettier."

"Much prettier."

They were still laughing when Avitr returned with a tray of soup, bread and strange vegetables for them to eat. Afterwards she took them down another spiraling corridor to a meeting room where four Ljósálfar sat with Gravnir and the Wanderer. The three Ljósálfar introduced themselves as Acristr, Ordavr, and Brandr, elders of their community. The fourth Ljósálfar, a woman called Namlr, explained their purpose.

Avitr translated. "The Elders wish to tell you the story of the Land you call Nyrland."

Llianna sat on the stone bench Avitr indicated and leaned forward eagerly. At last! The story she had been waiting for!

Namlr repeated the tale told previously to Gravnir. Llianna recognized some of it from Faeoia's story of the first people, but there were Threads in the Ljósálfar story that were different . . .

"The Landvördr are half Ljósálfar?" said Llianna, sharing a look of wonder with Gravnir. But what of the rest of the story?

"Are the Ljósálfar the people the Landvördr call Forn?" she asked.

Avitr nodded. "The Old Ones. You also have their blood."

"How could . . .?" asked Llianna.

Ah, the Warrior Queens! "The Queens were Ljósálfar?"

"Yes," translated Avitr. "The Queens were the only ones able to stop the dark magic of the Dökkálfar - the Noctimagi, as you call them."

Llianna's thoughts tumbled over each other. "But how . . .? Oh, my mother . . ."

Avitr touched Llianna gently on the arm. "We must decide if you are the one foretold," she said.

"How will you do that?" asked Gravnir, frowning at the Ljósálfr.

"There is a trial," said Avitr.

"A trial?" Llianna shivered. Would the Ljósálfar trial be was anything like the Keepers' Testing?

The Wanderer nodded, eyes alight with excitement.

Lunet looked frightened. "Is it dangerous?" she whispered.

Avitr crossed her arms over her chest, fists clenched. "It is the ancient testing for those called to the Warrior's path. It is the Way of the Warriors. It is necessary."

"Who will I fight?" asked Llianna.

"It is not a test of battle skills," said Avitr. "A Ljósálfr Warrior must know herself at best and herself at worst. She must walk the Way of Seven Thresholds and return."

"Where is this walk?" asked Llianna.

"The Way begins in the lower caverns, but it has not been walked for a thousand years. It is written that the chosen one will walk the Way and return."

"When can I start?" asked Llianna.

Lunet muttered prayers, Gravnir still looked worried, but the Wanderer rubbed his hands together and smiled.

‡

The next morning, Gravnir came to Llianna as she stood on the ledge of the Cavernacaeli, sipping warm fungus tea and watching the sun climb over the peaks.

"It is beautiful here," said Gravnir.

Llianna nodded and placed her bowl on the ground, her heart aching for what she knew was coming.

"I am leaving to warn my people," said Gravnir, taking her hands between his. "I pray that this does not make us enemies."

Llianna looked out over the mountains. "It seems that Fate decides where we will stand in this war neither of us wants, but we are still free to honor each other as friends."

Gravnir lifted her hands and kissed them. "We can, dear cousin. My hope rests with you."

"I wish you could take this trial with me," said Llianna. "If I can walk this Way of Warriors, then so can you. *Children of our race . . .*"

Gravnir shrugged. "It is needful that you are tested and named. I must go to my people. Fate will decide what might come after that."

They embraced, and Gravnir walked away to take his leave of the Ljósálfar.

Llianna sighed miserably, not sure whether to bless his journey or curse it. Like her, he had to do that to which he had been called, but she wished she could know if good or ill would come from it. Had she betrayed Rothmar and Hugo by telling Gravnir of the attack on Munstrond? Had she betrayed her husband and her beloved to their deaths, or had she helped a friend save his people?

She shivered. Whose ashes were being walked on, and how far into the future would the funeral pyre be lit?

Avitr came and led Llianna down a stairway into caverns below the main living areas. They spoke about the trial, but there was little Avitr could tell her. The Ljósálfar who had overseen the testing of warriors had left after the First Battle, and all that remained were stories - and Evenarlr's dreams.

"Evenarlr is of the line of ancient Healers," said Avitr, as they walked through passages and past several small caverns to reach the Healer's rooms. "She has much to teach, but I cannot compel her. She will speak with you if she chooses to do so."

Llianna hoped with all her heart that Evenarlr would speak with her. There was still so much she needed to know.

They arrived at a doorway leading into a small room with an open side like the main cavern, looking out to the valley between the peaks.

"Wait here," said Avitr. "I will find Evenarlr."

Llianna stood just inside the doorway, peering around the room. By the open side a colorful hanging moved in the breeze. Fascinated, Llianna walked over for a closer look. Crystals hung suspended on both ends of seven fine rods tied one above the other on a silver cord as fine as spider web, catching and reflecting the light. All the colors of the rainbow shimmered and sparkled as sunlight caught the hanging. Llianna recognized the clear crystal right at the top. As a child she had spent hours searching for quartz on the sea cliffs, gathering a collection of white rocks with tiny crystal points growing on them. She reached to touch the stones.

"It is one thing to step over my threshold uninvited," said a stern voice, "but quite another to presume to handle my belongings."

Llianna turned to see a tiny woman standing with Avitr by another door leading through to an even smaller room. The woman's silver hair hung to her feet, and silver bracelets circled her arms.

Llianna stammered an apology. "I didn't mean to trespass, only the crystals are so beautiful, almost like they were talking to me. I'm sorry."

"I accept your apology," said Evenarlr.

"I will leave you two to talk," said Avitr. She left through the outer door.

Llianna looked more closely at Evenarlr. The Healer was as small as a child, and she looked ancient, her face as wrinkled as an old apple. The only strong thing about her seemed to be her voice.

"Come sit and tell me what you know," said the Healer, pointing to a bench by the wall.

Llianna wasn't at all sure where to begin but found herself talking about Faeoia, the völva, and the prophecy, about Warrior Queens and the stories of the first people. Three hours later she was still talking, and Evenarlr was still nodding and murmuring to herself. Llianna felt greatly relieved to talk and be heard.

A Ljósálfr man appeared with food for Evenarlr, and the Healer sent Llianna away to find her own dinner.

"Be sure to come back tomorrow," she said.

Llianna did return the next day and the day after that, finally running out of words.

"Now we can begin," said Evenarlr. "Where shall we start?"

The old healer immediately began a rambling lecture on the healing properties of crystals.

Llianna sighed. Avitr had said the old healer carried centuries of wisdom, but it may be a challenge to focus her thoughts.

When Evenarlr paused for breath, Llianna was ready. "Avitr said you know of the Warrior's trial."

Evenarlr nodded and led Llianna over to study the hanging that had so entranced her on her first visit. The Healer's bracelets chimed like bells as she pointed at the crystals. The suspended rods moved in spirals that seemed to ascend and descend as the cord turned.

Evenarlr touched each stone as she spoke. "The red stones at the base are garnets, deep red for the bright blood of Life rooted deep in the earth. The next is carnelian, glowing vermillion for the ebb and flow of Life in the womb, the river of change moving, moving, moving. Then yellow citrine for warmth and light and Will, dancing through the body. And green for Love, tourmaline pulsing like the beat, beat, beat of the heart. Blue turquoise for purest Sound, vibration of Life. And for the eyes, for Seeing, lapis lazuli, indigo stone of Vision. At the top, clear crystal and amethyst, Immanence and Understanding."

Llianna absorbed the resonance at each level of the remarkable hanging. Evenarlr's words reminded her of the völva's lessons about the cycles of becoming: the interweaving cycles of birth and death, day and night, the cycles of the seasons, of summer and winter, youth and old age, and the cycles of the body, breathing in and out, bright blood flowing . . .

The undulating crystals led Llianna into the spirals until she became one with the patterns of life. There she found the Elements as vibrations preceding physical form, and she became the resonance of solidity with Earth, fluidity with Water, heat with Fire, movement with Air. Evenarlr showed her how to detect imbalance in the harmonics of the cycles and to clear the Elemental fields, restoring balance.

Llianna spent more and more time in Evenarlr's rooms, absorbing the Healer's deep wisdom. When she left she was restless, charged with a strange energy. She spoke of it to Avitr. "It's as if the cells of my body are not as solid as they once were, as if they are moving in a different way. It's strange; I want more and more of it, but it's changing me."

Avitr nodded. "We call it *dissolvo plurimi*, this experience. It is the first stage of initiation." She looked intently at Llianna, as if trying to determine just how deeply she had been taken.

"*Dissolvo plurimi*. It's a good name. It feels like that," said Llianna.

She spent the evenings with Lunet and the Wanderer, sitting beneath the stars on the steps of Cavernacaeli, listening to the haunting music of the Ljósálfar and talking about the coming trial.

"I have to do it," said Llianna for the twentieth time. "It is the old way of being named as a sacred warrior, strong in the inner battlefield as well as the outer. Evenarlr remembers initiates walking the Way, and she has taught me what she knows."

"What if it's not the whole teaching?" asked Lunet. "What if there's something she's forgotten?"

"It won't matter; it's as much a test of character as of learning," said Llianna. "Commitment, integrity, will, and the capacity to open to the rhythms of life and death."

"Sounds more like the path of a gothi than the path of a warrior," said Lunet.

"The path of the Warrior is a sacred path," said the Wanderer, staring into the night sky. "The power of the Warrior is rooted in the power of the Elements and the eternal rhythms." A look crossed his face, a fleeting memory of pain and sacrifice.

Llianna wondered about his response, but she did not ask; the Wanderer shared his stories when he was ready.

Later, after Lunet and the Wanderer had gone to their sleeping mats, Llianna sat alone, staring at the stars. The vault of the heavens covered her, and the night whispered secrets . . .

Days passed, and Evenarlr continued to guide Llianna on walking the path of the Warrior. The Way had not been walked for a thousand years, but the stories had been preserved . . .

"The initiate turned her attention from worldly matters to the Great Below." Evenarlr's voice took on the steady rhythm of sacred verse. "The Warrior-to-be turned her thoughts to the Great

Below."

"Is it Death?" asked Llianna. "Must the Warrior face Death?"

"Death is one way we name the deep mysteries," said Evenarlr. "In any sacred crossing something is relinquished, a death of sorts."

Llianna shivered. What would she be called to relinquish?

Evenarlr continued. "The Warrior-to-be gathered the seven strengths and prepared herself.

"She placed the helm on her head.

"She tied the first strand around her neck.

"She let the double strand fall to her breast.

"She wrapped the tunic round her body.

"She bound the shield across her back.

"She wore the gold ring.

"She took the staff in her hand.

"The Warrior-to-be turned her back on the light and entered the darkness alone."

Llianna shivered, as if ants crawled on her skin. Fear snaked through her body. But what was it that she feared?

She had never feared the dark, but the darkness beneath the mountain came with a crushing weight of stone . . .

"When the Warrior-to-be arrived at the first threshold, she knocked loudly.

"She called for the door to be opened.

"The Guardian of the Way opened the gate just wide enough for the Warrior-to-be to enter.

"And so it came to pass that at each gate the Warrior-to-be surrendered one of the seven strengths. Only then, naked and bowed low, could she face the deepest mystery."

Llianna's stomach tightened, her head throbbed. She glanced at the entrance to Evenarlr's room. She could run out of the cavern, leave the Ljósálfar halls, and return to her home. But what of the prophecy? Who would save the Land? The Nyrlanders? The Landvördr? She sighed and nodded for Evenarlr to continue.

"The Warrior-to-be faced the Dark and was judged.

"The Warrior-to-be faced the eyes of Death."

The breath left Llianna's body as if she already stood helpless in the darkness, condemned by her own weakness. Spots danced before her eyes like summer gnats. How could she walk such a walk and return?

Evenarlr spoke again, her voice slow. "You will now study the seven strengths. Bring them forth. Give form to them. Be silent and listen."

Days passed with Llianna sitting in Evenarlr's chamber, contemplating the journey ahead.

Strange images haunted her: *darkness, piercing eyes, dead bodies.*

Dreadful sounds assaulted her: *moans, shrieks, mad laughter.*

Terrible feelings assailed her: *pain, tremors, paralyzing fear.*

On the third day, Evenarlr brought her bundles of dried lichen and strands of tree roots.

"First you must shape the helm of the warrior."

Llianna studied the lichen and roots. How was she to make a helm fine enough to wear through the seven Thresholds? Evenarlr had brought her no metal or fine jewels . . .

Llianna's head ached, as if a weighty helm already rested there. She rubbed her scalp, feeling the softness of her hair. Gripping six long strands, she pulled hard, tearing them out. She ignored the stinging pain – *pain is strength for the true warrior* - and wove the hair with the root fibers and lichen to form a plaited rope. When the ends were joined, the garland rested lightly on her head, the fibers rough on her forehead. Would it be strong enough?

Llianna sat in Evenarlr's chamber, the woven helm resting on her lap.

"Let it speak," said Evenarlr. "Listen for the voice of the Warrior's helm."

Llianna listened. Faint, far-away sounds of life beckoned in the caverns. Her own breath whispered in and out. When Time had ceased to matter, a deep, thundering voice resonated in her body, as if the mountain were speaking: *That which is above is the same as that which is below; That which is below is the same as that which is above.*

The helm glowed with light.

"The Warriors call," said Evenarlr.

"Next comes the strand you wear around your neck. Let it speak."

Llianna closed her eyes and held the pendant in her hand, remembering the sea-green of the emerald, the sea-green of the ocean . . .

The strand whispered like the waves, speaking of possibility, of seeing through the visible world. *I am the womb of life. From me you come and to me you shall return. Nothing is wasted. Do not fear.*

Next Evenarlr told Llianna to listen for the voice of the malachite pendant.

Llianna held the stone and remembered Faeoia placing the pendant around her neck the day she left Gullhyrndr. Malachite for protection . . .

I am Tree growing. I remember being Seed, blown by the wind, riding the currents. I can still feel the first rains, moistening the earth, softening skin, awakening the life coiled in my heart. I am Tree growing roots deep into the earth, leaves dancing with the breath of life. I have seen the seasons come and go for a thousand years. Time passes.

I am Water moving down the stream. I was born in the mountain, under the mountain. I am Water rushing over the rocks, leaping in the air, glistening in the Sun. I am Water rising as Bubble from the mouth of a fish. I am Water returning to the sea.

I am Flame dancing in the fire. I remember sleeping in the heart of wood, a potential. I am Flame dancing in the fire, eating air, transforming it into the color of life. I am Flame dancing a dream of warmth and becoming.

I am Breeze blowing through the trees. I kiss the leaves and make them sigh, twirling and whirling, always moving, never still. I am Breeze soaring and dipping, touching the clouds, blowing up dust, ruffling hair. I am Breeze moving where I will, leaving a feather-like touch on your soul.

The malachite pendant shone with a soft light.

"The fourth is a shield that covers your heart, your breasts, your belly, and your sex," said Evenarlr.

Llianna held the Valkyrie shield on her lap. It was strong yet light, ancient yet the runes shone bright as a new day. It offered strength to cover and protect, strength to help her bear the shining light of truth . . .

Evenarlr traced the runes with her finger.

"Can you read them?" asked Llianna eagerly.

Evenarlr closed her eyes.

"A child will come from the Lady's line

Born in death, lost in time.

Strong and wild, swift and free

Her Fate is carved in Life's tree."

"That's it?" cried Llianna. "The runes just say that?"

"It is no small thing to be named in the runes," said Evenarlr. "The ancient writing only seems to begin in one place. Always it moves out in spirals, gathering meaning."

Llianna sighed. Meanings within meanings and none of them clear!

Evenarlr went on to name the next offering – a band of gold.

Llianna held her wedding band in the palm of her hand. The gold had been shaped with power from Sun and Earth . . . I *am the heart of life. From me comes the searing heat of desire. Nothing is unknown. Do not fear.*

The sixth offering was a staff. Llianna used Evenarlr's pigments to trace the outline of a snake on the wood of her short staff. Snakes lived on the ground, drank from the streams, rested in the Sun, moved in circles and spirals. Sybil, soothsayer, seer, the serpent represented wisdom, and wisdom could not be gained by following a straight path. Wisdom emerged from the twists and turns of Life . . .

"You must craft a garment to shed at the final threshold," said Evenarlr.

Llianna stitched chips of crystal to her tunic with threads made from her own hair. Drops of blood seeped from her fingers, staining the cloth.

Finally all seven offerings lay on the mat in Evenarlr's room. Llianna sat alone with them for three days and three nights. She ate nothing. She drank only water.

Strange images haunted her: *darkness, hooded eyes, dead bodies.*

Dreadful sounds assaulted her: *moans, shrieks, mad laughter.*

Terrible feelings assailed her: *pain, tremors, abject fear.*

The darkness and the eyes of Death waited.

Llianna's heart beat slowly, heavy as a rock. Her skin prickled as if the ants were back, biting her arms, her legs, her belly. Surely no one ever really died walking the seven Thresholds – did they?

‡

On the fourth night, when all was silent, Evenarlr came.

Llianna lifted the tunic and slipped it over her head.

She slung the shield across her back and placed the pendants around her neck.

She fitted the gold band on her finger and lifted the helm onto her head.

She took up the staff.

Was she really going to walk to the Otherworld? Did she truly have to face Death to be named Warrior? Llianna looked around. *Until the threshold is crossed there is still the possibility of turning away . . .*

. . . but what of the prophecy? What of the Warrior Queens who had sacrificed everything so she could be born?

Llianna took a deep breath and left the small chamber to follow Evenarlr through winding passages and down unknown stairways. Bare feet touched stone, the steps wide and worn in the middle. Others had walked this walk before . . .

Breathe.

Hands brushed the sides of the tunnel, the stone smoothed by the hands of others who had passed this way.

Breathe.

The steps ended in a cavern with a low ceiling. The walls glowed in the light of a fire burning in a bowl in the center of the room, filling the space with pungent fumes. Llianna turned to ask Evenarlr one more thing.

Where was she?

"Gone," said a voice like stone.

Llianna turned back to the room. The next Threshold lay three steps before her, darkness beyond that. Sweat dampened her palms. It became harder to breathe.

The coals died down.

The room darkened.

Three steps to the Threshold.

Llianna moved one foot. Moved the other. Stepped to the door. Her head reeled with the smoke, but she remembered to knock. Her knuckles barely made a sound on the wood. She pushed against it. Nothing moved. She hammered at the door with her fists.

"Who seeks entry to the Otherworld?" asked the voice of stone.

Llianna hesitated, her mouth too dry to speak. She licked her lips and swallowed, gulping down fear.

"I, Llianna, seek entry," she said.

"Wait," said the voice.

The last coal burned away. Cold seeped from the walls. Llianna reached for the deep inner calm Gravnir called *djuplogn*.

She met a wall of coldness so pitiless that she gasped.

"Enter," said the icy voice.

The door opened, revealing a passage lit by the glow of a single candle held by a grey-robed figure. Llianna strained to see beneath the hood of the robe, but there were only shadows.

She crossed the first Threshold.

The door slammed shut.

Hands grasped the helm she had fashioned from her own hair.

"What is this?" she asked.

"Quiet, chosen one. The Laws of the Way are perfect and may not be questioned."

The helm was lifted away.

Llianna's legs trembled, and she heard the voice thought of the helm: *That which is above is the same as that which is below; That which is below is the same as that which is above.* From above the weight of rock pushed down. From below that which waited pressed up. Llianna felt herself crushed, cracked like a piece of grain between grinding stones. Her bones snapped like twigs, and she fell into blackness.

Her thoughts returned to an absence of pressure. She shivered in the cold darkness. Had she slept? Had she fainted? She pressed her hands against the floor. The rock felt smooth and dry. It smelled musky, full of life. The helm was gone, but the Land remained solid beneath her hands. She picked up the staff and stood. The ceiling of the chamber was smooth and dry. *That which is above is the same as that which is below; That which is below is the same as that which is above.*

How long had she been there? There was no way to tell. She

remembered that she was meant to knock and reached out to find the next door. She beat loudly on the wood with her fists. The door opened. She walked through. Hands took the emerald pendant from her neck.

"What is this?" she asked, her teeth chattering.

"Quiet, chosen one. The Laws of the Way are perfect and may not be questioned."

Llianna's head spun as if she had been turning in circles. Why was this so difficult when she already knew the way of it? Dots of light flashed like stars, becoming brighter, bigger. One rushed at her and exploded against her forehead. She was on the ground again, head pulsing with pain like stabbing knives. Was it meant to hurt like this? Was she doing something wrong?

She stood on shaking legs to reach for the next door. Her hands met empty space ahead but found walls to both sides and a ceiling above. She picked up her staff and walked forwards into the chill. Her feet told her that the path sloped downwards, but her other senses were baffled, unable to tell how long she walked before meeting the next door. Surprised at the trembling in her body, the fearful thoughts in her mind, she hit her hands against the wood. The slapping sound and the stinging of her palms reminded her that she was alive.

The door opened. She walked through.

Hands took the malachite pendant.

The ritual words burst forth: "What is this?"

"Quiet, chosen one. The Laws of the Way are perfect and may

not be questioned."

A fight welled up in Llianna, fire and wind raging in her chest, her arms. A cry burst forth, wounding her throat. Why was it so hard? Surely this was what she wanted, what she had prepared for. She sat in the darkness, heat coursing through her body. When the fire and wind stopped, she rose and walked on. It was so dark she could not even see her fingers when she held them close to her eyes. The air shifted as she moved her hands, but she saw only blackness

She knocked on the next door. It opened. She walked through.

Hands grasped the shield, lifted it over her head.

"What is this?" she asked, her voice unfamiliar to her.

"Quiet, chosen one. The Laws of the Way are perfect and may not be questioned."

This time Llianna stood quietly as the dim light disappeared. There was no sound except the slow beating of her heart. Crossing her arms over her chest, she imagined the shield, sensing it as part of her body, something that could never be taken.

She moved more certainly to the next door and knocked on the smooth wood. The ring was taken from her hand, stripping skin, leaving her finger bleeding.

"What is this?" she asked.

"Quiet, chosen one. The Laws of the Way are perfect and may not be questioned."

Blood dripped onto the ground. The candlelight began to

flicker. Her eyes lost focus, and all dissolved into blackness

Llianna woke to dried blood and the absence of light, warmth or sound. Was she alive? Breathing? Slowly her chest rose and fell, the cold air moving in and out of her body. Could she lie there forever? Was that allowed under the Laws that now governed her life? And her death?

She stood. If Death lay before her, she would rather meet it on her feet, crossing yet another Threshold. That much Will was left to her.

Her head hurt. Spots danced behind her eyelids. Her hand throbbed as if her finger had been scraped raw, but she felt only unbroken flesh. Had it been fear alone that had weakened her?

Water dripped from the stone ceiling, landing on her face with a small, wet sound. Suddenly she was parched, her body desperate for water and life. She caught the drips of water on her tongue. It tasted of metal and earth.

Reason returned, and she knew no one had done her any harm. Fear alone had overwhelmed her. Perhaps that was the lesson: seeing through the power of fear to rob her of Will and Life.

She rolled to the side and stumbled to her feet. The illusion of flayed skin left like a sigh. She picked up the staff and moved steadily through the darkness until she found the next door.

She knocked against the wood. The door opened. She walked through.

Nothing. She peered into the faint light. Nothing. Then the staff was taken.

"What is this?" she asked.

The voice of night answered. "Quiet, chosen one. The Laws of the Way are perfect and may not be questioned."

Llianna walked to the final door and stopped. It may have been moments or days that she stood, wondering at the Threads, at the weavings that had brought her here. Had this final Threshold been waiting for her all the days of her life?

The silence deepened, as if the walls, too, were waiting. She reached out and knocked. Could she have chosen not to?

The door opened. She passed through. The Guardian took the grey robe, leaving her naked.

"What is this?" she whispered.

"Quiet, chosen one. The Laws of the Way are perfect and may not be questioned."

Llianna hesitated again at the last Threshold. What waited there at the end of the Way? Would Death take her? Would the Warrior Queens come for her? Hope and fear coiled like twin snakes up and down her spine. She thought of being seen by the eyes of Death, and her cheeks flushed, like a child caught at something shameful. It was not the lack of clothing; it was being seen by eyes that would reveal all her secrets, even those she did not know she held . . .

But enough! Now she must walk, naked, to meet whatever waited.

She entered the last room. The sudden brightness of candles

blinded her. She raised a hand to shade her eyes.

A circle of dark-robed men waited silently, heads bowed as if in prayer, robes absorbing light like a dark moon night. Was this Death?

As one, the men looked up. They had the look of Ljósálfar, but their faces were marked with patterns, and they watched Llianna like snakes, poised ready to strike.

One man stepped forward, sweeping back the hood of his robe. He stood taller than the rest and looked more like a sea-dragon than a common snake, eyes alight with swirling flecks of gold that spoke of worlds within worlds. His thick dark hair, streaked with silver, hung loose about his shoulders.

"I am Marsirg, Dökkálfar Elder. I acknowledge your passage through the Way of Seven Thresholds. The Guardian has recognized your claim as Warrior." His voice was deep and mellifluous, casting a soothing spell.

Llianna's skin crawled. *Dökkálfar. Noctimagi!*

The Elder extended his hands, offering her one of the strange dark robes.

She accepted the robe and raised her arms, letting the soft cloth slide down over her body.

"It is written that one who passes through the Seven Thresholds has earned the name of Warrior. It is written that one who passes willingly has this right." Marsirg did not tell her that none had done so for a thousand years, that he was speaking words of ritual that had not been spoken in his time as Master of the Inner Chamber. He did not tell her that the Watchers had sent urgently for the Master when they sensed her approach. He did not tell her that even now the other Elders debated the wisdom of letting her live, and only the Laws stayed their hand. The Laws that were perfect and may not be questioned.

Llianna did not know all that, but she suspected that these dark-robed men did not wish her well. Had Evenarlr and Avitr known they would be there waiting for her? Was this the test?

"I come by right of my mother's mothers," said Llianna.

"Who turned their power against their own kin," said the Elder.

"Who betrayed their pledge to serve," said another of the men.

"Who sided with our enemies."

"Who dishonored the Way."

"Who destroyed Sanctuary."

"Who violated the Laws."

"Who forfeited eternal life."

"Who are forever accursed."

The Noctimagi stared at her with loathing, as if she alone were responsible for all the betrayal, dishonor, destruction, and violation in the Nine Worlds.

Llianna shivered. If she was the first . . .

"You are the first in a thousand years to walk the Way. The first to be named Warrior since the days of destruction," said the Elder.

The others moved closer.

"What is this?" asked Llianna.

"Quiet, daughter of accursed mothers. The Laws of the Way are perfect and may not be questioned."

"The Laws say I must be named Warrior," said Llianna.

"We have fulfilled the Laws," said the Elder. "You are named Warrior. Nevertheless there is a price. Whosoever enters the Way belongs to the *Dökkálfar*. Or offers another in her place."

Llianna had no way of knowing the truth of his words, but the Elder spoke with conviction. She looked into the sea-dragon eyes.

"I can make no such offering," she said.

The man licked his lips. "We will accept your first child as an offering." A thread in the Tapestry hummed like the string of a lyre.

Llianna's fists clenched, her lip curled, and she snarled, like a she-bear defending her cub. It mattered not that the child did not yet exist; if one of the men moved towards her, she would tear open his throat with her teeth.

The Elder laughed. "You snarl like a she-bear, but you are no threat to us. We are Dökkálfar!" He raised his hands.

Llianna snarled again and lifted her hands to face his.

The man moved towards her, death in his eyes.

Llianna felt *djuplogn* take her, and fire blazed from her fingers.

Men screamed.

Llianna threw herself back through the low doorway.

Someone followed.

Llianna turned.

The Elder with sea-dragon eyes stood there, hands raised to

kill.

"Stop!" commanded the voice of stone.

Llianna ran.

‡

Marsirg heard the voice of stone and dropped his hands to his side. He had served in Sanctuary for six centuries, and never once had the Guardian of the Way spoken. Until now. To defend an enemy. Marsirg shook his head. What of the Laws?

"The Laws will be served," said the voice of stone.

Marsirg bowed low. It was not to his liking, but he knew better than to argue. He did not understand why the Halfblood woman had been allowed to leave, or why she had been allowed to enter in the first instance, but he would find the answers . . .

‡

In the dark, Llianna also heard the Guardian's words. She was not sure what they meant, but at least there was no mention of paying a price. She crossed the seventh Threshold.

And stopped. Her Ljósálfar robe awaited her, folded neatly. She took off the dark robe and dropped the grey one over her head. It settled softly on her body, bringing a deep inner security and stability, a warm solidity bestowed as a blessing on those who walk with courage and integrity. She stood tall, prepared to face

369

KELLIANNA & KAALII CARGILL

whatever might come in her life as Warrior.

Llianna walked slowly to the sixth Threshold. The door opened. She passed through and found the wooden staff with the image of the snakes, symbols of desire and intimacy, bonding and commitment. Gone now the fear and rage, helplessness and despair. Restored, opened, changed, she accepted the complexity of her desires and commitments, moving with newly found grace.

She came to the fifth Threshold. The door opened. She passed through. She raised her left hand to receive the golden ring. It shone with a soft glow in the pale light. She knew the certainty of who she was and her purpose in walking this sacred Way. Where there had been chattering doubts, there was now silence deep as Time.

She walked to the fourth Threshold. The door opened. The Valkyrie shield was returned to her. Gift of the Warrior Queens, the shield settled easily against her back. Peace filled her, arising from her heart's capacity to feel both love and grief, to open to the fullness of life and death, constancy and change.

She walked to the third Threshold. The door opened. She passed through. Hands restored the malachite pendant to her neck, and she released a sound that vibrated in every cell of her body.

She found the next Threshold close, the path fully revealed now, as if she had been walking it all her life. She stepped through the doorway. Hands placed the emerald pendant over her head, settled it around her neck. With a sudden sharp pain, the center of her forehead opened to a vista of light that existed beyond the horizons of time and space, revealing deepest wisdom. The Guardian moved aside.

Llianna walked on, guided now by light. She passed through the last Threshold, the first, and hands placed a circlet of gold on her head. In that moment, illusions of power and control fell away, and Llianna found herself inside the Tapestry, following the patterns that connected her to everything else. She rode the Threads more gracefully than ever before, yet she was unable to control anything at all. She moved in the limitless, boundless nothingness that encompassed the center of the Nine Worlds, and at the same time she sensed the solid rock surrounding her. She felt the simultaneous simplicity and complexity of knowing each and every person to be unique and separate and yet all one. She laughed with joy at the complex interconnections between all things.

With a bow of acknowledgement to the Guardian, Llianna emerged into the light of the cavern from where she had started the walk.

She stopped and stared.

Evenarlr and Avitr stood together, arguing loudly with Lunet, who was waving her hands in the air and shaking her head like a wild horse. The Wanderer sat to one side and seemed to be arguing with himself. They were all so intent they did not notice that she had returned.

"Of course we are going to find her," said Lunet. "It has been three days."

"Wait!" said Avitr. "We must wait a little longer."

"The ritual cannot be disturbed," said Evenarlr.

"The ritual be damned! I will disturb whatever I must to bring her back!" said Lunet, sounding fiercer than Llianna had ever heard her.

"I'm here," said Llianna.

Lunet cried out and hurried over to touch Llianna, to confirm that she was real. Then she saw the gold circlet, and her eyes widened.

Llianna surrendered to aching tiredness and sat on the ground.

"Has it really been three days?" she whispered. She retraced the time in her mind, but it made no sense.

"Time runs differently between the Worlds," said Evenarlr.

Avitr handed Llianna a bowl of water. "Come. Rest now. Enough that you are returned."

Llianna drank greedily, water running down her chin and wetting her robe. She handed the bowl back and sat quietly, eyes closed, savoring the silence and the absence of menace.

Evenarlr signaled for silence.

Llianna's heart settled, and she tested the newly awakened gifts of her ritual – the deep inner security of courage and integrity; the unbreakable twinned threads of desire and intimacy; the certainty of who she was in this moment; the fullness of love and grief, life and death, constancy and change; the haunting song of life; the light of her own deep wisdom.

She gave thanks for the gifts and opened her eyes to look directly at Avitr and Evenarlr. "There is something I must know. The men at the end, did you know they would be there?"

Evenarlr looked shocked.

Avitr gasped. "What men? What were they like?"

"What did they do?" asked Evenarlr.

"Ah. You did not expect them then." Llianna sighed with relief. The menace she had met in the final chamber did not fit with her sense of the Ljósálfar.

"Come," said Evenarlr. "You must eat and rest, and then you can tell us all that happened."

Llianna stood, holding Lunet's hand for support.

"I have walked the Way and seen many things, but the men were a surprise. They looked like Ljósálfar but darker, with markings on their faces."

"Dökkálfar!" said Avitr. But that is impossible! It has been so long . . ."

Llianna stood taller, remembering the gifts that were now a part of her. "If it happened, then it is not impossible. It was possible enough to nearly kill me."

"We must tell Acristr," said Avitr. "The Way must be guarded!"

"Why were they there?" asked Llianna.

"It is so long. Surely not. It is not possible . . ." Avitr spoke as if convincing herself of something.

"Stop saying that!" Llianna rejected the memory of reptilian eyes. "Whether it is possible or not, it happened."

Evenarlr put a hand on Llianna's arm. "Forgive us. It is a shock to hear that the Way is still tended by the Dökkálfar. Once they were the Watchers, but they violated the Laws."

"They used that word, *violated*," said Llianna.

"You spoke with them?" asked Avitr.

"Well, that was before they threatened to take my child."

"What child?" asked Lunet, eyes wide.

"My first child I haven't had yet." It didn't make sense, but it was the truth of what had happened in that inner chamber.

Everyone looked baffled.

"You need rest," said Evenarlr.

"We must tell the others," said Avitr, herding everyone out of the cavern, up the stairs, and along the passages to the living areas.

"I have never seen Ljósálfar move so fast," said the Wanderer. "You seem to have disturbed them."

"Well, it was disturbing. Imagine walking naked into a room to find eight men staring at you!"

"Naked?" said Lunet.

"Eight men? Eight Noctimagi?" The Wanderer sounded excited.

"Did you kill them all?" asked Lunet.

"I may have killed some of them," said Llianna, wondering if their deaths would haunt her like the Landvördr deaths.

She sat on a rug and hugged her knees to her chest. "Fire came from my hands, and I ran." It seemed like a dream rather than a real encounter where people might have died. Where she might have died . . .

She lifted the gold circlet from her head and turned it over in her hands. It proclaimed her sovereignty, but even a Warrior Queen could be achingly tired and desperately in need of rest.

Lunet brought a bowl of water for washing, and two silent Ljósálfar set down trays of food. Llianna washed her face and hands, sipped some broth, and curled up with her head on Lunet's lap. She smiled sleepily; she had passed the test and been named Warrior. That was good . . .

The Dökkálfar presence in Sanctuary shocked the Ljósálfar, and the caverns hummed like a disturbed beehive. The Wanderer was amused to see the Ljósálfar so agitated, but Llianna just felt a growing sense of dread.

Avitr came to lead her to a gathering the day after her return, and Llianna recounted her experience, giving as much detail as she could remember about the dark-robed men.

Her report stirred much discussion in the old language, the Ljósálfar all talking at once and gesticulating wildly. Avitr was too engrossed to translate, so Llianna had time to think about what it might mean that the forces from the First Battle were gathering again: Ljósálfar, Noctimagi, Landvördr, Nyrlanders. What had the Ljósálfar called the first people? *Aetas Gentis.* Were the Nyrlanders descended from these Aetas Gentis? Was there yet another dark secret hidden in that story? *Beware the lies of chroniclers and kings . . .*

Llianna sighed with frustration. There was still much she did not understand about the old battles, but one thing had become clear: the First Battle had not been a simple fight over the Land. It was more like one of the old stories told around the fireplace in winter: forces of light and dark battling for life and death. Llianna slapped her hand against her thigh. How was she meant to vanquish darkness and despair when the strands of light and dark had become so tangled and intertwined?

She gave up trying to unravel the knots and left the gathering to tell Lunet it was time for them to go home. She would leave the Noctimagi to the Ljósálfar, although she suspected that the Guardian of the Way - whoever he was - might be the one to determine who crossed between the Worlds.

Avitr farewelled them with blessings, and Evenarlr allowed Llianna to hug her close.

"Ah, Time turns again to the days of the Warrior Queens. I am glad to have lived to see it," said Evenarlr.

Llianna invited the Wanderer to ride with them to Ravensborg. "There is more I must know," she said. "I need you to help me sort through the stories and understand the prophecy."

He smiled. "I long to stay here with the Lost Ones, but my story is intertwined with yours. I will ride with you. Already I am blessed to have witnessed the crossing."

Two Ljósálfar escorted them beyond the mountains, following a convoluted path through passes and defiles so narrow that the way could be guarded by an archer or blocked with a rockfall.

Llianna rode away carrying deep blessings and a mountain-sized collection of unanswered questions.

When ill seed has been sown, so an ill crop will spring from it."
- The Saga of Njál, c.114

Gravnir had left the Ljósálfar caverns and ridden for Munstrond with fear burning in his stomach. He had no plan but to warn his people, but the cold dread in his belly told him he was caught in a double-tied knot: pull one way and the knot tightens; pull the other way and it tightens further. If he arrived in time to warn the Elders, the Ravensborg men would ride into a trap. If he did not warn the Landvördr, they would be taken by surprise, and the women and children would fare the worst. He was truly caught in an ever-tightening knot.

‡

Rothmar met Hugo on the road, battle weary and immensely relieved to hear that Llianna was safe. He greeted Hugo's information about Munstrond less than enthusiastically.

"So you would have us ride to the old city and take them by

surprise?"

"If we are fortunate," said Hugo.

"What did Llianna say to your plan?" asked Rothmar.

"She refused it. She said that destroying the Landvördr was not the way."

Rothmar frowned. "What if she is right about that?"

"How can she be right? The Landvördr are killing our people. This is our chance to stop them. We have to take it!"

"I suppose we do," said Rothmar, bowing to Hugo's certainty.

‡

Gravnir set his horse loose a league from Munstrond. The Ljósálfar had returned it to him to cross the Wastelands, but if he had any hope of entering the old city undetected, and therefore alive, it had to be on foot. He sincerely hoped the horse would return to the mountain pass and be found by someone who would care for it. The more likely event was that it would die of thirst before reaching the mountains, or be eaten by a mountain lion if it did manage to wander that far, but he could not take the beast with him, and there was nowhere safe to secure it . . .

Why was he wasting time worrying about a horse, anyway?

Because it was easier than worrying about Adelgunde, Abigahil, and the others . . .

He crept into the ruins of Munstrond in the darkest time of night, when the guards were bleary-eyed from staring at shadows, or so he hoped. He encountered no one as he made his way to where Adelgunde had set up home. A lamp glowed inside, and he breathed more easily than he had since leaving the Ljósálfar caverns. He pushed aside the rough cloth door covering and stepped into the corner room.

A brush of air warned him a moment before something solid hit his head. Pain flared, and his legs buckled.

Gravnir forced his eyes open through pain that brought bile into his mouth. Why did a thumped head always turn the stomach? He stayed completely still and squinted into the dim light.

" . . . there's no way of knowing," said someone to his right.

"He didn't announce himself, did he?" said someone on the other side. Bendeir?

Gravnir rolled his eyes towards the voices. Searing pain arrowed through his head, churning his stomach even more. What had they hit him with?

"I told you not to use the anvil. You could have killed him."

"No loss if I had. What's he doing prowling around in the dark without even announcing himself, eh? Never did trust the melrakki." Bendeir for sure.

But why was Bendeir calling him a white fox? Maybe the anvil had damaged his hearing . . .

"Let's take him to Olafeur."

They lifted him roughly and slung him over the shoulder of a hunter who smelled rank, the blood of his kills stiff on his tunic. Gravnir's stomach heaved. Bile spewed from his mouth, leaving a bitter taste. Maybe it would be acceptable for Rothmar to kill some of the Landvördr after all . . .

They dropped him on the ground at Olafeur's feet. At least Gravnir suspected they were Olafeur's feet; he could not raise his head to be certain.

"So, our seer returns secretly, stealing past the guards like a wraith. Did you just come to see your friends, Gravnir, or were you planning to report on your disappearance?"

"I came to warn you," said Gravnir, mumbling through the pain in his head.

"What?"

"I. Came. To. Warn. You."

"About what?" asked Olafeur.

"Ravensborg. Coming here."

"Ah. You play a warlike game for one so soft."

"No war. Get away. Leave . . ."

"Now you give us orders?"

Gravnir gave up the struggle with the pain and sank into unconsciousness.

‡

"More lives than a cat."

"Adelgunde?"

"There, there, Gravnir. You be safe now."

"How?"

"How be you hurt or how be you safe?"

"Why did they let me go?"

"Elders do as Elders do," said Adelgunde, probing his head through blood-matted hair.

"Owww! Bendeir hit me with an anvil."

"Hard-headed you be."

"Hmmph."

She cleaned the wound on his head, and he told her of the húskarlar attack.

"We be trapped here then," said Adelgunde, eyes wide with fear.

"We can leave, go North."

"There be monsters in the North."

"No monsters. The monsters are all here in Nyrland, I fear."

"But that be what the Elders say: *North of Munstrond be monsters.*"

"That is what everyone says when they run out of knowing," said Gravnir. "The lands to the North have not been mapped, and that is what mapmakers write when they do not know what to draw there."

"Do all monsters just be man's unknowing, then?"

"Possibly" said Gravnir. "There is an awful lot of unknowing in the Nine Worlds."

"Well, I don't suppose unknowing ever ate anyone," said

Adelgunde.

"Hmmph," said Gravnir again. It seemed a suitable sort of sound for his own vast unknowing.

‡

Llianna, Lunet, and the Wanderer arrived at Ravensborg with the cold winds that heralded the change of season. Thyvri sent the Wanderer to the kitchen and ushered Llianna and Lunet upstairs, where she organized warm water for washing, sent for food and drink, and had the beds freshly made up for sleeping. Faeoia was already in Llianna's room, sitting by the fire as if expecting them.

"Rothmar has been gone long this time," said Thyvri. "The fighting goes on and on." She pottered around the room, mumbling about the Förnir. Both Faeoia and Thyvri stubbornly used the old name for the Landvördr.

"Many blessings to you for looking after us, dear Thyvri," said Llianna. "I'm sorry for lying to you. I didn't want you to worry."

"You going out onto the roads where there be fighting, and I'm not to worry! Even if you had been riding to Rothmar, I would have worried, but you had something even more dangerous in mind, and it puts me in mind of Marina, and you so headstrong and . . ." Thyvri wiped tears from her cheeks with her hands.

Llianna hugged her, murmuring reassurances. Being a child of prophecy seemed to cause problems for everyone.

Lunet settled back into the life of the stronghold, but Llianna was restless. She tried to concentrate on the daily tasks of writing lists with Thyvri, managing household disputes, and planning provisions for the húskarlar and their families, but her mind wandered to the Wastelands and Munstrond, to Rothmar, Hugo, and Gravnir.

Giving up on the household tasks, Llianna sought out the Wanderer, who spent his days in the reading room, translating the manuscripts from the untidy pile she had not been able to understand. He listened to her concerns, but then he shook his head and went back to writing long, scrawling notes and muttering incomprehensibly.

At night the Ljósálfar caverns filled Llianna's dreams, and the Noctimagi always came, turning the dreams into nightmares. She woke with fists clenched, braced to fight. Her restlessness woke Lunet, who hurried down to the kitchen to bring mulled wine and a warm brick for the bed.

"Did they threaten to take your babe again?" she asked.

Llianna nodded.

"I've been wondering why they would want a babe . . ."

"Why indeed? Perhaps it's the bloodlines, something in my mother's mothers lineage that they want."

"But why not just keep you if that's what they wanted?"

"Perhaps a malleable babe is more to their liking," said Llianna. "Perhaps their infallible Laws prevented it. Who knows?"

The mulled wine and warm brick soothed her, and she drifted back to sleep to wander down tunnels in search of something she could never find.

Many a fine skin hides a foul mind." - Eyrbyggja Saga

Marsirg sat in Circle, leaning back with his hands laced behind his head, listening to the other Elders discuss the momentous arrival of the Warrior in Sanctuary.

"... a travesty that a Halfblood walked the Way of the Thresholds."

"Why did the Guardian allow it?"

"... a violation of the Laws ..."

"... Halfblood magic ..."

"Old blood ..."

Marsirg ground his teeth in frustration; he had been cultivating the Dökkálfar hatred of Halfbloods for three hundred years, and this random event must not be allowed to interfere with his plans.

"Our Ljósálfar cousins are not usually so bold," said Olandr, one of the senior Elders and a stickler for the Laws. "Perhaps this Halfblood carries true power."

Marsirg snorted derisively. "The Halfbloods are abominations, the cursed get of unholy unions between Ljósálfar and Aetas Gentis. Our cousins are grasping at shadows to send a Halfblood in the footsteps of Ljósálfar Queens."

"She used fire to kill," said Atargirn, scowling. "That suggests the blood runs true." She looked even more severe than usual with her grey hair pulled tightly into a knot. "It seems our cousins may have found the one who can bring them back from their long decline."

"The lineage of Warrior Queens was destroyed," said Marsirg. "This Halfblood is no true Warrior."

"But why now?" asked Millern, the youngest member of the Circle; if there was a question, Millern would ask it. "Their defeat and shame have kept them bound for a thousand years. There must be a reason they are moving now."

"It is the time of the prophecy," said Atargirn.

"Do we believe in prophecy now?" asked Marsirg, waving a hand dismissively. "Tales for children."

"Prophecy or not, there is no denying that the Way was walked by a Warrior of the old bloodlines," said Atargirn. "She used fire to kill. *Her power will come in anger born.* I believe that is what the children's tale says, is it not?" She glared at Marsirg.

The Elders continued to talk, voices rising and falling like the winds that echoed through the tunnels in winter.

"She killed three Watchers with her fire. She must have the old blood."

"It has been a thousand years since we faced the old blood

and were defeated."

"Just ashes. Nothing left in Sanctuary but ashes."

"The woman's attack is a serious matter," said Olandr. "Why do you stubbornly refuse to acknowledge her power, Marsirg?"

"It is not her power I deny," said Marsirg. "I refuse to acknowledge her right to it. She is a Halfblood and not worthy of the name of Warrior."

"Nevertheless, she passed through the Thresholds," said Olandr. "Our first commitment is to the Laws, and the Laws say she must be named Warrior. Long have you argued for us to return from the dark to destroy those who stood against us, but it is not our way to put personal ambition before our commitment to the Laws."

"Personal ambition has nothing to do with it," said Marsirg. "I speak of righting the great wrong done a thousand years ago when the Ljósálfar stood with the Halfbloods, and the Dökkálfar were driven into the shadows."

Olandr shook his head. "We lived through those dark days together, Marsirg, but I do not share your desire for revenge. Enough that we follow the Laws and serve Sanctuary. As we have served since the beginning."

Marsirg shook his head but said no more. He wanted to send a force to destroy the woman who had trespassed on sacred ground. It would reawaken the old enmity with the Ljósálfar, which served his purpose well, but the others must agree to it, and they were proving unusually resistant to his hints and suggestions. The problem was the Law that said Dökkálfar may not strike directly any who carry their blood; the debate turned on whether the Halfblood woman carried enough Ljósálfar blood to constrain them from killing her. Hours passed, and still they talked.

"The Laws must be obeyed," said Remlar for the fifteenth time, arguing against sending Dökkálfar to investigate the intrusion. "If the Guardian of the Way saw fit to let the Warrior pass, who are we to question?"

Marsirg ground his teeth and repeated his argument about diluted bloodlines, insisting again that there was nothing of the First Children left in the Halfblood woman, asserting that it was within the Laws to find her and kill her.

Others continued to argue for caution. After all, the Guardian had admitted her . . .

Marsirg seethed. He wished them well with their caution when the prophecy awakened and they faced a fully empowered Warrior Queen!

The Council meeting disbanded with no resolution of the issue, and Marsirg returned to his room to stare morosely at his reflection in the mirror. His face flickered in the light of oil lamps in sconces on the walls, and suddenly his plans seemed as insubstantial as his reflection. Could he proceed without the others? Could they stop him if he did?

He thought of Ariorn - scholar, warrior, renegade - with his righteous morality and unnatural interest in Halfbloods. Ariorn was one who could hinder him, but the renegade was away on one of his unsanctioned journeys in the Upper World, and there was nothing he could do if Marsirg chose to act now.

Marsirg walked slowly around his room, savoring the tapestries on the walls, the rugs on the floor, the furs on the divan. Like all the Dökkálfar caverns, the room had been hollowed from the rocky labyrinth deep in the mountains, and he had filled it with plundered symbols of ancient power.

A knock sounded at the door.

Marsirg stopped pacing.

Someone called his name softly.

Atargirn.

Marsirg frowned. It was unusual for the Dökkálfar to visit each other in their rooms except for consensual liaisons; privacy was one of their sacred tenets. For Atargirn to be at his threshold was unthinkable.

Curious, Marsirg opened his door.

Atargirn walked past Marsirg and turned to face him. "There is much that remains unexplained about the woman's crossing," she said in her clipped, superior voice.

Marsirg closed the door and waited. Atargirn risked much by speaking of Council business outside Circle.

Atargirn held his gaze, her lips curled into a sneer. "I do not like you or your scheming," she said. "But you are the only one who truly understands the necessity of destroying the Halfbloods. And the Ljósálfar."

Marsirg's eyes widened; this was daring indeed! It was against the Laws to speak of their own blood in that way, and Atargirn knew it as well as he did.

"The voice of the Guardian was heard throughout the Sanctuary," said Atargirn, watching his face.

Ah! He had not known that. He had thought the Guardian's command to stop had only been heard by the Watchers, and they had been too shocked by the Halfblood's attack to understand what they were hearing. If the whole Sanctuary had heard the Guardian, there would be talk about who the Guardian had been addressing, who had been about to violate the Laws.

Atargirn confirmed it. "Even now it is being asked who the Guardian was addressing, whose violation of the Inner Chamber called forth such a command. The Laws require that Circle find the truth."

Marsirg sighed. How had it come to this? All he had ever wanted was for the Dökkálfar to regain their rightful place as foremost of the First Children. He considered and rejected a number of strategies before responding.

"I thank you for bringing me these tidings personally," he said.

She narrowed her eyes. "I am not interested in your gratitude," she said harshly. "I have watched you work the Circle as skillfully as a fisherman hooking fish."

"What is it that does interest you?" asked Marsirg.

"I am here to help you construct a story that will satisfy those calling for the truth."

"Why would I need your help?" he asked. "I am accustomed to managing my own affairs."

"Because I know the truth," she said calmly.

"There are many truths but only one Law," he countered, calling on words he had used many times before.

"I was there," she said. "In Sanctuary."

Marsirg narrowed his eyes and studied Atargirn closely. She looked back calmly, dark eyes steady, face stern and proud. He had not seen her in Sanctuary when the Guardian spoke, but that did not mean she was not there. Yet there may still be a way . . .

"It is no matter. I will give a full account of the events in Sanctuary. Where you, a woman, dared to trespass."

Atargirn laughed. "I expected no less from you. You could do as you say, but then you would not hear what I am offering."

Marsirg bowed his head slightly. "Speak."

"We can begin by agreeing to provide each other with an alibi for when the Guardian spoke."

Marsirg began to admire her; she had a mind that worked so much like his own.

"Then we can agree that Halidor was the one to whom the Guardian spoke," she said.

Marsirg shook his head. "He was killed before the Guardian spoke, when the Halfblood attacked."

"I would call it more a defense than an attack, but let us not argue over irrelevancies," said Atargirn. She held up a singed cape. "The Watchers found this near the Threshold."

Marsirg frowned at Halidor's distinctive cape, sewn with falcon feathers, overlapping like scales. Halidor always wore it beneath the Watcher's robe, an idiosyncrasy that was tolerated because of his ability to enter the inner way of *Draumr,* the Watcher's sacred practice. Now the feathers smelled of fire.

Marsirg nodded to Atargirn with admiration; he had not known the Watchers answered to anyone but him.

"I could learn to enjoy having an ally," he said.

‡

Later that same night, Atargirn attended a different meeting. The four Elders who listened to the account of her meeting with Marsirg smiled grimly. They had him at last!

Happy is he who hath in himself praise and wisdom in life.
He hath need of his wits who wanders wide."- Hávamál, st. 5

Halidor had not died in the fire. He had been there in Sanctuary when the woman had emerged through the doorway, and he had seen her fling fire from her hands. He had dropped his cloaks and dived after her though the doorway, rolling to the side as Marsirg lunged past. He had seen the woman turn, seen Marsirg raise his hands . . . and he had heard the Guardian speak.

Halidor's heart had stopped for a moment, sending searing pain through his chest. How could one continue to live with that voice reverberating through rock and bone?

Yet he had lived, and he had followed the woman when Marsirg left. For some reason that still made no sense, he had been allowed to follow her through the Thresholds. He had witnessed the woman's reunion with her companions and had heard the Ljósálfars' shock when they learned of the Dökkálfar presence. He had stood alone at the final Threshold after they had all hurried away.

The final Threshold marked a crossing from the known World

into a World where the Laws were not upheld. Halidor hovered, one foot drawing him back, the other urging him forward. Back lay certainty and service; forward lay Ariorn and new possibilities.

He stepped across the final Threshold and set off to find his uncle.

Halidor slipped through the Ljósálfar caverns like a shadow. If any sensed his passage, he was gone before they turned at the hint of a strange shift in the air. He emerged from the caverns and headed north to find Ariorn.

‡

Ariorn drank from the Well of Memory. The water lay deep, but it could still be drawn up. It tasted sweet as the first morning, but he scowled at the name carved into the rock of the well. *Well of Memory*. The irony! The words had been carved into the rock in a time no one remembered.

Yet the well still offered sustenance, for which he gave thanks to the elementals who had faithfully guarded the place long after all others had deserted it. If he were willing to sacrifice an eye, as Óðin had done in the beginning of the Nine Worlds, would the well offer more? Would Mimir accept the sacrifice?

Ariorn looked into the shadowy depths of the well and decided to keep his eye.

The thorn trees growing on either side of the well offered scant shelter from the sun, so he hoisted his pack and walked on into the emptiness, searching the dust for impossible footprints . . .

The sky darkened towards purple, night approaching like a bruise on the horizon.

Ariorn's mind wandered in circles, like an old traveler whose walking brings him back to where he started. So much for the mind! If it could answer his questions, he would not be walking towards a bruised sky on bruised feet, seeking a cure for the ills of the world.

And off his mind went again: a bruise was just another way of bleeding, and bloodshed was one of the ills he hoped to cure . . .

‡

Halidor followed Ariorn's invisible path across the wasted land. He walked in the *Draumr*, the between place where night and day, birth and death, time and space dissolved. Dökkálfar Watchers were trained to enter *Draumr* through dreams or healing trance, but Halidor could enter *Draumr* at will, the legacy of a Magi grandmother and centuries of diligent training. He gave thanks for both as he tracked his renegade uncle across the Wastelands.

‡

Ariorn feared that his search was in vain; the Gods had abandoned the Dökkálfar, leaving their Fate to schemers like

Marsirg. There had been times when an Elder could summon a God, and a boy could look on in wonder. Now the boy was old enough to be an Elder, and he needed divine wisdom more than ever. The days of the prophecy were upon them, but Marsirg and others like him thought only of power, and the others just sat around repeating the Laws while the Tapestry of the Nine Worlds unraveled. What of the Dökkálfar who still valued life? What of the younger ones like Halidor, who sought truth but found only lies woven from the tattered threads of betrayal? Ariorn walked on, seeking answers on the wind, in the air, in the water, in the earth . . .

‡

Halidor followed.

‡

Ariorn crossed the last ridge of the wasted land and stepped into a dream: lush forests and rivers flowing from distant mountains towards a coast he could not see. If the old Gods lived anywhere, surely it must be here . . .

He walked down into the dream and stopped by a large tree with spreading limbs and pink aerial roots trailing in the breeze like stands of hair. How strange that his people had lost all knowledge of these northern lands, that this beauty and life had been out of reach for a thousand years. It truly did seem that the Gods must be closer here, yet Ariorn did not sense them. He sensed the birds and small creatures that scuttled away from the sound of his footsteps, and he sensed the elements weaving their balance, but he did not sense the Gods. He sat with his back to the trunk of the tree and closed his eyes. The breeze lifted his hair and rustled the leaves.

I am Breeze blowing through the trees. I kiss the leaves and make them sigh, twirling and whirling, always moving, never still. I am Breeze soaring and dipping, touching the clouds, blowing up dust, ruffling hair. I am Breeze moving where I will, leaving a feather-like touch on your soul.

Ariorn opened his eyes.

"Greetings," said Halidor.

"Ah, I sensed a presence, but I was foolish enough to hope it may be one of the Gods taking pity on me."

"Perhaps it is," said Halidor, sitting beside his uncle.

Ariorn raised one eyebrow, an expression that had frightened Halidor when he was younger.

"Something has happened. Something important," said Halidor.

Ariorn raised the other eyebrow.

"A woman passed through the seven Thresholds. I think she is the one named in prophecy."

"It is unusual, but our cousins may just be attempting to resurrect their past."

"She hurled fire from her hands."

"Ah."

"Yes, she is the one."

"Which line has been blessed with a child of prophecy? The Elders must be green with envy."

"She is not Ljósálfar."

Ariorn frowned. "Who is she? How did she come to the caverns?"

"She is a Halfblood of the line of Warrior Queens. The Ljósálfar brought her to be tested."

"How did they know of her before our own people? She should have been ours."

"That is what Marsirg thought, but he was constrained by the Guardian, and the woman returned to the Ljósálfar caverns."

Ariorn nodded. "She would have the favor of the Guardian if her mother's mothers were Warrior Queens."

Halidor sighed deeply. Now that his story had been told, the spirit that had sustained him drained away, leaving him exhausted. He slumped against the tree and closed his eyes.

Ariorn propped a cloak behind Halidor's head and bade him rest. "So the Gods have spoken after all. I am sorry to have made you follow me so far to deliver their message."

Halidor did not answer; he was asleep.

Halidor woke to birdsong and dappled sunlight. Memory stirred, so old it seemed like a dream: Dökkálfar children ran through a sunlit glade where grass grew deep and soft and warm breezes carried the scent of blossoms. The children were laughing, and there was a complete absence of fear.

Halidor described the vision.

"That is how it was," said Ariorn. "Before." He handed Halidor a leather flask.

Halidor drank, the water sweet and fresh like the world of memory. He ate three golden-skinned fruits and declared himself restored.

"I have never walked in *Draumr* for so long," he said.

"You have slept for five days," said Ariorn. "It is fortunate that you are young and strong; I have known travelers to pay a much higher price."

Halidor thanked Ariorn for caring for his resting body; without water and tending, a *Draumr* traveler might never wake from the deep sleep that took them. He stretched his limbs and made his way to the stream to wash. He would move slowly for a day or two, but he was alive, and he had seen the child of prophecy.

"Now you are well, you can help me find the old Gods," said Ariorn. "We must secure their help before we seek the child of prophecy, or this chance will end as the same way the last cycle ended a thousand years ago."

Ariorn led the way into the fertile land, speaking of the past and the future. Much had been lost, but there was still hope . . .

A learned man's heart whose learning is deep seldom sings with joy. - Hávamál

"I have it!" cried the Wanderer, holding a parchment in his arms as if it were a newborn babe.

Llianna looked up from her work, heart racing. At last!

The Wanderer placed the parchment on the table and weighted the corners with Llianna's inkpot and paperweights.

Llianna stood to see it more clearly. "What writing is that? It looks like birds have walked all over it!"

"It is very old, probably the oldest piece in the collection," said the Wanderer. "The ancient ones wrote in symbols. Each symbol could have many meanings, depending on where it was placed in relation to the others."

"Like letters?" asked Llianna.

He shook his head. "Nothing like letters as we know them. A letter is always what it is. We combine them in different ways to mean different things, but even the words are still just what they are. This writing is not fixed like that." He pointed to the bird tracks on the parchment.

Llianna remembered Evenarlr saying something similar in the Ljósálfar caverns - *The ancient writing only seems to begin in one place. Always it moves out in spirals, gathering meaning.*

"But can you read it?" she asked.

The Wanderer smiled. "Yes. See, these ones repeat. And these always follow these, and this always comes before this . . ."

"Yes, yes, I can see the patterns," said Llianna. "But does it say anything?"

"It says many things. This writing takes the mind outwards, like a spiral that begins in one place and circles out and out, gathering meaning. Our words spiral inwards to a fixed point, but these touch the whole of the Nine Worlds."

Llianna nodded; echoes of Evenarlr again.

"Just tell me what it says. Please."

"Oh, yes. It says this . . ." The Wanderer's finger traced the strange writing.

"*In Truth, without falsehood and most real: What is below is like that which is above, and what is above is like that which is below, to accomplish the miracles of one thing. And as all things have been derived from that one, by the thought of that one, so all things are born from that one thing by adoption. The sun is its father, the moon its mother. Wind has carried it in its belly and the earth is its nurse. Here is the origin point of every perfection in the world. Its strength and power are absolute when changed into earth; separate the earth from the fire, the subtle from the gross, gently and with great care. It ascends from the earth to the heavens, and descends again to the earth to join the power of the above and the below. By this means, you will attain the glory of the world. And because of this, all obscurity will flee from you. Within this is the power, the force of all forces. For it will overcome all subtle things and penetrate every solid thing. Thus was the universe created. From this will be, and will emerge, admirable adaptations. For this reason I am called Magi, having three parts of the wisdom of the world. What I have said of the sun's operation is accomplished."* [iii]

Llianna stared at the parchment. The words stirred the memory of Evenarlr's lessons and of walking the Seven Thresholds. *Above and below . . .*

The Wanderer smiled. "This belongs with the prophecy."

Llianna traced the bird track writing with her finger. *Its strength and power are absolute when changed into earth . . .* It spoke of balance, of the power of knowing the above and below as one, no separation between humanity and the Gods and Goddesses. No division between Heaven and Earth.

"Could it be that simple?" she asked.

"The truth is always simple," said the Wanderer. "The complexity comes when we try to live it and share it with others."

Was that true? If she could stand in that place of perfect balance, could she change the World? Was that her Destiny? Is that what the Warrior Queens were trying to do a thousand years ago?

Llianna asked the Wanderer to make a copy of the translation, and she read the words over and over until she knew them by heart.

Eyes can not hide a woman's love for a man. - Eigi leyna augu ef ann kona manni. - The Saga of Gunnlaugur the Worm-tongue, 13

Rothmar and Hugo returned to Ravensborg early in winter.

"Well come! I had not expected you back so soon." Llianna cried, running down the stairs to the forecourt.

She accepted Rothmar's embrace and Hugo's more sober greeting.

"Are you not riding to Munstrond?" she asked.

"I will not take the men on foot across the Wastelands in this weather," said Rothmar. "Either the Landvördr will be there in Spring, or they will have fled, but I will not march the men to their deaths. We have left men guarding the passes."

Hugo scowled and turned away to untie his saddlebag.

"Ah, I see," said Llianna. "If it is any consolation, I think that is a wise decision."

Rothmar held her hands. "You are always a consolation."

"Even when I ride out without you knowing?"

"Even then, although it would be more comfortable for me to

know that you are safe here. But then you would not be who you are, and that would be no consolation at all. Come, I would hear more of your adventure. Hugo tells me you have collected another stranger."

Llianna beckoned the Wanderer and Lunet down from the steps.

Rothmar sighed. "I see. It *is* becoming a habit."

Hugo mumbled something inaudible.

"This is the Wanderer. He has helped us," said Llianna.

"Mmmm. I am sure he has," said Rothmar, turning to the Wanderer. "My thanks to you. Do you have a name, or are you only known by the description of your activity?"

"Er, this is King Rothmar, my husband," said Llianna.

"Hmmph," said the Wanderer, looking from Hugo to Rothmar.

"Yes, well, perhaps the conversation will improve once I am rested." Rothmar smiled tiredly at Llianna.

She walked with him to his room, where Thyvri had a bath steaming.

"Sit with me and tell me what you have discovered," said Rothmar, shedding his riding cloak.

Llianna sat on the bed as he undressed. She knew his body now, the lean strength of his limbs, his finely shaped hands. He looked weary, and the scars stood out against the pale skin of his back and chest, but he was still a man to be admired . . .

Rothmar caught her look and smiled. Llianna sat close while he soaked in the tub, handing him Thyvri's special lavender soap and washing his back with a soft cloth. He closed his eyes and asked her to tell him all that had happened.

When she reached the part about meeting the Ljósálfar, he sat up abruptly, splashing water over the sides of the tub.

"Children's stories come to life! How wonderful! I would like to meet these people. You really area child of prophecy, aren't you!"

Llianna sighed. "Yes, it does seem that the prophecy will have its way with me, whether I agree or not."

"Well, you did ride out into the Wastelands, take up with another stranger, and go off with people from the old tales! I think you might have helped prophecy along a little," said Rothmar.

"Do you mind very much?" asked Llianna, feeling a frisson of shame.

"It seems irrelevant whether I mind or not," said Rothmar. "It is all so much larger than I am."

Llianna pursed her lips and raised her eyebrows. "Really?"

"Well, of course I would like a wife who stayed where I left her and who . . ." Rothmar stopped and reached for a drying cloth.

"Gave you sons?" said Llianna quietly, looking down at the floor.

Rothmar reached out and lifted her chin gently. "We are who we are, Llianna. I am grateful you are in my life, with or without sons, with or without this damned prophecy."

"Yes, but Ravensborg needs an heir."

"There is time," said Rothmar firmly. "Now tell me more about these beings from the old tales."

"Ah, the Ljósálfar. They hold much wisdom," said Llianna. "They say the Warrior Queens were from their people."

"What? They were Ljósálfar? But . . ."

"I know what our histories say, but the Ljósálfar tell a different story, a story of bitter struggles for power with the Noctimagi."

"Noctimagi!" cried Rothmar. "They are real?"

"Real enough," said Llianna. "The Ljósálfar call them Dökkálfar." She told him about her journey through the Thresholds.

"Naked?" said Rothmar, just as Lunet had.

"Why did they want the child?" he asked when she had finished.

"I think it's my bloodline, my mother's mothers' bloodline."

Llianna rose to pour more mulled wine, not wanting to think any more about the child she should be having.

"The Ljósálfar sent three of their most powerful Warriors to stop the Noctimagi and save the Land," she said, handing Rothmar the wine. "The Warrior Queens."

"They made the Wastelands," said Rothmar.

Llianna nodded. "They stopped the dark magic of the Noctimagi, but there was a terrible cost."

"So Ronja's mother's ancestors were Ljósálfar?" whispered Rothmar.

"So it seems," said Llianna. "Does it trouble you?"

"Not in itself, although it explains the light that shines in you and your . . . er . . . difference. No, I am more worried about the Keepers hearing of it. They would consider it an abomination."

"What would they do?"

"At the very least, they would declare you unfit to bear sons for Ravensborg. At the worst . . .? I am not sure."

Llianna shivered.

"We must not speak of this," said Rothmar. "We can trust Lunet, but what of Gravnir and this new person you have found, the Wanderer?"

"They are no friends of the Keepers, but I will ask them to tell no one."

They spoke some more about the Ljósálfar and Llianna's journey, and then Llianna asked about the fight with the Landvördr.

Rothmar sighed tiredly and rose from the tub. Llianna handed him a drying cloth and took another to wipe his back.

"We do well enough against the Landvördr, but the men are tired of being away from home, and the small battles wear them down. It is the same all the way East. We must be grateful the Landvördr cannot affect sea trade. Some of the strongholds are using small craft to sail to Gullhyrndr for trade rather than using the roads. It is changing the seven fiefdoms."

Llianna ran the cloth down the long muscles of Rothmar's back to the curve of his buttocks. She dropped the cloth and wrapped her arms around him, clasping her hands over his heart.

"It's good to see you safe," she said.

Rothmar turned and held her close. "How I have missed you!"

Later, as they lay together on the furs of the bed, their talk returned to the Landvördr.

"So you think Hugo is right to attack Munstrond?" asked Llianna.

"I gather that you do not," he said.

Llianna shrugged her shoulders. "I don't believe that more killing will restore the Land or right the wrongs that have been done, but I know Hugo is determined."

"It is trying to bear two loyalties," said Rothmar tiredly. "Hugo is called to fight this battle, even as you are called to your path."

"Yes, I see Hugo's position, but you and I need not be divided on this," said Llianna. "Their warriors provoke us to kill or be killed, to fight regardless of the damage that is done to the Land. This is not the way to vanquish darkness and despair."

"I am not as different from Hugo as you imagine. I also want to vanquish the Landvördr and relieve our men of this endless fighting, but perhaps your vision is more encompassing," said Rothmar. "I would hear more."

Llianna marveled again at his graciousness; was that what came from crossing so close to death? Her own crossing in the Ljósálfar caverns had brought blessings, yet it had also left her struggling with complexity, troubled by how many things in her life seemed beyond her control. She shook her head to clear the thoughts.

"Are you winning the argument this time?" asked Rothmar.

Llianna shrugged again. "I think it's an argument that can't be won. Something else will have to arise, something I can't even imagine right now." She smiled to acknowledge Rothmar's attempt to lighten her spirits, but she was troubled. Trying to be a Warrior Queen brought terrible responsibility; how could one person possibly save her people, save the Landvördr, save the Land, and vanquish darkness and despair? Not to mention running a stronghold and having babies!

Rothmar left the bed to dress in soft, indoor clothes. "You know we must ride for Munstrond in Spring."

Llianna gathered her courage and told him about Gravnir leaving to warn his people.

Rothmar was quiet for a long time. "You risked much telling him of our plans."

Llianna nodded, suddenly ashamed. "I was hoping he could warn them and they could leave."

"To fight us another day," said Rothmar. He sounded exhausted.

"I'm sorry," said Llianna. "Being a child of prophecy is proving very difficult."

She left the bed, dressed, and joined Rothmar on the bench were they had sat on their wedding night.

"It is good to be clean," he said. "I hate the dirt and blood so much I fear that I can never again be a true Warrior King."

"You are a good King," said Llianna.

He smiled and drew her close.

A knock on the door announced Hugo, and Llianna rose to pour wine for them all. Rothmar and Hugo spoke at first of Ravensborg and the Western strongholds.

They fell silent, and Rothmar looked intently at Hugo. "You are my closest cousin and heir to Ravensborg until I have sons," he said.

Llianna went as still as a mouse in the presence of a cat. If she had whiskers they would have been twitching. What was Rothmar about? Why was he saying this now?

. . . *You are my closest cousin and heir to Ravensborg until I have sons . . .* Rothmar's words played through Llianna's mind. *Closest cousin. Heir to Ravensborg.* What did he mean? Rothmar was wise in the ways of love and loss, and he had alluded to the true leanings of her heart more than once. But Hugo knew his position and carried the role of King's second honorably – he had saved Rothmar's life at Gullhyrndr and stood beside him in battle

"I have wandered the land of the dead," said Rothmar softly. "I am not bound by worldly things as some Kings are."

Hugo did not meet Llianna's eyes, but she could see that he was troubled. He bowed to Rothmar and took his leave, back straight, shoulders rigid.

Llianna waited until the door closed and then sat beside Rothmar and brought his hand to her lips. "I think I understand your meaning, but you do not need to do this."

"You are right. Ravensborg needs an heir," said Rothmar. "Long have the Keepers sought to control our Land, but my father and the Kings before him forged their own Laws to resist the Keepers. Yet the Keepers grow stronger, and Ravensborg will need to become stronger as well."

Llianna bit her lip. "I'm truly sorry we don't yet have a child."

"You must stop apologizing for what you cannot change," said Rothmar. "Ravensborg has not resisted the Keepers just to treat women like broodmares. That is their way, not ours."

"But . . ."

"I know enough of women's ways to think that you might give Ravensborg an heir if you were able to be with the one Fate has chosen for you."

"Hugo," she whispered.

Rothmar nodded.

"Is there no part of you that minds what exists between me and Hugo?" asked Llianna.

"Of course I mind!" said Rothmar, standing to pace the room. "I am a man and a King! My blood heats every time I see you with him, when I see you thinking of him with that faraway look, but what can I do?"

His voice softened. "You did not choose this, and it is true - I would have an heir for Ravensborg before I die."

"You are an unusual man," said Llianna, stroking his cheek.

Rothmar smiled. "I assume that is a compliment?"

Llianna returned his smile. "You know Hugo's honor will never allow it."

Rothmar stroked her fingers. "And yours?"

"There are different kinds of honor, even as there are different kinds of love," said Llianna. "My honor is about living in truth with myself and my Thread in the Tapestry. Your honor comes from a nobility of soul, a generosity with no trace of meanness. Hugo's honor is more about what is morally right according to his precious Warrior Code, and he can't bear it when he falls short. He is so unforgiving of himself, I wonder if he has ever known any love or tenderness in his life."

Rothmar nodded thoughtfully. "Hugo has always been deeply concerned with right and wrong. He is like a bloodsworn warrior from the old tales. It is what makes him such a formidable fighter, but he demands too much of himself. It scares me sometimes."

"Why is he like that?" asked Llianna. "What happened to him?"

"The sins of the fathers," said Rothmar, shaking his head.

"Huh?"

"Hugo's grandfather was Hemgen, a great fighter. He led the West against the Raiders and won himself a King's daughter for a wife, but he betrayed the Code and died for it, shaming his family. Hemgen's three sons all became great fighters, but their father's shame haunted them. Hugo's father was the best swordsman I have ever met, but he was a hard man. He had Hugo reciting the Code before he could walk."

"You trained with him," said Llianna. "Marina told me."

Rothmar nodded. "He was good enough to me, but he treated Hugo differently. It was as if he was trying to beat Hemgen's sins out of him, just in case."

Llianna shivered.

"Someone walking on your ashes?" asked Rothmar gently.

Llianna sighed. Why did Fate have her longing for a tragic, honor-bound warrior, when she was married to this sweet, noble man?

She set her thoughts of Hugo aside and spent the rest of the afternoon in Rothmar's room. He had furnished it comfortably with woven rugs and carved chairs, and they spent the day talking quietly, eating pastries, and making love again in the gentle way that moved Llianna to tears.

"I love you," she murmured, as they lay together on the bed furs at the end of the day.

"You have no idea how happy it makes me to hear you say that," said Rothmar. "I think I have always loved you, since I first saw you as a child."

Llianna smiled. She did love her gentle, wise King; he was the steady hearth fire that welcomed her home, warmed her, and held back the dark. It was not a love that moved the moon and stars, but it helped subdue the blazing, impossible passion she still felt for Hugo.

‡

The day after Rothmar's talk of heirs, Hugo left Ravensborg to gather support from Gullhyrndr for the spring assault on Munstrond. He had not slept well, troubled by Rothmar's talk of heirs and ashamed of the sudden desire that had flared when Rothmar seemed to be suggesting . . . but, no, he must have misheard him; no King would open the way for another man to be with his wife. Hugo had left his bed to pace the ramparts; better he not sleep when sleep brought dreams of Llianna, dreams that took him beyond ideas of honor, dreams in which he betrayed his King and his father's name over and over again.

‡

Llianna had not said farewell to Hugo, but she counted the days he had been gone; thirteen days, the moon changing from full to a thin crescent. He would return in time for the new moon . . .

The new moon.

Oh!

Llianna counted again, a different number in mind.

Yes, her moonblood was three days late . . .

She dropped her attention into her body. Could it be?

Yes. Life pulsed in her womb.

She tapped her fingers, counting back; if she were with child, the baby would have been made welcome by her body the afternoon she had spent with Rothmar in his rooms, the afternoon they had spoken of heirs. Llianna went to Faeoia, who confirmed her sensing and told her it was written. Llianna just nodded and sipped the raspberry leaf tea Faeoia made her, too stunned to rail at Fate in her usual way.

She swore Faeoia to secrecy and went to her room, claiming a fever as the reason for missing the evening meal. What she really wanted was time to enter the Tapestry and find this new Thread, to come to terms with this child who had found a way to enter the story whether she was ready or not. She settled into the deep inner state that led to the Tapestry and found her Thread glowing brightly. There, a new Thread, glowing blue, like the sea in summer, so beautiful . . .

Ripples of darkness twined across the blue, like the shadows of clouds on water. Llianna cried out. Something threatened her child! Her body tensed, and killing rage surged. But where was the threat?

She lost connection with the Tapestry and leaped to her feet, braced to fight an invisible foe, arms raised, lips pulled back in a snarl. She sucked in a breath and dropped her arms. Whatever that strange darkness had been, it was beyond her now. She calmed herself, sent blessings to her child, and spent the rest of the night wondering at the fierce love and terrible vulnerability that had besieged her.

She told Rothmar the next morning and was humbled by the bright leap of joy in his eyes. How could she have been denying him a child of his own blood? He had been kind and generous to her in every way possible, and this was fair beyond words. So be it; she would be the mother of Rothmar's child, and let Fate have its way with her.

Hugo returned two days later, the Gullhyrndr troops ready for spring. He attended Rothmar at the end of the morning's petitions, and Llianna sat quietly as Rothmar told him about the royal baby.

Hugo offered congratulations, but Llianna saw the tightness in his jaw and the flash of pain in his eyes. She could not regret this child, but her heart and body still dreamed of a response to the fire of *inn mátki munr*.

Later that day, she found Hugo in his room, unpacking his saddlebags. She hesitated in the doorway.

He turned, silhouetted against the window. A warrior, strong and proud.

Then fire arced between them, turning the room golden.

Llianna crossed to him and reached for his hands. She brought them to her lips and kissed the warrior's calluses.

He pulled away. "I offer my blessings."

Llianna knew he offered true blessings, but surely there was more . . .

"Oh, Hugo! I do not begrudge Rothmar this child, but I still dream of you."

Hugo sat heavily on the bed. "What are you saying? You are with child, the King's child. It is as it should be." He dropped his head into his hands and groaned.

Llianna, trained by a völva, wanted to object: a woman's body was her own to share as she willed. But she was also a King's daughter, and she knew her words would be seen as madness, yet . . .

"You had better go," said Hugo, voice cold.

"Oh, Hugo . . ."

"Go!"

Llianna backed out of his room and ran to her rooms on the other side of the stronghold. What was wrong with her? Had she truly thought that Hugo would forsake his precious honor? Did she really want him to? She ground her teeth in frustration and paced her sitting room like a caged bear.

"Are you unwell?" asked Rothmar at dinner.

Llianna shook her head, but she ate nothing and left the table early. Sleep eluded her, so she wrapped herself in the blue cloak and went to knock on the door of Faeoia's small sleeping chamber.

"Enter," said Faeoia, as if she had been waiting. She sat on a low stool at the foot of her bed, shuffling cards in her lap.

Llianna sat at her feet.

"Ah. You have chosen," said Faeoia.

"I did not choose, not really. My body chose, lulled by Rothmar's decency and the love I bear him. My desire for Hugo still burns."

"Yet you hold Rothmar's child."

Llianna nodded. She knew the women's lore that said she could still refuse this babe a home in her body, but she could not bring herself to do that. It was not the child's fault that she desired Hugo.

"Ah! As you hold to this son, so he will hold to you all the days of his life," said Faeoia in the singsong voice of a true telling.

Llianna shivered. "Why do you say 'all the days of his life' and not 'all the days of my life'? Will I have to mourn this child one day?" She thought of the shadows in the child's thread and shivered.

Faeoia sighed and looked down at her lap. She lifted the cards.

Llianna had loved this game as a child: Staffs, Cups, Swords, Coins; King, Queen, Warrior, Child.

She reached for a card. Hesitated. Took another.

Queen of Swords.

"Power and sorrow in equal measure. Doing what is known to be right rather than what passion demands." Faeoia spoke the card's meaning slowly, pausing between each word.

"Warrior Queen," said Llianna, frowning at the card. "I'm not much of a warrior at the moment."

"It is written . . ."

"Don't say it!" Llianna glared at Faeoia. Maybe a rant about Fate would help after all.

‡

Spring announced itself too soon. The men prepared to ride to Munstrond, and Llianna was torn between wishing them safe and hoping Gravnir had reached his people in time to avert a battle. Hugo had looked at her coldly when he had learned of Gravnir's intention to warn the Landvördr, but she could not regret it. It was Hugo's Destiny to carry this fight to the Landvördr settlement, but it was hers to save almost everybody!

For once Llianna did not want to march with the húskarlar; Sigfinn had been right when he had said that battle was pain and blood and death, and now it was about to erupt between people she was called to protect. What had Rothmar said? *It is trying to bear two loyalties . . .*

Hugo and Rothmar rode out with the húskarlar eager for battle. Hugo's farewell was constrained, and she tucked the fire of *inn mátki munr* away in a corner of her soul. Rothmar's farewell was bittersweet: the sweetness came from the shared joy of the growing babe and the gentle love that flowed between them; the bitterness from the shadow of death that had hovered since the attack on the road to Vadsted.

Rothmar held her close, pressing his face against her hair.

"You are bigger," he said. "Rounder."

"Of course," said Llianna. "The babe is growing."

Rothmar placed a hand on her belly. "Yes, but it is hard for a man to believe in the mystery of life. To us it is always a miracle."

Llianna offered blessings for a safe return and took herself back to managing the stronghold and waiting . . .

There is mingling in friendship when man can utter all his whole mind to another. The summer moments always pass quickly.
- Hávamál, 113

The Ravensborg troops joined the Gullhyrndr húskarlar on the road to the mountains. Dagmar led the Gullhyrndr men, with Falden his second, both eager to crush the Landvördr. The combined forces crossed the Wastelands and arrived at Munstrond in a cloud of dust.

Rothmar scowled at the distant ruins. Between him and the old city lay the natural barrier of a deep, dry riverbed.

"Good defenses," he said to his horse.

The horse snorted.

Hugo organized the encampment and deployment of guards a safe distance from crumbling walls that might conceal archers. If the Landvördr were still there, they had the advantage of position, but they had proved themselves more skilled at random attacks than engaging a concentrated force. Hugo radiated confidence, strengthening the men's resolve to destroy the Landvördr for all time. Dagmar shared his confidence, and the two leaders worked together to plan an attack that would end the war of attrition waged by the Landvördr. No matter if the enemy had received warning; as long as they were still at Munstrond, victory would belong to Nyrland . . .

‡

Gravnir heard the troops arrive, an echo in the ground like thunder. He would not be called to fight, a relief of sorts. He did not want to fight, but it still rankled that he was not trusted; *white fox*, they had called him, and a white fox changed its color with the seasons. His warning had been received with wariness, and he had been banished from Council. In that first meeting, he had urged the Elders to take the Landvördr back to the mountains, but their talk suggested there was something back there that troubled them. Gravnir had thought to mention the Ljósálfar, but what if the Landvördr warriors decided to fight them as well? He had shuddered and kept quiet about his time in the Ljósálfar caverns.

To be fair, the Elders had debated the wisdom of crossing the plains, but pitched battle had never been their strength, and the Seafarer's forces may already be in the Wastelands. Gravnir had listened to the debates until the Elders made it clear that his presence was no longer welcome in Council, and he left to find his friends. He was resolved to die with his people, but, like a fox, he still sought a way out of the teeth of the trap that was closing around them.

He gathered Adelgunde and her extended family in a sheltered area near the northern wall. Thirty-four in all, they carried small bundles of food and clothing, and they waited quietly for his signal that would take them over the wall and away from the fighting.

Did it make him a coward to want to run rather than fight? The warriors would call him a coward and kill him painfully for it. He wondered what Llianna would call it, but she was lost to him, on the other side of the tide of destruction that threatened to engulf the Landvördr. Would he live to see the prophecy unfold, to see Llianna fulfill her destiny as a Warrior Queen?

Gravnir pushed away the regrets; at least he had stood with her in the place of the Warrior Queens, and he had sat in Cavernacaeli and heard the Ljósálfar sing.

Rothmar watched the first assault as dawn turned the ruins golden. The húskarlar sent hundreds of flaming arrows over the broken walls. It was a warning only; there was nothing to burn in Munstrond. At least they found the Landvördr still there; they answered the assault with a barrage of arrows that barely made the distance. And so the first day unfolded with few deaths and much posturing from both sides. *Would that battle was always so benign . . .*

The night seemed relatively friendly, with lamps and fires on both sides and even some songs from the húskarlar. Rothmar sat apart to allow his eyes to adjust to the darkness. Not that he expected to see much, but it helped him think. His warrior-trained senses shouted warnings, but his mind could not decipher them. Something was wrong, but it was nothing he could name. He gazed across at the flickering fires in the Landvördr settlement; they covered a large area. The Landvördr had gathered a sizeable fighting force behind the ancient walls . . .

He settled for sleep wrapped in his riding cloak, counting stars instead of Landvördr fires.

‡

"We can't reach them." Hugo paced restlessly in an arc around where Rothmar sat poring over battle plans he knew by heart. "Every advance is met with arrows and rocks and fire. They have the advantage of position, and with enough things to throw, they can hold us off forever." He glared in the direction of Munstrond like an eagle thwarted from seizing its prey.

"Good defenses," said Rothmar.

Dagmar glared at them both. "We can't just leave, but we can't stay forever. What will we do?"

Rothmar gestured for them both to sit. "We wait until something happens. We have supplies and can send for more. They must run short of food before we do. We are not experienced at this sort of fighting, but we know from our training that sieges are won or lost on small turnings: someone inside opens a way for the enemy; the needed rain does not fall, and their water runs low; a leader dies. We wait for the small turning that will end this. In the meantime the Landvördr are no longer attacking farmers and killing children in Ravensborg and Gullhyrndr."

So they waited, sending men towards the ruins in small numbers and large, by day and night, defeated every time by the natural defenses surrounding the old city. A few Landvördr could hold off the húskarlar from all seven fiefdoms as long as they had enough arrows and men to aim them.

A month passed, then two. Spring gave way to Summer, and the húskarlar used their tents for shade rather than warmth.

‡

The Landvördr also waited. The ruins were more crowded with the warriors at home, and Gravnir took long walks through the deserted parts of the old city to avoid meeting anyone who might suddenly decide to hit him with a heavy object. One anvil to the head had been enough to give him recurring headaches and bouts of double vision; he doubted he would survive another encounter like that.

He had made four attempts to lead people out of Munstrond, but he had been thwarted at every turn by the guards. He had appealed to Olafeur to evacuate the women and children, but the Elder had insisted that he had foreseen a Landvördr victory, and everyone was to remain in the ruined city to support the warriors.

"It be our Fate to stay here," said Adelgunde. "The Elders will see us safe."

Gravnir told the fox to accept its fate, but still it nosed around, seeking a way out of the trap.

‡

By mid-summer Rothmar's small turning had still not happened. Ravensborg and Gullhyrndr men had walked for days to find a crossing that would bring them unseen to Munstrond's far walls, but the city had been cunningly built in a double curve of the river, and the approach from all directions invited a hail of arrows.

Hugo stared morosely at the ruins. "The babe will be coming in two moons," he said to Rothmar. "You could ride to Ravensborg."

Rothmar smiled sadly. "I would like nothing better, but the men look to me, and I did not bring them here to abandon them. They have families, too, and some will have had babes born while they wait here with me. How can I ask it of them and not of myself?"

"You are King," said Hugo.

"All the more reason I must be here with them."

The nights became colder as Summer waned, and the men prepared for yet another Winter away from home.

Silent and thoughtful and bold in strife
the prince's bairn should be.
Joyous and generous let each man show him
until he shall suffer death. - Hávamál: 15

The leaves changed to gold, and Ravensborg prepared for winter with wagonloads of wood, stores of onions and squash, and long days of harvesting and preserving the last of the summer crops.

Llianna worried about feeding the stronghold and sending enough supplies to Munstrond. Rothmar's letters arrived with travel-weary messengers, who returned with supplies of food and bedding and anything else Llianna could send to support the men.

The latest consignment had just left when she felt the first birth sign. It was not exactly a pain, although some of the women had told her to expect pain. It was more like the surge of power like she had felt when she had called Aegir all those years ago. Or like the wave of heat that had passed between her and Hugo that morning in the stream.

Llianna collected her thoughts. Why was she remembering her

encounter with a God and the passion of *inn mátki munr*? Was that what the völva had meant when she talked about the life-giving power of women?

Ah! The life-giving power *was* like calling a God or being taken by *inn mátki munr*; it was immense and glorious and it was happening to her now . . .

Llianna delighted in herself for some time before deciding to let Thyvri and Faeoia know that the baby was coming. By the time Thyvri had taken her to the birthing room, gathered the women, and prepared the herbs, Llianna was pushing her son into the world.

Faeoia lifted him and placed him in Llianna's arms. He opened his eyes and looked up, and Llianna fell in love. He moved his lips as if kissing the air, and Faeoia gently guided him to Llianna's breast. He opened his mouth and fastened his lips to her nipple.

"Oh!" Heat pulsed from her breast to her womb, forging a bond as deep as life itself. Llianna sighed, ecstatic and tired and loving the tiny creature suckling hungrily at her breast. How could there be so many ways to love?

Thyvri insisted that Llianna stay in the birthing room for five days. Llianna felt well enough to take Marri out to see the rest of the world, but Thyvri was adamant.

"The child's soul is still hovering between the worlds. You must be still so he can find his way here."

Llianna believed her. She had looked into Marri's eyes and glimpsed the vastness of eternity. She sent a messenger to

Rothmar and waited patiently, sleeping and eating and watching her son come into being.

‡

Rothmar received the message at the end of another day of waiting.

"A boy. I have a son!" He ordered extra rations of mead for the men and sat alone to give thanks that Llianna and the babe were well.

He watched the sky darken and the stars appear, and he looked across at the Landvördr lights, lanterns and fires around which families gathered. Were there mothers with newborn babes there? Did they give thanks as he did?

Rothmar spoke earnestly with Hugo and wrote at his camp desk until the encampment settled for the night, guards keeping double watch. Sleep was elusive, so Rothmar walked the perimeter. Something felt different, but he could not place the feeling with anything tangible. He called himself a fool jumping at shadows, and finally he made himself settle down for sleep. He welcomed the night hours when he could roam in his dreams.

‡

"That's it!" cried Rothmar, scrambling to his feet.

"What's it?" asked Hugo, who had been sleeping lightly nearby.

"No shadows."

"What? Are you fevered?"

"Their fires were not crossed by shadows tonight. They burned steady. The Landvördr are not there."

"Then where are they?" asked Hugo, strapping on his sword.

"I fear we are about to find out," said Rothmar. "Rouse the men and alert the guards."

Alerted, the guards peered into the darkness for the expected attack. Martri, second cousin to Lunet, shared his watch with his boyhood friend, Gurhyr. They had been excited to march on the enemy settlement; finally, an end to the interminable skirmishes along the roads. The excitement of ending the fighting and returning home had given way to boredom as the siege continued, and now the boredom had given way to trepidation with word of a surprise attack by the enemy.

"Where will they come from?" whispered Gurhyr. "There's nothing out there."

Martri peered into the dark. A troop of mountain giants could be moving out there for all he could see. At least mountain giants would make some noise, but the Landvördr could be creeping up on them, silent as death. He strained his ears for any sound, but the night was eerily quiet, as if waiting for something . . .

"Can you see anything?" asked Gurhyr.

Martri shook his head. "Maybe they can fly."

Gurhyr bent his head back to stare at the sky. Clouds moved

across the stars like great winged creatures from the old tales. Martri shivered; *someone walking on his ashes* . . .

"What's that?" Gurhyr spun around and raised his sword.

An axe split his head like a winter squash.

Martri cried a warning to the others and raised his sword to fight the enemy who emerged from the ground like the restless shades of unburned dead, fierce warriors armed with swords and knives, axes and staves. Martri felt the absence of Gurhyr, who had fought at his back since they were boys. Instead of Gurhyr he found an enemy sword and died calling his friend's name.

Rothmar cursed as his men struggled against the tide of warriors rising from the ground. Munstrond had been built of stone; it stood to reason that there would be mines beneath the city, tunnels hollowed out by the ancient builders. All the Landvördr had to do was extend them a little further . . .

Why had he not seen it?

"Over here!" cried Hugo, cutting a path through the Landvördr fighters.

Rothmar rallied himself and joined Hugo, their swords rising and falling together, slicing and stabbing, working as a team as they had trained to do, shields up, their moves too fast to parry. Landvördr warriors fell around them, and Rothmar felt a rush of something he had thought gone forever: fear. For the first time in a long while he very much wanted to live.

The Landvördr melted away as suddenly as they had appeared,

although no signal had been heard by the Nyrland men left standing. Hugo and Rothmar leaned on their swords and caught their breath.

"Where did they go?" asked Rothmar.

"Why did they go?" asked Hugo. "They could have won this."

"Ah!" Rothmar's eyes lit with understanding just as the arrows began to fall.

‡

Gravnir led Adelgunde and the others through the darkened ruins, finding the pathways he had mapped with the children. The passages were free of guards. They left the city through a tunnel on the opposite side from the fighting and emerged into a barren plain stretching north to the horizon. The children were quiet, but they could have been howling at the moon, and the noise would have been lost in the clash of metal, the wild battle cries of warriors and the screams of dying men and wounded horses. By the time the death cries faded to eerie silence, Gravnir and his band of survivors were a long way from the ruins of Munstrond.

Where fault can be found, the good is ignored - Fár bregður hinu betra ef hann veit hið verra. - The Saga of Njál, 139

When the time came to leave her room, Llianna felt strangely reluctant. The haven of warmth and timelessness had been a precious gift, but the distant promise of Spring had brought the usual flurry of activity and new life, and it was time to take Marri out into the world that would one day be his. Llianna dressed herself in leggings and tunic, dressed Marri warmly, wrapped him in a soft woolen blanket, and walked slowly down the stairs to the kitchen.

"Oh, here he is!" The women gathered round, cooing like doves. "Isn't he handsome!"

Llianna laughed. She adored Marri with a passion that amazed her; he was sweet and button-nosed and smelled like warm bread, but he was far from handsome. She was still laughing when the messenger rode in.

She slowly followed the others out to the forecourt. The silence should have warned her, but she was filled with love and joy and the promise of Spring.

The messenger stood by his horse, talking to Thyvri.

"No!" Thyvri screamed and threw her apron over her head.

Llianna stopped in the doorway, holding Marri close. What was wrong? Why were people crying?

The message whispered across the yard to where Llianna stood.

"Rothmar. Dead."

Ah.

The black lines in Marri's thread.

The Queen of Swords.

Sorrow.

Llianna turned and carried Marri back to the warmth of her room.

‡

Hugo rode in two days later with Rothmar's body and a clamoring litany of guilt. It should be him strapped to the horse, still as death, covered in a riding cloak; it should be him carried home to a pyre on the cliffs. The attack on Munstrond had been his idea, and the failing was his; he should have anticipated the enemy attack from beneath the ruined city, he should have anticipated the ferocity of the attack, he should have anticipated that last cruel flight of arrows. It should be him dead and Rothmar alive, returning to his Queen, welcoming his son . . .

At least the messenger from Ravensborg had arrived in time for Rothmar to hear of his son's birth; perhaps Loki had granted him laughter as he went. Or perhaps not. Dying did not seem to be a laughing matter.

Hugo had been beside Rothmar when the arrow struck. He had just asked his question - "Why did they go?" - and had been answered by the flight of arrows. He had flung up his shield, expecting Rothmar to do the same. Rothmar had been slower, and the arrow had taken him through the throat. If Hugo had held his shield higher, might he have deflected the arrow? Might Rothmar be riding in now to see Llianna and the babe?

Darkest of all were the thoughts that told Hugo he had wished his cousin dead, that he had wanted the way clear to be with Llianna. That he had betrayed every article of the Warrior's Code: courage, truth, honor, fidelity, discipline. That he was just like his grandfather, after all. Surely he could have covered Rothmar or pushed him to safety . . .

Had he hesitated for a fatal moment?

Despite the battle experience that told Hugo there had been no time to do anything but lift his own shield, the ragged thoughts attacked as viciously as the Landvördr had attacked from the hidden tunnels.

Hugo saw Llianna standing in the forecourt, cradling the babe in her arms, her face etched with grief. Had she come to truly love Rothmar? Had she found a way past the fire of *inn mátki munr* to give her heart to Rothmar? Hugo hated himself for even asking the question, but there it was: jealousy, desire, love. Enough to kill for? Enough to let an arrow find its mark? Enough to hold back for a fatal moment? Enough to betray everything?

He handed the reins to a stableboy and stalked off to find oblivion in a barrel of ale.

Llianna watched Hugo ride in, and her heart leaped to see him alive. Was it wrong for her heart to leap like that? Could a heart be wrong?

He barely looked at her, and she could guess something of his torment. She knew his pride and his bone-deep sense of honor, the Code by which he had lived since before he could walk. She could imagine how much he wished himself dead and Rothmar alive. Why did Fate persist in torturing them like this? Why were they pulled apart by forces too big for ordinary men and women to bear?

Hugo sobered up enough to give a full report of the battle at Munstrond, and Llianna despaired to hear of the surprise attack and the number of Ravensborg men lost. She grieved also for her brothers, Falden dead, Dagmar seriously wounded, and for the grief her father must be suffering. That any had survived was testimony to Hugo's leadership, to the men's discipline and skill at arms, but the battle had left the húskarlar of Gullhyrndr and Ravensborg depleted and disheartened. When Rothmar fell, Hugo and Dagmar had ordered the remaining men to retreat, and they had limped home in the cold, bearing the wounded on the surviving horses.

"The Landvördr lost many as well," said Hugo finally. "There were no real victors at Munstrond, but our loss is great."

The remaining chiefs nodded sadly. Rothmar had been well loved, and his son was so young. They looked to Hugo as Rothmar's second, but he walked away to continue punishing himself.

The pyre built for Rothmar rose to the sky, a fitting farewell for a good King. Did Marri watch the flames with any sense of what had been lost to him? Llianna held him close and wished with all her heart that Rothmar was being welcomed joyfully by the maidens he had told her about from his time near death. He once said that he could hear them talking and laughing, waiting for him to return.

‡

Spring moved through the stronghold like a sullen child, the usual exuberance blighted by loss; bedding flapped less vigorously in the spring breezes, and children played less joyously in the soft sunshine.

Llianna returned to managing the household, waiting for Hugo to take up his role as Rothmar's second. She was more than capable of running Ravensborg, but a man's presence was essential for negotiations with the Council and the other fiefdoms. And to appease the Keepers.

Rothmar had encouraged her leadership and independence, but he had always stood firmly between her and the rest of Nyrland. How would the other fiefdoms respond if Hugo refused to step into his role as regent for Marri? What would the Keepers do if Hugo waited too long?

Llianna had sent messages of love and sympathy to her father and brother at Gullhyrndr, but she had not yet asked for their help with Ravensborg. They had their own troubles, and surely Hugo would drink himself through the grief and guilt to take up the responsibility Rothmar had expected of him . . .

Days passed, and Hugo stayed away. Llianna paced restlessly, increasingly worried; it was unheard of for a woman to be left alone to manage a fiefdom. She resolved to seek her father's support, but first she went to beseech Hugo to leave the ale jug and step into his place as Rothmar's second. He responded in monosyllables and never met her eyes. Llianna was too heartsore to challenge him further, and she watched in dismay as he retreated further, drinking more and refusing to engage the promise of Spring in the air. She sent a second messenger to Gullhyrndr.

‡

"Everyone expects you to marry Hugo," said Lunet. "He is cousin to Rothmar, and he can hold Ravensborg for Marri until he is of age."

Llianna shook her head. "Hugo carries too much honor and too much guilt, and he's a stubborn fool. No, I will not marry. I will wait for Hugo to step up as Regent, and I will rule as Queen until he does. I have sent to my father for help."

"It is not the custom for a woman to rule, even for a short time," said Lunet.

"Custom be damned!" said Llianna. She would do without a man until her father sent help, or Hugo came to his senses.

Then the Keepers arrived.

Four Keepers rode in, uninvited and unannounced. With them came ten húskarlar in the colors of Aereskobing. It soon became clear that this was no ordinary deputation; three of the Keepers wore grey robes edged in purple, and the leader was resplendent in a full robe of deep purple. Pole bearers supported a casket draped in more purple cloth - the Book of Law.

The First Keeper had come with his Second, Third and Fourth.

Unheard of.

Terrifying.

Llianna silently cursed Rothmar for dying, Hugo for drinking, and herself for taking so long to send for help, but she managed to greet the Keepers courteously.

"We come to offer support in this grievous time," said the leader, the First Keeper, who introduced himself as Solvaldr. "A woman cannot be expected to carry the burden of a stronghold. We are here to relieve you of the burden."

Llianna's heart thumped painfully and her throat tightened.

Relieve her? What did that mean?

Solvaldr requested an immediate audience, but Llianna claimed urgent stronghold business and arranged a meeting for the following morning. The man's manner warned her that this was not going to be like the previous visits when Rothmar had managed the Keepers so well. There was something terrible in Solvaldr's eyes, a darkness that made Llianna's bones ache.

She retreated to her room and paced until her legs gave out. Rothmar had named Hugo as his Second, Regent if the child were a son, King if the child were a girl. But had he written and sealed it? Or had stupid, stubborn pride stopped him from formalizing it?

Llianna sighed miserably. *Inn mátki munr* had already taken more than Rothmar wanted to give, but surely he would not let pride stand in the way of protecting Ravensborg . . .

Llianna roused herself to walk to Rothmar's rooms and search for documents that would secure the Kingship. There was nothing. She sent for the Council, but the messenger returned to say the Councilors could not be found. Llianna sighed in frustration; she had worked to win the Councilors' trust, but the men had looked to Rothmar for leadership.

She went to the stables and searched through the saddlebags that had returned from Munstrond, but Rothmar's held only rumpled clothes and her letters. She held the letters to her chest and wept for how much had been lost. Then she wiped away the tears, cursed all men, and went to ask Faeoia's advice.

The old nurse just rolled her eyes and muttered her usual

insults about the Keepers. Llianna left frustrated; how could Faeoia have so underestimated the Keepers' power? How could she be so wise yet so wrong about this?

Llianna shook her head and called herself nine kinds of fool; Faeoia's wisdom had never been about worldly things. She saw everything through the words of the prophecy and, as Llianna well knew, prophecy was no guarantee of good outcomes. She gave up on Faeoia, borrowed Lunet's inconspicuous cloak and went in search of Hugo.

She found him at the húskarlar settlement, sitting alone, staring into a mug of the local brew. He looked dirty and disheveled, like someone in mourning. But weren't they all in mourning?

"I need you at the stronghold," said Llianna, standing over him with her hands on her hips like an aggrieved wife. "Rothmar intended that you be Regent."

"Go away," said Hugo, slurring and bleary-eyed.

"The Keepers are here! They want to *relieve* me of the burden of Ravensborg."

"By Óðin's balls!" Hugo staggered to his feet and glared at her.

"Exactly."

He slumped back onto the stool and emptied the mug. "No happening without a Keeper."

"I need your help, Hugo. Now."

"Haven't I done enough?" he slurred. "Ishn't killing my King enough? Ishn't it enough that I coveted hish wife? Ishn't it

442

enough that I betrayed the one pershon who never doubted me?" He dropped his head into his hands.

Llianna couldn't tell if the shaking that racked his body was caused by tears or mad laughter. Either way, he was lost to her while he wallowed in guilt and self-loathing.

"You didn't kill him," she said quietly.

"Hmmph."

Llianna leaned closer. "Did you loose the arrow? Did you push him into its path?"

Hugo looked up and shook his head. His hair fell over his eyes, lank and greasy.

"Then why are you punishing yourself? I miss him, too. He was a good man and a good King. I wish with all my heart that he hadn't died, but it wasn't you that killed him."

"Yes, it was." Did he sound more sober?

"Explain that! How exactly was it your fault?"

"The battle was my idea. You said it was wrong. Rothmar did not want it. I insisted."

"It was wrong, but he wanted it as much as you."

"He did?" Hugo raised bloodshot eyes and looked at her suspiciously.

By all the Gods, he was beautiful, even in this wretched state. Llianna banished the echo of *inn mátki munr* and thumped her fist on the table.

"He wanted the Landvördr defeated and the fighting finished. He told me he wanted to go to Munstrond, so stop trying to drink yourself to death, have a wash, change your clothes, and help me with these cursed Keepers!" She yelled the last words, furious with Hugo and equally furious with Rothmar for dying.

"People are staring," said Hugo, hiding behind his hair again.

"Of course they are!" said Llianna. "You look like a drunken Raider, and I'm the tragic Queen. Half of them pity me, and the other half are hoping something interesting will happen so they can talk about it until next season."

"Hmmph." Hugo drained the mug and refilled it from the jug on the table.

Llianna wrinkled her nose. The local brew smelled like horse piss, but Hugo didn't seem to care.

"Hugo?"

"I haven't finished drinking." He turned away from her and emptied another mug.

"*Paska!* They will appoint someone else, you stubborn fool! What of honor? What of fidelity? Perseverance? What of your Warrior's Code?"

Hugo refilled the mug and raised it as if offering a toast. Llianna grabbed it, threw the horse piss in his face, and stormed off muttering about self-indulgent males, stubborn fools, and the sheer stupidity of Laws that said men were more suited than women to rule.

She locked herself in her room, fed Marri, and prayed that the Keepers would respect Rothmar's wishes about Hugo becoming Regent, even if he was too drunk to attend the meeting.

The next morning Llianna dressed in her widow's grey, left Marri with Lunet, and walked resolutely to the King's solar. Perhaps she could just wish them all dead like she had the Landvördr . . .

Solvaldr and his fellow Keepers entered at the appointed hour and seated themselves opposite Llianna. They were joined by the Council of Ravensborg, eight merchants, and the chiefs and landowners who had served Rothmar well as advisors over the years.

Llianna bowed her head to the Ravensborg men. Hallmund acknowledged her with a nod, but the others kept their eyes fixed on the Keepers.

Solvaldr steepled his fingers and peered at Llianna with cold eyes. "The Law requires you to marry a man of our choosing, or stand down for a Regent."

Llianna acknowledged his words with a nod. "King Rothmar named his cousin, Hugo of Brodrup, as Regent until our son is of age."

Solvaldr looked around the room. "And where is Hugo of Brodrup? A King's word is only as strong as his reign. Rothmar is dead. His wishes cannot supersede the Law unless he wrote the succession and sealed it."

Llianna bit the inside of her lip so hard she tasted blood. Why had Rothmar let this happen? Why had he not written the succession and marked it with the royal seal? Surely he was not so proud as to leave her without protection. And what of Hugo's sworn vow to defend her and all she held dear? Her seething thoughts must have shown in her face because Solvaldr raised an eyebrow and smiled thinly.

"It is incumbent upon us to relieve you of the burden of Ravensborg," he said. "In the absence of a suitable candidate, I will act as Regent."

The Ravensborg men whispered to each other, but none seemed overly surprised by the Keeper's announcement. Even Hallmund did not speak out against this travesty. A shiver rippled up Llianna's spine. Had the Keepers already met with the Council to secure their support? Was that where they had been when she called on them? What had the Ravensborg men been promised for their cooperation?

Solvaldr signaled, and the Second Keeper arranged paper, quills, and ink on the table. Solvaldr wrote a few lines and then looked up at Llianna.

"Furthermore, you are to be relieved of the burden of caring for the King's son."

"No!" Llianna surged to her feet. "You cannot take my child."

"It is my duty to protect the future King," said Solvaldr. "It is already done."

Llianna started for the door.

Four húskarlar stepped forward to stop her.

"What . . .?"

"You are to be held for Questioning."

"About what?" asked Llianna, pushing past the húskarlar to confront the Keeper.

He sneered. "Your true nature is revealed. You dare to speak to me with anger! A woman's place is not to question the Law. It will be noted."

Llianna drew in a deep breath and slowed her frantic thoughts. "I beg forgiveness, Keeper. A mother is always fierce in protection of her child."

Solvaldr waved dismissively. "It is too late to feign submission. There is evidence that you used dark magic to ensorcel the King. Why else would he have granted you more power than is fitting? Why else would he have defied the Keepers to give you too much freedom?"

Icy dread took Llianna's breath. Too late she realized that this was about so much more than appointing a Regent; the Keepers meant to destroy her and take full control of Ravensborg.

"I would hear this evidence," she said.

Solvaldr gestured, and the door opened to admit Lunet. She walked with her arms crossed over her chest, her eyes on the floor.

Lunet? The evidence came from Lunet? Llianna's fear coalesced into something sharp and painful. A cold tear ran down her cheek.

"We will hear the evidence, and you will be put to Questioning at . . ."

"By what right do you decide for Ravensborg?" Hugo stood in the doorway, washed, groomed, and dressed in Ravensborg black and red.

"Hugo of Brodrup," said Solvaldr coldly.

Hugo bowed his head slightly to the Keepers and took the King's seat. "Rothmar entrusted me with the care of Ravensborg," he said.

"We have heard nothing of this," said Solvaldr. "By what right do you sit in the King's chair?"

Hugo closed his eyes as if in prayer. "My cousin, King Rothmar, died fighting beside me at Munstrond. I am his Second and, by his wish, will act as Regent for his son." He opened his eyes to fix the Keepers with the look of ice and fire that Llianna knew so well.

To Llianna's surprise, he also produced documents attesting to his claims. When had Rothmar written those? Had Hugo held them all along? She took the first deep breath since the meeting began.

"Why not marry the Queen and claim the throne?" asked Solvaldr. "You are well placed to do so."

Llianna's skin crawled with warning. Where was the Keeper going with this? What did he know?

"The Queen does not wish to marry so soon after her loss," said Hugo.

"The Queen's wishes are not our concern," said Solvaldr. "The Keepers' sacred task is to maintain the Law in Nyrland. The whims of women have nothing to do with the Law."

"Nevertheless, I will serve as Regent according to King Rothmar's written and sealed command," said Hugo. "Will that be all?"

Solvaldr scowled and beckoned Lunet forward. "Tell us what you know of the Queen's relations with Hugo of Brodrup."

Lunet kept her eyes on the floor and spoke in a whisper. "They be lovers, meeting behind the back of the King, bringing dishonor to Ravensborg."

Llianna gasped. Lunet didn't sound like herself at all; what had they done to her? She spoke as she had when she first came from Settlement. Had they hurt her?

"How long has this travesty been happening?" asked Solvaldr.

"It began even before she wed the King."

"Not true!" said Llianna moving towards Lunet. Two húskarlar took hold of her arms, holding her back.

"This is false witness," said Hugo. "Never have I dishonored my King."

Solvaldr signaled again.

Two more húskarlar entered and came to stand before the Keepers.

"Report," said Solvaldr.

One of the men stepped forward. "It be on the road from Gullhyrndr to Ravensborg that it happened, taking Llianna of Gullhyrndr to Ravensborg to be married to King Rothmar. Graller and I had the watch in the small hours, and we escorted Llianna of Gullhyrndr to the stream to bathe. As were the orders, she went alone to the water, but we had to keep watch. I saw her meet him there, and Graller did, too."

Graller nodded.

Llianna glanced at Hugo, but dare not meet his eyes. He had gone still as a hare trapped by dogs. She closed her eyes, as if that would block the words as well.

"Who did she meet at the stream?" asked Solvaldr.

"Hugo of Brodrup," said the húskarlar, pointing.

Hugo sighed like an old man. "It is true that my Queen unknowingly came upon me bathing, but nothing happened between us that dishonored the King."

"You were bathing fully clothed?" asked Solvaldr.

"Of course not, but the accidental sighting of a naked man is not evidence of wrongdoing."

Hugo was calling on all of his cold arrogance and disdain, but Llianna knew what would come next, and snakes of fear coiled around her body.

"Continue," said Solvaldr to the húskarlar.

"She, Llianna of Gullhyrndr, went to him in the water. They embraced." Graller nodded again.

Llianna stepped forward. "I was a girl, not yet married. I admired my future husband's cousin, and I acted impulsively and foolishly as a child might. My husband's cousin did not encourage me or take advantage of my foolishness. In fact, he rebuked me and apologized for any impropriety. I did not dishonor my father or my husband to be."

"An embrace with a naked man did no dishonor? Your idea of honor is strangely warped." Solvaldr licked his lips.

"I remained clothed, and nothing more happened than a brief embrace. It was foolish and wrong, but I came to my marriage untouched." Llianna said the words, but her whole being rebelled. Why should she disclaim what had passed between her and Hugo that morning? Why should it be diminished by this farcical questioning? Heat flared in her belly, rising up to her cheeks.

"Your guilty blush suggests otherwise," said Solvaldr. "There is more than enough evidence to warrant Questioning. Bring them both."

Hugo drew his sword and stepped back to make room to swing it.

Solvaldr nodded, and one of the húskarlar holding Llianna pulled a knife from his belt and held it to her throat.

Llianna reached for *djuplogn*.

The guard dropped the knife and fell to floor screaming.

"Stop!" Solvaldr pointed to the door. A woman Llianna had never seen held Marri before her, his face screwed up in fear or pain. A húskarl stood beside the woman, holding a knife to Marri's throat.

"Surrender or he dies. Ravensborg can do without a whore's son."

Marri cried out, as if he heard the intent in the Keeper's words. Llianna pulled up more power. Could she kill the húskarlar without harming Marri? Could she kill them all?

Solvaldr nodded. The húskarlar pricked Marri's throat and held the knife poised for another cut. Marri screamed, and blood welled on his neck.

Llianna released her connection to the killing power and let them take her. Three húskarlar held her roughly.

Hugo surrendered his sword and hung his head. They bound his wrists tightly with cord and pushed him towards the door.

Llianna sobbed brokenly, calling Marri's name, but his screams drowned out her voice.

Solvaldr stood and crossed to stand before her.

"That display of abominable, forbidden magic makes our task so much easier. You will be treated like the vile sorceress you are."

Llianna spat in his face.

He laughed and slapped her so hard she blacked out.

Hugo growled like a bear and struggled against the men who held him, but the ropes binding his wrists and ankles held.

You don't have to put out the fire when all is ash. - Unknown.

The sky soared in shades of blue like the ocean, the clouds like great sea creatures swimming in the depths. Llianna's thoughts drifted with the clouds, imagining her father's welcome and the pony she would choose for Marri; a round, dappled pony like her faithful Vaskr . . .

No, that was wrong; she wasn't on her way to Gullhyrndr. Llianna pulled herself back from the strange dreaming. Her head hurt horribly, and her stomach burned as if she had swallowed poison. Had she been drugged?

She lay on her stomach in a dark room. *Where was she?*

Memory flooded in. The Keepers. The meeting. Lunet's betrayal. Hugo. *Marri!*

Llianna opened her eyes and moved to sit up. She couldn't do it; her hands were tied behind her back and roped to her ankles. Even thinking of moving sent pain like fire through her arms and legs. She turned her head, desperate to see where she was held.

It was as dark as a mid-winter night.

She listened for familiar sounds; if she was being held at Ravensborg someone might come to help her. Faeoia? Hallmund?

But Hallmund had been at the meeting, and Faeoia had probably been taken. Or worse. A wave of despair washed over Llianna, leaving her shivering and more alone than she had ever felt. How had it come to this?

She groaned.

"Lli?"

"Who's there?"

"It's me. Lunet."

Llianna groaned again. Had the Keeper's slap knocked her silly?

Lunet sobbed and spoke all at once, her words coming out in a rush. "They made me do it, Lli . . . they said they'd kill Marri! I'm so sorry. I would never hurt you. Or Marri. Oh, what have I done?"

Llianna sucked in a deep breath, and her heart unclenched a little. "Ah. I should have known."

Lunet sobbed. "I shouldn't have opened the door . . . I thought it was you come back, but it was that woman and two guards . . . they took Marri."

Llianna breathed through the terror and rage that threatened to consume her. *Pain is strength for the true warrior.*

"Are your hands tied?" she asked Lunet.

"What?"

"Are you tied up? Can you move?"

"My hands and feet are tied, but I can move a bit."

"Good. Come over here."

"Where are you? I can't see."

"I'll make noise so you can find me."

Llianna hummed tunelessly, and Lunet made her way awkwardly across the stone floor, scraping and groaning. When she finally bumped her head into Llianna's shoulder, they both screamed.

Llianna whispered instructions. "I'm stuck on my stomach and my hands are tied to my feet. Wiggle down so your hands are next to mine."

With much grunting and groaning, Lunet lay against Llianna and touched her hands.

"Can you loosen the ropes?" asked Llianna.

Lunet scrabbled at the knots. She picked at a strand, and eventually it started to loosen. After that it was easier to undo the rest, and soon they were both rubbing their wrists and crying with relief.

"I don't know why we're so relieved," said Lunet miserably. "We're still stuck in some cellar, and Marri's still gone."

"And Hugo's been taken," said Llianna. She was alive, but how could she keep living when her heart had been torn from her chest?

"And we're dying of thirst," said Lunet.

"Let's find the door," said Llianna.

They crawled together to a wall and set off in opposite

directions to follow the wall around until one of them found the door.

Llianna listened to the scuff of Lunet's feet on the stone and moved slowly along, searching with her hands for the way out. The stone of the wall was smooth, and she wondered if others had been trapped here before . . .

She bumped into Lunet, and they both screamed again. There was no door.

"If it's a cellar, the door could be in the roof," said Lunet. "The root cellar at Ravensborg has a trapdoor and a rope ladder."

"A perfect prison," said Llianna.

"Do you think they mean to leave us here?" asked Lunet.

"I suppose it would suit them for me to disappear," said Llianna. "Although Solvaldr seemed eager to have a Questioning, whatever that is." She shuddered at the thought of his cold eyes and mean mouth.

"Something horrible, I'm sure," said Lunet, shivering. "But there'll be no one to question if they don't come soon."

Llianna sat against the wall and settled into the internal state she had learned with the völva, sending her senses out into the stone walls. The stone was dense and cold and ever so tightly fitted. Why would anyone make a cellar so like a fortress? It didn't seem like anywhere she remembered at Ravensborg. How long had they been drugged?

The stone offered no answers, so Llianna extended her senses beyond the stone to soil and twining roots, earthworms and moisture . . .

"Lli!"

Llianna pulled herself back. "What?"

"Can you hear that?"

Screaming, muffled by the stone.

"*Marri?*" Llianna staggered to her feet, gasping for air.

"That's not a babe," said Lunet.

"A man . . .?" Llianna's heart clenched and pain shot through her body as if it were she being tortured. By all the Gods, how could she bear it?

"We don't know who it is," said Lunet. "It could be anybody."

"It could be us," said Llianna, sobbing.

They huddled together in the floor, Llianna flinching at each terrible cry. What would make someone scream like that?

Lunet sat up. "Listen! What's that noise?"

They crawled towards the scraping sound, moving slowly, like dogs following a scent.

"Here," said Lunet. "It's here." She tapped her knuckles on the floor.

The scraping sound stopped.

She tapped again: one, two, three.

The floor answered: one, two, three.

One, two, three, four.

One, two, three, four.

There was someone there!

The scraping started again, and Llianna felt along the floor for some sign of a trapdoor or irregularity in the stone. If someone was trying to get in, there must be something . . . but she could find nothing at all.

Time passed, and the scraping grew louder. The tortured screaming stopped, but Llianna feared what that meant for the poor soul who had been crying out. Hugo? She called up the glorious blue of his eyes and the blessed wonder of the golden light that joined them. Surely she would know if that light went out . . .

Llianna held Lunet's hand and curled listlessly on the floor, trying to sense through the rock to whoever or whatever was making the scraping sound, but she was so thirsty and tired, her breasts heavy with unused milk.

Her mind wandered, and she began to think they had just imagined the sound. This place was so different from her journey through the seven thresholds; that journey had been deep and dark and lonely, but it had been filled with purpose and meaning. What meaning was there in dying in a cellar, her babe and fiefdom stolen, her men lost?

She reached for the Tapestry to see if this was where her Thread stopped . . .

The floor erupted in a shower of stone. Llianna and Lunet scrabbled away from the hole.

Light appeared, a lamp held aloft by a small man who climbed nimbly from the hole.

"Ah! Here you are! I am in time then."

"In time for what?" asked Llianna, voice croaking, back pressed against the wall.

"In time to save you," said the man, who looked like a grubby child and spoke like a mummer.

Llianna thought sadly of Hugo, who had not been in time to save her.

"Do you have water?" asked Lunet.

The man unslung a leather flask from his shoulder, and Lunet scuttled forwards to grab it and drink thirstily. She finished and handed the flask to Llianna.

Llianna drank in great gulps and poured water in her cupped hand to wet her face. She sighed with relief to feel her body revive a little. She still trembled with the horror of what the Keepers had done, but where there was life . . .

"Who are you?" Lunet asked the man.

"I am Demenor, a friend of the one you call the Wanderer."

Ah! Llianna had almost forgotten the Wanderer since Marri's birth and Rothmar's death. It seemed he had not forgotten her.

"Shall we go?" asked Demenor.

He lighted the way for them to scramble down the rough steps that led from the hole he had opened.

The steps ended in a domed corridor, and Demenor signaled for them to wait while he climbed back up. A sound like thunder rolled down the steps, and he returned in a cloud of dust.

"No one will follow us," he said.

Llianna shook her head in disbelief. Marri and Hugo were both somewhere on the other side of all that rock . . .

Demenor urged them away from the steps and guided them through tunnels shaped around the natural rock, a crude echo of the Ljósálfar caverns.

"Did you really think I had betrayed you?" whispered Lunet.

Llianna sighed miserably. "I didn't know what to think. It was all so sudden."

"That's how they work! Turning people against each other, breaking down trust. I hate them." Lunet slapped the rock wall as if she could squash the Keepers like she would cockroaches.

"Can you forgive me for doubting you?" asked Llianna.

"If you can forgive me for saying those things, I can certainly forgive you," said Lunet.

"And so the power of the Keepers is broken," said Demenor, looking back at them.

"Huh?"

"When people see through their trickery and hold to each other, the Keepers can no longer control them. They work by dividing people, breeding mistrust, as you say. When we work together, they cannot beat us."

"Who is 'we'"? asked Llianna. "Who are your people?"

"I hark from Aereskobing. I worked in the mines there, rose to supervisor, and then the Keepers decided to cleanse the workers. I was lucky to get away."

"What does that mean, to cleanse the workers?" asked Llianna.

"They send in Keepers to determine who lives according to the

Law, but what they really want is power and wealth. They take a few away for Questioning, and everyone else is so scared they agree to whatever the Keepers want. Higher tithes. Mining rights. Property. My name was marked for cleansing, but I got word of it in time."

"I have never heard of this," said Llianna. "It doesn't happen at Gullhyrndr or Ravensborg."

"King Bekkr and King Rothmar, and their fathers before them, they all held their own against the Keepers," said Demenor. "It called for courage and cunning, but they all had plenty of that. Oh, there are still places in Gullhyrndr and Ravensborg where the Keepers extract their dues, but you have suffered less than the other fiefdoms."

"Not any more," said Llianna. "They came down like vultures when Rothmar died, and they're blaming it on me and my dark magic." She fought against the despair that threatened to consume her. How had it come to this?

Demenor patted her hand. "Don't be too hard on yourself. The Keepers have likely been planning this since before you were born. They spin and weave and cut Threads as if the Tapestry was theirs to weave and snip. This was a long time in the making."

"Rothmar warned me about the Keepers, but he didn't expect this," said Llianna.

Demenor shook his head. "Rothmar likely underestimated their greed, their cunning, and their malice. He was a good King by all accounts, and goodness is no match for the likes of Solvaldr. The First Keeper lives for power, and he stops at nothing to get what he wants."

Llianna shuddered. Solvaldr had elected himself as Regent for Marri; she could only hope that meant he would keep Rothmar's child safe. But what did it mean for Hugo?

‡

Hugo commended his soul to the Valkyrie and prayed for death. The Aereskobing húskarlar had delivered a very skilled beating, but the damage was no worse than he had earned in battle. It was Solvaldr's personal attentions that had him asking for death. What man could live with the foul touch of a Keeper on his skin?

There was always a risk the Valkyrie would not come for a man dying without a sword in his hand; if they did not come, he would be lost. The warrior's pledge he had made to Llianna bound him to her, alive or dead, for as long as she lived; it would hold him this side of death unless the Valkyrie took pity on him and led him through the veil between the Worlds.

Hugo woke from another raging nightmare and opened one eye. He groaned to find himself alive. If being shackled to the wall of a stone cell could be called living . . .

Hugo felt a rush of cold dread for Llianna and Marri. What had Solvaldr done to them? Is that why the bastard Keeper was keeping him alive – to gloat over his helplessness? Wasn't that what men did in war: humiliate the conquered men by raping their women and killing their children? Hugo shuddered. What more could they want from him? Hadn't he handed them Ravensborg on a platter? Hadn't he betrayed any trust that had ever been given him? Hadn't he forsaken his sacred vow to protect Llianna and those she cared for?

No wonder the Valkyrie had not come. The sacred ones were probably watching in disgust as he slowly died the miserable, ignoble death he deserved.

A small, sane voice pointed out that the Keepers would not have recognized his claim even if he had presented it to them on a golden shield as they rode though the gates. It was just so unbearably humiliating to have played into their hands and aided them in their schemes!

The small, sane voice said, "Stop wallowing in self pity and do something."

Hugo groaned.

He tried to open the other eye, but it was crusted with blood. What could he do with one eye, a broken nose, shackled hands, and bound feet?

He sang.

"Alone by the fire, a warrior I knew
Told me this tale, and I pray it is true.

From far Ansteorra our dragon-ship came

To fight for good Halidar on Lilied plain.

My sword I had lent seeking honor and fame

Or Óðin's great hall in the fray.

We charged into battle, the sun beating high,

Our battle-horns sounding a victory nigh.

Our spears crossed their arrows like hawks in the sky,

Leaving many men dead on the way.

Sing me no songs of angels I pray,

For a Valkyrie found me in battle that day.

The battle was long and the sun was like fire.

The heat drove us down like a funeral pyre.

Though many I'd slain, now my bloodlust did tire.

Struck down by the heat of the day.

The battle moved onward from where I was laid.

I drew of my helmet to rest in the shade,

When a soft even tread, like the wind in a glade.

Brought a daughter of Asgard my way.

Sing me no songs of angels I pray,

For a Valkyrie found me in battle that day.

She gave me cool drink 'till my wits came again,

Before I could speak she was gone like the wind.

Had I but died, I could follow her then,

But I lay with the living that day.

Long I did search, a full year I have mourned,
And told all my brothers this love I have borne.
But she is of Asgard, and I of this shore,
So here with my brothers I stay.

Sing me no songs of angels I pray,
For a Valkyrie found me in battle that day.

True to this dream like the tale I have told,
Close to my heart, a small pouch I still hold,
And in it a lock of her hair pure as gold,
This I carry to battle this day.

Alone by the fire, a warrior I knew
Told me this tale, and I pray it is true . . ."[iv]

"Óðin's balls, Hugo! That has to be the worst singing you ever did."

Hugo shook his head to be rid of the vision of Emryn, the big, capable húskarlar chief who had carried Rothmar's body home from Munstrond. Emryn was standing in the cell, arms on his hips, scowling like he had just found two warriors in the furs together. Was Emryn dead, too? Had he come to carry Hugo's body away?

Emryn pulled his axe free and raised it over his head.

Hugo sighed unhappily. He wanted to die, but why was Emryn doing the killing? It added grievous insult to have a friend kill a man.

The axe fell.

Hugo held steady, though he wept that it was Emryn delivering the death stroke.

The axe severed the chain, and Hugo fell free of the wall. He landed on his face and stared up at Emryn with his good eye.

Emryn cut the rope binding Hugo's feet and pulled him up to lean against the wall.

"They messed up your pretty face," said Emryn. "Can you walk?"

Hugo took a step and collapsed. Emryn caught him and hoisted him over his shoulder.

"Play dead," said Emryn, carrying Hugo out of the cell and along a narrow stone passage.

Playing dead was easy. Through his one eye Hugo watched the walls move past and caught a glimpse of guards in Aereskobing blue.

"Another dead one," called Emryn.

"Take him to the cart," said a guard.

Emryn climbed a flight of narrow stairs and carried Hugo out into the blinding light of a fine day. He ducked behind a low wall and lowered Hugo to the ground.

"You have to walk or we'll never get out of here," he whispered, rubbing Hugo's feet to bring them to life.

Hugo pulled himself into a crouch and wondered where Emryn was taking him. Why did he have to walk to Valhalla? And why was it Emryn taking him instead of a Valkyrie? And why was Emryn wearing Aereskobing colors? Another fever dream?

"Now or never," said Emryn, hauling Hugo to his feet and walking away from the wall with an arm around his shoulders as if they were friends out for a stroll. He held Hugo tightly, keeping him upright.

Hugo could not feel his feet, which must be what happened when you died. He remembered how to walk, though, and he talked himself through it: Lift. Step. Down. Lift. Step. Down . . .

It seemed to be working.

They walked across a yard towards a double gate.

"Keep walking," said Emryn.

Hugo turned to frown at him. This did not look like Valhalla.

"Stop!" called a harsh voice. "We'll take him from here."

Emryn tensed. "Damn!" he muttered.

Three húskarlar took Hugo from Emryn. "Take him on to the infirmary," ordered the harsh voice. When they're done with him, bring him back to the cells. The Keepers aren't finished with this one."

The húskarlar carried Hugo away.

Ever would Ódin
on earth wander
weighed with wisdom
woe foreknowing,
the Lord of lords
and leaguered Gods,
his seed sowing,
sire of heroes. - The Legend of Sigurd and Gudrún

The first light of the sun slipped over the horizon, a soft, golden promise of clear skies and warm breezes.

An old man stood by the Well of Memory, his gnarled hands grasping the stone rim. A sound of music rode the breeze: deer hide frame drums, mouth harps, goat horns, lur, fiddles and tagelharpe, making music to raise the dead and entice the living. The old man turned his head to listen. A single tear rolled down his papery cheek. When the music stopped, he turned from the well and walked into the sunrise.

He walked all day and into the night. When his legs buckled, he slept beneath a yew, sheltered by the sacred tree. He rose before the dawn and continued his pilgrimage. The sun set and rose again before he saw the domes of Asgard glowing in the morning light. For a moment he imagined the others there; he could almost hear them, chanting and laughing. He hurried towards the gate, hoping to find someone who remembered his name. It had been so long since he had heard it spoken, in song or prayer.

He entered through the eastern gate, feet barely touching the ground. The place was deserted, but for dogs and pigeons. He wondered if they, too, were waiting for Gods who no longer came. He walked slowly through the ruins, lured by the cool green of a giant ash tree. Older than the oldest story, the tree sheltered a well beneath its spreading branches. The old man lowered himself to the ground and sat next to a discarded bundle of rags.

"What are you doing here, old man?" asked the bundle of rags, in a voice like pebbles in a dry riverbed.

"Resting," said the old man, turning his back on the beggarwoman.

"Not here, you old fool," said the beggarwoman. "Here. In Asgard. Here."

The old man went very still. The beggarwoman's voice had softened, like water flowing cool and sweet from the mountains. He wanted to turn and look at her, but his longing had played tricks on him before. He closed his eyes and sighed.

The beggarwoman moved to sit before him. He opened his eyes to see a beautiful face, golden hair, just like . . .

"Frigg?"

"Who do you think it is? Of course it's me!" The rags fell away to reveal the Goddess in all her glory: luminous eyes, golden hair cascading around her voluptuous body, rosy-tipped breasts.

The old man began to cry.

"I know. I know," said Frigg, voice soft as swanskin. She stroked his face. *"They have forgotten us."*

"I thought I was the last," said the old man. *"I thought you had gone."*

"You were the last," said Frigg. *"I missed you. We all missed you. I came back to find you."*

"Say my name," said the old man. *"Let me hear it again."*

Frigg laughed. *"Which name shall I say? There are so many! Aldaföðr – Father of Men! Foldardróttinn – Lord of the Earth! Sanngetall – Finder of Truth! Angan Friggjar – Delight of Frigg! I like that one,"* she said.

The old man nodded. *"More,"* he whispered.

"Draugadróttinn – Lord of the Undead! Arnhöfði – Eagle Head! Biflindi – Spear Shaker! Asagrim – Lord of the Aesir! Báleygr – Flaming Eye! Itreker – Splendid Ruler! Böðgæðir – Battle Enhancer! Ein sköpuðr galdra – Sole creator of magical songs! Faðmbyggvir Friggjar – Dweller in Frigg's Embrace! Another of my favorites," said Frigg, leaning closer.

"Limbultýr – Mighty God! Grímnismál – Wanderer! Göllnir – Yeller! Hangi – Hanged One! Oski – God of Wishes! Hrafnagud – Raven God! Hveðrungr – Weather Maker! Jörmunr – Mighty One! Rúnatýr - God of Runes! Svidur – Wise One! Uðr – Beloved."

The old man remembered what it was to be a God. He straightened his back and took a deep breath.

"Say my name," he said, eyes twinkling.

"Óðin," she said and kissed him on the lips.

A gentle breeze lifted the spirits of men and women toiling to feed their children. Merchants stopped counting their money and gave food to the hungry. Mothers walked with swaying hips and a secret smile on their lips. A woman left her sorrows and danced, moving to a rhythm as old as time. Two men searching for the Gods turned back to the World.

"Come," said Frigg. "The others are waiting."

The God and Goddess left together, dissolving in the old way, like mist in the morning sun.

Never laugh at the old when they offer counsel, often their words are wise. - Hávamál: 134

After searching for most of a year, Ariorn reluctantly accepted that the old Gods had abandoned Nyrland. If this cycle were not to end in disaster, he would have to do something other than wander around in circles.

"It is time to find the child of prophecy and lend what help we may. If the old Gods will not help us, we must help ourselves."

He and Halidor retraced their steps and set out for Ravensborg.

‡

Gravnir sat away from the others, watching the stars and wondering if any of the other Landvördr at Munstrond had survived. The Ravensborg forces were more than a match for the Landvördr warriors, and it was hard to imagine them being merciful when King Rothmar's own sister had died so horribly. Gravnir sighed and renewed his determination to lead Adelgunde and the others to safety. It was a far cry from his old desire to save his people, but it was better than nothing. Although it still might amount to nothing if the Wastelands did not end soon.

He was still watching the stars when two men appeared out of the night to stand before him. Gravnir leaped to his feet and brandished his staff.

"We bring no harm," said the older man. "We are curious to know who else wanders this dreary land."

Gravnir lowered his staff. If they had wanted to harm him they could have done it while he was stargazing.

"Well come to the night camp of the wandering Landvördr. I am Gravnir."

"Ariorn. And this is my nephew, Halidor."

"You are named for birds. Is that the custom of your people?" Gravnir peered at the men; they had the look of Ljósálfar, but there was something . . .

"No, it is more of a family custom. Our family have ever been different from our brethren."

"Ah, I know how that is," said Gravnir.

"You say the *wandering* Landvördr. Has something happened to bring this about?" asked Ariorn.

"A battle at Munstrond. The Landvördr warriors have been harassing the fiefdoms, and two of the Kings attacked the Landvördr settlement. I brought these few out, but I fear for the others."

"So the outcome of this battle is not known," said Halidor.

Gravnir shook his head. "Does anyone ever really win a battle?"

Halidor looked sharply at his uncle.

"I have asked the same question," said Ariorn. "Yet there are always those who want to fight."

Gravnir warmed to Ariorn in the same way he had warmed to the Wanderer. Was this man one of the Old Ones, too?

"How old are you?" asked Gravnir.

Ariorn's smile chased away the shadows from his face. "An interesting question! Do you always ask strangers how old they are?"

"Not always, but you remind me of a friend, and he is as old as the Ljósálfar."

"Ah, you have encountered our cousins. We are a long-lived folk."

Gravnir let go of the question of age, and invited the men to share the last of the ale he had carried from Munstrond. They told him of the fertile land five days walk away, and Gravnir began to believe his people would survive.

They were still sharing stories when the sun rose and the Landvördr began to stir. Gravnir saw his nighttime visitors in the dawn light and gasped in surprise. Their tattooed faces marked them as Noctimagi, yet their manner had nothing of the fearsome menace Gravnir had been taught to expect.

"We are Dökkálfar," said Ariorn. "It is long since our people have shared ale and talked around a fire."

"You surprise me," said Gravnir. "I have only heard the tales told to scare children. It has been a welcome pleasure to speak with you and find the tales untrue."

"Like any people, there are Dökkálfar about whom the tales may be true," said Ariorn. "I am also pleased to have spoken with a Landvördr who remembers the meaning of the name your people bear."

Gravnir reluctantly farewelled the Dökkálfar and rallied his people for another day's march. "Five days more and we can rest under trees and not have to dig for water."

Their spirits lifted, and even the children walked faster, but Gravnir's thoughts stayed with the two men who walked south. They had spoken of the prophecy and the woman who had walked the way of the Sacred Warrior, but he had said nothing of what he knew. He was not surprised that Llianna had emerged from the crossing in the Ljósálfar caverns as a named Warrior; she was the child of prophecy.

It troubled Gravnir that he had not told the men of his part in Llianna's journey. Did he fear the Dökkálfar men, or did he fear the pull of the prophecy and the unknown effect on his people? Or was he just so unaccustomed to trusting others that he did not know how to tell what he knew?

He finally decided it was due to all the reasons, and he regretted the unspoken words; they rattled around in his head, urging him to find the Dökkálfar and start again.

Three days away from the promised safety, he sought out Adelgunde and Gaurol and explained why he must leave.

"I know my path lies with them. I must ask you to lead the

others to safety. Three more days, and you will reach a land rich with food and water."

Adelgunde smiled. "Of course you must go. We have been waiting for you to leave us since we set out."

"You have?" Gravnir wondered yet again why he made things so difficult for himself.

"You have done well by us, dear Gravnir, but your Destiny lies elsewhere. Go with our blessings."

He left that night and walked under the stars, letting his feet find the path. So great was the pull to find the Dökkálfar that he walked through the next day and night, resting only long enough to sustain himself. He came upon them on the third morning, just as they were setting off for the day.

"Ah, our Landvördr friend," said Ariorn, as if he had been expecting him.

"I can take you to the woman you seek," said Gravnir. "Her name is Llianna, and she is the daughter in the line of the Warrior Queens." He told them of his time with Llianna, but he kept secret his own link to the Warrior Queens; the prophecy, after all, was not about him.

He was relieved to follow the Dökkálfar along a path that skirted Munstrond. They in turn were relieved when he showed them a way through the mountains that avoided the Ljósálfar caverns.

"It seems we are all outcasts," said Gravnir.

"It is only from outside that one can see clearly," said Ariorn.

"When we are inside the problem, we call the problem reality, and we are caught. Outside, we can see through the problem, and there is hope."

Gravnir smiled. This was the sort of wisdom he had been seeking! Ariorn spoke like the Wanderer, as if he saw through the veils to another World where Laws were based on balance and completeness rather than ideas of right and wrong, love and hate, kill or be killed. Why did these men roam on the edges when they should be invited to the councils of Kings?

Halidor had his own wisdom to offer, and the three-way discussions carried them through the mountains towards the road to Ravensborg. Each day they gathered their food from the Land; eggs from nests, honey stolen from the bees, and berries eaten as fast as they were picked.

They left the mountains, and the roads became busier. Ariorn and Halidor raised the hoods of their cloaks to hide the markings on their faces.

"People are looking at you," said Gravnir. "No one wears hoods like that in daylight."

Halidor mumbled something unintelligible.

"They would run screaming if they saw our tattoos and knew that two Dökkálfar walked among them," said Ariorn.

Gravnir shivered. He really was walking with figures from his dreams!

Dreams or not, Gravnir did not want to risk trouble, so he persuaded Ariorn and Halidor to conceal their faces with a simple spell that made the tattoos look like age spots or scars, neither of which would draw undue attention from the increasing number of travelers on the road.

"Ravensborg must be prosperous," said Halidor, pointing to the travelers.

"The roads are busier than I remember," said Gravnir, frowning at the carts and laden mules making their way to the stronghold. "The battle at Munstrond must have gone badly for the Landvördr." He felt sick.

"Why did your people not heed your warning and leave the ruins?" asked Halidor.

Gravnir shrugged. "I am not the most trusted among them, but I think they believed they could win. The defenses at Munstrond were built by the Ljósálfar in a past age."

"Most warriors go into battle believing they can win; that is what keeps the battle grounds ripe with corpses," said Ariorn.

"Do not fear the worst until the worst is upon you," said Halidor. "Why not ask these people what brings them to Ravensborg?"

Gravnir approached a farmer leading a herd of goats.

The farmer frowned at him. "Must have been somewhere strange not to hear the goings on."

Gravnir nodded. "I have been in the mountains."

"Ah, a prospector."

Gravnir nodded again; the description was close enough.

"Something's happened, all right!" said the farmer, leaning

closer to Gravnir. "King be dead, Queen be taken for dark magic, and there be a Keeper up there as Regent! Can't say I like it much, but it be good for business."

"Rothmar's dead?" Gravnir staggered.

The farmer took hold of his arm to steady him. "Yes, a shock it is. Killed fighting the Förnir."

Gravnir groaned.

"He was a good King," said the farmer. "But goodness never did save anyone from dying."

"Who won the battle?" asked Gravnir.

"Seems like there be no real winners with King Rothmar dead, but the blasted Förnir have stopped their attacks, so that be a victory for all good folk."

"Hmmph." Gravnir bit back the words he could have said and asked the farmer about Llianna.

"The Queen be gone, taken by the Keepers, and her son with her. The First Keeper be calling himself Regent, so the child must live still."

"The First Keeper?" Gravnir frowned at the walls of the Ravensborg stronghold.

"Solvaldr by name. A nasty piece of work, if you ask me. But no one be asking common folk about the doings of Kings and Keepers."

"More's the pity," said Gravnir, clasping the farmer's hand. "I thank you for telling me the way of things."

The farmer nodded and continued on his way. Gravnir walked

slowly back to where the others waited.

"Bad tidings?" asked Ariorn. He led Gravnir to the side of the road.

Gravnir repeated the farmer's tale, voice raw with grief.

"He was a friend," said Gravnir. "A good man."

"I am sorry for your loss," said Ariorn. "The Keepers have wasted no time in securing Ravensborg. We need to know whether their actions are prompted by the prophecy, or whether this is just about taking over Ravensborg's mines."

"What difference does it make?" asked Gravnir. "They have Llianna and the child!"

"It may mean the difference between life and death," said Ariorn, pacing beside the road. "If they are acting to thwart the prophecy, then they may try to use Llianna's power for themselves. If it just about greed and power, they do not need her alive."

Gravnir groaned.

"Come. Let us see what the Keepers are about," said Ariorn, leading them towards Ravensborg.

They entered the stronghold with the farmers' carts and milling goats. The market filled the square, and they made their way past stalls of produce, tables laden with steaming pots of soup and fresh-baked bread, and pens of goats and chickens and pigs.

"Come and hear what the Norns have woven for you today," called an old woman sitting between two carts.

She risked a beating or worse for peddling fortunetelling in a stronghold run by Keepers, but it was none of Gravnir's business. He ignored her and turned to show Ariorn and Halidor the way to the King's quarters.

The old woman swung her stick hard against Gravnir's shins.

"Aargh! You old . . ." yelled Gravnir.

Ariorn and Halidor turned in time to see Gravnir fall to his knees and grab the old woman's hands.

"Faeoia! Where is she? Where have they taken her?"

Faeoia looked over his shoulder at the two men and scowled. "Strange company you keep, Landvördr."

"A friend of yours?" asked Ariorn.

Faeoia waved her stick at him. "What concern is it of yours, dark one?"

"They are friends, Faeoia," said Gravnir. "They have come to see Llianna." He beckoned Ariorn and Halidor closer.

"Never have Noctimagi been friends to us," said Faeoia, waving her stick at Ariorn again.

Ariorn smiled. "Many of them have not been friends to me, either," he said.

Faeoia glared at him, scrambled to her feet, and hobbled away behind the carts, waving for them to follow.

Gravnir hurried after her, beckoning the others.

"Llianna? Where is she? Can you take us to her?"

"Some things are written, Landvördr," said Faeoia. "I will take you to her."

She led them through the back of the market where children

scavenged for scraps of food. Some of the children looked curiously at the warded men, but Faeoia waved her stick and scowled at them, and they scampered off. From the market Faeoia took them to the stronghold stables.

"Where are you taking us?" asked Gravnir. "Is she here?"

Faeoia shook her head and led the way to the practice yard. Ariorn and Halidor waited in the shadows by the gate while Gravnir spoke with the húskarlar chief. He returned to them looking grim.

"The Keepers took Llianna and Hugo to the Dmavar Sanctuary for questioning."

"Hugo?" asked Ariorn.

"Rothmar's cousin and Second. He was named by Rothmar as Regent, but the Keepers have taken it from him."

"Will the people let this happen?" asked Halidor. "Are they not loyal to their King?"

"There are few who will risk themselves when the powerful are fighting each other," said Ariorn.

"Hallmund will," said Gravnir, pointing back to where he had spoken with the húskarlar chief. "He attended the Council where Llianna was taken, but he could do nothing then. Now he is arranging horses and supplies for us."

"All of us?" asked Faeoia.

They left the stronghold before the gates closed, four travelers with riding cloaks and laden bags hanging from their saddles.

"Where is Dmavar?" asked Ariorn.

"It lies a league off the road between Ravensborg and Gullhyrndr. The Keepers have Sanctuaries in every fiefdom, and Dmavar is one of the smaller ones."

"She is not there," said Faeoia.

"What?" Gravnir turned to stare at the old woman. "Hallmund said that is where she was taken."

Faeoia nodded. "Taken there and taken away. They still have the Black Wolf trapped, but she is gone."

"The Black Wolf?" asked Ariorn, looking from Gravnir to Faeoia.

"Hugo," said Gravnir, remembering Llianna claiming him in the Wastelands, remembering the fire that arced between them. "We must free him."

Their camp that night was more comfortable than their previous resting places, with food to eat and thick cloaks to rest on. They reached Dmavar late the next day.

"What now? Do we just ride up to the gate and ask them to release him?" asked Halidor, scowling at the Sanctuary walls.

"Not if you want to get him out alive," said someone from behind them.

Gravnir turned.

"Emryn?" He knew Rothmar's man from his time at Ravensborg, but what was he doing there?

Emryn acknowledged Gravnir with a nod. "Friends?" he asked, gesturing to Ariorn and Halidor.

Gravnir nodded and did the introductions.

"I have tried to get him out, but they watch closely. I was nearly caught two days ago. They torture him and then take him to the healers so they can do it some more." Emryn clenched his fists and looked hopelessly at the Sanctuary.

Faeoia muttered something about the foolishness of men and proceeded to tell them exactly what they would be doing.

It is not fated that we should live together. I am a shield-maiden. I wear a helmet and ride to war with Warrior Queens. I must support them, and I am not averse to fighting. - adapted from Brynhild, The Saga of the Völsungs

Igmund wanted to be a Keeper. Keepers wore soft robes and fine boots, they ate fresh-baked bread and meat every day, and they slept in real beds. He would be a good Keeper, rising early, attending holysong in the chamber, eating in the common room, doing his allocated chores, studying the Laws . . .

"Wake up, dullard. Open the door!" The First of Dmavar kicked Igmund, shattering his dreams and bruising his leg.

Igmund scrambled to his feet and took the key from the hook. He fumbled before fitting it in the lock of the heavy door, earning another kick. The First strode thought the door and glared at the shackled man hanging limply in the cell. The Second followed a step behind.

"Revive him," said the First. "As long as we have him, the bitch will be lured back."

"There is no sign of her?" asked the Second.

"She used foul magic to escape, and she uses foul magic to conceal herself, but she is out there waiting. She will not forsake her unholy lover to torture and death."

"He is very weak," said the Second, scowling at the prisoner.

"Bring healers and see that he lives."

The Keepers left, and Igmund locked the door. He resigned himself to a busy day, with Keepers and healers coming and going . . .

The healers arrived before Igmund had time to scratch; they came with a húskarl, but at least none of them kicked him. Strange ones, the healers, hiding inside their hooded robes.

"Unchain him," ordered one of the healers.

Igmund took down another key and undid the shackles. The prisoner fell to the floor.

The húskarl hefted the filthy, battered prisoner over his shoulder and carried him out of the cell, following the healers towards the infirmary. Igmund yawned and rubbed the bruise on his leg. It might be a quiet day, after all . . .

Emryn waited with Ariorn and Halidor until the guard turned the corner, and then he carried Hugo to where Gravnir waited on the wall, casting shadows to conceal them. They pushed and pulled Hugo up and over the wall, scrambled over themselves, and managed to mount the horses and ride into the trees before the guard returned. It had all happened exactly as Faeoia had said it would.

They rode for an hour, Emryn holding Hugo before him, with Gravnir riding close to support the dead weight of the unconscious man. Gravnir felt sick; what had they done to Hugo? What was wrong with people that they had to kill and maim and torture each other? He held Hugo's limp body and wept for Rothmar and Llianna and the Fate of the World.

They stopped by a stream, and Faeoia prepared the herbs Gravnir remembered from the ride to Gullhyrndr with Rothmar so deathly ill. She dripped the bitter tea into Hugo's battered mouth, and Gravnir hoped for the same healing miracle that had restored Rothmar.

Gravnir helped Faeoia wash the blood and filth from Hugo's body, stitch the worst of the cuts, and wrap him in a spare cloak she produced from her saddle bag. Hugo groaned and clutched at the air, but he did not wake.

They rode on, making their way through the trees, avoiding the road. When the night became too dark, they stopped and slept, taking turns to watch for Keepers.

Hugo opened his eyes two days later, just as Faeoia had forced more herb tea into his mouth. He raised his head and spat the tea out.

"Aaargh! Poison!"

Gravnir helped Hugo raise himself to his elbows.

"You!" Hugo groaned and dropped back down to rest his head on the blanket Faeoia had folded for a pillow.

Gravnir nodded. "Yes, me."

"Hmmph."

"I will take that as an expression of your appreciation for saving you from the Keepers," said Gravnir.

"You sound like Rothmar," said Hugo, closing his eyes.

"He will live," said Faeoia.

Hugo struggled up again and looked around. "Llianna?"

"Faeoia is taking us to her," said Gravnir. "We hope."

Faeoia glared at him and stalked off to gather comfrey to bind Hugo's cracked ribs.

Emryn walked over from tending the horses.

"Ah. It was not a dream," said Hugo. "You came to get me."

Emryn smiled. "Just promise me one thing," he said to Hugo.

"What?"

"No more singing."

Hugo tried to smile, but it ended in a grimace of pain. As well as cracked ribs, he had a broken nose, a sprained wrist, cuts, bruises, and burns all over his body, and a fierce, raging anger at the Keepers.

That night he managed to sit propped against a tree and eat the broth Faeoia fed him, and the next day he rode double with Emryn, although he brought them to an abrupt stop when he fell unconscious from the horse. They stopped for the day, and Faeoia tended Hugo with poultices and herbs. The next morning, he declared himself fit to ride on; he wanted to reach Gullhyrndr, see Llianna safe, and plan his revenge on the Keepers.

King Bekkr stood in the yard to welcome them. He embraced Hugo, kissed Faeoia on the cheek, and turned to Gravnir.

"It seems I am once again in your debt. I thank you for the life of Hugo of Brodrup."

Gravnir nodded. "My companions are also to be thanked for rescuing Hugo from the Keepers."

Emryn, Ariorn and Halidor stepped forward.

Bekkr acknowledged Emryn with a nod. He looked at Ariorn's tattoos and gave a wry smile. "I see that the old tales are all true. I thank you for your help."

"Hugo?" Llianna ran down the steps and stood before him. "Oh, what have they done to you?"

He reached out and wiped a tear from her cheek. She was pale and thin, dark circles under her eyes.

"Marri?" he asked.

Llianna shook her head and clasped her hands to her breasts.

Hugo sighed miserably. "I am so sorry."

"The Keepers have been planning this since before we were born," said Llianna. "If you start blaming yourself for all that has happened, I will kill you." She fixed Hugo with a dark look that made him scowl.

Then she looked over his shoulder.

"Gravnir? Is it really you?" She threw herself into Gravnir's arms and cried like a child.

"Rothmar . . ." she said through the tears.

Gravnir nodded and held her close.

She caught her breath and stood back.

"Long have the Keepers coveted Ravensborg's mines," said Ariorn, stepping forward.

Llianna cried out and held up her hands to fight. "Noctimagi!"

Ariorn stepped back. "You know my people?"

"I have met some. They were not friendly," said Llianna.

"He says most of them be not his friends, either," said Faeoia, hurrying over to Llianna.

"Oh, Faeoia! I feared for you. How did you get away?" Llianna hugged her close.

"They never saw me," said Faeoia. "Foolish men."

"Not so foolish, after all! They have Marri," said Llianna. "And they have Ravensborg." She sobbed again, tears running down her cheeks. "He's just a baby! Everyone wants him for his bloodline, but he's just a baby. The Noctimagi wanted him even before he was born."

"My people threatened your child?" said Ariorn, moving closer to Llianna.

Llianna nodded. "They said I must pay a price to return from the Way of the Warrior."

Ariorn frowned, a fearsome look with his tattoos. "Long have my people guarded Sanctuary, but that was not done according to the Laws. I would hear more of your story." He bowed his head as if to a Queen.

King Bekkr interrupted and ushered them all inside. "Please come and rest. We can hear everyone's tale, and we will see what can be woven from this."

"Did you know this would happen?" whispered Lunet to Faeoia, scowling at the old nurse. "Did you foresee it?"

"Seidr cannot be forced," said Faeoia, sounding like the völva. "There be nothing anyone could have done to change this weaving."

‡

Solvaldr smiled when he heard of the prisoners' escapes; more rope, but this time it would be Gullhyrndr that would be caught in the noose . . .

‡

Cleaned and fed, Llianna and Hugo sat together on the bench where she and Marina had often sat to whisper secrets. Hugo still hurt all over, but he rejoiced to see Llianna safe. They did not touch, although the familiar fire still arced between them, fire with a life of its own. The Valkyrie shield, kept safe by Hallmund and given to Faeoia for safekeeping, rested against Llianna's knees. She would rather have had Marri back in her arms, but Fate had brought her a Valkyrie shield, and Fate had returned it to her.

Llianna sighed and looked down into the courtyard where she had first seen the dark-haired stranger.

"It all seems so long ago," she said.

Hugo frowned, thinking his own thoughts about the day he had looked up from the Gullhyrndr courtyard to be taken by *inn mátki munr*. A lifetime ago, by some counts . . .

"Demenor told me the Keepers have been planning this for a long time," said Llianna, trying to reach past Hugo's dark mood. "A weaving with many strands, threads within threads."

Hugo shrugged. "All weavings have many strands."

Llianna set the shield against the wall and stood to pace in front of the bench. "My father knew what he was doing when he married Ronja and brought her and Faeoia to Gullhyrndr; he knew I would be born. He wanted a Warrior Queen to stand against the darkness."

Hugo shrugged again. "*Child of golden light.* It sounds like a blessing, but it is a curse to carry such a Destiny."

Was he thinking of his own Destiny as well?

"Yes, Destiny is double-edged," said Llianna. "But my father hoped the prophecy would unfold in his time. He and Rothmar's father wanted to reclaim Nyrland from the Keepers."

"So you think the Keepers are the real enemy?" asked Hugo. "What about the Landvördr warriors who came from the ground like undead wraiths to murder our men?"

Llianna's skin crawled; she had her own memories of Landvördr warriors. "They killed Rothmar and Marina and so many others, and the Noctimagi I met in the caverns weren't exactly friendly, but . . ."

"When darkness comes from mountain halls . . ." said Hugo.

"The prophecy names the Landvördr."

"I've been thinking about that," said Llianna. "What if it's a way of naming the times, not the enemy?"

Hugo looked puzzled.

"It could mean that when the Landvördr rise, the time of the prophecy is upon us. The prophecy may not be saying that the Landvördr are the only enemy we face." Llianna brushed at her arms to shed the memory of Fangar's touch. "The Landvördr are dangerous, and it is natural to name them as enemies. The Keepers are part of our history, part of the fabric of Nyrland. How do people fight the threads of their own weaving?"

Hugo shook his head. The lock of black hair fell forward over his startling eyes, and Llianna was sixteen again, seeing him for the first time.

"Oh, what are we to do?" she asked, looking out over the walls as if the answer might appear on the wind.

Hugo shrugged. "I am not subtle enough to unravel these tangled threads." He told her then about his dream, the dream of the bloodsworn warrior, sacrificing his eyes in the old way so he could truly see, truly live within the Warrior Code . . .

Llianna sat beside him and held his hand. It felt cold, as if the dream had turned his blood to ice.

"You think the dream binds you to a life of sacrifice?" she asked.

"What else is there to think? I have dreamed that dream, walked that walk, a thousand times since I was a boy. It would come night after night, and then it would not be there, and I would think it gone. I would begin to imagine a different life, and then three nights or thirty nights later, it would come again, always the same. It has shaped me, even if the Old Ways are no more."

"Dreams do not always guide us truly," said Llianna, remembering some of her own.

"Perhaps you are right. Perhaps there is choice," said Hugo. "But I seem to make the wrong choices, and people die. It would be a relief to have no choice; if there were no choice, then everything is already written, and nothing I did would have kept Rothmar alive."

"Nothing you did would have kept Rothmar alive," said Llianna, emphasizing each word as if talking to a child. "It is a conceit to think differently! Such thinking places us with the Norns, weaving the Tapestry. That's what the Keepers do, and it is wrong."

"What are any of us doing when we desire something and try to make it happen?" asked Hugo.

Llianna smiled sadly and shook her head. "We act as if we can, and we find out where we can't. Then we try to live with the inevitable defeat. We really are very tiny Threads in a vast Tapestry."

"I live with that defeat every day," said Hugo. "I have lived with it all my life." The bitterness was back, burning like lye.

"No!" cried Llianna. "You punish yourself for your human failings and the failings of your forefathers. That's not the same.

Blaming ourselves maintains the illusion that Fate is ours to weave." She wanted to shake him, but instead she reached out to brush the stray lock of hair from his eyes. "I once thought I could weave my own Fate, but there are forces greater than we are. There is choice, but some Threads are already woven. I think it might take a lifetime to know the difference, so we keep trying to find out where it is ours to do and where it isn't." Grief tugged at her heart for the Threads that had been broken.

"But what if it was mine to do, and I failed?" asked Hugo. "How would I know?" he murmured, asking the question that haunted him.

Llianna sighed. "I'm not a wisewoman, but I think we have to start by asking if there were other Threads in the weaving, stronger threads than ours perhaps. You did not loose the arrow that killed Rothmar! Don't you think I've tormented myself with what else I might have done the day they took Marri?"

"Exactly!" said Hugo. "What if I had been there from the start, holding Ravensborg as Regent?"

"It would have made no difference. Haven't you been listening? The Keepers have been planning this; if we had not given them the rope they needed, they would have woven it themselves."

"You truly believe that?" asked Hugo.

Llianna nodded. "I do, but it's painfully humbling to admit it. I wanted to shape my own Destiny, but it seems some things are Fated after all."

"Like us?" asked Hugo, the fire of *inn mátki munr* flaring

through the loss and despair.

"Yes, like us," said Llianna. "I have struggled with *inn mátki munr* every day since I first saw you, but it's much bigger than I am. And that's not all. The prophecy says I have to save everyone, and how am I meant to do that? My power comes and goes of its own accord, and I couldn't even use it to save Marri. What if I had unleashed the killing power and harmed him? What if I destroy everything like the Warrior Queens in the First Battle? For all the fine words of the prophecy and the gifts of walking the Way of the Warriors, it turns out I'm just a game piece on the Keeper's tafl board! It's a bitter drink to swallow."

"Bitter, indeed," said Hugo, standing to look out over the yard. "There must be something we can do now, some way to stop them! Some way to get Marri back." He hit the railing so hard Llianna winced.

"I must leave Gullhyrndr," said Llianna. "Every day I am here places everyone at risk. The Keepers will come, and I must be gone when they do."

"Where will you go?" asked Hugo.

"To Angan Eyeland to find my mother's people. I want you to find Marri and bring him to me."

Hugo nodded, but he sighed like an old man.

"You pledged yourself to protect me and mine," said Llianna.

"I did," he whispered. "Instead I have seen your husband die, your son stolen, and your stronghold taken. Perhaps my pledge is not worth the breath with which it was spoken."

Llianna sat up straight and called on all her strength; she wanted to offer Hugo comfort, but that was not what he needed now. "Nevertheless I hold you to it. Only time will tell what your pledge is worth."

Hugo bowed his head.

Dagmar called from the yard below, "Llianna! We are meeting in the Council room."

Llianna stood and slung the shield across her back, although what she really wanted was to curl up and sleep for a year.

"I wish Rothmar were here," said Hugo quietly. "He managed the Keepers well enough."

"Not so well in the end," said Llianna sadly.

They walked together to the Council room, hands not quite touching, souls tangled in threads of love and loss and stubborn hope.

Continued in Book Two of the Warrior Queen Chronicles

ACKNOWLEDGEMENTS

Kellianna: To my mother who asked many years ago to hear the story of the Warrior Queen's life. To Devin Hunter for inspiring me to finally do this trilogy after 10 years of thinking about it. To the Goddess Conferences in both Glastonbury, UK, and Australia for bringing women together from all over the World to meet, collaborate and create. To my beloved Christopher Marano for encouraging me in all my mad endeavors. And to Kaalii Cargill for being such an intuitive and brilliant co-collaborator!

Kaalii: Wonderful synchronicity brought us together to write The Warrior Queen Chronicles, and grateful appreciation goes to the personal agents of that synchronicity - Lyndel Robinson and Tricia Szirom in particular. A huge thank you to the circle of readers who encouraged us, made creative suggestions, and picked up the inevitable typos – Jan, Julie, John, Kat, Mary, Patrick, Taren (the remaining errors are not their responsibility). Blessings to Leslie Baker who collaborated on cover design and art work. And heartfelt appreciation to Kellianna, sister, co-collaborator and genius songwriter/songstress.

THE AUTHORS

Kellianna is an American Neo-Celtic singer and songwriter internationally renowned for her powerful performance of song and chant inspired by myth, magic, sacred places and ancient times. With guitar and vocals she brings to life the stories and saga of the Gods and Goddesses. Using frame drum and chant she honors the Earth and the Ancestors with primal drumming and soaring vocals. Since 2003 Kellianna has performed her music in 9 countries on 3 continents, with regular visits to Canada, the United Kingdom, Western Europe and Australia.

Discography:

Lady Moon 2004

I Walk with the Goddess 2007

Elemental 2010

The Ancient Ones 2012

Traditions 2013

Fairy's Love Song 2015 by Lady Moon Duo

The Green Album 2016 Multi-Artist Compilation

Chronicles, Volume One 2016

www.kellianna.com

kellianna@kellianna.com

Kaalii Cargill is an Australian writer, artist, and psychotherapist. Kaalii writes fiction and non-fiction that asks "What if . . .?", exploring possibilities and alternative ways of seeing and experiencing the World. Her PhD investigated ancient women's mysteries, and her art takes shape in three-dimensional forms using feathers, fabric, snakeskin, and mythic images. Kaalii co-developed a therapeutic modality – Soul Centred Psychotherapy – a combination of ancient and contemporary healing practices. As well as writing, Kaalii teaches, works with dreams, and continues to explore possibilities. She lives in Melbourne with her family and a diamond python.

Books:

Don't Take It Lying Down: Life According to the Goddess 2010

The Element Series (fantasy trilogy) 2012

Daughters of Time (historical novel) 2013

Why Goddess Feminism, Activism, and Spirituality? 2015 with Helen Hye-Sook Hwang (Mago Books)

http://kaalii.wix.com/soulstory

kaalii@kairoscentre.com

Notes

[i] Adapted from *Retribution* by Henry Wordsworth Longfellow

[ii] From Kellianna's 2007 CD release *I Walk With The Goddess*

[iii] From *The Emerald Tablet*, a piece of Hermetica reputed to contain the secret of the transmutation of matter – original source unknown.

[iv] *Song of the Valkyrie*, composed by Mikal the Ram (Mikal Hrafspa) of the Society for Creative Anachronism. Lyrics in Public Domain.

Made in the USA
Las Vegas, NV
23 July 2021

26929012R00282